Daniel Rosenbaum leads a predictable life. He's a professor at Lobell, a small liberal arts college in the Hudson Valley, where he spends his days teaching classes and doing research alongside his friends and fellow professors, Colette and Mario. The biggest change Daniel's routine has seen in years is when car trouble leads him across the Hudson and into an unexpected romantic encounter with local mechanic Tony.

When tragedy strikes in the form of Mario's murder, Daniel's orderly life is thrown into chaos. Not only is his friend dead, it seems Mario was keeping secrets that could cause rifts in Lobell's close-knit community. At first, Daniel's intensifying relationship with Tony is the only way he can find solace from his grief and confusion. But all too soon, the trail of Mario's secrets leads Daniel to the same place he's been seeking comfort: Angel Automotive, the auto repair shop run by Tony's family.

Before long, Daniel is forced to question everything: his friends, his job, the way he lives his life, and the relationship he's not even sure he's in yet. Only one thing is for sure: Daniel is falling heart-first—in love or into mortal danger.

HEART FIRST

A Hudson Valley Murder Mystery,

Book One

S.B. Barnes

A NineStar Press Publication

www.ninestarpress.com

Heart First

CONTENT WARNING:

This book contains sexually explicit content, which may only be suitable for mature readers. Discussion of a university student's attempted suicide (side character, off page), discussion of cannibalism; guns/gun violence, murder, power imbalance/harassment, alcohol use, grief, stalking.

For B. and K.

Prologue

With his hands stuffed deep into the pockets of his hoodie, he'd rather be anywhere but here, standing in a corridor of the film department's building, waiting for her under the flickering fluorescent lights.

"How many times?" he asks.

She rolls her eyes. "When did you last take a shower?" She's almost dismissive, but there's still a hint of concern in her voice, a shadow of caring.

He's going to lose that if he keeps going. He's well aware, but he needs to know. If he doesn't know, he can't keep track, and if he can't keep track, he won't know how much...

"Did you hear me?" she asks. Snaps, really.

"I don't know; sometime this week," he mutters.

"I'm really worried. This isn't good for you." Her dyed-dark hair swings into her eyes, and she pushes it behind her ears angrily. One strand catches on her nose ring. "Can I take you to counseling?"

"No," he says instantly. He's been too many times, and it's humiliating and tiring, and he can *fix this* if he can only keep count. He's sure of it because she's told him so; she's told him this is the right track to fix everything and make it all return to how it used to be. "I just need to know—"

"It's *my life*," she tells him with an air of finality. "You may not agree with my choices, but you can't keep doing this."

"How many times?" He steps closer, forgetting he's taller than her until he's towering over her, angry and desperate and all the things he didn't want to be.

She shrinks back. "You're scaring me."

"Just...tell me!"

Mutely, she shakes her head. "If you won't let me help, leave me alone."

She turns on her heel and disappears toward the office she came from.

"Damn it," he mutters. That's twelve that he knows of.

"Twelve," he repeats to himself. "Twelve." He counts his steps as he leaves the building, twelve at a time. Twelve steps at a time as he walks toward his building.

In his room, he sinks to his knees in front of the picture. He lets his fingers trace across the words carved into the floor as he picks up the bread. "Twelve," he mumbles to himself, counting out his bites. Twelve of them. He needs new bread.

It's not her fault, and she shouldn't have to hurt for it. If he eats, she's free.

"I will eat your sins," he promises.

Chapter One

"Hello?" Daniel calls out into the seemingly deserted garage. "I, uh...I brought my car in?"

He winces at himself. Of course he brought his car; it's an auto repair shop. What else would he have brought? A tricycle? There's something about places like this that make him acutely self-conscious of his own ignorance. There's probably nothing seriously wrong with his car, and he's already bracing for some guy with a mustache and a baseball cap to tell him condescendingly he could have easily fixed it himself.

"Just a second," a voice calls back, much closer than Daniel expects. He flinches and looks around, trying to find the source.

There's a clanging noise, like someone dropped a tool on the floor, immediately followed by the sound of wheels scraping over asphalt. From beneath the sleek black car parked to the left, a guy in a pair of washed-out jeans and a stained white tank top emerges.

He has a mustache.

Daniel called it.

Granted, he also has a beard, which makes the mustache less out of place, but still.

"Hi," Daniel says and waves awkwardly.

"Hey," the guy says. "Wasn't there someone at the front office?"

"There was." Daniel bristled a little. "She told me to come here."

The guy rolls his eyes and pushes a strand of hair out of his eyes. The rest of it is in a short ponytail at the back of his head, with the once close-shaved sides grown out a bit. With the mustache, it's an intense look.

"Fuck," the guy says. "Uh, sorry. I'm guessing she didn't give you any paperwork?"

Daniel shakes his head. Mostly, the goth girl at the front desk snapped her gum and said "Uh-huh" when he tried to describe the sound his car started making this morning on the drive over from Rhinebeck. When he finished, she pointed him wordlessly toward the garage. She didn't look up from her phone once during the interaction.

"I wish I could fire her," the guy mutters to himself, wiping sweat off his forehead with his forearm.

It gives Daniel an unobstructed view of his arms, which are really nice.

Not the time, he chastises himself. Hitting on a mechanic in an auto shop in a dinky little town in upstate New York sounds like a neat way to get himself in trouble, and anyway, making a move on someone while they're at work is just bad manners. Besides, that mustache is really something, and while it does suit the man's face, Daniel's not sure how he feels about it.

"Sorry, I'm Tony. I should probably have led with that."

Daniel grins. "Hi, Tony. I'm Daniel, and I'm having trouble with my car."

"Well, you're in luck. I happen to be a mechanic."

"Wow, what are the odds?"

Tony shrugs and gestures to the rows of different-size chains hanging on the wall. "You walk into a setup like this, it's an even split— mechanic or sex worker."

It shocks a laugh out of Daniel. He gets the impression he doesn't need to worry about homophobia here if Tony's using respectful language, which is a relief.

"So, what's wrong with your car?"

Daniel winces. "It's been making this weird noise all morning. Like a kind of irregular clunking?"

"All the time or just when you go over a bump?"

"Um..." Daniel considers. The roads are pretty shitty between Rhinebeck and Lobell College anyway, so he wasn't exactly sure how frequent the noise was. He didn't hear it much on the better-paved way into Kingston, but he was also focused on finding the garage and wasn't really paying attention.

"Your muffler might be loose," Tony tells him when he fails to answer the question.

"Okay," Daniel says slowly. "And that's...bad?"

Tony blinks. "Not a car guy, huh?"

"No," Daniel says quickly. "Computers guy. Classic literature guy. Fourth season of *Buffy the Vampire Slayer* guy. Very much not a car guy."

A frown line draws tight on Tony's forehead. "That's a really bad season, which, okay, no one's perfect. Here's what we'll do. Technically, we're booked totally full today, but you're here now, and I don't feel great about sending you away when we don't know for sure what's wrong with your car. I'm gonna take a quick look at it to see what's wrong."

"That would be amazing," Daniel says. "Thank you so much. I'm sorry to put you out." It figures they'd be busy. He chose this place because it's the only auto shop in a twenty-mile radius that takes walk-ins, and he couldn't quite work up the motivation to call somewhere. He's probably not the only one.

Tony waves a hand. "Don't worry about it. Just don't tell my boss or Mrs. Cooper when she comes to pick up her car in an hour." He nods toward the car he's been working on, and Daniel taps the side of his nose.

For a long moment, they grin at each other widely. Tony has really nice eyes. Daniel's always thought brown eyes exuded warmth, and Tony has exceptionally long eyelashes. There's something kind in there, in the crinkles around the corners. He must laugh a lot.

"I, uh, I'll need your keys," Tony says.

"Oh, right." Daniel fumbles for his pocket like an idiot. "Of course. Sorry."

"That's cool."

He hands over the keys. Their fingers brush, and oh shit, Daniel has really done a full one-eighty here on the whole *it's probably a bad idea to hit on this guy* thing. It's still a really bad idea, but now Daniel wants to do it anyway.

"So, do I wait in the office?" Daniel asks, trying to sound casual and not at all like he's wondering what those calluses on Tony's fingers would feel like if they were to touch more intentionally.

Tony's teeth flash white as he grins. He has dimples. Daniel is really coming around on the mustache. "You can. If you want to enjoy my sister's charming company some more. Or…"

Daniel raises an eyebrow, a neat trick it only took him about two hours to learn when he was fourteen. "Or?"

"Or you could stay here and keep me company."

This is how Daniel finds himself sitting on a plastic stool, ogling an inconveniently hot mechanic bent over the popped hood of his '98 Honda Civic. "So, the receptionist is your sister?" he asks because it's better small talk than *Did you buy those pants specifically to drive me insane?*

"Unfortunately. Worst receptionist we've ever had." Tony stands up, stretching. The planes of his back and shoulders are very clearly outlined, and Daniel appreciates it a lot.

Trying to sound polite and not at all like he's ogling Tony, Daniel says, "She did seem a little, uh...uninterested in customer service."

Tony snorts and walks around the car to look at the rear. "That's a very nice way to say that she's driving away customers."

"I mean, I'm still here," Daniel points out.

"Clearly, you're an exceptionally patient person," Tony says with a wink over his shoulder.

"Somehow, I think Mrs. Cooper would disagree."

"Eh." Tony shrugs. "What she doesn't know..." He comes back around the car. "So, it's definitely your muffler. That's an easy fix, just tightening some bolts. I'm going to change your oil, too, though. It looks like it's been a while."

Daniel winces.

"Really not a car guy." Tony shakes his head. He's smiling, though, so Daniel doesn't take it personally. "If I ask you to hand me a wrench..."

"I will tell you I am only 85 percent certain what a wrench is," Daniel admits. "I could have fixed this myself, couldn't I?"

Tony brushes past him on his way to get the long silver thing Daniel had been pretty sure was a wrench. He smells like engine oil and sweat, and it makes Daniel a little dizzy. "I'm pretty sure *you* specifically couldn't have, sweetheart," Tony tells him.

Okay.

It's a little condescending, but Daniel's knees are officially weak.

"Sweetheart, huh?"

"Too much?" Tony pulls his rolling bench thingy over from the car he was working on before Daniel's car and disappears between the wheels.

"Nope," Daniel says, popping the *p*.

The wrench on the bolts makes a really satisfying sound, and then Tony's rolling out from under the car. "Glad to hear it." He rolls under the front of the car, presumably to change the oil. Daniel would be lying if he were to say he cared about anything besides the way Tony's thighs strain against the seams of his jeans when he bends his knees.

"All right." Tony comes out from under the car. "The oil needs to drain now. That should take a while."

"Okay."

"While we wait..." Tony looks Daniel over. He wipes his hands off on a towel.

"Yeah?"

Tony closes the hood of Daniel's car and leans against it. "Well, either I try to salvage what's left of my professionalism and get back to work on Mrs. Cooper's car, or you come a little closer."

Daniel licks his lips. "I won't get you in trouble?" He steps a little closer.

"Can't say I really care if you do." Reaching out, Tony grabs Daniel by the belt loops of his chinos and tugs him close. Just in time, he tilts his head to the side, and their mouths collide in a slick slide.

It's instantly wet, deep, and not how Daniel would kiss a first date. Fitting, for a run-in this unprecedented. Daniel swore off hookups when he was twenty-three and it stopped feeling good or convenient to go out on the pull, but there's a nostalgia to it now. It's electric to click this well with a stranger, to skip the pleasantries and the not-so-pleasantries of getting to know someone. His hands find Tony's hips on instinct and push the tank top up until he can run his thumbs along warm skin.

"You're sure?" Daniel asks when they pull apart for a moment.

Tony smiles. It makes him look a little less dangerously sexy, a little softer. "I won't get in trouble; I promise. Sweet of you to care."

Daniel leans forward to nip at his lips. "I'm not that sweet."

"We'll see about that." Tony grins.

Daniel has all kinds of ideas as to how he could prove it, and he would get started on them right away, but Tony's hands are firm on his waist, and Daniel really likes the prickle of Tony's mustache against Daniel's own shaved upper lip.

He's missed being kissed.

Tony is warm and his arms are pretty much as muscular as they seemed, something he proves by twisting them around until it's Daniel leaning against the car. The base of Daniel's spine bumps awkwardly against the side mirror, but to be honest, he doesn't care. He cares about the soft, spiky feel of the shaved parts of Tony's hair under his hands. He cares about Tony's shaky inhale when they part for breath. He cares about how red Tony's mouth looks now he's been kissed.

"I—" Tony's staring at Daniel. His eyes are dark, or maybe that's the lighting. "Um."

Daniel waits a moment, but Tony doesn't add anything.

Daniel leans forward and kisses him again. It's hesitant this time, gentle. Daniel's probably reading way too much into things, but he wonders if maybe between the two of them, he's the one who's kissed more strangers.

He tilts his head, kisses Tony's jawline, the side of his neck. Tony exhales sharply, a little gasp, and Daniel instantly wants to hear more. He lets his teeth trace lightly down the line of Tony's neck and—

The door between the front desk and the garage slams open.

Tony stumbles away from Daniel so fast he trips and nearly falls.

A woman's voice shouts, "Yoo-hoo! Anthony!" so loudly it rings through the entire garage.

"Mrs. Cooper," another voice says. That must be the receptionist. The sister. "I told you to wait—"

"Oh, I only want to see how my baby's doing."

She pats the hood of the car next to Daniel's. He realizes he's still pressed uncomfortably against his passenger side door and steps away from it hurriedly.

"Hi Mrs. Cooper." Tony's smile is apologetic. "You're early."

"Just a smidge." Mrs. Cooper is at least forty-five, charitably, and her wispy brown hair is up in a chignon that was probably really nice this morning. Her eyeliner is a tad too dramatic, and her smile is extremely wide. "How is she?"

"Almost done," Tony promises. "I'm running a little late today."

"I can wait," she says breezily and sits on the stool Daniel occupied previously. "I see I'm not the only one."

Daniel smiles politely and tries not to think about how his lips are tingling. He especially tries not to look at Tony, who's bending down over the hood of Mrs. Cooper's car.

"Are you from the area?" she asks him.

Daniel blinks. "Uh, no, I'm from California." He's on autopilot, hoping it's not too noticeable that his heart is pounding and the back of his neck is flushed unattractively. "How about you?"

"Kingston born and raised," she says cheerfully. "What brings you to our neck of the woods?"

"I have a teaching job over at Lobell." Too late, he considers he should probably ask what she does. He's not really used to nonacademic small talk anymore.

Her face doesn't fall, which is already better than a good half of staunchly conservative Hudson Valley residents who think it's a travesty that Lobell staff and students skew the vote blue. "Oh, that's wonderful. What subject?"

"It's called digital humanities." Daniel winces internally. This is where he always loses people. "Basically, it's about how to connect fields like literature and philosophy with IT and computers and things."

"Sounds *fascinating*. Any projects I'd have heard of?"

He laughs self-deprecatingly. "Probably not. My last project was creating an immersive digital world for the works of Geoffrey Chaucer."

She purses her lips and wags her head. "I'm afraid I've never heard of him. I'll have to look him up."

"It's pretty niche. The other thing we're planning on starting this semester is pretty cool though. Sounds of the Hudson Valley." It's a project Daniel's starting with a class this semester, one of the first anthropology crossover projects for the digital humanities group.

"Oh, like birdsong and the river?"

"That too." He walks away from her car slowly as if that will make him look less suspicious. "But also human sounds, farmer's markets, and apple-picking trips. Inside local businesses, if they agree to us recording there. We want to create a sort of digital sound-map of the valley."

"I love that," she says decisively. "You know, I have a friend who runs a coffee shop here in town. I bet she'd be thrilled. She has a lot of local singer-songwriters perform. Here, let me give you my card; I'll set it up!"

Daniel's willing to bet the cross section of local singer-songwriters and anthropology students is large enough to get him an in with or without Mrs. Cooper's number, but he goes along with it anyway and slides her business card into his wallet. She's a social worker, apparently. Who knew social workers cared about their cars so much?

Mercifully, before she can keep asking him about his job, Tony interrupts. "All right, Mrs. Cooper. I think you're just about set. Let's have a look at her to make sure."

"Oh, Anthony," she says and, horrifyingly, winks. "I know you took good care of her. You always do."

Daniel stares at the floor to avoid eye contact with Tony.

Even worse, Mrs. Cooper then gets to her feet and goes to examine the car. Right by the side mirror on the driver's side, she pauses to bend down and examine the paint job. For balance, her hand is pressed to his car, right where Daniel's ass was not five minutes ago.

"Beautiful!" she exclaims. "I can practically see my reflection."

Looking up, Daniel catches Tony staring straight at him like a spooked horse. He wonders what the chances are of a portal to another dimension opening up under him to swallow him whole.

Thankfully, the receptionist-slash-sister chooses that moment to snap her fingers in Daniel's direction. "Hey, you."

Daniel's pretty sure he hears Tony mutter, "Jesus Christ, Gianna," under his breath.

"I gotta ring you up; come on." She walks back through to the office, the door slamming shut behind her.

With a last glance over at Tony, who's watching Mrs. Cooper inspect her car, Daniel follows.

"What'd he do?" The receptionist—Gianna—is chewing gum again and staring straight at her computer screen through her thick black bangs. It's hard not to feel like she hates him personally.

"Uh…" Daniel scrambles around his brain for the word Tony used. "It was, um…my muffler."

"Fixed or replaced?"

"Fixed."

She nods and types a few keystrokes.

"Oh, and he changed the oil," Daniel adds.

"We don't charge for that," she says dismissively.

Weirdly, the way she says it makes Daniel feel bad for not knowing.

She types for a while. Daniel's unsure if he should be adding any information, like his name or what kind of car he has, but she doesn't ask.

Eventually, he realizes he's probably supposed to make friendly small talk. That's what you do in the Northeast when talking to strangers—unless you're in New York City.

"So," he says. "You're, like, a proper family-run business."

She doesn't respond.

He perseveres. "That must be cool."

It gets him a shrug at least. The points of her shoulders are sharp in the incredibly oversized dark sweater she's wearing. "It's not the worst."

He suspects, from her, it's a ringing endorsement.

She rings him up. It's surprisingly cheap for car repair. Of course, the last time Daniel had his car looked at was two years ago when his ex-boyfriend, Jeff, started setting out statistics about regular car maintenance and automobile longevity at the breakfast table. Daniel's been driving on his winter tires all year round since then.

"Thanks for squeezing me in on such short notice," he says, mostly to be polite. Their website does indicate they take walk-ins.

Gianna shrugs again. "Thank Tony. He should be ready for you any minute."

Daniel swallows around a sudden lump in his throat. He coughs. "Thanks." He tries very resolutely not to interpret anything into the words *ready for you.*

He waits for another minute or two, but she's taken out her phone again and started to tap out hurried messages with chewed-down fingernails. Taking it as a goodbye, he heads to the garage.

True to Gianna's word, he's just in time to see Tony driving Mrs. Cooper's car onto the lot. She waves cheerily at Daniel as she follows it out.

He smiles weakly. "Nice to meet you," he says into the empty garage.

In the two minutes it takes Tony to return, Daniel's palms start to sweat.

Was he always like this? Vaguely, Daniel remembers a time in his life where he enjoyed flirting with handsome men. Probably it also made him nervous then, but this nervous?

"So," Daniel starts.

"Sorry about Gianna." Tony grimaces. The apples of his cheeks are pink, and Daniel's pretty sure he left a tiny mark on Tony's neck.

"Oh, no, she was—fine."

"Good."

For a long moment, neither of them says anything.

The phone in the office rings.

"Right, so, um, you're all settled up?" Tony asks.

"Yeah. I—"

"Great. I'll drive your car out."

It's probably a good thing Daniel can't think of a way to segue into what they were doing before. Tony works here. Still, he feels a pang of regret as he follows his car out to the lot.

"Thanks," he says as Tony gets out. He's not sure whether he means *thanks for driving my car out*, *thanks for fixing my car even though you didn't have time*, or *thanks for making out with me*.

Probably the latter, if he's being honest.

"Anytime." Tony gives him a weak smile.

Daniel really doesn't mean to, but the words just slip off his tongue. "I might hold you to that."

He's almost certain he sees Tony grinning in the rearview mirror.

Chapter Two

It's not that Daniel thinks of Tony constantly after he drives his perfectly functioning car back across the Kingston-Rhinecliff Bridge. He's not like that; even as a teenager, he was pretty chill about crushes and boyfriends, more practical than anything else.

Definitely not someone who has impromptu make-out sessions with a stranger in broad daylight in their place of work.

That's probably why he finds himself thinking of it every now and again, like a song stuck in his head. It was unusual; it was risky. Sure, Daniel's met guys at bars or clubs and gone home with them in the past, but that's what you expect to do at bars and clubs. You don't expect to randomly hook up with a mechanic at an auto workshop. It was so far out of the wheelhouse of Daniel's regular behavior that it thrills him in hindsight to think of it. It's not so much about Tony, he decides, as it is about *himself* and this unprecedented ability for spontaneity.

Not that Tony wasn't great, of course.

He was really handsome, actually. The mustache was kind of unique, but the long hair in a ponytail at the back of his head, the close-shorn sides, the warm brown eyes, the nice ass... It wasn't like he had six-pack abs or perfect features, but Daniel is impressed someone like that had gone for him. Outside of drunken hookups in his undergrad years, Daniel is pretty aware his most attractive feature is his brain. He's not a troll or anything; he's average.

It's flattering, that's all.

Maybe it shouldn't still be flattering or thrilling to think about three weeks later, but Daniel can't quite help that it is. He's not obsessing or anything, but when he hears an engine rev loudly somewhere behind the rickety row of old stone buildings that house most of the literature faculty as well as the social scientists, he can't help but grin at the memory it invokes.

"What's got you so happy?" Colette Ravel, anthropology professor and Daniel's downstairs neighbor, asks.

Daniel coughs. "Sorry. Just thinking."

"I hope it's about how to get our students around the Hudson Valley without us having to drive them." She leans back in her creaky office chair, eyebrows raised. He's so envious of her easy poise. She looks like a professor, even though, like him, she's barely past thirty. Maybe it's her style; it seems she has an endless supply of slinky, silky blouses in jewel tones that pop against her dark skin. She wears them with high-waisted slacks and understated jewelry, and somehow, she always looks relentlessly professional, elegant, and competent.

Daniel has two pairs of work pants he doesn't hate, and if he ruins one in a way he can't fix, he's fucked.

"Ugh," he groans. "Why are there no car-sharing apps on campus?"

"Because Lobell is barely a real place," Colette returns seamlessly.

"I had three books go missing in the mail before I started ordering them to my home address instead of to the office."

"Okay, but is that the mail or is that buildings and grounds?"

"Shh," Colette admonishes. "If you say that too loud, they'll hear you."

"Anyway, the only reason you get your books now is because I always sign for your packages."

"Yeah, well, you spend way too much time at home." She shrugs. "Sorry for having a life."

It's a terrible Americanism absolutely butchered by her French accent. He tries not to be insulted by the content as well because she's not wrong.

There just isn't a lot to *do* in Rhinebeck, and Daniel doesn't love socializing enough to drive a half hour to Germantown to attend the opening of an obscure documentary in the freezing cold independent theater with Colette and Mario from the film department. The last time he did, it was about some horrific Welsh myth involving horse skulls, and he had to drive home alone in the dark, and he couldn't sleep for hours.

Worse yet, he could take the train down to the city on the weekends and hang out with Paul, his best friend from grad school. It's not that he doesn't have fun when he does, it's that he spends the next week and a half recovering from it. It's very much a once-a-semester pleasure.

He's getting older, and as an old guy, it turns out he really likes staying home in his cozy apartment with his bad-tempered cat, watching Netflix and reading. It was a more acceptable character trait when he was still living with Jeff, but he's working on owning being a hermit.

It's either accepting his fate or making ill-advised public hookups a habit. Sternly, Daniel tells himself the latter doesn't sound attractive at all.

He's lying.

Sighing, he stretches. The second chair in Colette's cramped, top-floor office is not that comfortable. "So. Transport."

"Right," Colette sighs. "I mean, we can set aside a session or two for fieldwork and drive the students around then, but nonetheless, there are two of us and twenty-five of them."

"Also, the syllabus is jam-packed," Daniel reminds her. He's a little skeptical about the three classes reserved entirely for the theory of participant observation. Most of the students taking the class are interested in crossing off their social science credit while getting another class for their concentration in digital humanities, with only a handful of actual anthro majors signed up. It's not that Daniel doesn't respect Colette's expertise; it's that he's pretty sure the ethics of anthropological research will be lost on a bunch of kids for whom sitting in a coffee shop in Tivoli, New York, population 1021, with a recording device, will form the sum total of their efforts.

"I can't do weekends," Colette tells him.

"I won't do weekends," Daniel tells her.

They stare at each other, helpless.

"I guess we have to hope a couple of them have cars and they can carpool?" he offers.

"I guess," she agrees hesitantly. She drums her fingers on her desk for a second, staring out the door as someone walks past. Then, far too loudly, she yells, "Hey, Mario?"

Daniel cringes.

Seconds later, Mario's head pops in through the door. "It's-a me-a."

"I have a question for you," Collette says, while Daniel rubs at his mouth to hide that he's smiling at the joke. Mario's ego is big enough, and he's made the joke so many times Daniel really shouldn't still think it's funny.

"Shoot." Mario leans against the doorway with his arms folded. He has his shirtsleeves rolled up, and his dark hair is perfectly coiffed. If only he weren't so straight, Daniel thinks, not for the first time. Mario is distractingly good-looking and pleasantly even-tempered and funny. Students flock to him; staff and faculty admire him. Daniel wonders if Colette is immune to it because she's not into men; she seems to like him in a much less fawning way than everyone else.

"We're going to need to arrange transport for our students around the Hudson Valley. Could you help us drive around with the van?"

Mario's lips twist. Even that looks good. "Depends on when."

"We were thinking of using a class slot, so a Tuesday or Thursday morning sometime late in the semester."

He nods slowly. "That ought to work; my classes are in the evenings."

Right, Daniel remembers. The bane of the film studies teacher: late classes for evening screenings. A terrible fate.

"Thanks," Colette says. "We owe you one."

"And I would like to cash in." He grins. "Will you give me a lift home later?"

Colette looks to Daniel. They live in the same building and almost always carpool—for a given value of the word "carpool." Colette's value, as far as Daniel can tell after two years, is "Daniel drives, and Colette occasionally gives him gas money or pays for brunch."

"Sure," he says. "What time are you heading back?"

Mario groans. "I have an intro section till four. After that, I would like the sweet release of death, but I will take a ride home and a stiff drink."

"I can offer the latter, but I'd prefer not to murder you."

"Sweet." Mario makes a dorky little fist pump. "Hey, uh, Colette?"

"Hm?" Colette hums, not looking up from the calendar app on her computer, probably trying to imagine which part of their syllabus she can squeeze another appointment into.

Rubbing the back of his neck, Mario seems hesitant. "Andrew Clayfield stopped by my office again."

Colette makes a face. "Still about…"

Mario nods.

She sighs. "I suppose we can't dissuade him if that's what he really wants."

"Is this the cannibalism guy?" Daniel asks.

"Yeah," Mario says. "He took Colette's class on pre-Christian practices in Christian religious ceremonies last year, and it got him really obsessed."

"Pre-Christian is an inexact term." Colette examines her fingernails, a clear sign she's trying to project disinterest even though the point is probably at the heart of what she was trying to teach in that class in the first place. Sometimes, she's just as much a nerd as the next academic. "Not all religions are pre-Christian, nor are all other spiritual practices that get mixed up in it."

"Forgive me." Mario's tone is dry. "I was distracted by the student trying to sell me on the short film about a man-eating corpses."

Daniel shudders.

"Do you think he'll actually make the film?" Colette asks.

Mario shrugs. "In terms of talent, not really. I mean, he can make *a* film, but it won't be good."

"He's a student; I'm not expecting a Scorsese. What about in terms of content—is it doable?"

"You want to see it," Daniel realizes.

"It would be interesting," Colette defends. "There's a lot of cannibalistic imagery in Christianity, and the sin-eater is such a fascinating concept—"

"The sin-eater," Daniel repeats. "It even sounds like a third-rate horror movie."

"Which is what it would be." Mario doesn't even look at Daniel. He's studying Colette intensely, a smile playing around his lips. "If you co-chair the board for his senior project, I'll let him do it."

Colette snaps her fingers. "Deal."

Daniel shakes his head. "You're both severely messed up. And it sounds like that student needs to go to counseling."

"Such an American." Colette clucks her tongue. "Sometimes our darkest impulses reveal our greatest capabilities."

"And sometimes we create terrible student films about cannibalizing corpses," Mario finishes.

"We have a responsibility to our students," Daniel tries. "To—"

"To support their full creative potential." Colette's tone is serious, even if she's smiling a little. They're going to spend weeks debating this; Daniel can already tell. "I fully agree."

"I'm finished with you both." Daniel sits forward. "I'm going to try to forget this conversation ever happened." He levers himself up out of the creaky chair, ducking so he doesn't hit his head on the slanted roof of Colette's office. She gives him a lazy salute as he starts to head toward the door, but his exit is blocked by five foot nothing of Stacy Allan. She may be a full head shorter than Daniel, but she makes up for it with sheer presence. It's not her dress style—classic suburban mom, all jeans and T-shirts with dumb slogans—or the rest of her appearance, although she has the kind of bangs that look strangely girlish and bouncy on a woman who must be well over forty. It's her personality.

"Rhinebeck gang!" she says in an overly cheerful tone. "Did I just hear you arranging carpools?"

Colette and Daniel trade a look.

Among a slurry of other responsibilities, Stacy chairs the Digital Humanities Program as well as being dean of the English department. She will decide if their project gets continued after this year, so it's in both their interest to suck up to her. Whether or not that's worth spending a fifteen-minute car ride with her is yet to be decided; Colette can't stand Stacy and might actually kill someone if she spends too long in close proximity.

"Yeah." Daniel plasters on a smile, feeling very much like he's arranging his own funeral. Hopefully not one at which any corpses get eaten. "You need a ride?"

"Oh, if it's not too much trouble." She smiles her toothy smile.

"Not at all. Gee, did no one else drive today?"

"Well, my husband needed the car," Stacy begins, and Daniel braces himself for a long, involved story about Stacy's husband being unable to manage simple tasks without Stacy rearranging her entire life around him—depressingly, all her stories are like that, and for a literature professor who teaches close reading, she's alarmingly unaware of it. He thinks it's sad; Colette thinks it's infuriating.

"My car's in the shop." Mario blessedly interrupts her. "Fender bender a few days ago."

"Oh, no!" Stacy gasps. "Are you all right? Was anyone hurt?"

"Well, funny story." Mario walks away from Colette's door toward Stacy's office. "I was driving home after class, and it was pretty dark…"

Stacy follows him, hanging on his every word. Over his shoulder, Mario throws them a wink.

Thank you, Colette mouths at Mario. Daniel shakes his head, waves at both of them, and heads over to his office.

He has to set his feet sideways as he walks down the narrow staircases. He's incredibly grateful he's a new enough hire that he got an office over in Condelmuir, the somewhat newer brick building down the road.

Well.

Daniel says road, but he means footpath. Lobell's campus isn't big enough to have much car traffic, and the student body is a bit too granola to drive when you could walk or bike instead. That's how he and Colette got into this whole mess regarding transport.

He scheduled all his classes for the morning or midday slots this semester, so he's free until Mario's ready to head home. That is, he has time to prepare his classes and work on his own research, but if he's being honest with himself, that probably won't happen today. It's only one week until Thanksgiving, all his class preparation is done until then, and he taught two back-to-back comp lit sections this morning. His brain feels like jelly.

Maybe he should unclench and take some afternoon classes. He just hates when he only finishes teaching at four, or even worse, six. It really blocks him from doing anything else productive all day.

Fuck, he's really going to end up like the old guy at the grocery store the other day who counted out his quarters and complained about how everyone paid in plastic these days.

Daniel's willing to bet that guy never kissed a hot mechanic in the middle of a garage though.

Not that they actually did anything illicit, it was only kissing.

Which is a shame, because if they'd done more, it would have probably been great.

Daniel could break one of his side mirrors and go back to get it fixed. That would, however, be insane.

He's just going to have to keep reminding himself that he has the capacity, buried somewhere deep within himself, to do spontaneous, exciting, stupid things and to be desired by someone who wants to do them with him.

The thought is a warm ember in the pit of his stomach as he slogs through answering emails from students.

Dear Lily,

If you're concerned about finishing the paper on time, let me know 24 hours before the due date to arrange an extension. It's still a ways away, though, and you have loads of time. Try not to worry too much and keep up with the readings! If you're having a hard time with the class, or just in general, feel free to stop by my office hours on Wednesdays from 2 to 4.

Sincerely,

Daniel Rosenbaum

Assistant Professor of English Language and Literature and Digital Humanities
Lobell College
30 Lobell Road
NY 12504
daniel.rosenbaum@lobell.edu
845-596-7928

Afterward, he rewards himself by responding to Mari Hoffman's latest email from Santa Cruz; he hasn't seen her since a conference last year, and she wants to know if he'll be at an event put together by a grad school friend of theirs in a few weeks. Seeing Mari and Paul is worth the trip down to the city, and he hasn't been since March, so Daniel tells her he'll be there and RSVPs to the event. Then, he downloads a series of articles from JSTOR about the anthropology of sound that Colette put on the syllabus for their joint class as required reading for next week. She's the one teaching those bits, but he likes to know what's going on.

He makes it about halfway through the second one by the time her class lets out. It's a lot more interesting than he thought it would be. Who knew there was so much to say about the anthropology of the senses? He did actually know that scent is the sense most strongly tied to memory from watching way too much *Criminal Minds*. He hasn't thought too much about hearing specifically and how that affects perception. He has a solid idea of how to design this project or they would never have gotten the class approved. But he didn't consider how different it would be to have only the sounds online rather than sound and visual like most streaming services and, regrettably, social media sites offer. He emails the rest of the papers to himself. Looks like his evening plans are set. He doesn't want to let Colette down by not being ready, after all, and if they can get Stacy to approve, they can continue this project for at least another year. Working with Colette is great.

Of course, he debates with himself as he walks toward the car, he could always do the reading over the weekend and do something else tonight. It's weirdly warm out. There is a storm forecast for later, and the air pressure niggles under Daniel's skin. Maybe he should get out of the house more. Meeting Tony feels like a callback to an earlier time in Daniel's life, a time before Jeff, before Lobell, before Daniel's life was as calm and structured as it is now, and it's made him hungry for more.

That doesn't make it a good idea.

The drive to Rhinebeck is comfortably familiar by now, even with the darkening sky and the rainclouds drawing up. Sure, Daniel wishes there was decent public transportation, but it's only twenty minutes at the absolute worst. Driving a full car, even with Stacy in it, reminds him of his own student days. It's kind of nice.

He tells them about Lily's email, funny in a very sweet sort of way. "I mean, there's concerned and then there's asking for an extension three weeks before the paper is even due!"

Mario hums in agreement. "She was in one of my classes last semester. Really earnest girl, very dedicated. I hope she's all right."

Daniel sighs. "I told her to come to my office hours if she's struggling. I hope she does."

"It's so good to hear what a concerned and engaged staff we have," Stacy muses from the back seat.

In the rearview mirror, Daniel sees Colette's expression. Murderous would be putting it lightly. Hurriedly, he says, "Well, I'm just doing my job."

"Still—" Stacy unbuckles her seatbelt as he pulls up in front of her house. "We should really do more to appreciate your hard work! I'll be sure to bring it up at the next faculty council. Bye everyone; have a good evening! Hope you're all bright-eyed and bushy-tailed tomorrow! We should really carpool more often."

She closes the door behind her, way too gently on the first go and then barely hard enough with a little squeak.

Almost as soon as Daniel has pulled away from the curb, Colette groans. "I hope Andrew Clayfield eats her corpse."

"Oh, come on," Mario cajoles. "She means well."

"You say that because she loves you," Colette tells him.

"She loves *everyone*, that's her whole thing," Daniel points out. "It's kind of a lot." With Colette listening, he doesn't want to admit he finds it comforting. He has a limited bandwidth for it, but he does appreciate it.

"She's the faculty Title Nine rep," Mario says thoughtfully. "If she didn't get along with people, that would be pretty bad."

Daniel considers for a moment to which authority figure on campus he would feel most comfortable going in case of something discriminatory happening to him, and it's Stacy by a mile. "She is ridiculously well-suited for that job."

"And it *would* be nice to get more recognition," Mario adds.

Colette shakes her head. "I can like all her ideas and still find every word she utters incredibly grating."

"I don't even like all her ideas," Daniel says. "Recognition sounds like a faculty retreat."

"Homebody," Colette accuses.

"Guilty," Daniel agrees, although everyone knows the worst part of a faculty retreat is not that he has to leave his apartment; it's the ice-breakers.

He pulls into the parking lot by their building. Because the ground floor is a store for upcycled knickknacks and the owner always bikes to work, there's plenty of space. If he'd taken the job in Albany or returned to California like his parents wanted, he would be struggling for parking and affordable rent right now. Upstate New York is quiet and cheap and charming in a quaint sort of way. If there were someone who agreed, who wanted to share that kind of life with Daniel, that would make it perfect. Until then, he'll have to make do alone. Or maybe invent some more car troubles.

It wouldn't be that weird to drive over the Hudson to Kingston and ask if maybe he should change his tires, hypothetically. Daniel knows he should change his tires; he just doesn't want to deal with it. It would be expensive, but it's an expense he's known about and put off for a while.

He'd get to see Tony again.

Maybe.

"You want to come over and have a drink with us?" Colette asks. Somewhere in the last five minutes, she and Mario decided a Wednesday evening drink was in order.

Daniel considers, but he still has those articles to finish, and he doesn't really like drinking during the week. It makes him sleep even worse than usual. Distantly, thunder rolls and makes up Daniel's mind. Storms are for being cozy and at home, or for chasing a real adventure.

"Maybe later," he says, by which they both know he means "no." If he knows either of them at all, and he does, they'll eventually decide it's too boring to hang around at home, and depending on how much they have to drink, they'll either drive to Kingston to see a movie or walk to the nearest restaurant.

"Boo, Rosenbaum." Though Mario's tone is serious, his eyes are twinkling. "Live a little."

"Your loss." Colette shrugs.

Mario waves goodbye as he and Colette peel off to her apartment on the second floor, not without reminding Daniel of their standing dinner date on Saturday. It's his turn to cook. Colette's a vegetarian, and she hates mushrooms, so he has his work cut out for him.

"Worf," he calls as he opens his apartment door. "I'm home."

There's a noise, less of a meow than a bleat, and then the thump of a slightly overweight cat hitting the floor.

By the time Daniel's got his shoes off, Worf has trotted over to receive his daily butt scratches.

"How's your day been, huh, boy?" he asks, rubbing at Worf's tailbone. He purrs like a creaky hinge. "Yeah? Good?"

Worf makes a tiny chirping noise that is the cutest thing Daniel has ever heard. He would pick Worf up and cuddle him, but Worf hates to be picked up.

"I think it's snack time for you, mister." Daniel sets his bag down by the couch and heads toward the kitchen. His mom sent him a bunch of candy in a decorative basket two years ago for some holiday or other, either Easter or Hanukkah, and it has since become a cat treat basket. Daniel tries not to have human treats in the house as much as possible; his self-control is nonexistent.

He selects the tuna and cheese crunchies and takes a handful, then crouches to let Worf sniff at his hand and lick at his palm until he manages to get a treat into his mouth.

"You are so spoiled," Daniel tells him, ignoring the fact that he is the one doing the spoiling right at this very moment. "You are the most spoiled cat I have ever met."

This is the nice thing about living alone. When Jeff lived here, he complained about how much Daniel talked to the cat, and about the cat in general. Daniel adopted Worf when he moved to the Hudson Valley, six months before Jeff arrived for a temporary adjunct position. Jeff had no right to complain about the cat; Worf was here first.

And Worf won out in the end, Daniel reminds himself, given that Jeff is gone.

He really needs to stop dwelling on Jeff. Their breakup barely qualified as a life event. Their relationship had been at least 60 percent convenience and comfort as opposed to any sort of passion. Anyway, they both knew from the start that Jeff's position was temporary, and when he got a tenure-track position teaching pre-law at Ohio State, they were in agreement instantly that it wasn't worth trying for long-distance or, god forbid, a spousal hire.

Daniel still gets lonely, living by himself.

Just not lonely enough to get plastered on a Wednesday or, worse yet, download Grindr and dodge being matched with his students all night.

Worf purrs loudly, crunching on his treats. Daniel tips the rest into his dish and gets up to wash his hands. It's only four thirty, and he's already hungry, so he's going to have to occupy himself for the next hour and half until he can have dinner.

Or he could have a snack, brush his teeth, and head to Kingston. Maybe he'd have to tiptoe down the stairs to avoid Colette asking any questions. Maybe it would be worth it.

What are the other options anyway? Reading a bunch of anthropology papers, eating the disappointing veggie burgers in the fridge he planned for on Monday and now doesn't really feel like, and then watching *Criminal Minds* until he gets too tired or it gets too scary?

He's been progressively watching the whole show sequentially as background noise for months, but the current season has been hard to get through, largely because the actor playing Hotch left and the influx of new characters is threatening to lose his interest.

Maybe he could do something with his addiction to procedural crime dramas. An interactive map of every fictional serial killing on network television. That would be fun.

Interesting, too, actually; there's a point in there somewhere about the sensationalizing of human misery and what patterns might be revealed about where crimes occur, fictionally, versus where they occur in reality. With his laptop fired up, he makes a note in his to-do list. He should absolutely write a grant proposal for this. Maybe after this semester, once the Hudson Valley soundscape thing takes off and needs less constant babysitting.

He would absolutely love to teach a few classes on the history of the murder mystery too.

Daniel looks outside. If he times it just right, he could make it to Kingston before the storm hits. He catches a glimpse of himself in the hallway mirror. It'll do; his hair actually looks okay today. *Criminal Minds* and participant observation can wait. He's going to Kingston.

He's in the process of putting his shoes on without untying or retying his laces when his cell rings.

"Hello?" Daniel clenches the phone between his ear and shoulder as he grabs his keys. He didn't even bother checking caller ID with not enough hands and eyes available to multitask that well. He hopes it'll be a quick call.

"Hi, Danny," his sister says brightly.

Not fast, then. Shit.

"Hey, Meredith. What's up?"

"Not much. How about you?"

Reflexively, he shrugs. "Same old. Students, research, all that."

"Sounds like a blast." She sounds sarcastic.

"It is. We're running a new project this year. Digital sound mapping of the Hudson Valley. The class is going well so far, and the dean seems pretty happy with our work."

He doesn't know why he does this, praising his own work. She never cares. He still has this uncomfortable urge to let her know he's doing well, precisely because she never seems to care.

"That sounds great." She seems earnest, but she doesn't ask or add anything.

There's a pause where he doesn't want to outright ask why she's calling, and she clearly doesn't want to segue right from his life stuff into whatever it is.

Then, eventually, she says, "Hey, I wanted to ask you something."

"Okay?"

"About Christmas—"

He can't help himself; he sighs in exasperation.

"I *know*," Meredith says. "But mom's been asking me to ask you, and you know how she gets."

"Why wouldn't she just ask me?"

Meredith makes a noise that sounds a lot like she's tutting at him like their mom used to. "Because you're going to say no."

"We're Jewish!"

"I *know*, but it's not like we were ever really practicing. We never even got mitzvahed or whatever. I'm just thinking; it would make her happy."

"I'm coming for Thanksgiving, aren't I?" Daniel hates flying over the holidays. It's crowded, full of people coughing and sneezing with every-thing from allergies to seasonal flus, crying babies, and stress. Doing it twice in a month is way too much, especially for a holiday they shouldn't even celebrate. Adding to which, he's already going down to the city for one conference in December.

"That's four days, Danny."

Daniel sighs. "I'll think about it, okay?"

"Thanks. Anyway, you used to love Christmas."

He did used to love Christmas. It seemed a lot more fun than being Jewish, based on the two times Daniel went to the synagogue with his grandparents. Then he grew up and started to hate commercial bullshit and, ever so slightly in the back of his mind, to resent the lack of access to religion his parents provided.

Anyway, Daniel and Meredith both know he means he'll put off telling her he won't come for Christmas by an extra week or two but will inevitably do it anyway.

He wishes his parents would come visit him sometimes too. He might not be married with kids like Meredith, but he does have a life here, and it isn't always convenient to fly out to the Bay Area. His parents are retired. He's not.

"How are the kids?" Daniel asks, for lack of a convenient end to this conversation.

"They're great!" She's enthusiastic for the first time. "Well, I mean, Davy broke his arm, but that's what you get for doing expressly forbidden backflips on the trampoline."

Daniel forces a laugh. He hasn't seen Davy since June. "Poor guy. I hope he gets some candy to make up for it."

"Shh, not so loud; he'll hear you."

They chat a while more about Meredith's kids, a safe topic of conversation in that they both love them. Daniel makes a mental note to send them a care package soon. As much as the conversation irks him, Daniel finds himself glad to hear her voice. It's nice to talk to Meredith, even if it's hard too.

When they hang up, it's started raining.

Daniel looks down at his shoes, which are properly on by now. He looks at himself in the hallway mirror again.

There's a fine horizontal line starting to form on his forehead. He thinks his hair looks okay today, but that's only if you don't look at it for too long, in which case it's getting a bit shaggy because he's been putting off going to the hairdresser. He has too many cowlicks to really allow for that. His eyes—well, he's never thought they were his best feature. He has his mom's eyes, blue and worried. He's getting crow's feet.

His stomach grumbles.

The auto shop Tony works at is probably about to close up anyway. And what would Daniel gain from it? He and Tony might kiss again. They might do more. Or Tony might not even be there today, or he might regret what happened last time. And either way, at the end of it, Daniel would be heading back to his empty apartment.

Instead, he heads to the kitchen and sticks his burger buns in the oven. As he sets about slicing a tomato and washing off two leaves of lettuce, Daniel tries to keep his mind on the question of whether the plastic packaging on his veggie patties negates the positive climate impact of the patties themselves.

He still can't quite seem to forget Tony's smile in the rearview mirror.

When the burgers are done, he sets his cutting board and frying pan in the sink and runs water in to rinse them. It pools in the sink basin, trickling down the drain very slowly. Daniel sighs. He should really call a plumber. He puts it on his mental to-do list for tomorrow.

Downstairs, he hears a door click open. There's the low rumble of Mario's voice, Colette's answering laugh, footsteps down the stairs.

Daniel takes his plate and heads to the couch. Drawing a blanket over his legs he breathes in deeply and listens to the wind howling outside for a moment. Then, he presses play on *Criminal Minds* and rests a hand on Worf's big, flat head.

"Guess it's just you and me tonight, buddy."

Chapter Three

Daniel sleeps restlessly. It keeps raining all night, and by three in the morning, howling winds and the sound of tree branches slapping into windows have woken him twice. Worf is no help, stalking through the apartment and jumping loudly from furniture before hitting the floor with a massive thump. Daniel can't blame him; the first big storm of the season is always loud and upsetting.

Waking up in the morning is a challenge. It takes two cups of chai before he's even slightly functional, and it's Thursday, which means he has to be mentally composed enough to teach the anthro class by ten. Especially given that Colette will probably be hungover.

Daniel checks his email while sipping his tea. There's not much, just the daily email announcement blast from Lobell about what activities and events are happening that day and an email from Stacy about this year's info session for freshmen looking to pick a major who have no idea what "digital humanities" even is.

With a sigh, Daniel clicks on the email.

Hi Digital Humanities fam!

I hope everyone is heading into the last month of the se-mester well! It's been a wild one so far, but I know you're all hanging in there :)

Don't forget this Friday afternoon is our yearly Cake & Questions event for students interested in our wonderful field. Daniel, Patricia, and Juanita, you're on cake—I'm on questions!

See you all on Friday!

Stacy Allan

Dean of English Language and Literature / Faculty Title IX coordinator
Lobell College
30 Lobell Road
NY 12504
stacy.allan@lobell.edu
845-596-7923

Someone needs to tell her she should stop using words like "fam." It makes her sound even more like someone's mom. Which, Daniel supposes, she is. Someone also needs to tell her to stop sending emails at 11:00 p.m. Logically, Daniel knows this is why she's the dean and not him (well, that and seniority), but the thought of caring so much about everything that you're writing group emails that late makes him shudder.

Sighing, he puts "cake" on his to-do list for the day. He'll make a batch of brownies. Not a lot that can go wrong there.

At nine, he puts his mug in the sink, slips on his shoes, pets Worf on the head and gives his tailbone a little scritch, and heads out the door. The sky is still dark, and it looks like it will be raining on and off all day. Frankly, it's a little rude that classes haven't been canceled due to inclement weather, but administration already pulled that one during hurricane season in September, so it looks like they'll have to pull through today.

Daniel knocks on Colette's door and then pulls out his phone to check the traffic report while he waits. There's a fallen tree on the 9G, so it looks like they're taking the 103 instead.

Three minutes later, Colette opens up.

"Wow," he tells her. "You almost look not perfect."

She narrows her eyes at him for a second, parsing his words. Finally, her face clears, and she says, "Thank you," with great dignity.

It's truly unfair that she looks like this after a night of drinking. Today's blouse is a deep fuchsia with some sort of loose, tie-like construction around the neck in the same shade. Her slacks are dark blue, and there isn't a single crease on her.

"I don't know how you do it," he complains as they head down the stairs and toward the parking lot. "I look like shit, and I didn't even go out last night."

"You do not look like shit," she tells him solemnly, which is nice, if untrue. "Anyway, you're a white man; the standards are so low for you."

"And yet, I continually fail to meet them," he says cheerfully, pulling the hood of his raincoat over his head as they leave the building.

It's really awful outside.

"Fuck, I hope I can drive in this." He peers up at the sky as if looking at it will make the storm front magically disappear. "I'm guessing you're not interested in playing chauffeur today?"

Colette sniffs disdainfully. Their carpool arrangement is more of a gas money arrangement; Colette thinks all American drivers but a choice few (one of whom, Daniel is proud to admit, is him) are not fit to be behind the wheel, and she avoids sharing the roads with them whenever possible. Daniel can't claim she's wrong, and on a day like this, it will be especially bad.

"By the way," he warns, tilting his head to see her a little better with the hood on, "Stacy sent an email about the faculty event tomorrow."

Colette groans. "How many exclamation points did she use?"

"I don't know. As many as there are sentences in the email." Daniel shrugs. "Anyway, you'll probably have to attend that event if we want to keep this project going—oh, *fuck*!"

He pauses, dismayed, in front of his car. There, lying across his windshield like the proverbial French girl, is a massive branch from a nearby tree.

Okay, maybe it isn't massive.

It's a lot larger than Daniel wants things lying on his windshield to be, though, especially given the velocity of the wind last night. Carefully, he pulls the branch aside, wincing at the sound of it scraping across his car.

"Okay..." He tries not to panic. "Okay, this is fine. It's just a crack."

Just a big, long crack running vertically up his windshield, with other, smaller cracks spiderwebbing off of it. This is not good.

"Okay," he tries again. "Okay, I don't have afternoon classes. I can take it to a shop then. We'll take your car, and...Colette?" He turns to where she was standing a moment ago, searching. She's nowhere to be seen. Maybe she already went to get her car keys while he was freaking out?

"Colette?" he calls again.

The only answer he gets is a scream.

Everything is a blur after that: Sprinting over to find Colette in the narrow alleyway between their building and the bakery next door, hunched over and throwing up in the gutter. Following her line of sight down to the prone body lying on the asphalt by the trash containers. Kneeling beside the body with a sick feeling of recognition in his gut, he paws at the familiar leather jacket, the slick dark fabric wet with—oh, it's not rainwater, it's blood sluicing off of Mario's chest toward the gutter.

Feeling as if he's acting through a thick veil of fog, Daniel uses his index and middle fingers to search for a pulse. Mario's skin is ice cold. Rainwater cold. There's no pulse, but Daniel could be wrong; Daniel can never find his own pulse; maybe he's doing it wrong. He stumbles away, grappling for his phone, and dials 911.

After, he can't remember what he tells them, only that it takes minutes—twenty, fifteen at least—before he hears the sirens coming.

"We need to call the college," he gets out through numb lips.

"I'll do it." Colette has her arms crossed over her stomach, shivering in her thin, stylish jacket. Her feet must be wet through by now. Daniel's are, and his legs and his face and any part not covered by his raincoat.

Colette steps out of the alley to call the registrar's office. It doesn't help; Daniel hears every word. He hears how her voice breaks when she finally speaks. "Mario Lombardi has been hurt," and he hears how wooden it sounds when she adds, "Professor Rosenbaum and I will not be in today."

Daniel should email the anthro class, let them know class is canceled. He looks down at his phone, still clenched in his hand, waiting on some sort of emergency service to arrive. He's never called 911 before, so he doesn't know what to expect. Will it be police? An ambulance? Both?

The students will probably figure out class is canceled when neither of them shows up. Most of them live on campus anyway, and it's at most a five-minute walk back to their dorms if they show up to an empty class-room. Daniel's hands are shaking too badly to type out an email right now. Raindrops cover his phone display. The hand not holding his phone has Mario's blood on it.

What would he even write? *Sorry Anthro 206. Class is canceled due to unforeseen death.*

The sirens get closer, and Colette starts waving her arm and jump-ing up and down, splashing dirty water up her pant legs. A police car pulls into the lot sharply, lights flashing, followed almost immediately by an ambulance.

Several men in a variety of uniforms swarm out of the vehicles and Daniel is so relieved he starts crying. It's the stupidest thing he's ever felt, relief at the sight of uniforms, but he doesn't know how else to pro-cess everything that's happening.

"Holy shit." A police officer shines a flashlight into the alley. "Oh, fuck."

Dimly, Daniel realizes the Rhinebeck PD doesn't see a lot of violent crime.

"I made the call," he says dumbly. "I think he's—I think he's dead."

The last word makes his stomach turn, and he only just manages to avoid following Colette's example of throwing up in the gutter.

"Are you gonna let us through sometime today?" A bad-tempered EMT stands at the entrance of the alley, holding a stretcher. The police officer steps aside.

The EMTs roll Mario's limp, unresponsive body onto the stretcher. Daniel stares down at the dark patch where Mario's body was as the blood slowly washes away.

"Hey, wait, don't you need to examine the scene or something?" he blurts out.

For a moment, everyone freezes, and Daniel wants to kick himself. All his information comes from crime procedurals, and he probably shouldn't go around advertising that fact.

Then, the police officer says, "Fuck."

With Mario—the body—fully loaded up onto the stretcher, the EMTs carry him to the ambulance. Daniel follows, unsure of what else to do, Colette close behind him. Under the harsh, fluorescent lights of the car, they confirm what Daniel already knew: Mario is dead.

Colette makes a noise that sounds like it's ripped from her throat.

Before he knows what he's doing, Daniel wraps an arm around her shoulders. It's the kind of comforting, emotional gesture he rarely makes because touch does not come naturally to him. It's the kind of gesture he doesn't expect Colette to need or want. But to his surprise, she turns to him, buries her head in his shoulder, and takes long, shuddering breaths as he tries to soothe her, stroking gently down her back.

The police officer, who appears to be younger than some of Daniel's students now that Daniel's looking properly, walks over to them. "The sheriff's department is sending someone over. We're going to need both of you to stick around, and if either of you has an umbrella, that would be great."

It takes another twenty minutes for a team from the Dutchess County Sheriff Department to get there. Daniel spends the time holding an umbrella carefully over part of the crime scene while Colette waits in the ambulance with Mario's corpse.

Finn, the officer who answered his 911 call, asks Daniel a few basic questions, standing on the other side of the scene holding a second umbrella. How did he find the body, did he know the deceased, what did he do when he found the body, that sort of thing. Daniel answers on autopilot and tries not to stare at the water slowly, inexorably, washing Mario's blood off the pavement.

They get driven to the sheriff's department, after, in a black-and-white cop car. Daniel gets rainwater all over the seats. He wonders if he should have asked for a minute to run up to his apartment for a change of clothes; he's cold and wet, and he has no idea how long this will take. He feels shaky, like he's had too much caffeine and not enough to eat.

When they reach the sheriff's office, a friendly detective wearing an outfit not too different from Colette's (before she stood out in the rain for half an hour) leads them into an office away from the bustle of the main room. The bullpen, Daniel thinks, if real cops call it that.

"I'm Detective Taylor," she tells them, smiling kindly but not too much, as if she took a class in appropriate facial expressions for a murder investigation. "Can I get you a cup of coffee? Something to eat?"

"Coffee," Colette replies before Daniel can react at all.

He nods silently. He hates coffee, but he wants this over more than he wants anything else.

"All right." Detective Taylor sets down two Styrofoam coffee cups in front of them as well as sugar and cream. Daniel dumps enough into his coffee to make it drinkable. "Why don't you tell me what happened this morning?"

Colette takes a deep sip of her coffee, so Daniel starts.

"I knocked on Colette, uh, Professor Ravel's door at nine. I do every day; we carpool to Lobell. She came out around three minutes later, and we went down to the parking lot."

Setting down the cup, Colette continues. "There was a branch on Daniel's windshield from the storm." She wraps her arms around herself. Daniel forgot about his car entirely. He's going to have to take care of that. "He was inspecting the damage. I thought I would need to get my keys if we couldn't take his car, so I turned back to the building."

"I didn't even notice," Daniel said. "I was...I was looking at the car."

Detective Taylor nods for them to continue.

"I saw a strange shape in the alley." Colette toys with one of her braids. She's not prone to nervous habits, and it strikes Daniel as if she needs the haptic input to keep from panicking. "I thought someone had left their garbage next to the container. I went to check, and then I saw— I saw—"

"I heard her scream," Daniel picks up the thread quickly. "I went to see what was wrong, and then I saw the, the body. I...I touched his shoulder to wake him up, and then I checked for a pulse. I couldn't find one, and then I called 911." He doesn't need to stress so often that he touched Mario, he thinks distantly. It's not like fingerprints will stick in this weather. He takes a deep breath to try to calm himself down.

Detective Taylor nods. "All right, thank you very much. I gather you were both acquainted with the deceased?"

"Yes," Colette agrees. "Mario was a colleague. A friend."

Wordlessly, Daniel nods.

The detective notes something on her pad. "And when did you see him last?"

"Yesterday." Daniel thinks back to the afternoon, trying to line up the facts. "I drove him and Colette and Professor Allan home around four p.m., and then I went up to my apartment and Colette and Mario went to hers."

Detective Taylor smiles. "Crime buff, huh?"

He blinks. "How…"

"You keep giving me the times things happened," she tells him. "It's very helpful."

"Oh. It wasn't on purpose." Daniel does keep track of the time pretty well though.

"So, Professor Ravel, Professor Lombardi came over to your apartment?"

Colette nods slowly. "Yes. We had a drink, and later that evening, we went to dinner at Terrapin. He came back to borrow a DVD afterward, and he left sometime after midnight. I was in bed by one."

The detective takes more notes. "Were you and Professor Lombardi in a relationship?"

"We were friends." Colette's finger is still idly toying with her braids. More notes.

"We're not certain what kind of case we're looking at right now." The detective steeples her fingers, looking serious. "So please understand I'm only asking this to be thorough. But did Dr. Lombardi have any enemies?"

"No." Colette's response is instant. "He was very well regarded in his faculty and his field. His students love him. Loved him."

Detective Taylor looks to Daniel.

"I can't think of anyone either," Daniel agrees. "Was he murdered?"

The metal legs of Colette's chair squeak against the linoleum floor as she flinches.

"I'm sorry," Daniel says. "That was probably a stupid question." Mario was shot. In the chest.

"Not at all." The detective smiles tightly. "But we can't make a call about that until the autopsy report is in. I'd still like to ask you both where you were last night, just for the record."

Daniel shrugs. "Like I said. I went to my apartment, and I stayed there. I did some reading, watched TV. I went to bed about midnight."

"Any witnesses?"

"Just my cat."

"And you, Professor Ravel?"

Colette sighs. "As I said, Terrapin, then my apartment with Mario, then he left. I didn't leave the apartment until Daniel came by at nine this morning."

"No witnesses?"

"I suppose the Terrapin waitstaff might remember."

"I heard them leave her apartment to go out for dinner if that helps." Daniel remembers the sound of their laughter, the door falling shut. Maybe it's a good thing he didn't go to Kingston after all, last night.

Detective Taylor sighs and puts her pen down. "Thank you both very much for your statements. Could I take your contact information in case anything else comes up?"

They fill in the forms she provides, and then suddenly, unceremoniously, they're done. The police, she tells them, will inform the college and give the two of them a ride home.

Colette doesn't speak at all in the car. Daniel's never seen her quite so shaken. He follows to her apartment as a matter of course; he doesn't think either of them should be alone right now.

Eventually, when he's made them both a cup of tea and they've both changed into sweatpants and dry socks, she asks, "Do you really think someone murdered Mario?"

Daniel swallows hard. It's a frightening, awful thought. "The detective said she wasn't sure."

"But?"

"But Mario was shot in the heart."

Colette bites at her upper lip, another uncharacteristic nervous habit. "It could have been an accident."

Daniel wants to ask her whether a lot of people fall heart-first onto bullets, but that seems unnecessarily callous. "It could be. I guess we'll find out."

"I hope so," she says.

The shrill ring of her phone makes them both jump.

She scrambles for it and grimaces when she sees the caller ID. After accepting the call and turning on speakerphone, she sets her phone on the table.

"Colette!" Stacy Allan's bright voice is on the line. "How are you? You poor thing!"

"I'm all right." It's not true, of course, but Colette clearly doesn't want condolence from Stacy.

"Florence—you know, from the registrar's office—she said you *found him*." Stacy's voice lowers dramatically as she says the last words as if they don't all know what she means.

"Yes." Colette's fingers reach for her hair again, as if guided by an unconscious reaction every time she has to relive this morning's events. "We did. Daniel and I, that is."

"Oh, and how is he? I couldn't reach him."

Daniel winces and pulls out his phone. Sure enough, two missed calls from Stacy. Good thing his phone is on silent.

"I'm fine, Stacy," he tells her. "I had my ringer off."

"Well, let me know if you two need anything! Anything at all, I'm your neighbor after all. Don't worry about tomorrow either; the President canceled all classes and events for the rest of the week."

"Oh." Daniel hadn't even thought about the mixer. It makes sense.

It's what happens when tragedy strikes in such a small community. "That's good. I don't think I would have managed to bake a cake."

Stacy's bright, tinkly laugh floats down the line and fills Colette's somber living room. It grates on Daniel's every nerve. "Daniel." Her voice is so full of sympathy Daniel kind of wants to hang up the phone immediately. "You're such a sweetheart. I'll be in touch. Rest up, you two, and if you need it, counseling is doing walk-in hours all day tomorrow."

Mercifully, she hangs up the phone, and Daniel sighs in relief.

"She's not wrong," Colette says eventually. It's a first for her.

"About counseling?" That would probably be a good idea for both of them.

"And rest."

"Oh. Yeah. I guess. Shit, you must be so tired."

Colette nods. There are tears glistening in her eyes, and Daniel realizes that as close as they are, this is too close for her.

"I'll let you get some sleep." He gets up to leave. "And if you need anything, you know where to find me."

It draws a weak smile to her face. "You too. I'm sorry to be throwing you out. I just…"

"No, I understand. Take the time you need. I'll even put my phone on loud so you can reach me whenever you're ready."

Before he leaves, she gives him a fierce, tight hug.

He makes it all of two hours alone in his apartment.

Criminal Minds is out of the question right now. So is work. He can't concentrate on anything for more than five minutes put together. He makes himself a PB&J—it's long past lunchtime, and he should probably eat something. It doesn't taste of anything.

After an hour, he realizes he doesn't want to be alone.

He could call his parents.

The thought floods his body with anxiety and relief all at once. If he could only hear his mom's voice, tell her about what happened...

But if he does that right now, he'll end up agreeing to a visit over Christmas, which would mean more berating about when he's going to move back to the Bay Area. It would mean more questions about why he isn't using his "computer skills" to get a job in Silicon Valley and more unsubtle hints that he's getting old enough to settle down and provide a few grandchildren already.

It would be a very short-lived comfort.

He could call Meredith, but she would tell their parents, thinking she was doing him a favor. That would get him the same end result.

He could call Jeff in Ohio.

Jeff never really liked Mario, and he wasn't exactly clear on why. Daniel was left with the uncomfortable feeling that Jeff knew how attractive Daniel found Mario and resented it. Either way, he hasn't talked to Jeff since their breakup a year or so ago, and he's surprised by how little he misses it. That doesn't seem like an auspicious start to a phone call with your ex, especially when the reason for it is that someone died.

There's always Stacy.

Daniel could probably go over to her house, with its overstuffed, plush furniture and the kids leaving their sports equipment and toys all over the place and Stacy's husband a permanent feature on the couch, watching some sport or another. He's about ten years older than Stacy, almost as old as Daniel's parents, and at that age men get to where they nap all the time. As sad as it is, it reminds Daniel of home. Stacy would feed him something delicious and smother him with commiseration.

It would be really cathartic, and Daniel probably should call Stacy.

She's a little much, but she's the perfect person to talk to right now.

He doesn't.

Maybe it's because he's in shock, maybe it's because he's feeling a little too raw to let himself go for the kind of healing Stacy can offer.

Either way, what he ends up doing is taking a quick but thorough shower and pulling on a nice button-up and his least objectionable pair of chinos. He rinses out his mouth with mouthwash, feeds the cat, and then he gets his second raincoat—the one that's not still dripping from this morning—out of the closet, puts his shoes back on, and gets into his car.

Usually, the drive to Kingston takes about twenty minutes, maybe twenty-five if traffic is bad.

Daniel takes forty.

He's acutely aware the whole way that he can only partially see out of the windshield. The wind is so strong he feels it pushing at the car on the bridge. For a second, white-hot terror floods him at the image of his car careening off the sides of the bridge and hitting the Hudson, hundreds of feet below.

By the time he pulls into the lot at Tony's auto shop, he's shaking.

He has to take a few deep breaths before he can get his legs to work enough to walk into the reception area. There's no one there; Tony's sister must be on a break.

Daniel rings the bell.

He's utterly unprepared for Tony to step in from the divider to the garage only seconds later.

A broad smile stretches across Tony's face. "Hi," he says.

Daniel licks his lips. "Hi."

"What can I do you for?"

Daniel's whole throat goes bone dry. "How are you at windshields?"

Tony's lower lip sticks out in an exaggerated pout. "And here I thought you were coming to visit me."

Leaning an elbow on the counter in what he hopes is a flirty way, Daniel jokes, "Well, I was thinking about breaking a side mirror to have a reason to come here, but the storm took care of that for me."

Tony clutches at his heart. "Property damage, for me? You could have just called."

"If I had your number, I would have."

Raising a finger, Tony nods slowly. "You make a good point." The creases around his eyes are all crinkled up with his smile. He has really nice eyes; Daniel wasn't remembering that wrong.

His hair is a little messier today, strands escaping from his ponytail. Daniel wants to tuck them in. Or pull at them. He could go for either.

"So." Tony gets to his feet. "Let's take a look at this windshield."

They walk out onto the windswept parking lot together, and Daniel realizes his is the only car there. "Shit, did I catch you at closing time?"

Tony checks his watch. "Maybe a quarter of an hour out?"

"Oh god," Daniel groans. "I'm so sorry. I can come back tomorrow. I didn't even— It's been kind of a terrible day; I didn't even think."

"Hey, chill out." Tony smiles as if he isn't at all put out by an idiot customer not valuing his time. "I wouldn't have had time for you earlier anyway. This is good. I'll take a look."

"But it's the whole windshield. It will take—"

Tony shakes his head. "I'm not even doing anything, just looking."

"Seriously though, if you're not on the clock anymore—"

Tony rests a hand on his shoulder. He has big hands. Firm. Warm.

Daniel's not sure he ever really warmed up after this morning.

"Let me take a look, sweetheart." Tony lets go to walk around the front of the car. He looks at the crack from different angles. "Jeez, I'm surprised you made it here in one piece."

"Believe me, so was I. Not my favorite way to drive."

"So, we'll definitely need to replace this. It's not actually a huge deal, maybe forty-five minutes, tops, for the work itself."

Daniel breathes a sigh of relief. "That doesn't sound too bad."

"The problem," Tony continues slowly, "is that I'm gonna need to order you a new windshield. That'll take a few days."

"Oh."

Distantly, Daniel's aware there are a myriad of problems he should be concerned about. Driving with a broken windshield for a few days. Getting home in the dark with a broken windshield. Going home to his empty, quiet apartment, knowing his friend got murdered just outside last night.

Being disappointed that he won't get to watch Tony work today shouldn't even make the list.

"Tell you what." Tony leans in close over the windshield. "Come in for a second while I order the part, and then we'll figure out when we can get you your car back."

"Okay, sure," Daniel agrees, too fast and too eager to spend more time with Tony. He tacks on, "But only if that won't make you late closing up shop."

Even in the rising dark, with rain and wind whipping past them, he can see Tony wink at him.

"You can make it worth my while."

Daniel experiences something like déjà vu, leaning against the counter across from Tony as he taps away at the keyboard like his sister did last time. The only differences are the running commentary on how annoying placing orders is without Gianna there and the fact that Tony clearly needs glasses for computer screens because he keeps squinting at the monitor. It's kind of cute.

"She left midway through her shift," he grouses, tapping at the mouse as if that will make the site load faster. "I know she's going through a lot right now, but she didn't even say anything."

"What's she going through?" Daniel asks, watching as Tony scrolls through a list of identical-looking windshields. "I mean, if you don't mind me asking."

Tony shrugs. "She had to drop out of college in the summer. It was really rough on her; she has bigger dreams than this." He gestures to the shop around them.

"I'm sorry to hear that." It feels awkward to add anything more, sitting pretty on his tenure-track assistant professorship.

"Eh." Tony smiles over at him. "I think she'll find something she wants to do more than this sooner or later. But it's our dad's garage, and between you and me, he's a pretty lenient boss."

Daniel smiles, a little charmed despite himself. "Proper family business, then?"

Tony nods, entering an employee key to place the order. Daniel looks away a second too late and tries to forget that the key was clearly someone's birthday. People really need to work on their password safety.

"Do you ever have...bigger dreams?" Daniel asks the wall.

"Nah, not really. Maybe someday, if the Jiffy Lube over on Ulster Ave starts encroaching on our territory or something. I'm good here for now though."

He must have finished the order because he logs out of the computer and powers it down. He doesn't get up though. Instead, he looks at Daniel for a long moment.

Daniel swallows, wishing he could think of something to say.

"So." Tony stuffs his hands in his pockets. "You're not driving home in a storm with a busted windshield."

For a wild, crazy moment, Daniel thinks this is it; this is when Tony will invite him over to his place; this is when all his problems are solved or at least become ignorable.

"Let's find you a car for the weekend." One of the rolls on the desk chair squeaks when Tony gets up and heads for the garage.

Right. Of course. That's a thing people do in auto shops. They lend out cars while yours is being repaired. Daniel is an idiot. He follows Tony through the door.

"Sure you want to get rid of me so fast?" Daniel asks, which is up there on the list of the boldest things he's ever said. Probably also on the list of the stupidest things he's ever said.

Tony flashes him a smile over his shoulder. "Not at all. Just wanna make sure you're taken care of." He crouches to take a look at the car he's in front of, probably to see whether or not Daniel could borrow it.

"I seem to remember something about making overtime worth your while," Daniel points out.

It feels as though Tony's being slow about inspecting the car on purpose. He turns when he's done and leans against the driver's side door with his arms crossed. The swell of his biceps under the shirt fabric is really something. "I was kidding." Tony doesn't quite look at Daniel, more at the air over his left shoulder. "I wouldn't hold you to that."

"And if I wanted you to?"

There's something self-deprecating about Tony's shrug. "Then I'd probably say something really dumb about how I was hoping you'd come back."

"If you want," Daniel carefully picks his way across the garage toward Tony, avoiding tools and cables as he does, "we can skip all the parts where we talk about it."

Tony lets his arms fall open, making space for Daniel to step into place right in front of him. The heat of Tony's body is intoxicating and thrilling and exactly what Daniel was hoping for to help him forget—everything.

"You wanted me to come back, huh?"

"Let's definitely skip the talking." Tony's smiling, and his big hands settle on Daniel's hips.

Kissing him is as good as Daniel remembers. The scratch of his mustache is still exciting, and beneath it, his lips are soft and plush. He seems shy about it, and it makes Daniel chase after the touch of his lips.

"I thought about you too," Daniel whispers between kisses. It feels like a confession, the acknowledgement that their interrupted encounter left such an impression on him. No wonder Tony doesn't want to talk about it.

Apparently, though, Tony wants to hear about it because he groans, a soft little noise, and bends to kiss Daniel's neck.

It makes a full-body shudder run down Daniel's back.

Determined to give as good as he gets, Daniel runs his hands down Tony's sides and then up under the thin fabric of his shirt. He must be freezing. Except he's not, skin warm to the touch, and Tony immediately pushes himself closer to Daniel's touch.

Daniel takes advantage, letting his hand slip down to Tony's ass in his ridiculously tight jeans. He winces as his hand gets caught at the car door handle.

Tony makes a frustrated noise and pushes Daniel away before relocating a foot and a half to the left, practically on the hood of the car. "Come on." His voice is already rough and low. "Make it worth my while."

He drags Daniel in closer as he leans against the hood with his legs spread to make room for Daniel between them. Daniel inhales deeply for a moment, savoring, taking in the scent of motor oil and Tony's cologne—subtle but present. On the list of porn-adjacent fantasies in the back of Daniel's head, this is not one he ever saw coming true. Might as well make the most of it.

"Challenge accepted." Daniel sinks to his knees.

It's easy, with Tony's legs already spread, for him to make space between them. It's even easier to unbutton Tony's jeans and lower the zip carefully over the bulge of his cock where it's already pushing against the fabric of his boxer briefs.

Looking up at Tony from under his eyelashes, Daniel sucks at the line of his cock through the fabric.

"Fuck, sweetheart." The pet name should not be making Daniel's stomach flip. He's over thirty, and it's kind of condescending. Unfortunately, it's also really doing it for Daniel, and he should nip that in the bud, or he might be in danger of getting attached.

"Told you last time I'm not that sweet. You got condoms?" he asks, toying with the elastic waistband of Tony's underwear.

"Uh, yeah. Fuck, my wallet's somewhere..." Holding his pants up as if they were in any danger of slipping, even open, Tony pushes himself off the hood of the car and gets his wallet off the workbench at the far left of the garage. He pulls a condom from inside it, then hands it to Daniel as he settles back on the hood.

"You know the friction in your wallet can rub holes in the latex, right?" Daniel asks before his brain to mouth filter can engage.

Tony blinks. "No, I didn't. I haven't got any others. We don't have to—"

Daniel waves him off. "Sorry. It's not that likely, and it's not like you're gonna get my mouth pregnant. It's just one of those things you learned once—"

"And then you can never not think about it," Tony finishes.

Daniel blinks up at him, surprised. "Yeah, exactly."

A hand settles at the nape of Daniel's neck, warm and careful. Tony's been working with motor oil and probably all sorts of other stuff today, and Daniel should have a lot more issues with Tony touching his hair than he does right now.

"We could do this somewhere more comfortable," Tony suggests.

Daniel grins. "Like where? The back seat?"

It gets a laugh out of Tony, which is nice because it means Daniel and his stupid condom factoids didn't entirely ruin the mood.

Shuffling forward, Daniel presses a kiss to the outline of Tony's cock. "I think it's kinda hot like this."

The hand at Daniel's neck flexes. "You're kinda hot like this."

"Only kinda?" Daniel pouts. "I guess I'll have to try harder." He pulls down Tony's boxer briefs with his teeth and wraps a hand around his cock. It's a decent size, not so huge Daniel's going to break his jaw or anything, but big enough he'll feel it. He strokes a few times, getting Tony fully hard, and then rips the condom open and rolls it down his cock.

It's been a while since he's given a blowjob with a condom. He and Jeff got tested so they could go without one a couple months into the relationship, and Daniel hasn't been with anyone since. Not for lack of wanting, more a lack of opportunity. The Hudson Valley isn't exactly a hotbed of queer activity, especially if you're looking to avoid Lobell students.

Tony has been a welcome surprise.

Enough so that Daniel can deal with the starchy taste of latex as he wraps his mouth around the head of Tony's cock. He can even enjoy it, along with the stretch of his jaw, the bite of Tony's fingernails on his neck, the hiss Tony lets out.

He pushes himself down, takes as much of Tony as he can manage. His cheek bulges out, and he's already starting to drool. Judging by the noise Tony makes, he's into it. With one hand wrapped around the base, Daniel sets a smooth rhythm, pulling back and tonguing the head, leaning in to go as deep as he can. He rests a free hand lightly over the zip of his own fly, just to have something to rock against.

"Sweetheart," Tony breathes above him. There it is again. "You mind if I pull your hair?"

It's a wrench, but Daniel pulls away. "Just don't choke me." He's already a little hoarse. Fuck, it's been *way* too long.

Tony's hand slides up immediately and tugs at the short strands of Daniel's hair. "Baby, you're doing so good."

Daniel isn't proud of how that makes him moan around Tony's cock.

"Yeah, you like that, huh." Tony keeps going, totally unaware what his voice is doing to Daniel. "When I tell you how good you're doing, how nice you feel."

When it comes to blowjobs, Daniel would ordinarily argue that *nice* is kind of damning him with faint praise. He's willing to make exceptions for really hot guys, though, and Tony is really hot, as is the uninterrupted stream of praise slipping from his lips. It trickles down Daniel's spine like liquid-warm honey and settles in his balls, making him whine and rock up into his own hand.

"Fuck, Daniel," Tony moans out. "So good—you're so good—" He trails off into a breathless gasp, and that's Daniel's cue to pull off entirely.

When Tony manages to get his eyes to focus, blinking in barely denied pleasure, Daniel's smirking up at him.

"Told you I wasn't sweet," he says.

He's not expecting Tony to actually growl and haul him up by the arms.

"You're kind of a little shit, aren't you." He's so close to Daniel's mouth Daniel can feel his lips move.

"What are you gonna do about it?" Daniel asks.

Burying his hand in Daniel's hair again, Tony kisses him fiercely.

Daniel goes with it gladly, surrendering to the heat of Tony's mouth and hitching his hips closer to Tony's. His goal might have been to tease Tony a little, but fuck if it didn't get him going like crazy.

He yelps in surprise when Tony starts pushing him backward slowly.

"I gotcha," Tony mutters and then goes right on kissing Daniel senseless.

Daniel's back hits...something, maybe a wall, maybe a workbench, fuck if he cares. Tony takes instant advantage, pushing him further and running his hot mouth down Daniel's neck.

A really awful sound leaves Daniel's throat, somewhere between a hiccup and a whine.

With one hand, Tony works Daniel's pants open, and it's a relief and torture at the same time because his fingers brush against Daniel's cock so softly Daniel wants to cry. He knew those calluses would feel good.

"Please," he gasps.

"Sweet." Tony flashes him a grin, which is not fair at all.

"Asshole." Daniel wraps a hand around both of them. He pulls the condom off and tosses it, a problem for future Daniel, and then he pushes his hips up against Tony's.

His eyes nearly roll back in his skull.

"You're so wet," Tony groans. "You're dripping, baby, all for me?"

Something in Daniel gives. He has no idea where this guy came from or how he managed, within two meetings and a cumulative three-quarters of an hour at most, to precisely pinpoint the brand of condescending, praise-heavy dirty talk that gets Daniel off the most, but he can't resist. "Yeah," he pants. "Yeah, just for you, please, give it to me."

"Fuck, yeah, I'll take care of you, sweetheart, lemme make it good." Tony's hand joins his around their cocks, and fuck, that's even better, the friction only bearable thanks to how much Daniel's leaking, turned on and desperate for it.

"Tony," Daniel manages, and that's about it. Tony's calluses are barely on the right side of too rough against the sensitive skin of his cock. He's hot and hard and pressed tightly to Daniel.

"Yeah," Tony whispers back, breath hot against Daniel's neck.

Heat rises in Daniel's gut, and he grabs blindly for Tony's jaw to kiss him messily. It's the only thing that keeps him from making noise when he comes suddenly, sharply, all over Tony's hand and his cock. The thought of it—that he's making a mess of Tony, that Tony's jerking them off with Daniel's come—sends an aftershock spiking through Daniel's balls, pleasure so sharp he nearly doubles over with it.

"Baby," Tony pants, and then he grunts, and his grip goes tight and hot and liquid as he comes as well, panting into the crook of Daniel's neck.

"Fuck." Daniel gasps for breath.

"Yeah," Tony agrees, still slumped against him.

It takes them a minute to catch their breath and catch their bearings.

This is when Daniel realizes they're leaning on a van. "Oh, shit." He steps away. It's a gray, eight-seater van. Daniel wouldn't know the brand if the CEO called him in person.

He knows this car though. He's seen the faded anti-NRA bumper sticker at least twenty times. And worst of all, he recognizes the figurine stuck to the dashboard.

It's a little golden Oscar statuette on a suction cup.

Daniel gave it to Mario in the faculty white elephant gift exchange in the first holiday season he spent at Lobell three years ago. Mario thought it was funny and also as close as he would ever get to an Oscar. He put it in his car, and that was when they became friends.

Now he's dead, and Daniel had sex up against his car.

They left a long, perfect streak of come right by the driver's side door.

Mario did mention he had a fender bender.

A snort breaks out of Daniel's nose first, and then a full laugh.

He's only saved from sounding hysterical by Tony following his line of sight and starting to laugh as well. Tony crosses the floor to a sink in the corner, where he washes his hands thoroughly before wetting a rag and using it to wipe down the car door.

"There." He finishes cleaning. "No one will know."

Laughter threatens to crawl out of Daniel's throat again. He can't quite tear his eyes away from that golden figurine on the dashboard. "No one," he repeats. It's true, although Tony doesn't know it yet. Mario will never find out what happened up against his car because Mario will never pick up his car.

"You don't need to worry." That sentence alone is proof Tony doesn't know Daniel at all. "We're well past closing time now; no one's gonna come back here."

From somewhere deep in his untapped reserves of interpersonal capabilities, Daniel summons a weak smile. "So long as I didn't get you in trouble."

Tony steps in close. "Not in any way I wasn't asking for." He presses a kiss to Daniel's cheek.

Frantically, Daniel wonders if anyone has done studies on how the human heart reacts to emotional whiplash. It might be life-threatening.

"How are you at driving stick?"

"What?"

"Stick? Like, a manual transmission?"

"I've never tried."

Tony grimaces. "Right. Well, then, I guess you're taking my car."

"*What?*"

"Relax." Tony's dimples transform his whole face, make him seem boyish. He's probably a couple years younger than Daniel. When he smiles broadly, he looks it. "There's no way you can make my car worse than it already is."

Daniel blinks. "You're a mechanic."

Tony just shrugs. "The windshield should be ready by Monday at the latest. What's the worst that could happen?"

The worst that could happen is that whoever shot Mario is lying in wait outside Daniel's apartment, and when he gets home, it will be him next.

"Here." Tony lays a gentle hand on Daniel's shoulder. He hands over his phone. "Put your number in. I'll text you when you can pick up your car. And in the meantime...well, you need some way of getting around, right?"

"That's really generous of you."

Again, Tony shrugs.

"You have to let me pay for the windshield repairs before I leave."

Tony's expression sours. "I feel really weird about asking you to pay a bill after—"

"I feel really weird about *not* paying after. Especially if I'm borrowing your car."

"Well, I don't know how much it will be yet," Tony points out. "I can charge you for the part, but I haven't actually done the work yet."

Daniel sighs. "All right, fine. But—"

Tony presses a brief whisper of a kiss to his lips. "It will be fine. I trust you."

Though it seems like an error in judgment on both their parts, Daniel can't help but reply, "It's mutual."

With nothing else left to talk about, Tony hands over his car keys, and then they're out in the parking lot again. The wind has settled, but it's already dark.

More than anything, Daniel wants to ask if they can forget about him driving home, if he can stay the night, here, with Tony, where he feels something approaching safe. For a wild moment, he considers telling Tony about it all—finding Mario's body, the police station, the van in Tony's garage that will never be picked up.

"Drive safe," Tony says.

Daniel swallows down all the words he nearly said. It would only scare Tony off.

"No worries. I'll take care of your car."

A line tightens on Tony's forehead. "Not just the car, mister. I'm looking forward to seeing you again."

"Me too. I had a great time today."

At that, Tony's expression loosens a little. "Me too."

Because he might as well, Daniel leans in close and presses another close-mouthed kiss to Tony's lips.

When he steps away, Tony's smiling at him, eyes sharp and shrewd. "I knew you were sweet."

Daniel's not sure it's a compliment.

Chapter Four

That night, Daniel doesn't sleep.

It's only a little past seven when he gets home. Driving is an experience, no matter how well Daniel knows the route. Tony was right; his car is a piece of shit. The windshield wipers squeak, and it takes way too long to speed up past twenty miles per hour. How Tony gets around in it is a mystery. The seats are so low it makes Daniel feel like a senior citizen when he tries to clamber out.

Colette's car is parked where it always is. There's a light on in her apartment, which he can see from outside.

He texts her: *How are you doing?*

She doesn't respond.

Daniel could order something to eat. Probably, he should, as he hasn't eaten much today, and there's not a whole lot in the fridge. He just can't stomach the thought of human interaction with someone he doesn't know. The idea of opening the door to a stranger or, even worse, stepping outside the door to meet someone, is more than a little terrifying. There's a family-size bag of Hint of Lime Tostitos in the back of one of his cupboards. It's way too easy to decide that will be his dinner instead. He doesn't have dip, so he makes an unholy combination of tomato paste, sour cream, salt, and shredded cheddar, using up the last reserves from the fridge.

He tries watching TV, but the constant ad breaks make him unexpectedly, violently angry.

He tries to read those articles he downloaded yesterday, but reading them makes him think of Colette, which makes him think of Mario.

Maybe he should have told Tony about Mario. Who else will do it? The van could be sitting in Tony's garage for weeks. Months, even. It depends on if Mario's death makes the news.

But then, he'd have told Tony how he knew, and then Tony would have asked why Daniel's reaction to his friend's death was to have sex with a virtual stranger in said stranger's place of work.

Daniel's still working that one out himself.

He's pretty sure it counts as an unhealthy coping mechanism.

Not the sex; sex is very healthy, and sex with Tony is definitely something Daniel would be interested in revisiting. He's rarely felt so in the moment. There are a lot of think pieces out there about good sex being entirely about communication, and as a queer academic, Daniel has probably read a good 60 percent of them. After this afternoon, he's starting to wonder if there might be some flaws in the theory or, at least, some pretty significant statistical anomalies. Being with Tony, a man he's only met once before and barely communicated with about what they were doing, is...electric. It's not fair to compare it with Daniel's most recent experience prior to Tony; his relationship with Jeff was all about comfort and mutual respect, and it was nice. The sex was more of a regular perk than a main feature, and trying out anything even slightly out of the norm was an occasion. Jeff was always self-conscious of every word he said and noise he made during sex, and it made Daniel nervous in turn. They tried dirty talk, but it was too fraught for either of them to get really into it. No way would they have been spontaneous enough for frotting against a car door in a semipublic place.

Apparently, without Jeff, Daniel is a lot more spontaneous than he thought.

Unfortunately, all the spontaneity in the world doesn't stop him from turning every aspect of the interaction over and over in his mind for half the night.

The worst of it is Mario's car.

Around nine, Daniel starts thinking about the afterlife. He's always been pretty sure it doesn't exist, or if it does, it's so irrelevant to his human existence that it might as well not. The perks of being raised in a mostly lapsed Jewish family include pretty staunch agnosticism. Life after death, when Daniel thinks about it, is a problem for the future. The only thing he can really do about it now is to live as good a life as he can manage, and if there is anything afterward, hope that whoever's running it takes that into account.

At least, those are the guiding religious and philosophical principles by which Daniel usually lives his life. Now, for some reason, he can't help but imagine Mario's ghost watching Daniel have sex up against his car.

What a welcome to the afterlife that would have been. A part of Daniel thinks Mario might have actually applauded him for it—after all, the last thing he ever said to Daniel was that he should "live a little." He even offered to go down to the city with Daniel after he and Jeff split, to help him find a rebound fuck.

Colette scoffed and called Mario crass, although, to be fair, Colette probably misses Jeff more than Daniel does. There's an unfortunate dearth of professors of color, even (or maybe especially) at an institution as liberal as Lobell, and she and Jeff had a kinship over being Black non-Americans.

Whether or not she rejected Mario's suggestion out of respect for Jeff, at the time, Daniel agreed with Colette. He didn't feel any need to rebound like that. Maybe he should have; maybe then, he wouldn't have routed what must be his own messed-up feelings about Mario's death into a hookup that Freud would have a field day with.

One of Daniel's missions in life is to stay off the radar of the world's few remaining Freudians.

He wonders if Mario would have been angry if he was still alive and Daniel were to tell him. It's possible, although Daniel never saw Mario get angry. It seems more likely he'd have thought it was funny, that he'd have clapped Daniel on the shoulder and asked for details in a way Daniel would have found slightly invasive but preferable to getting yelled at.

He wonders if his tryst with Tony would have even happened if not for Mario's death. It's not the kind of behavior within Daniel's comfort zone. At least, it isn't anymore; Daniel likes to think he outgrew quick and risky hookups when he started living in his own place, affording him and his partners some privacy. But people react to grief in all sorts of ways. Daniel knows this even if he hasn't really experienced it before. Maybe his reaction is risky, juvenile behavior.

On the other hand, maybe Tony is just really hot, and Daniel likes him. Maybe it's not all that complicated and psychological, and maybe Daniel is driving himself crazy. The most bizarre part is how having thoughts he can't quite forget makes him think of Tony and the way his eyes crinkle when he smiles, like when he smiled down at Daniel after Daniel spouted irrelevant facts about condom wear and tear.

Colette still hasn't texted him back.

There's one window in the bedroom from which he can see the alley where Mario was shot. Daniel spends most of the evening trying to avoid looking right at it, but as ten ticks into eleven and he starts to get tired, he decides he ought to face it head-on.

He wonders if he heard the gunshot, last night, and mistook it for the wind whipping the tree branches into windows. As an experiment, he lifts the window up a little bit. All he hears is a car passing on the street.

Below him, the alley with the garbage cans is as narrow and dingy as always. The ground remains wet from the rain. All the garbage cans are in the wrong places from the police reorganizing everything to sort out the crime scene.

What if Daniel had woken up properly last night? What if he heard it and went to look out the window? What if he saw it happen, and he was in time to save—

Daniel takes a deep breath and closes the window.

"No," he tells himself.

He brushes his teeth and gets ready for bed.

It's very quiet when he lies down.

The sheets rustle when he turns.

Worf jumps onto the bed heavily and curls up behind Daniel's legs, weighing down the covers.

Daniel is slowly drifting off when another car passes by, the lights pushing through the gap he left in the curtains.

With a sigh, he pushes himself upright and closes the curtains properly.

Next, it's that the bedroom door is fully shut. If whoever shot Mario comes back, what if they come into the building this time? What if

Daniel doesn't hear them, and they go after Colette? What if they creep up the stairs and into his apartment, and it's too late because he's sound asleep?

He cracks the door to his bedroom.

Then, he triple-locks the door to his apartment.

Then, he gives up, makes a cup of tea, and turns on the TV.

Weirdly, *Criminal Minds* is comforting now, with all the lights on. Watching JJ and Morgan tag-team a suspect in the interrogation room makes Daniel feel like there's a chance Mario's murderer will be caught. It only works as long as he actively and harshly pushes aside literally everything he knows about the real US police force.

After about half an episode, Worf follows him out to the couch. He plonks down on Daniel's legs and starts purring like a very small, fluffy guard dog.

By about five in the morning, the sky has gone from pitch-black to dark gray and Daniel has listened to Rossi read six or seven inspirational quotes over stock footage of the *Criminal Minds* team's ridiculously expensive and wasteful private jet.

He drifts off to the sound of the DVD menu looping and wakes up at eleven. The TV has put itself to sleep, and the DVD player logo is bouncing off the sides of the screen.

Worf, still sprawled across Daniel's legs, is watching it idly. Daniel's feet have fallen asleep from being in the same position with a reasonably heavy cat on top of them for so long.

He groans and pushes himself upright.

Instantly, Worf snaps into action. He gets up, stretches, and starts to meow but interrupts himself halfway through with a yawn.

"Sorry, buddy. You must be hungry." There's a crick in Daniel's neck the size of an oxbow lake. He hobbles to the kitchen as his feet wake up.

"You're in luck; it's tuna time."

If Daniel let him, Worf would eat nothing but tuna all day, every day. Thankfully, he would also eat everything else, so Daniel tries to keep the tuna for special occasions out of a halfhearted hope he's somehow helping with climate change and chronic overfishing at least a little bit.

For about an hour, Daniel manages to pretend he's about to start working.

Then, he gets an email from the university president announcing classes have been canceled for the entirety of Thanksgiving week and counseling hours have been extended due to the tragic death of Professor Mario Lombardi.

On his way downstairs, Daniel knocks on Colette's door.

"Colette?" he calls. "Are you home?"

He knows she is. He would have heard her leave, and her car is still in the lot. He can see it from the kitchen window.

"I get that you need time," he adds. "I just...kind of need a friend."

He gives it five minutes.

She doesn't answer.

Somehow, Daniel has managed to forget he's now driving Tony's car despite spending the hours of the night he wasn't obsessing over Mario's death, obsessing over Tony. It's still awful. He has to hunch to get into the driver's seat, and then he has to fiddle with the settings because, in a mysterious and irritating turn of events between yesterday evening and this afternoon, his foot has moved too far away from the gas pedal for comfort. He tries to turn on the radio and gets nothing but static.

"How does he live like this?" Daniel mutters to himself.

He could have walked; it would have been easier. Possibly also faster.

Stacy lives in a house in the suburbs, which is wild. Rhinebeck is barely a dot on the map; how it can have suburbs is a mystery. And yet, Stacy and her family managed. It's probably cheap real estate, or it was ten years ago when they bought it. Daniel can only dream of owning a home someday. Even in upstate New York, it's not likely on a single salary.

At least, it's not likely without owing the bank money for the rest of his natural life, which Daniel is not into as a concept. He got away with a ludicrously small number of student loans by attending a UC school and burning through his entire college fund in undergrad, then working as a TA throughout grad school. But he's very aware that's an incredibly privileged position to be in. And he's still paying off those loans. He's not really interested in spending his whole life in debt.

Not that renting an apartment is all that dissimilar from debt.

Either way, he doesn't see himself in a free-standing four-bedroom house with a large, squat garage on the side.

The yard is a little unkempt, and a section of it appears to be dedicated to a variety of plastic toys that should not have been left out in the storm two nights ago but definitely were.

Daniel eyes it as he walks up the drive and to the door. He's not sure how old Stacy's kids are, but judging by the toys, at least one is in the single digits.

He rings the bell.

It takes Stacy about three minutes to answer, but she calls from inside to let him know she's coming no less than four times.

"Oh, *Daniel!*" she cries when she opens the door. "It's so good to see you!"

"Hi," Daniel manages before being wrapped up in a massive hug. For such a small person, it's amazing how firm her grip is.

"Come in, come in." She beckons him into the house. This was

Daniel's intention in coming here—talking to another human being about what happened, maybe feeling a bit comforted—but he feels weird and intrusive about following her into the house and toeing off his shoes. He's only ever been here for faculty dinner parties once a semester with four or five other colleagues.

Stacy seats him on the living room couch, which takes up a solid third of the room and is a little too worn through to be really comfortable. "You want something to drink? I can make coffee, or cocoa, or—"

He tries to tell her he's fine, but he ends up with a cup of cocoa and a plate of toast with sausage links left over from the Allan family breakfast anyway.

"How are you holding up?" Stacy leans in a bit too close as he eats. She has her own cocoa, but she's not touching it.

Daniel shrugs awkwardly and swallows. "I've been better. I thought maybe...I don't know, I needed to be around people. I hope that's okay."

"Of *course*, Daniel." Stacy pats his shoulder. "Do you want to talk about it?"

Daniel pushes a bite of sausage around his plate. The Allans are syrup on sausage people, apparently, and it's disconcertingly sticky. "Remember parents' weekend last year? When the film department did a screening of student films and—"

"Oh god." Stacy grimaces. "Do I ever. The registrar's office was getting phone calls for *weeks*."

"Mario stayed till three in the morning cleaning up all the stains after the students, um, innovated 5D filmmaking."

She shakes her head ruefully. "I didn't know that. Not gonna lie; I still wish he intervened *before* they sprayed an audience of parents, students, and *other professors* with ketchup."

"He had a lot of feelings about artistic freedom." Daniel makes a face at the memory, somewhere between a smile and a grimace. "I can't claim I agreed with all of them, but..."

"You talked to him a lot about stuff like that, huh?" Stacy leans back on the couch and takes a long sip of her cocoa.

Daniel shrugs again. "I guess. We're academics; it's part of the business, right?"

She shakes her head again. "I think I'm too old for that. Or maybe it's the kids; I don't know. Feels like I'm always running around taking care of them, or I'm running after administration and students."

It would probably be tactless to agree that she's a good ten years older than him and Colette and Mario. Probably, he should say something else, but he can't think of anything. He eats more toast instead. It's gone soggy after sitting around all morning.

"Do you remember the faculty retreat two years ago?" Stacy asks.

Daniel nods around his mouthful.

"It was such a disaster."

"It *was*?" Daniel asks. "I mean, *I* thought so because I hate faculty retreats. But everyone else..."

She sets down her mug and stares at him. "Daniel, we debated the ethics of professor-student relationships for *six hours*. The motion against it failed by *two* votes, and now everyone is still upset about it."

"Isn't that just normal academic posturing?"

"I guess." Stacy looks out the window at her dreary yard. "Like I said, I don't get much of that these days. I remember Mario went out on a snack run midway through the second hour, and he kept handing them out to everyone, filibustering on both sides."

Daniel laughs. "He loved chaos, I guess."

"He did." Stacy makes a noise that might be laugh if it were happier. "Did he think it was funny? Or was he actually interested to hear what people were arguing?"

"Probably some combination." Daniel sets his plate aside. "Hey, Stacy?"

"Hm?"

"I...I feel like I should be thinking about him all the time, and I am. I'm also... Is it really selfish that I'm terrified whoever did it will come *back*?"

Stacy blinks for a second, and then she gasps. "Oh my god, Daniel, I didn't even *think* about that. It was right by your apartment building, wasn't it?"

He nods.

She pats his shoulder again.

It does make him feel better. "Hey, I have a good one. Lobellpalooza, last year."

"Oh boy," Stacy groans.

"Yeah."

Lobellpalooza is the campus-wide festival weekend right after the seniors hand in their senior theses. There's a fund for musical and performance acts, which would be outrageous in any reasonable society, but for a liberal arts college, it's on the small side. The whole thing is a nightmare for Residence Life and Housing as well as for Health Services and Counseling. So much alcohol poisoning, so much nonconsensual groping.

The students not affected by either of the former love it.

Last year, the favored main act turned them down (hearsay has it she took a gig playing her bizarre electronic music at a billionaire's yacht party instead, and given what Daniel knows about Lobell's financial situation, who can blame her). The planning committee came up with an alternative, JimmyJamz, a flash-in-the-pan R&B star from a tiny island in the Caribbean. He had one hit when Daniel was still in undergrad.

"So, I wasn't on campus, obviously." Daniel makes it a point to be as far away from Lobellpalooza as he can without inconveniencing himself. Seeing his students drunk, high, or both would be embarrassing for everyone involved.

Stacy purses her lips. "Lucky you."

He raises an eyebrow.

"Oh, Title Nine stuff." She waves her hand dismissively. "I would *love* not to have to witness Lobellpalooza, especially given all the senior theses I have to read right about then, but every time, I get a call on Friday evening at some point about something terrible that happened to someone."

"Ah." Daniel picks at his fingernails. "Well, that makes this story less funny."

"No, no, I bet if you're not tied up in all that, it's a great time. So long as you're not...you know, affected."

"Sure," Daniel agrees slowly. "Well, Mario and Colette liked to check it out from a distance when it was late enough the students didn't notice the professors being about. Last year, he called me three times from the JimmyJamz concert to keep me updated."

Mario spaced the calls apart over forty-five minutes while Daniel was trying to sleep, which made the whole thing more of an exercise in FOMO than a friendly gesture. It was only the following morning when Daniel listened in to the two extra voicemails Mario left after he turned his phone off that revealed JimmyJamz arrived several hours too late for his own concert and then proceeded to play his only hit in a loop for a solid hour.

Mario still sometimes talked about it.

"That concert was a disaster." Stacy groans at the mere memory, and from an administrative perspective, Daniel knows why. Lobellpalooza stories really are only funny from a comfortable distance. "I can see why he'd call."

"Oh, yeah." Daniel snickers. "Half an hour in. *Hey, Rosenbaum. Just wanted to let you know he's playing the same song. If he weren't so off-key, I'd think this is an Ashlee Simpson situation.*"

Stacy snorts and then covers her mouth as if she hadn't meant to laugh.

They sit in silence for a while after, apparently both out of Mario stories. Daniel has a few others, but they mostly involve alcohol or Mario intentionally creating chaos of some sort, or both. And Stacy seems as though she doesn't appreciate that given her memory of the faculty retreat incident. Daniel's starting to wonder if now is the time to extricate himself from this situation, now that he's eaten her food and let her comfort him like some sort of emotional sponge. He should probably offer to help out with whatever fallout is happening at Lobell first.

A key twists in the lock, and then a sudden influx of noise alerts Daniel to the fact that Stacy's family must be home.

"Stace?" a man calls. "Stace, are you here? Can you take Jason to soccer?"

Stacy's eyes close briefly. "Hi, honey." There's a level of cheer in her voice that was absent a moment ago. "I'm sure I can make it work, but I thought you were going to?"

Stacy's husband pokes his graying head into the living room and waves at Daniel. "Yeah, but only because I thought you couldn't. It's been a *day*. Some kid threw up in the locker rooms again; had to call the janitor back after hours to deal with it."

Daniel shakes his head. "The American public school system."

"You said it, man." Stacy's husband makes a "right on" gesture with his fist, which makes it seem as if he and Daniel have a lot more in common than they do.

Daniel feels pretty comfortable about having forgotten his first name because there's no way he remembers Daniel's. Daniel has curated a lifelong ability of being utterly unmemorable to PE teachers, and he's sticking to it.

"I'll be ready in a second, Mom," the kid that must be Jason calls from somewhere in the house. "I just gotta find my cleats!"

"No problem." Stacy's voice has gone high and hectic, the way it does right before some major faculty event. "I'll make it work. I should drive over to Lobell again anyway while Jason's at practice."

"You're a star," her husband says with an incredibly sleazy wink. It would be less weird if he weren't ten years older than her and a PE teacher, Daniel's pretty sure.

"That's my cue." Daniel gets to his feet. "Thanks for having me, Stacy."

"Anytime. And if you need anything at all—"

"I should be saying that to you." He's firm, trying not to give her husband the stink eye. "Let me know if there's anything, at work or otherwise."

It might be his imagination, but he's pretty sure she hugs him extra tight before they both get into their separate cars, her with her awkward, pimply teenage son and him with a wince as he remembers again how terrible Tony's car is.

He checks his phone before he drives.

Colette still hasn't answered him.

Does he go home to his apartment now and watch more bad crime shows? He should probably go shopping first, while it's light enough that he doesn't fully psych himself out.

It's only four in the afternoon. There's a lot of day—and night—left for Daniel to get through. He's groggy from having slept weirdly, and he can already feel himself edging toward last night's panic at the idea of getting through the rest of the day alone.

A new text comes in on his phone.

hey Daniel, my windshield guy came through superfast. wanna work overtime with me again today?

It's followed by a winking emoji, and then by *this is Tony btw.*

Daniel's not proud of it, but he breathes a sigh of relief. He doesn't have to spend the rest of the day in his apartment alone.

Anything to stop driving your terrible car, he texts back, adding the emoji with its tongue sticking out so Tony can tell he's mostly kidding. He puts the car in drive and, after a quick pit stop at home to change into a nicer shirt and grab a few supplies, he heads for Kingston.

The weather is, if possible, worse than it was yesterday. The bridge is still nightmarish, and dark clouds are piling up overhead. But Daniel feels more like himself when he pulls into the parking lot at the garage than he did yesterday. That, he reflects, is both a good sign for his mental health and a bad sign for his ability to seduce a hot mechanic. What if Tony was only into him yesterday due to the slightly unhinged vibes?

He takes a deep breath. Tony invited him this time. He checks his hair in the rearview mirror, realizes there's nothing he can do about it, and gets out of the car.

The reception area is empty, the computer already turned off. Gianna must have left early again, or maybe the shop closes at four; Daniel didn't look it up. He's trying to power through by not letting himself think about the actual practical ramifications of Tony's life. If he did, he'd have started googling Tony, the store, and everyone else who works here obsessively yesterday, and that would have been stupid. He pushes open the door to the workshop and goes straight through.

There, bent over the hood of Daniel's car, is Tony. He's lifting the broken windshield out carefully, concentrating fully on what he's doing. There's a little frown line at the middle of his forehead. He must have been wearing a flannel shirt for most of the day because it's crumpled up on the workbench in the corner. Tony is down to a white tank top and his jeans, and both have motor oil stains on them. Daniel's not sure why he's so attracted to the sight, but he's not complaining.

He waits for Tony to place the windshield down carefully, leaning it against the wall, before he says, "Hey."

Tony straightens immediately. "Hi." He waves, then looks at his own hand, clearly realizing he's still wearing heavy-duty gloves. "Uh…"

"How's it going?" Daniel asks.

"Good. We are right on schedule with your windshield. How'd my girl treat you?"

Daniel takes a seat on the stool he sat on the first time they met. He's not going to start thinking of it as his place or anything, but it's nice to feel like he could have a regular seat in Tony's garage. "Absolutely terribly. As I'm sure you know."

Tony laughs and starts scraping what looks like old rubber out of the sides of the hole where Daniel's car used to have a windshield. "You gotta treat her right, and she handles fine."

"You're kidding." It sounds rude as soon as it's out of Daniel's mouth, but he can't help himself. "You're not one of those guys who's into the whole…cars as women thing, right?"

For a long moment, Tony's quiet as he concentrates on cleaning the last of the gunk out of the windshield hole. Daniel's terrified he's stepped on some secret mechanic's code of honor.

Then, Tony straightens and grins at him. "Yeah, I'm messing with you.”

He walks over to the workbench, close enough that Daniel can smell his aftershave, and picks up something that looks, to Daniel's untrained eye, like a paint gun.

“Your face does a really funny thing when you think I'm being mildly politically incorrect though,” Tony informs him. “Like you can't figure out if you have a moral duty to be mad at me. It's kind of worth it.” He cocks his not-a-paint-gun and grins at Daniel, waggling his eyebrows.

“Okay, what is that thing?”

“Just my caulk.” Tony's voice is innocent.

“Your *what*?”

Laughing, Tony explains, “It's a caulking gun. I couldn't resist.”

Daniel rolls his eyes to hide that he still doesn't really know what it is.

“I'm gonna put a new layer of urethane down, and then we can get your new windshield in,” Tony tells him and does just that.

It's all over remarkably fast. In Daniel's head, replacing a windshield was a long and complex project (and if he were the one doing it, it probably would be). Why he'd driven over yesterday afternoon thinking Tony could magically get it done is anyone's guess. Daniel wasn't thinking clearly at the time. It's good to know he's not taking up a full workday for Tony though.

When it's all said and done, the actual work takes only a little over half an hour.

Tony carefully sets the rubber seal around the edges of the windshield and steps away from the car, admiring his handiwork. “There we go.”

“So.” Daniel's voice is as casual as he can make it. “You said it takes an hour to dry?"

Tony turns to him. "I did say that, didn't I. And you were wondering what we could do in the meantime."

"I don't remember wondering that."

"It was implied." Tony winks.

Daniel moves toward Tony as if drawn magnetically. He loops his arms around Tony's neck and leans in, a hair's breadth away from a kiss.

Thunder rumbles so loudly above them that, for a second, Daniel thinks the garage roof is going to cave in.

He pulls away, startled.

"Another storm?" Tony peers out the garage door. "Jesus fucking Christ."

"Is it bad?"

"It's not good." Tony gestures Daniel over.

Rain sheets down so hard Daniel can hardly see ten feet ahead. The streetlights are the only hazy point of light ahead of them. It looks like the world is ending.

Daniel pulls his phone out of his pocket. He has a text from Stacy and one from his mom. His weather app has sent an alert for inclement weather. There's an extra exclamation point on it, which means at least one road has already been closed. He's supposed to drive in that in an hour.

"Okay." Tony speaks slowly, as if afraid he'll spook Daniel. "I'm gonna suggest something really crazy, but hear me out."

Turning to him, Daniel raises an eyebrow.

"If you drive in that, you're gonna fuck up your brand-new windshield. Or, you know, get in an accident. Let's get a motel room."

It's almost exactly what Daniel was hoping for secretly, anything to keep him from spending the night alone in his apartment.

"Don't trust me enough to take me to yours?" Daniel jokes weakly.

Tony grimaces. "I live with my parents."

That tracks with the whole family business thing. It should probably be a red flag, given Tony looks to be in his midtwenties, but Daniel's too busy being relieved it's nothing to do with him that Tony didn't ask him over. He peers outside again and tries to picture driving across the bridge in this weather, if it's even still open. The Hudson is so big its waters are usually placid. In this, it will be terrifying. "I don't care if it's crazy. I've been having the most insane week of my life anyway. Let's do it."

Tony pumps his fist once in victory.

After locking up the garage, he drives them—slowly, carefully— through the rain. Irritatingly, he drives his car so smoothly Daniel nearly forgets how bad he was at it. They end up at a dinky little place called the 9W Motel, which is scraping the bottom of the barrel as far as Daniel's concerned. Naming the motel after the road it's on is tantamount to admitting its only claim to fame is being better than sleeping rough.

Tony sends him in to get a room key, saying the receptionist knows his mom, and he doesn't need that. Small-town woes.

Daniel's going two for two here on the questionable sexual decisions with this guy. He thinks this as he unlocks the door to their room and pulls Tony in, out of the rain. Shacking up for the night in a skeevy motel room with a mechanic he's only met twice. He doesn't know Tony's last name or much of anything about him beyond that he has a potentially strained relationship with his sister and doesn't like the fourth season of *Buffy*. Daniel doesn't even have a change of clothes with him.

Somehow, he doesn't mind so much when Tony pushes him against the closed door and kisses him.

The thunder still roars above them, but the room is warm and not totally hideous, and Tony's mouth is slick and wet against his. Daniel officially doesn't care about anything outside of these four walls, at least until tomorrow. He kisses Tony back and runs his hands up under Tony's T-shirt.

"Fuck, you're so hot," Daniel mutters between kisses, utterly distracted in the best way.

"Me?" Tony laughs incredulously. "Fuck, baby, look at you."

Daniel doesn't think he's anything special, but Tony kisses both of his cheeks, licks a hot line up his neck, mouths at his collarbone. All the while, he undoes Daniel's shirt button by button until it's hanging loose and open, and then he stops and gazes at Daniel.

"Look at you," he repeats, quieter.

Daniel's every instinct is to cross his arms over his stomach, to make a self-deprecating joke, but he can't think of anything at all to say. Not when Tony's looking at him like this, all hunger and honest, open desire.

He has nothing to be ashamed of; it's just his body, and someone likes it.

He cups Tony's jaw in one hand and rests the other on his hip as he kisses Tony, slow and deep, with every ounce of appreciation he can muster for this wild, wonderful night.

When they pull away, Tony turns a fraction to press a kiss to his palm.

Daniel's heart thunders in his chest. "What are the chances of you fucking me tonight?" he blurts out.

Tony's eyes slide shut. "Really fucking good, sweetheart."

"I was hoping you would say that." Daniel pulls the condom and single-use pack of lube out of his pocket and throws them on the bed.

Tony whistles. "Boy Scout."

Daniel shrugs. "I knew I was coming to see you, didn't I?"

He pulls the hem of Tony's tank top up. and together, they get it off. Daniel lets his fingertips skim lightly over the paler skin of Tony's chest and sides. "Ticklish?" he asks when Tony flinches.

"Little bit," Tony admits, a smile pulling at his lips.

Daniel takes ruthless advantage, and the ensuing tickle fight propels them across the room toward the bed. On the way, Daniel's shirt falls off his arms, and they both kick their shoes off.

The bed has loud springs, but it turns out Daniel doesn't give a shit what motel patrons in Kingston might think of him. When Tony kneels between Daniel's legs, blankets Daniel's body with his own, and nips at his collarbone, he throws his head back and groans.

"What do you want?" Tony murmurs in his ear.

"I don't want to feel anything but you," Daniel tells him. "I want to be overwhelmed."

"Wow."

Daniel looks up at Tony. Should he play it off as a joke? Should he rephrase? He can—

"Tall order, but I'll see what I can do." Tony grins. "Big brain like yours, college boy? I don't see it turning off easy."

"I think you can do it."

"Challenge accepted," Tony says, and that's the last they talk for a while.

That doesn't mean Daniel doesn't make noise.

He moans into Tony's mouth while Tony kisses him hot and wet and slick and sloppy as they rock together, going from interested to desperate in a matter of minutes.

He hisses when Tony moves down his body to toy at his nipples, sensitive and pebbled with arousal.

He sighs when Tony strokes his sides, which are a little too soft in his own image of himself but apparently just right for Tony.

His breath hitches when Tony reaches for the lube and sets one wet finger at his entrance.

He's hard by then, hard and dripping against his own stomach, but Tony bypasses his cock entirely.

It really doesn't bear thinking about the noises he makes as Tony stretches him open, first one finger making him sigh and groan, then two making him produce the strange stuttering groan Tony appears to be an expert at drawing out of him. Finally, when Tony slips in a third finger and angles them up to stab right at Daniel's prostate, he shouts up to the ceiling.

"Enough," he pants, barely able to catch his breath. "Please fuck me."

"Hmm." Tony lets his free hand stroke gently down Daniel's side. "I don't know. You don't seem overwhelmed yet."

He repeats the motion of his fingers, and Daniel nearly cries. The third time he does it, Tony licks once, delicately, at the head of Daniel's cock, and Daniel can barely *think*.

"Wish we had a second condom," Tony says wistfully. "I'd get you off like this once, and then again on my cock."

If he were at all in his right mind, Daniel would tell Tony that he's wildly underestimating Daniel's refractory period, but right then, Tony pulls his fingers out and all Daniel can seem to do is whine for more.

"Shh, I got you." Tony fumbles with the condom wrapper and then slots himself into place between Daniel's legs, warm and heavy and solid.

It takes Daniel's breath away, that first slide of Tony's cock into him. He's not as ready as he thought he was, or maybe it's been too long, but it's so much at first that he can barely even see.

Tony seems to get it, and he holds steady, unmoving at first.

It's only when Daniel finally gets his eyes open and sees the clench of Tony's jaw that he realizes how much effort it's taking him. He's shaking with it.

Daniel hooks his heels together behind Tony's back. "C'mon," he demands, with a taunt in there somewhere—*show me what you've got, make me feel it*—but he loses his words and his breath all over again when Tony starts fucking him properly.

It's not only the movement of his hips, the slow slide in and out, the gradual build of pleasure; it's his words.

"You feel so good, baby," Tony croons. "You're so perfect for me like this."

Praise drips from his tongue like honey, and Daniel laps it up, urging him on with pleas and his heels, digging into Tony's back to get him to move that tiny bit faster.

Before too long, his thighs start to cramp, and he has to let his legs fall open on either side of Tony. Tony takes it in stride, pushing Daniel's knees toward his shoulders, and oh fuck, Daniel wasn't aware his body still did that; it's been a hot minute since he was stressed enough to try yoga, but the *angle* of it...

"Please," he moans, "right there."

"I gotcha," Tony pants, and he does. He's doing so good; he's fucking Daniel steady and thorough and *hard*, and Daniel isn't thinking of anything at all but the rhythm of their bodies and how turned on he is.

He scrambles to reach between them, to stroke himself a little, but Tony's too close to him, he can't get a hand in between. It's devastating to feel this much pleasure and have nowhere for it to go, and Daniel feels tears build behind his eyes.

"Oh, you're ready for it, aren't you," Tony says, and then he's pulling out and away, and Daniel reaches for him desperately.

"Shh, no, wait a second," Tony tells him. "Get on your knees, yeah?"

With Tony's help, Daniel manages to turn over shakily, propped on knees and elbows, and then Tony slides into him again, and he makes a sound like he's been gutted.

Tony's hand wraps around his cock, and pleasure slams into Daniel so suddenly he knows it'll all be over in a matter of seconds.

"Wait," he breathes, and Tony pulls away.

"What's wrong, sweetheart?" Tony asks, hips stilling.

"Don't want it to be over," Daniel manages.

Tony laughs. He starts to move again, just as fast, and god, whether or not he's touching Daniel, it feels like Daniel might explode.

"But you're so ready for it," Tony murmurs in his ear. "Look how wet you got, baby. You want it so bad you're dripping with it. Lemme make it good for you."

Daniel whimpers.

Tony's hand snakes around his cock again, and fuck, there's no stopping it now. His balls tighten and clench; Tony fucks in at exactly the right angle, and Daniel comes with a strangled groan.

He's used to orgasm being a moment of stillness, but even through his clenching and writhing, Tony keeps fucking him. It would have been a good orgasm, but with Tony continuing to pound his prostate ruthlessly, Daniel can't seem to stop coming. He shoots rope after rope of come onto the tacky bedspread and then all over Tony's hand, and Tony keeps going. Each new thrust sends another shockwave of pleasure through Daniel's gut, and he knows he has only seconds until it turns to painful oversensitivity, but it's so good he's still panting and moaning and gasping like he's being filmed.

"Oh my god," Tony mutters into his skin, shell-shocked and shaky.

"Oh my god, Daniel."

"Come on." Daniel reaches behind himself to rest a hand on Tony's hip. "Fill me up."

With a guttural groan, Tony follows the order instantly.

Daniel has never felt more powerful or more desired in his life.

Not even the lukewarm hotel shower can dim his buzz in the aftermath, nor the smell of stale cigarette smoke that lingers in the sheets. It's a queen-size bed, big enough for two, but it should be weird, sharing a bed with someone new.

It's not.

"Fuck, I needed that." Daniel groans as he stretches out on the bed, Tony curled beside him, propped on an elbow and watching.

"Seemed like it," Tony agrees. "Anytime you have another crazy week, let me know."

Forcibly, Daniel rejects the thought of his week. He turns onto his side, back to Tony, and lets himself fall asleep.

Chapter Five

Daniel wakes up with a dry mouth, a headache, and an inextinguishable sense of unease. For a moment, he thinks he's hungover before he remembers he didn't drink any alcohol yesterday. He did go for another round with Tony in the dead of night, that time with Tony fucking his thighs and jerking him off slow and steady and perfect. He also didn't drink any water, which is probably why he feels like death.

The sight of Mario's dead body flashes before his mind's eye, and Daniel sits bolt upright in bed.

Behind him, Tony groans, jostled by Daniel's movement.

Oh shit. Tony.

"What's going on?" he slurs, still half asleep.

"Nothing. Sorry." Even to himself, his voice sounds all wrong, tense and tight and scared.

Tony pushes himself up slowly, yawning. "Baby?"

"I just, uh…" Daniel doesn't know how he's going to finish it.

Wrapping his arms around Daniel's middle, Tony hooks his chin over Daniel's shoulder. "If you wanna talk about it…"

Daniel shakes his head. "I mean, I do," he corrects hurriedly when he realizes that might come off as douchey. "But it's really heavy, and a lot, and we had such a good night." He doesn't say, *and I barely know you*, but he thinks it loudly enough he's pretty sure Tony hears.

Tony kisses his shoulder. "Yeah, we did. I don't mind heavy though."

Daniel takes a deep breath, but he doesn't answer.

After a moment, Tony slides out of bed and starts pulling on yesterday's clothes. Daniel heads for the bathroom. There are no toothbrushes, but there is some complimentary toothpaste, so he makes do by swirling that around his mouth. He debates drinking from the faucet to do something about his persistent dry mouth and the fact that his brain feels like a shriveled raisin, but Hudson Valley tap water tastes so intensely of chlorine Daniel would rather be thirsty.

He's not sure what the etiquette is here. Do they go their separate ways? It's the done thing for a one-night stand, probably, only Daniel's dependent on Tony to get him back to his car. He's also not 100 percent on the whole one-night stand thing. On a technicality, they're already disqualified by having had sex before. On less of a technicality, the way Tony looked at him last night makes Daniel want to see if there might be something more there.

It's probably meaningless, he tells himself sternly. Some people are really good at making other people feel special, and that's a quality that gets you laid. Anyway, if Daniel breaks a side mirror now to have an excuse to return, Tony will absolutely be onto him.

"So." Tony rocks on the balls of his feet when Daniel comes out of the bathroom. "I don't want to rush you, but I have to be at work in about ten minutes."

"Shit." Daniel scrambles for his phone to check the time. "Is it already that late?"

Tony shrugs. "Guess so. Believe me, I'd rather stay in bed with you."

It charms a laugh out of Daniel. "You're insatiable."

Spreading his arms wide to indicate his innocence, Tony says, "Hey, I'm just being practical! Who knows when you'll next have car trouble?"

"I could give you my address so you could come by and slash my tires or something."

"Tempting." Tony scratches his chin. "But how would you get here on slashed tires?"

Daniel nods slowly. "You raise a good point. You do have my number, to save us the logistical difficulties."

Tony points at him. "Clever. Very clever. However..." He pulls open the motel room door, ushering Daniel out. "I texted you, so you have my number too."

Daniel walks over to Tony's godawful car, squinting against the sunlight. For some reason, he was expecting it to be as gray and rainy as yesterday, but it seems the storm has finally completely passed. The sky is clear and beautiful, and the air is sharp and cold. The car looks even worse in bright lighting—the paint job must be getting on in years. Tony's not after a one-night stand, then. Maybe he's angling for more of a fuckbuddy situation? Daniel is by all accounts too fucking old to have a fuckbuddy, but he did make a New Year's resolution to try something new every month. Granted, he meant foodwise at the time, but still.

He sits in the passenger seat, buckles his belt, and then slides out his phone so he can save Tony's number to his contacts. Uncharacteristically, he's considering texting Tony before they've even said goodbye...

When he's done, Daniel sets the phone on the dash and flicks the radio on.

—and this just in. We've received breaking news that Lobell College announced the sudden death of faculty member Mario Lombardi several days ago. The circumstances of Dr. Lombardi's death are still unclear, but we here at WBPM send our heartfelt condolences to the Lobell community and especially to—

Daniel flicks the radio off again.

He's shaking, he realizes absently. His hands are, at least. And his legs, a little.

Out of the corner of his eyes, he looks over at Tony to see if he noticed.

Tony's knuckles are white on the steering wheel, and his jaw is clenched tight. "Did you know him?" he asks roughly.

There's a lump in Daniel's throat he can barely speak around. "Yeah. We were friends. I found him—I found his body. Day before yesterday."

Something like a snort forces its way out of Tony's nose. "Jeez, you weren't kidding about it being a weird week."

"Yeah," Daniel says hoarsely. He wants desperately to add something about how he didn't come see Tony because of Mario's death, but he's not sure that would be true. Either way, it would sound desperate.

They pass two intersections in silence before Tony pulls into the garage lot. "I'm sorry." He puts the car in park. "About your friend." His voice is tight and controlled, nothing like he sounded a minute ago.

"Thanks." There's probably more Daniel could or should answer, but he can't think of a single word.

"You can wait in the main office for a sec. I'll get your paperwork from the back." Tony practically jumps out of the car and heads for the garage.

"Right," Daniel tells his retreating back, feeling oddly as if he's the one who did something wrong here. The turn of events has left him discombobulated. There's a reason he didn't tell Tony about Mario, which is largely that he was in shock and didn't know how to, but also that it seemed like too much to put on a guy who is, for all intents and purposes, a stranger. Now, he's wondering if that was wrong and if he should have. Tony clearly seems to think so.

It's not as though he was using Tony or something, Daniel rationalizes. He was genuinely in need of a new windshield, and it's not as if Tony got nothing out of it. They both enjoyed yesterday.

Of course, there's also the van.

Mario's van that they had sex against two days ago, which Daniel realized at the time and Tony's maybe only now realizing. Shit, Daniel should have said something.

He pushes open the glass door of the main office and stops dead when he sees Tony's sister sitting at her spot behind the desk.

Of course she's there. She works there, and if she weren't already in, the door would have been locked. He's just surprised to see her, given what Tony said yesterday.

"Hi," he says.

"What can I do you for?" She doesn't look up, and she sounds incredibly bored. Tony said it better.

"Um, I got a new windshield yesterday." Daniel will presumably never not feel like an idiot talking about anything to do with cars. It's a wonder Tony even wanted to see him again. "Tony said he'd be right in with the paperwork and stuff."

She does look up then, frowning. Her eyes are red-rimmed. "What time did you get here?"

"Uh, pretty late, almost six." Daniel wonders if he should ask if she's okay, but his interactions with her so far have not given him the impression she would take kindly to it. He feels like the power of her scorn would decimate him on the spot, so he decides discretion is the better part of valor.

One of her well-groomed eyebrows raises, the one with the piercing. She doesn't say anything about the time, she only asks for his name and address. She pushes up the cuffs of her oversized sweater to reach the keyboard.

"You're not going to send me a ton of coupons or something, are you?" he asks suspiciously.

"Not unless you're really into two for one on spare tires."

She does talk a lot like Tony, but she lacks his warmth. His crinkly-eyed smile. His little ponytail.

"Paper or plastic?" she asks, and while he's distracted fumbling his debit card out of his wallet, she adds, "You're the one he lent his car to, huh?"

Daniel drops his card to the floor.

"Yeah." He bends down to pick it up.

"Hm. Drives terribly, doesn't it?"

"Yeah." Daniel manages a forced laugh.

"First car he ever got. You'd think he'd have traded up by now, working here. He's had it more than ten years. But he's attached or something."

Daniel tries not to smile. It's not cute. It's not. "Well, I'm glad he got the windshield in early. I'd be scared to drive his car for too long. Who knows what I'd do to it."

Finally, she cracks a smile. It doesn't meet her eyes.

Tony pushes aside the curtain separating the garage from the front desk. "Morning, Gianna." He presses a kiss to the top of her head.

"Ew." She scowls at him. "You're supposed to be mad at me for leaving early the other day."

Tony doesn't answer, just shakes his head. "This is for Daniel's bill." He hands her a sticker with a bar code.

She scans it in and prints the bill. It's less expensive than Daniel thought it would be, but he did also think it would take hours and hours of work.

"So," he tries, once he's paid and signed. "Um. Thanks?"

"Yeah." Tony smiles, but it's tight and awkward. "Yeah. Sure. I gotta... I'll drive your car out onto the lot in a second?"

"Okay." Daniel puts his wallet away again. He wonders if he's supposed to kiss Tony goodbye, but with his sister watching and whatever it is that changed so intensely in the last ten minutes, he doesn't want to.

When no one else says anything, he heads out for the lot.

Peering back through the glass door, he sees Tony clutching his sister's arms hard enough to pull the neckline of her sweater clear off her shoulder and looking at her intently. She's staring at the floor. Daniel probably shouldn't be watching, but he is because Tony so clearly wanted him to get out, and Daniel is the kind of person who needs to understand things. Maybe Tony's sister doesn't know he's into men?

She's clearly still upset. He can barely see through the door how she reaches up to wipe fresh tears away from her eyes.

Daniel really hopes finding out her brother slept with a man doesn't cause that reaction. He turns away to give them some privacy. It only ends up being a matter of minutes before Tony drives his car out anyway, so it can't have been too serious a conversation.

The goodbyes are awkward, stilted words by the open driver's side door.

"I guess I'll hear from you?" Daniel hears himself asking.

"Yeah. Yeah, definitely. Drive safe."

The other side of the Hudson is not exactly an odyssey, but you wouldn't know it from the finality of how he says it.

Daniel plays it over in his head while he drives, how the mood changed so suddenly after the radio turned on—as soon as the reality of Daniel's life set in, as soon as Tony realized he had more going on than a fun fuck every now and then.

It's hard not to feel a little insulted.

Maybe he's not giving Tony the benefit of the doubt though. Maybe Tony has a lot going on himself. He certainly seemed terrified Daniel would say something wrong to his sister. He's probably a run-of-the-mill closeted guy who was more worried about his sister seeing his male lover than about being nice about Daniel's very traumatic experience. Although, if Tony were all that concerned about it, he wouldn't have hooked up with Daniel in his place of work, especially given his whole family also works there.

Still, Tony did claim he didn't mind heavy, and then very clearly did.

He might really feel used, Daniel decides, reconsidering his earlier line of thought. Daniel very clearly showed up the day before yesterday because he wanted a distraction, not because of Tony himself. The windshield was incidental. And then they had sex up against a dead man's car. Daniel's still pretty upset about that, so he can't imagine how Tony might feel. That would be understandable, and given they don't really know each other, it would be extremely flattering if Tony were that upset about Daniel not having the clearest of intentions toward him.

As he sets his blinker and turns toward Red Hook, Daniel shakes his head at himself. If it makes him feel that good about himself, it's probably not true. He won't know what's eating Tony until Tony tells him. Tony has his number—Daniel tries not to wince at himself about how obviously he was angling for Tony to text him first—and if he wants to see Daniel again, he'll have to use it.

Right now, Daniel needs to get his life together and deal with what happened. Starting with grocery shopping. He pulls into the Hannaford parking lot and takes his canvas bag out of the trunk before checking his phone for his shopping list.

There's a missed call from Colette.

He nearly gasps out loud in relief. *Finally.*

Hot on the heels of relief comes anger, unexpected and hot, clawing up the back of Daniel's throat. Before he realizes it, his thumb is hovering over the return call button, and he's almost ready to give her a piece of his mind for ignoring him for a full day right after their friend died, and—

He stops himself and takes a deep breath.

In the normal course of things, he doesn't necessarily talk to Colette every single day. It's not like he's been good company the last day or two. It's not fair to expect her to process the way he does: with company.

Anyway, he promised he would keep his phone on loud and be there if she needed him, and now he's missed her call. If anything, *he's* a bad friend. He wonders if telling her where he was and what he did would make it better or worse.

He opens his messaging app to apologize, but she's already sent him a message an hour ago.

What are my chances of you coming over and making me brunch.

100%, Daniel texts and makes a beeline for the eggs. *I'm at the store now. I'll be there in half an hour.*

He hurries through the store, irritated at the realization that it's Saturday morning and thus full of pensioners shopping incredibly slowly. Hannaford's is always a culture clash, with hungover Lobell students buying snack food, the handful of professors who dare shop in such close proximity to the college, and the locals.

There's a woman ahead of Daniel in the checkout line who apparently could not get through the shopping experience without opening and drinking a smoothie. He doesn't know which of the three groups she belongs to, but the length of time she takes considering buying a magazine featuring a Kardashian sibling prominently on the cover doesn't endear her to him.

He's being an asshole, he realizes. Granted, it's only in the space of his own head, but he should probably get over himself and his anger at Colette, most likely rooted in his disappointment in Tony, before he sees Colette. She doesn't deserve the version of him who makes classist assumptions at the grocery store because he's feeling impatient and uncertain of himself. He takes a deep breath and doesn't tap his feet or clear his throat while the lady in front of him takes ages clearing the checkout counter. He drives exactly the speed limit on the way home, and he feeds Worf and waits around until he's eaten up before he heads down to Colette's.

Colette answers the door in the same sweatpants she was wearing the day before yesterday. Her long braids are tied together loosely behind her head. Daniel becomes aware that usually when he sees her, she's subtly but perfectly made-up because today, she isn't.

Before he can come in, she wraps him up in a tight, fierce hug.

"Oh." He's surprised, and he can't really hug her back with the groceries in the way, so he just stands there for a while as she hugs him. "I'm sorry I missed your call," he tells the side of her head.

"I'm sorry I sent you away." She steps away and drops her eyes as she lets him in. "I was...I needed..."

"It's fine."

"I'm sure you needed support too." It rubs him the wrong way, if only a little bit. She's not wrong, but she talks about it like it's an immutable fact that he would, and he doesn't like how sure she is. "And I...told you to leave. I've been...a mess. I don't like...being seen like this."

"It's seriously okay." In point of fact, he's still not sure it is, but he's not sure anything at all is okay right now, so he's willing to let it slide. "Anyway, I'm here now. What do you want for brunch?"

"Anything. I haven't eaten much since...you know. I'm starving."

Daniel hasn't eaten properly since his pilfered breakfast yesterday afternoon. At some point in the night, Tony pulled on his pants and got them an assortment of shitty snacks from the motel vending machine, but they weren't what Daniel would call nourishing. (He thought it was nice, actually, splitting Fritos and a Snickers for dinner, licking the taste out of each other's mouths. He needs to stop thinking about it.)

He pulls out the eggs, flour, maple syrup, baking powder, buttermilk, and sugar and sets to work.

Pancake batter is quick work, and frying them while he boils an extra few eggs for something savory is easily managed. He longs a little forlornly for bacon, but Colette can't eat it, and anyway, Daniel probably ought to stop eating meat properly instead of occasionally sneaking a real burger and then feeling guilty about it.

"How are you?" Colette asks him. She's sitting on a bar stool in her kitchen, watching him cook. Her hands are clasped around her coffee cup.

"I'm all right, I guess. I don't know. The first night was...bad. Maybe I'm starting to process? Or maybe I'm just exhausted from having feelings."

She nods slowly. "I think it was the shock that made me react so badly. I don't think I've really understood that he's actually dead." The words make her mouth turn down. She looks so tired. "I keep thinking...what if it was an insane accident, you know? He was pretty drunk that night. What if he had a gun, and it misfired? You know, a lot of gunshot injuries in this country are accidental."

"I guess." Daniel wonders how best to phrase his skepticism. "I don't think he had a gun though. Mario had a bumper sticker that said 'F U NRA,' remember?" He hopes she doesn't ask how he remembers it in such detail.

Colette shrugs helplessly. "He could have changed his mind."

"Yeah." There's not a lot else to say. Daniel debates bringing up Occam's razor as gently as possible to remind Colette that the simplest explanation is usually the right one, but he can't make the words come out in a way that won't sound condescending. Instead, he plates up their brunch and sits across from her at the high kitchen table.

He's only halfway through his pancake stack when the doorbell rings.

Colette stands to answer, and even a room away, he can hear from her tone of voice that she's letting whoever it is inside. With a sigh, Daniel sets down his fork and drains his orange juice. At least his brain is starting to feel less like a raisin.

"Oh, hi, Detective," He gives a little half-hearted wave as Colette leads Detective Taylor past the kitchen toward the living room.

"Professor Rosenbaum." She sounds pleased and surprised. "Well, I guess that saves me interviewing you separately."

Daniel wonders briefly about professional ethics; shouldn't she interview them separately? What if they were lying to her? What if they're suspects? If he gets arrested on murder charges, his parents are definitely never coming to visit him.

Then he remembers that he isn't actually a murderer and doesn't want to be interviewed separately anyway. It's the detective's problem if her procedure is wrong, not his. And he should probably not be thinking of it as "wrong" but as "not how they do it on TV."

He follows them into the living room. "I would offer you some pancakes," he lies, "but we're all out."

Detective Taylor waves him off. "That's fine. I already ate. A cup of coffee, though...?"

"Oh, of course." Colette heads for her tiny moka pot, sitting right by the stove.

Daniel takes a seat on the couch opposite the detective.

"Do you live here?" she asks.

"Upstairs."

"But you and Professor Ravel aren't..."

He shakes his head instantly. "No, we're just good friends." He doesn't elaborate; outing himself to local police seems like poor judgment, especially when it's not relevant to the investigation. Unless it becomes relevant in the worst way and Detective Taylor starts thinking he's some sort of gay predator who killed Mario because he wasn't interested—

Daniel interrupts the train of thought. There's no reason for him to be accused here; he needs to stop imagining all the horrible ways it could happen. "So, what brings you here?"

"A few follow-up questions." Detective Taylor clasps her hands together. "Professor Lombardi's family lives a few hours away, and it seems you two were his closest friends in the area. I'm trying to get a sense of his life and his habits."

Daniel frowns. His closest friends? Colette was close with Mario, certainly, but Daniel wouldn't have thought he was. They were friends, but not exactly close. Sometimes, Mario joined him and Colette for dinner on Saturdays, and every now and again, Daniel went to the movies with them, but that was about it. Their only commonality beyond Lobell was that Colette was close with them both.

"We'll do anything we can to help, of course." Uncomfortably, he thinks of the current location of Mario's car, but doesn't offer any further information. If she needs to know, the detective will ask. No point in attempting to explain how he knows without revealing more than he wants to about himself and Tony both.

In the kitchen, he hears the moka pot burble, and shortly after, Colette emerges with a steaming cup.

"Sugar or milk?" she asks.

"Milk would be great," Detective Taylor says.

Colette sets down the cup on the coffee table and then gets the milk from the fridge. She's judging silently. She would never taint an espresso with milk.

Detective Taylor takes a long sip and closes her eyes in pleasure. "God, we should get one of whatever you have over at the station. Good stuff."

Colette smiles, tight-lipped. Coffee comes shortly after driving, healthcare, and police brutality on her list of things wrong with America.

"So-" The detective sets down her cup. "I have a few more questions about Professor Lombardi. For starters, do you—"

She's interrupted by the doorbell going off again.

Daniel stands to press the buzzer this time.

"Oh, Daniel," Stacy calls up the stairs. "I was hoping you'd be here! How *are* you?"

"I'm holding up," Daniel tells her weakly, although he'd like to say, *you literally saw me yesterday.* "Listen, the—"

"I brought some cookies." Stacy huffs a little as she climbs the stairs to Colette's door. She's wearing a purple raincoat and rubber boots even though it finally stopped raining. The coat swallows her short frame almost whole. She proffers a gigantic Tupperware in his direction. "Double chocolate chip."

Daniel smiles as he takes them. "Thanks, Stacy. This is really nice of you."

At the door, Colette has appeared. "Hello. The police are here right now, but I'm sure you can come in all the same." Her tone of voice is friendly, but Daniel knows she's hoping Stacy will take the hint. It's unlikely; Stacy is impervious to subtext unless it's in a James Joyce novel.

"Oh, if you're sure I won't be in the way." Stacy's already walking through the doorway before she's finished speaking. She waves to Detective Taylor. "Hi, I'm Stacy Allan—"

"With the college, right?" the detective asks. "I was meaning to talk to you next."

The expression on Stacy's face is almost worth how hard Colette is clenching her jaw to avoid being impolite.

"Oh my." Stacy's hands flutter up and down, as if looking for something to do. "Did I do anything? Is everything all right?"

Detective Taylor smiles kindly. "Have a seat, Professor Allan. It's only that you three were the last people to see Professor Lombardi."

Stacy breathes out in relief. "Of course. And what a terrible thing. I just can't believe this has happened. And here! You know, my husband and I moved up here from the city because it was supposed to be much safer."

Colette rolls her eyes behind Stacy's back.

"I'm sure it *is* much safer here." Colette reclaims her seat on the couch. "We don't even know how Mario died."

She's sticking with the accidental gunshot idea, then. Daniel swallows his commentary, sets the Tupperware on the coffee table reverently, and opens it up. He takes a cookie and starts nibbling at it.

"Unfortunately, after the autopsy, we're certain we're looking at murder or manslaughter." Detective Taylor takes a cookie as well. "The final verdict will take a few more days as our coroner doesn't have a lab on standby for this kind of stuff."

"That's *horrible.*" Stacy is aghast, eyes wide and bright. "Who would *do* that?"

The detective holds up her index finger as she chews and then swallows. "I'm hoping to figure that out." She takes another long sip of her coffee. "There were a number of calls on his phone records in the last few months from an auto repair shop in Kingston. Angel Automotive? Do you know anything about that?"

Daniel sits up straight so suddenly the blood rushes in his ears. "I'm sorry. For how long?" His lips feel numb.

"A few months. Since about September."

Daniel opens his mouth to answer something, anything, but what could he say? He knows Mario's car was there, but he doesn't intend on telling the police what he did up against Mario's car, especially since that doesn't explain the calls dating back to September.

"He was in a fender bender." Stacy nibbles on one of her own cookies, clearly over her anxiety at the police presence. "Just a few days ago. He said his car was in the shop on Wednesday, remember? That's why we carpooled."

"Yes, that's true," Colette agrees. "His van was always giving him trouble, so maybe it was getting fixed more often?"

Daniel nods mutely and tries to calm his heart rate.

The detective asks for information about Mario's class schedule and students, which Daniel knows next to nothing about. He lets Stacy and Colette talk, explaining that his film classes were late, that Mario was incredibly in demand as a faculty advisor, and that his classes were usually full.

As they talk, Daniel wonders whether Mario had anything else to do with Angel Automotive. He was probably getting his car fixed there, same as Daniel. Mario was about Daniel's age, and the draw of a shop that didn't require a phone call to make an appointment is pretty convincing to their generation. Mario was probably a regular customer. Maybe that's why Tony was so spooked this morning—he recognized the name. Maybe Mario hadn't paid his latest bill yet or something.

Except something doesn't add up. Daniel goes over the moment in the car that morning when he turned the radio on and the way Tony asked gruffly if Daniel knew Mario—that doesn't seem quite right. Tony could have been a lot more sympathetic. A lot kinder. He could have expressed condolences much, much earlier, but he waited almost two full blocks. It made Daniel feel bad for having known Mario. Tony also didn't mention that he knew Mario himself.

Then afterward, when Daniel saw Tony impressing something on his sister, her upper arms clenched in his big hands—that seemed suspicious. Daniel thought it was about him, about her figuring out that Tony was maybe less than straight. It struck him at the time as desperate. But she was already crying before Daniel and Tony even got there. What if instead of being worried, she wasn't reacting to their little overnight getaway as Daniel assumed? Did Tony actually have some reason to react so badly to the news about Mario, both to Daniel and to his own sister?

What if Tony had something to do with what happened to Mario?

That would be ridiculous.

That would be horrifying.

He doesn't seem like someone dangerous, but if Daniel has learned one thing from crime shows, it's that killers rarely do.

Daniel needs to not think about it. It's probably all coincidence. And either way, Tony didn't seem interested in seeing Daniel again this morning. Daniel will be totally uninvolved no matter what. Unless Tony texts him, of course.

Should he answer if Tony texts him? Should he see Tony again?

Would it be dangerous?

He thinks of how reverently Tony undressed him last night and then how his eyes crinkled when he laughed so hard that he couldn't breathe when Daniel demonstrated the only correct way to eat Skittles (sorted by color). Daniel's probably not in any danger from Tony. Maybe he can find out more, though, on the off-chance Tony wants to see him again. It would definitely be worth a look if he could check the computer at Angel Automotive for Mario's name. Just for his own peace of mind, of course. He could make sure the only connection really is Mario's shitty van. What are the other options anyway? Telling the police?

It's not like there's a good way to admit that Daniel also has a connection to the shop, and he's concerned about the mechanic from the shop being involved in the murder based entirely on him reacting weirdly to the news. It would make him sound utterly insane, and in the worst case, it would get Tony in trouble and torpedo Daniel's chances with him.

He'll wait for Tony to text him, and if he doesn't, then he'll know Tony isn't interested in more than a secret fling in a shady motel. That would be fine; then Daniel won't have to go to the shop again and worry that Tony's somehow involved. If he does text, Daniel will check it out a little bit, enough to be sure there's nothing shady going on. It will be fine.

Tony's definitely not some criminal mastermind; he's only a mechanic.

Of course, Daniel could always text first and arrange another hook up. To get a feel for things. So he has an answer and doesn't drive himself crazy.

"Daniel?" Stacy rests a hand on his knee.

Daniel flinches.

"We lost you for a second there, sweetie." She pats his knee and then mercifully pulls away.

"Sorry." Daniel rubs at his eyes. "I didn't sleep well." He slept great, actually, his back pressed into the warm, solid chest of a potential murderer.

"You poor thing." Stacy offers him the Tupperware container. "Have another cookie. God knows, if I take them home, my husband will eat them all."

"What was the question?" Daniel takes another cookie.

"We're trying to establish Mario's daily routine," Detective Taylor recaps. "Just to know where he might have been in the days prior to his death."

"His class schedule and his office hours are easy enough to come by," Colette points out. "And the dean of the film department will know about faculty meetings and all that."

"He went to the pool a few times a week," Daniel remembers. Sometimes, Daniel would be huffing away at the ellipticals upstairs in the campus gym, staring blankly through the windows to the pool, and he'd see Mario dive into the water elegantly. He wore speedos and apparently saw no issue with that. They met in the changing rooms sometimes too. Daniel remembers how they joked about the out-of-use sign on the sauna doors in the men's changing rooms.

"Was it really a hotbed of gay activity?" Mario asked, wriggling his eyebrows on the word "hotbed."

"According to Kevin in the Poli-Sci Department," Daniel answered with a shrug. "And honestly, if he was involved, I'm glad I didn't check it out."

They laughed about it, and every time they saw each other at the gym, Mario found some new pun about heat and steam. In all honesty, it made Daniel uncomfortable; it felt like Mario was constantly reminding him he's gay, as if Daniel didn't know.

"There's one more thing." Colette fiddles with the end of one of her braids again, speaking slowly and nervously. It pulls Daniel out of his memories. "There's a student, Andrew Clayfield. He was...becoming quite intrusive about a project."

Right. Corpse cannibal guy.

"How so?" the detective asks.

"He wanted to work on a very specific film project for his senior thesis. It's to do with a Welsh funeral tradition. It's...well, never mind. I'm just concerned this student will...try to involve himself. He has a preoccupation with death."

The detective pauses in her note-taking. "Could you elaborate on that?"

Colette sighs. "I taught a class about nonliturgical elements in Christian ritual last semester. Andrew focused on the Welsh tradition of the sin-eater for his final paper."

There's a pause in which all the nonanthropologists in the room attempt to look both interested and as if they have no clue what she's talking about, prompting her to continue.

"In the traditional sense, the practice features a person taking part in the funeral rights for a deceased community member and eating and drinking something, usually bread and beer, to symbolize taking on the sins of the deceased so they can continue on to heaven. Andrew argued the practice was reminiscent of the bread and wine as the body and blood of Christ in Catholic services and formed a quasi-cannibalistic aspect of Christian practice. The belief is that eating something which represents the body of someone else leads to taking on their characteristics."

Colette fidgets briefly before admitting, "It was an excellent paper. Andrew is wasted on film studies. However, ever since then, he's been asking Mario to support a senior thesis project in which he takes the subtextual cannibalistic aspects of sin-eating and turns them into text."

"He wants to make a movie about someone eating corpses," Daniel translates. "He's been very pushy about it; Mario was getting creeped out."

Looking more than a little disturbed, Detective Taylor makes a note on her notepad. She thanks them all for their cooperation and tells them she may return for further questions some other time.

On her way out, she takes another cookie.

Colette leans back into the couch cushions, clearly exhausted again. "What a mess. Who would kill Mario?"

"You just made a solid case for Andrew," Daniel points out.

Colette winces. "I don't want to get him in trouble. I'm only worrying that the idea of an easily accessible corpse will do bad things to him."

"It's not easily accessible. It's in a morgue."

"That student sounds very disturbed indeed." Stacy makes a face that tells Daniel everything he needs to know about how she feels about cannibalism films. "Have you considered sending him to counseling services?"

Manfully, Daniel resists the urge to say *I told you so.*

"Having an interest in death is not a mental illness," Colette responds sharply. "He's barely twenty years old; he's still figuring out who he even is."

Stacy subsides.

Colette softens slightly. "I can't think of anyone else with anything *like* a motive though."

"I can't imagine it," Stacy agrees.

"I can't imagine going to class after the holiday as if nothing happened." Daniel tries very hard not to think of Angel Automotive and what motives might be hidden there. "What do we even say to the students?"

Stacy grimaces.

"There's been a lot happening on campus, huh?" Daniel guesses.

She nods. "We've had a lot of calls from concerned parents. A lot of students taking prolonged Thanksgiving breaks. You know how it is."

Daniel was planning on screening a film for the two or three students who actually show up to his Wednesday Comp Lit II section. Now that he's able to process the information that classes have been cancelled for the week, he's intensely grateful he doesn't have to. He knows how it is. "I hope counseling isn't totally overrun."

Colette clicks her tongue. As little as she personally seems to believe in the importance of counseling for students obsessed with cannibalism, she also thinks the lack of available mental health resources is another American travesty. "That's what they're there for. Better those who need it take advantage than not."

"I was thinking." Stacy is hesitant, as if she hasn't steamrollered them about everything so far. "We ought to do something—as a college. To commemorate him, you know? Maybe we could hold a service in the chapel? Or a vigil or something? And anyone who wants to speak about him could get a chance."

It's pretty much exactly what Daniel thought she would want to do. Something cathartic and healing for the community. It's why he went to see her yesterday and why he left feeling better. For a moment, he's overwhelmed with gratitude that people like Stacy, with their unending, bottomless desire for kindness, exist.

"That's a good idea," he agrees. "We should probably ask the film department first. So we don't step on any toes."

Colette nods slowly. "That sounds lovely." She seems surprised by it herself. "The film department isn't very good at event planning, and they'll be glad of the help."

"Great." Stacy claps her hands together. "I mean, not great. You know what I mean. I'll get out of your hair and go send a few emails. Probably not next week, with the holiday and all, but maybe the week after."

"You're not in our hair." Daniel's protest is weak at best, but she's already putting her rubber boots back on and doesn't seem to notice.

"You two take it easy this weekend," she warns them sternly. "And let me know if you need anything at all, okay?"

"You too," Daniel tells her. "Give yourself some time. You don't need to plan everything right away."

Stacy smiles weakly and rests a hand on his arm for a moment.

"Thank you for everything, Stacy," Colette says with supreme dignity. As the door falls shut behind Stacy, she breathes a long sigh of relief.

"Come on," Daniel cajoles. "That was nice of her."

"That's the problem." Colette sniffs. "It was *too* nice. She can't leave well enough alone."

Daniel shakes his head. "You're too harsh on her. We could all use some niceness now. Anyway, who ever heard of someone who was too nice?"

"It's not only that she's nice. It's that she wants everyone else to know how nice she is. It's infuriatingly false."

They wander toward the kitchen, to their half-eaten, gone-cold brunch. As Colette picks up her fork and keeps eating, Daniel continues the argument.

"Does motivation really matter? Surely, if she's doing something good, it's the outcome that matters?"

"That depends." Colette's mouth is full of pancake. She still manages to project a level of dignity Daniel will never possess. "The ends she achieves for others might justify her means, but the ends she achieves for herself do not."

"And what ends does she achieve for herself?" Daniel asks before shoving a bite of cold and slightly syrup-soggy pancake into his mouth.

Colette licks her lips and daintily slices more pancake before answering, "Relentless and grotesque self-satisfaction for being a good person. And, of course, validation from others that she is."

"I don't see you planning a memorial service. Doesn't she deserve some validation for putting in the effort?"

The corners of Colette's mouth draw downward. She cracks the top of her boiled egg with her spoon and starts peeling it, clearly stalling for time.

In his pocket, Daniel's phone buzzes, saving her from having to respond.

Hey, sweetheart, I'm sorry I was so weird this morning. Can I make it up to you?

Daniel reads the message twice. Maybe his initial read on Tony being a regular closeted guy who freaked out about things being a bit too real in the morning was right. It's nice that he wants to make it up to Daniel.

Either that, or he's a crazy psychopath who wants to kill Daniel as well for knowing too much.

Then again, Daniel doesn't really know anything. He texts back:

And how would you do that?

There's no harm in asking, after all.

"Who was that?" Colette asks, studying him intently.

"My sister."

Colette shakes her head. "Try again. You hate getting messages from your sister."

"No one you know, okay?" Daniel feels a hot flush creeping up his neck.

"Intriguing. I won't push if you don't want me to."

"I don't," Daniel says hurriedly.

She shrugs. "All right then." She polishes off the last of her food and stretches. "You know what we could use the long weekend for?"

"Hm?" Daniel hums absently. He's still considering the pros and cons of meeting up with Tony again. Pro: Figuring out Mario's connection to Angel Automotive. Con: Possible death. Pro: Hot guy who appears to actually be into Daniel. Con: Potentially closeted guy with whom Daniel probably doesn't have a future.

"We need to collect some material of our own to use as an example for the class on Tuesday." Colette picks up her plate and puts it in the dishwasher. "Our timeframe just shifted by a class, and we only have a month left before the semester ends."

"Shit." Daniel had forgotten about all of his real-life responsibilities. They need to start researching, and fast, and he'll need to code an example onto their website so the students will know what to reproduce with their own audio samples.

"Yeah," Colette agrees.

"Would it be wrong of us to work after...?"

Colette drums her fingertips against the table. "I don't know what I'll do all day if I don't occupy my brain somehow."

Daniel's phone buzzes again.

Any way you want ;)

An idea that's either very stupid or absolutely ingenious begins to form in Daniel's head.

Chapter Six

Andrew Clayfield is waiting in front of Colette's office building when they get there.

It's Monday.

To be more precise, it's 7:00 a.m. on Monday morning, a time Daniel didn't even know existed when he was in undergrad.

Andrew looks up in something like relief when she gets there, pushing his too-long hair out of his eyes. "Professor Ravel. Do you have—"

"Let me get in first, Andrew." Colette sounds far calmer than Daniel feels as she unlocks the door to the building.

Andrew subsides, shrinking into his gray hoodie. The drawstrings are tangled, thready, almost like he's been chewing on them. He's of average height and a bit pudgy, with glasses and too-long brown hair. In all fairness, he looks not unlike Daniel did at that age.

"I'll speak to you after Andrew's finished, Professor Rosenbaum?" Colette asks.

Daniel nods intently so that Andrew knows he'll be waiting. He's not sure what either of them is imagining Andrew will do or say or what Daniel would do if Andrew did or said it, but it doesn't hurt to be cautious.

Andrew follows Colette into her office without asking first. It's presumptuous. With nothing better to do, Daniel wanders around the building. It's weird to be there this early; all the doors are closed. Lobell's staff isn't immune to the college's hippie roots, and most everyone keeps their door open when they're not in a meeting. He's never read all the cartoons taped up on the doors before.

Mario's door, all the way across campus in the film studies building, has a Far Side comic of three people and a dog staring at a blank wall with the caption "In the days before television" taped under the sign-up sheet for his office hours.

Of course, it's probably a crime scene. Crime scene adjacent. Something. Daniel couldn't go there and look at the space Mario used to work in now. Although, by that logic, the alley next to his apartment should also be a crime scene, and it isn't, apparently. Maybe the police decided the rain had washed away too much. Either way, Daniel doesn't want to stand around in Mario's old office, chasing ghosts. It would only make him sad. Sadder.

Daniel swallows around the lump in his throat and heads back to Colette's office in time to hear Andrew yell, "You don't *get* it" as he storms out.

"Mr. Clayfield," he calls after Andrew, utterly ineffectually.

"It's all right." Colette waves an exhausted hand.

"Are you sure?"

She nods. "He's not doing well with the news."

"Are any of us?" Daniel asks with a snort.

For a moment, he thinks he crossed a line. Colette's expression doesn't so much change as it freezes and then melts sharply into despair. But in an instant, she pulls it together.

"Sorry," he starts, but when she holds up a hand, he asks instead, "What did he want?"

"He wants me to advise his senior thesis."

"And?"

She sighs. "I told him he should consider whether now is really the time to make *that* project and reminded him he still has time; he's only a junior."

Daniel peers out the window. Outside, Andrew kicks a lamppost so hard it flickers on and then off again. "Yikes."

Colette follows his line of sight. "He's...very insistent."

"Did he say anything about..."

She draws her arms tight around herself. "He said he needs to do it *because* of what happened to Mario. He said the project, the... The sin-eater needs a real death. To eat."

Dan sits down on Colette's uncomfortable guest chair. "What the fuck."

"Agreed."

"I know you think I'm overreacting about him." Daniel phrases it cautiously, unwilling to push Colette too far. "But if he comes back, or if he stays...insistent, would you think about calling security? Or counseling?" He doesn't ask her to call the police. He's not convinced that's the right call, and Andrew will already be on their radar after the conversation they had with Detective Taylor.

"Fine."

The relief lasts him through their planning session and up to around eleven when he drops her off at their apartment building and heads toward Kingston for Tony's promised favor. He can't help the unease that creeps up on him during the drive, no more than he can help the pounding of his heart when he parks his car outside Tony's garage. He tries to tell himself he's just doing research—anthropologically speaking—but the knowledge of his actual plan keeps creeping up on him. Excitement and adrenaline rage through him at the thought he might actually find something. He might be the only person in a place to know enough about Angel Automotive to figure out what happened to Mario. Quickly, though, his excitement is replaced by anxiety that he could either ruin things with Tony or get murdered himself.

It's a very tense drive.

Arriving at the garage is kind of a letdown.

"Okay, so what do we do first?" Tony asks, bouncing on his heels. "Are you gonna, like, record me while I work, or do we talk about it first, or..."

"Whoa, slow down." Daniel laughs.

"Sorry. No one's ever wanted to *research* me for *science* before."

"Wow. You are really into this."

Tony smiles. His eyes crinkle like they always do, and Daniel can't help noticing how his cheeks dimple. It's adorable.

No way this man is a cold-blooded killer.

No way to *tell*, Daniel corrects himself. It's not like he's an expert, and he wants to like Tony. He's better off trying to get information than making assumptions.

"I just want to get it right," Tony tells him. "So how do we start?"

"Well..." Daniel takes out his cell phone. "I'll press record, and then I'll ask you a few basic questions about who you are and what your business is, and then I'll record you for a while as you work."

"That sounds pretty easy." Tony seems almost disappointed it's not a more involved process. "I guess I'm not supposed to flirt with you while you're recording though?"

"Afraid so."

Tony sighs. "What a bummer."

"Hey, you're sure your boss won't mind this?"

"Dad?" Tony laughs. "He wouldn't get what I'm talking about if I tried to explain this to him, so why would he mind?"

"Well, it'll be public. Online."

Tony shrugs. "That's basically advertisement."

"Okay, then." It's not going to be Daniel's problem if this blows up in Tony's face. "Here we go." He presses record. "Introduce yourself, please."

"Um, hi," Tony begins. He's clearly nervous, and Daniel nearly ditches his plan out of sheer affection. "I'm Tony d'Angelo, and I'm a mechanic here at Angel Automotive."

"Tell me a little about the shop," Daniel encourages.

"So, Angel Automotive is a family-run business." Tony leans against the front desk. This is safer ground for him than talking about himself. "My granddad founded it way back in '73, and my dad took over in the '90s. These days, my dad and I and one other employee run the shop, and my mom and my sister handle the front desk."

Daniel whistles. "That really is a family business." He already knew all of this because he researched the shop extensively in advance of this excursion, and it feels a lot like lying to pretend this is the first time he's hearing it.

Tony looks away, bashful. "I know it's pretty old-school, but it works for us."

"And what sort of work do you do?"

He tunes out as Tony reels off all sorts of specific types of car repair and improvement the shop handles, wondering instead how to segue into his next question.

When Tony's words peter out, he goes with, "And how would you describe your clientele?"

"Varied," Tony answers after a moment. "We've got our regulars, of course, local folks who've been coming here for years. But we also get a lot of people passing through, you know, taking the scenic route up to Boston. And every now and again, a professor from over at Lobell gets lost and ends up in our garage."

This is Daniel's opening. "Oh?" he asks airily. "That happen a lot?"

"Once or twice."

"So I'm not the first to end up here?"

Tony grins, sharp and almost predatory. "We're happy to serve all customers, but it is always a special pleasure when someone from your hallowed halls finds their way here."

"Is it, now. And here I thought only I got special treatment." Daniel's heart is in his throat. Is this flirting? Or is Tony referencing whatever happened with Mario?

"I couldn't possibly tell you that, could I?" Tony affects innocence but instantly proves himself wrong by winking.

Daniel clicks pause on the recording. "Okay." He tries not to sound too disappointed. "I think that's enough for an intro. I guess next we record you working."

"Awesome. This is really exciting."

"I can tell. But also, remember you're not allowed to talk to me while we're recording the next bit."

Tony pulls a face. "I'm not very good at that."

"Just act like I'm not there."

Drawing close, Tony drops a whisper of a kiss on Daniel's lips.

"Impossible," he says, low and husky.

Definitely not a murderer, Daniel's heart pounds out in his chest. Definitely not a murderer, his gut instinct tells him.

He's not here to follow his gut though.

"I can always wait at the front desk," he suggests, trying to sound as though it's an idle thought. "It's only a quarter of an hour."

"You sure? Won't you get bored without my scintillating company?"

"Of course. But I'm prepared to suffer that fate in the name of science."

"I respect your professionalism." Tony's voice is solemn; his expression is anything but.

Daniel sets up his cell phone to record on a stool next to the car Tony's working on. The radio in the corner of the garage is on low volume, only so loudly it can still be heard but won't overtake the sound of Tony working.

"I'll leave you to it." Daniel disappears behind the door separating the garage and the front desk.

It's closed right now as the rest of the family are on their lunch breaks. This makes it the perfect time to record a bit, with only the ambient noise of the garage and, according to Tony, no one roasting him for what he says on tape. Daniel thought the shop would be busier on a Monday, but Tony informed him most people bring their cars in early in the morning and pick them up late.

This also makes noon the perfect time for Daniel to snoop.

The computer is still on and the last user is logged in. Why wouldn't they be? It's only Tony in the shop, and he's family. Daniel did enough googling to figure out the birthdays of everyone in the family, just in case, but it turns out he doesn't even need to guess whose birthday might be the password Tony used last week. One of the icons on the desktop is a folder marked "Records." Daniel clicks on it.

Each file in the folder is marked with a last name and a number. He searches his own last name and finds two files. Two bills, for the two times he brought his car in.

He searches for "Lombardi."

Nothing.

He tries "Mario."

Still nothing.

He scrolls through the last three months, and there are no files that can be connected to Mario at all, unless the shop used an alias for him. His car is definitely in the shop, so there must be something.

Unless Tony deleted whatever paper trail Mario left. Daniel wonders how he'll justify those calls to the police, then.

Daniel wonders what other reason Mario wouldn't be in the shop records under his actual name. He searches a few misspellings of "Lombardi" just in case, but he keeps coming up blank. There's nothing in the computer trash files either, which means Mario's van was never recorded. Or it was deleted thoroughly, properly.

Is it incriminating to not have files on someone? Should Daniel call the police? Mario's van is here, after all. Daniel imagines trying to explain to Detective Taylor how he came to be in the garage she mentioned and how he gained access to their computer and immediately discounts the idea.

There's a loud clanging from the garage. Daniel jumps what feels like about a foot in the air and hastily closes all the windows on the computer. He checks his watch. It's only been ten minutes, but that feels like long enough. He goes back into the garage as if staying in the office is some sign of his guilt.

"We're all set," he announces, turning his recorder off again and sitting down on the stool.

Tony emerges from under the hood of the car. "Great. That was super weird. I've never thought about what kinds of sounds fixing cars makes."

"That's the point of the project. We accept a lot of ambient noise without really thinking about it, but when you only focus on one sense, you can learn a lot."

"I can't wait to check it out." Tony sounds so earnest.

It's probably all a mix-up. Maybe Detective Taylor confused Angel Automotive with any one of the dozen or so other auto shops in Kingston, and Mario only brought his van here after something weird happened there. Maybe Mario's bill went missing in the system, or Gianna forgot to ring him up. Maybe the computer wasn't working the day Mario came in. Maybe...

Daniel remembers Colette trying to reason her way into Mario's death being accidental.

Occam's razor, he reminds himself.

"Give it a few days." Daniel tries to stay on topic and keep his thoughts out of his voice. "I still need to write the code for the website to put this up." He does have a draft of it saved that he wrote over summer break when he and Colette were still planning this project. But experience has taught him that actually implementing it with content the way he wants it to look will be a headache and a half, let alone making it user-friendly enough that students who aren't double majoring in computer science can recreate it.

"You're so smart," Tony tells him.

Daniel laughs, caught off guard and pleased.

Tony shakes his head. "No, no, I'm being serious, baby. It's incredibly sexy." He presses a wet, smacking kiss to Daniel's cheek, and Daniel turns to catch his lips in a real kiss.

Tony's not a murderer, he decides. There's nothing connecting him to Mario beyond what's probably a police screw up. Occam's razor does not account for every eventuality, and a lot of problems have complex solutions. Tony's a great guy who likes Daniel, and Daniel is catastrophizing and trying to find reasons not to go for it. He would be an idiot to keep going down this road rather than to see where pursuing this thing with Tony could take him. The police can follow up on their own information and Daniel can stop getting himself involved.

"So hey," Tony says bashfully when they pull apart. "I was thinking..."

He doesn't continue, so Daniel prompts with, "Oh?"

Tony rubs a hand on the back of his neck. "Well, it's about time I take my lunch break. And, uh...I was thinking maybe I could take you around Kingston? Show you some other places that sound good?"

"That sounds like a date." It's out of Daniel's mouth before he's thought twice about it. Ordinarily, it would make him nervous. With Tony, he's had so many other things on his mind that asking what they're doing here seems like the least of his concerns.

On Saturday, when he left in the morning, he was pretty sure Tony just wasn't that into him and all the baggage he's currently toting. They're from totally different worlds, and Daniel's still not sure whether Tony's out to his family (although he engages in some really risky behavior at work if he's not). Today, after having gone through a full day of thinking Tony might be a murderer, which gets stupider the longer Daniel realizes how insane it is, he's fully ready to decide all of his previous thought processes were wrong.

Daniel doesn't really give a shit that he's a professor and Tony's a mechanic, and why would Tony? Tony wants to take him around town, the town where he lives. If he's not out, it seems like he's ready to be. Daniel likes Tony, and he likes how much Tony likes him. Maybe he needs to stop self-sabotaging.

"I was hoping it would be a date," Tony admits. "I mean, if that's not something you want—"

"No, it is," Daniel says quickly.

"Great."

For a long moment, they grin at each other stupidly.

"Uh, let me get my jacket, and then we can..." Tony indicates something with his hand that Daniel takes to mean "date."

He nods quickly, and Tony gets his jacket, locks up the garage, and they head off.

Most of the time when Daniel heads over to Kingston, he goes to the mall for some necessity or other. Maybe the movies. Once or twice, he ventured to downtown Kingston when he and Jeff still went on dates to restaurants instead of staying in every day. He hasn't actually seen all that much of the town itself though.

First, they stop by the bagel shop next door for food. It's not a place Daniel would have gone on his own; it's run-down and tiny. Tony greets the cashier by name and orders his usual, which turns out to be an everything bagel with schmear. Daniel opts for raisin in the optimistic belief that his preferred bagel flavor (onion) would be a hindrance later on.

The weather has cleared since the storm; it's still cold, but the sky is blue, and the winter sun is bright. Tony parallel parks perfectly in a free spot on a street right off Broadway before leading Daniel down a series of smaller, quieter streets. It's a pleasant surprise they don't drive the whole way.

"You get a lot of birdsong here." Tony scuffs his feet against the sidewalk. "Off the main drag, I mean. I dunno—I like that it's quieter here, you know?"

"I live in Rhinebeck," Daniel deadpans. "Trust me; I get liking quiet."

Tony laughs a little. "Come on. I hear there's a hopping yoga center there."

"Hey. They do yoga *and* Pilates."

"How could I forget. You ever do stuff like that?"

"Not really. My friend Colette goes sometimes, and she makes me come with her once in a blue moon."

"Huh." Tony looks over at Daniel.

"What?"

"Nothing." Tony affects utter innocence. "Just picturing you in yoga pants."

Daniel elbows him lightly. "What about you? I'm guessing yoga's too hippy for you?"

"Hey now." Tony puts his hand to his heart, mock-offended. "I grew up ten miles from Woodstock."

"So you *do* like yoga?"

"I don't know. I've never tried. Looks pretty chill, but it always seemed like something guys don't really do."

Shrugging, Daniel says, "Some guys do. I'm not one of them. I don't like people watching me when I exercise. But you should give it a try if you're into it."

Tony hums, agreeing, and Daniel wonders if he could ask Colette to take Tony with her once or twice.

He needs to cool it.

A week ago, he thought Tony was a fun one-time hookup he'd never see again. Two days ago, he was pretty sure Tony was too scared of his family knowing he's into men to pursue anything with Daniel. An hour ago, he thought Tony might be a murderer. He barely knows the guy; he shouldn't go setting up meetings with his best friend.

"This is the elementary school district." Tony gestures to his right toward the empty playgrounds beside large, square buildings lined with windows covered in brightly colored Thanksgiving decorations from the inside. "Great soundscape, lots of screaming and laughing."

"Oh, I wish. But we'd have to get permission from all the parents of the children we record."

"You probably could if you go through the principal. Mrs. Mazzeti's the best."

"Is this your school?" Daniel asks, charmed.

"Yeah." Tony's dimples are showing again. Daniel imagines him as a little kid, elementary-school-aged. He must have been adorable. "She was my math teacher before she got promoted. Schools around here are pretty proud to be part of historic Kingston, you know? I bet they'd love your project. Local history, local color, that sort of thing."

"That does sound nice." Daniel knows, vaguely, that Kingston has a historic city center but hasn't really seen much of it before now.

"You're not from around here, right?"

"No, not at all. Piedmont, California."

"Never heard of it."

"No one has." Daniel is used to this spiel by now. "Basically, right by San Francisco."

Tony whistles. "Big city kid, huh?"

"Eh. I mean, we had buses and BART back home. Less driving. But SF was still kind of a haul."

"I wish we had more buses and trains around here." Tony has the hand not carrying their bagels in his pocket. Daniel wonders how he feels about holding hands. He wonders if there's a good way to ask whether or not Tony's family knows he's gay. If he even is. He could be bi.

There's no good segue to that though. "I thought you were a car guy," Daniel teases instead.

"I am," Tony says easily. "But I also like all this, you know?" He gestures to the trees lining the street, the park to their right. "I love this town, but I think it'd be better if we drove less."

"Wow. That's— I agree, but you work in an auto shop."

Tony shakes his head ruefully. "I keep trying to tell Dad we should start doing electric stuff, too, but he's not there yet."

"I hope that works out."

They walk in silence for a bit around a curve. Daniel realizes they're pretty much completely alone out here, nothing but winter-bare trees and the occasional car passing them by.

"Where are we headed anyway?" he asks, trying not to sound anxious. He really needs to get his shit together here. He just decided he's sure Tony has nothing to do with Mario's death; he needs to be way less suspicious.

"I thought we could go down to the park." Tony gestures to the woodsy area ahead of them. "It's right by the Hudson. Prime picnic spot. I know it's pretty cold—"

"That sounds great." It is pretty cold; Daniel wishes he brought gloves. It's worth the chill though. "Kind of romantic."

"That's what I thought."

The park is empty this time of year, with the grass and the trees all showing the season. It's strange what a difference a few weeks can make. "You know, I started to love this place my first autumn here." Daniel sits down on a bench by the water, Tony sliding into place beside him.

"Yeah? It is pretty special."

"It's magical. We don't get that at home at all—no seasons. I went to grad school in the city, and that's not the same either, not with all the pollution. But being down by the river in autumn..."

"Makes me wish I could paint or something," Tony agrees. "I've taken, like, three hundred pictures on my phone that all look the same, trying to capture it."

"I do the same thing."

They smile at each other as they unwrap their bagels, and they eat, staring out at the water. "I just hope it doesn't all freeze over before Thursday," Daniel says.

"Why's that?"

"I have to get home for Thanksgiving. The train down to the city gets canceled sometimes if the tracks freeze over."

"Aw, shit. That does suck. You really fly all that way for four days?"

Daniel chews and swallows, considering his words. Tony's close with his family, after all. "My mom would be disappointed if I didn't. And I don't like going there for Christmas, so."

"You don't?"

"My family was Jewish at some point. I mean. Technically. We never practiced, and my parents did do Christmas when I was a kid. But I still think it's weird they never even tried to do the Jewish holidays instead. Every time I go now, I have to justify coming back before the new semester starts, and they start in on how I should move home to California, and it isn't very fun."

"Oh." Tony winces in sympathy. "Sorry. I didn't even think..."

Daniel waves him off. "That's fine. Let me guess; you're Catholic?"

"What gave me away? Was it the Italian surname or the inability to imagine people not celebrating Christmas?"

"Mix of both. Also, we passed two different Catholic churches and one Catholic school on the way here."

"Well, like you said. I don't practice much. It's kinda hard, what with..." Tony gestures between them. Daniel takes it to mean, *what with being into men.* "My mom would kill me if I didn't go to church for holidays at least, though. I mostly fudge my way through all the confession bits."

"I would never want to tell a rabbi what we did up against M—that car."

Tony laughs so hard he almost chokes on his bagel.

"This is the nicest date I've been on in years."

Tony's face softens. "I'm glad. I know we don't know each other well yet, but I have this thing where I really want you to like me."

"That's mutual." Again, words Daniel would worry over in any other situation slip out before he can consider them. No matter what else is going on, he likes Tony enough to overcome his own perpetual overthinking, and that has to be worth something.

He's surprised when Tony's cold, slightly rough hand cups the side of his face and cradles his cheek gently as Tony leans in and kisses him. It's a soft, close-mouthed thing, a first kiss long after they've passed by other firsts.

When Daniel's eyes blink open after they separate, the first thing he sees are Tony's warm brown eyes smiling at him, and beyond that, Tony's windswept dark-brown hair falling out of its ponytail and the light sprinkling of freckles barely visible against his ruddy cheeks. Slowly, as Daniel recovers from the heart-clenching softness of that kiss, he begins to remember where they are. The choppy, rough sight and sound of the Hudson in winter, the few trees surrounding them, still bravely baring leaves, come rushing into Daniel's senses.

He's going to remember this.

The crisp scent of cold air, the sound of the river, the sight of Tony smiling nervously. The sense memories will stay, and the feelings Daniel associates with them. Wild, giddy excitement and the pounding of his own heart.

It really is a good first date. They stroll to Tony's car, elbows and shoulders brushing together. Tony tells a few more stories about growing up in Kingston; Daniel trades more of his first impressions of the Hudson Valley when he moved here, three and a half years ago. They warm up in Tony's car, the heating on full blast as they hold their hands in front of the air vents. Their fingers brush in front of the front console, and they can't stop smiling at each other.

Daniel's never been quite this stupid over another person.

It's a chore to keep his face straight when Tony pulls up behind the garage and he realizes he'll have to walk through the shop to get to his own car.

"Hi, Dad," Tony calls when he tests the door handle and finds it already open.

"Hiya, kiddo," a voice answers from under one of the cars on the lot.

"I thought you were gonna stop doing undercarriage work for your back." Tony sounds disapproving, as if he's had this conversation several times before.

"I thought you were gonna be back from your lunch break ten minutes ago."

Tony winces and trades a guilty look with Daniel. "I'll be right there, Pa. Let me put my jacket away." He grabs Daniel by the elbow and leads him out toward the shop entrance.

"Hi, Gianna." Tony hangs up his coat. "How's it going?"

Gianna spins around on her chair, and they both stop dead. Her eyes are red-rimmed again; she's clutching a half-disintegrated tissue. "Oh." Her voice is thick with emotion. "It's you again."

"Hi." Internally, Daniel groans at himself. He should have said nothing at all rather than just that; it's not like he has a follow-up.

"Gigi." Tony isn't as reproachful as he was with his dad a moment ago, he sounds kind and gentle and caring, exactly like he did with Daniel down by the river. "Hey, if you need more time, I bet we can call Kyle—"

She shakes her head. "Kyle always fucks up the orders; you know that."

"You can take some time," Tony argues.

"Um." Daniel hates to interrupt, but he's pretty sure this is none of his business. "I'm gonna..." He points to the door.

"You work at the college, right?" Gianna turns the full force of her watery eyes at him. "I used to see you there. Did you know—"

"Gigi," Tony says sharply.

She subsides.

"Jesus H. Christ," Tony mutters under his breath. He grabs Daniel by the elbow again and leads him out to his car. "Sorry about that. I know you're going through it right now about...your friend. You don't need that."

Feeling very much like he missed a step walking up the stairs and his feet are dangling over screaming nothingness, Daniel asks, "What's wrong with her?"

Tony shakes his head. "She, uh—she took a few classes with your friend. Lombardi?"

"Oh. I didn't know she went to Lobell." She must recognize Daniel from campus. Daniel assumed the whole d'Angelo family stayed on the

Kingston side of the river for some reason. He knows Gianna was a student, though, and her brother is clever and interested in learning about the world around him. It stands to reason she would be, too. The only reason he hasn't considered it before is he assumed, wrongly and lazily, that families like the d'Angelos sent their kids to community college or state schools.

"She quit after last semester. Damn shame; she only had a year to go."

"And she knew Mario?"

"Yeah." Something bitter and ugly crawls into Tony's voice. "She's… really broken up about what happened to him."

"I'm sorry. You know, I don't mind talking to her—"

"Maybe some other time?"

With no other option without seeming suspicious, Daniel agrees, "Sure. Of course."

"Sorry. I just…I don't wanna mess her up more. And I don't wanna mess this up, either."

Daniel softens. "Of course. Um…I'll call you, I guess? Or text?"

"Please." Tony sounds like he means it.

He doesn't kiss Daniel goodbye.

As he drives across the Kingston-Rhinecliff Bridge, Daniel stares straight ahead and tries not to think. He can't seem to help the way thoughts intrude on his brain like the clouds slowly covering up the midday sun once again. Maybe his search on the computer at the garage was completely above-board and accurate; maybe Mario wasn't a client. Maybe the calls were personal. Maybe someone had a reason not to charge him for the repairs on his van. And, well, who is it that spends all day sitting by the phone at Angel Automotive? Who is it that files all the bills?

Tony's not a murderer. He might be the nicest guy Daniel's ever dated. He's so nice, in fact, that he's absolutely the kind of guy who would help his sister cover up a murder.

Chapter Seven

Daniel mops up a bit of extra gravy with his second slice of challah. "You've really outdone yourself, Mom. This is fantastic."

"Thanks, honey," his mom says. Her frizzy hair is pulled back with a scrunchie, and maybe it's because she's been cooking all day, but somehow, the bags under her eyes and the way her frame seems to keep going bonier the older she gets stands out even more than it did the last time he was here.

She put up the string of hand turkeys Daniel made in elementary school that she keeps carefully preserved in her box of seasonal decorations, along with a few hollowed-out gourds. She's probably going to spend Sunday taking it all down and putting up twinkly lights and the menorah she likes to put in the window right next to the light-up reindeer.

It's not that he doesn't respect her dedication to secularizing the holiday season academically, it's only that he wants it to feel like it did when he was seven and really proud of his hand turkeys, and it doesn't anymore.

The table truly is a masterpiece. It's the same old dining room table Daniel sat at three times a day from age five to eighteen but with the addition of a fold-out table at the end for the aunts and uncles and a few nieces and nephews not doing Thanksgiving with their spouses. Every inch of both tables is groaning with food. There's the turkey, an enormous masterpiece, golden brown and somehow not completely dried out, and beside it, bowls and bowls of stuffing. The good kind, made with Mom's three-day-old challah, resting in pottery she hand-painted when Daniel and Meredith were both small enough to love painting their own mugs and bowls. There's even a veggie bowl with no turkey innards, just in case Daniel stopped eating meat. Apparently, his mom is never sure. There's cranberry sauce and brussels sprouts fried up in turkey drippings, and gravy and fresh bread, and sweet potato mash covered in walnuts and brown sugar. The trip home was worth it for the food alone.

Maybe he *should* come visit over winter break.

"Glad to see you're still eating meat after all." It's the first thing Daniel's father has said since the meal started, and Daniel groans internally.

"I told you; I'm not a vegetarian." Daniel mentions this every time he's here. "I'm trying to reduce meat, that's all."

His dad doesn't answer. Daniel's dietary choices, as well as his career choices, remain a mystery to him, Daniel can tell. Academia is all well and good, but that's in fields like medicine and law, not something as weird as "digital humanities."

"Well, it's good you're making an exception for the holidays." Daniel's mom is all forced cheer. "It's so nice we're all together today, isn't it!"

"Definitely." Daniel hopes his smile doesn't come off as fake.

"Except Benjamin."

"Oh, such a shame he had to work, and on Thanksgiving!" Daniel's mom agrees. "Meredith, do you think he'll be by later?"

The heat now firmly on Meredith, Daniel pulls his phone out under the table and opens his messenger thread with Tony.

Happy thanksgiving

Only seconds later, Tony answers.

hpy t-day hope ur having a good time in cali

Daniel tries not to let anything show on his face—happiness at the quick response, confusion at Tony's sudden lapse into textspeak, continued conflict at how he's supposed to handle this. He hasn't seen Tony since their impromptu first date on Monday, and he doesn't know if he should angle for a second. Tony certainly is; he asked on Monday evening if Daniel was free before he had to leave for Thanksgiving, and Daniel lied and said he wasn't.

He wants to see Tony again; he wants it so badly he has trouble remembering why he probably shouldn't.

The problem is he looked up Gianna's records at the registrar's office. She took a class with Mario in the fall semester last year. Her transcript is nothing special, a solid B-minus/C-plus student, but her dropping out is not explained in any of the official documentation.

The problem is Daniel needs to know why she dropped out and why she's so affected by the death of a professor she took one class with a year ago. He needs to know why she was calling Mario in the weeks leading up to his death.

The problem is Daniel lay awake three nights in a row, feeling guilty for not telling the police about Gianna and her possible connection to Mario out of fear of hurting Tony if she is involved.

The problem is Daniel woke up way too early three mornings in a row, feeling guilty for not asking Tony about his suspicions.

The red-eye flight into SFO this morning was almost a relief; at least he has an excuse for how tired he is.

"Put the phone away, son," Daniel's dad says, snapping Daniel out of his reverie.

"Sorry." Daniel does as he's told.

They've moved on from interrogating Meredith about her absent husband to Aunt Silvia's work stories. Aunt Silvia's work stories range from utterly baffling to absolutely horrifying, so Daniel tunes in long enough to hear about her coworker who was caught doing meth in a supply closet.

Aunt Silvia works in an elementary school.

Dinner peters out slowly. Daniel manages to nab the last bit of the good stuffing—the stuffing that was in the bird, that is, as opposed to the three dishes of excess stuffing his mom baked in her neighbor's oven. There's just something about all that soggy bread and celery when it's mixed up with the liver and the heart and all the other bits Daniel doesn't ever eat on his own. He might as well make the most of it.

He offers to help his mom with the dishes about twelve times, but she turns him down each time, and the aunts bustle their way into the kitchen to help without asking. Once he's carried all the plates and dishes into the kitchen, Daniel's out of a job unless he wants to help his dad find a football game or an insanely boring documentary on TV.

Instead, he steps out back onto the porch.

"Traitor," Meredith says from where she's looking out at the yard they used to play in.

"They were about to start ganging up on me."

"So you threw me under the bus?"

"Who else was I gonna throw? The dog died three years ago."

"I miss Harley."

"Me too."

They smile at each other. It's only when they're both at their parents' house that they get along like they used to—when Meredith isn't stuck playing messenger for their parents, and Daniel isn't stuck disappointing her by proxy.

"So, who were you texting under the table?" she asks, turning to lean against the porch railing. She's not wearing any makeup, which she never used to do before she had kids. Her brown hair is pulled up in a tight bun. Her forehead has creases now. She's only four years older than him. Emily is asleep in the crib their parents still keep upstairs for her even though, at three, she's almost too big for it; Davy's in the living room with Dad, probably learning to swear at football players. It's the most relaxed Meredith has looked all evening.

"So, where is Benjamin?" Daniel parrots.

Meredith scowls at him. "I still think that was a low blow."

"Sorry. Just trying to get Mom and Dad off my back."

"Mom and Dad would get off your back if you called more."

"They would not, They'd get on my back some more over the phone."

"So you tell them what they want to hear a bit; where's the harm?"

Daniel laughs darkly. "I tell them I want to live in Cali again someday? I tell them I want to follow your example and procure some grandkids so they can at least pretend I'm not gay?"

"Daniel!" Meredith looks shocked.

"It's true. They've hated every single guy I've brought home."

"Because they were all pretentious douchebags," Meredith tells him, which is rich given that she's married to fucking *Benjamin*. "They're not *homophobes*."

"They literally think my life isn't worth as much, and I can uproot it any time because I don't have kids." It's an effort to keep his tone even and his voice low so no one inside hears him. Daniel's not ready to have this discussion with his parents. Not again, and definitely not so soon into the holiday.

"So that's it. You're...never coming home?"

"You too, huh?"

She shrugs. "I kinda thought... I don't know. We're all here."

"I like my life," Daniel bursts out. "I like my apartment and my friends and my job. I worked really hard to get a PhD before I was thirty, and I know none of you give a shit about my career, but it means something to me. I don't get why this is so hard to grasp."

"Oh my god, shut up about your career already."

"Excuse me?"

"It's all you ever talk about. Do you have friends? I don't know! Are you seeing someone? You'd never tell me! All you ever talk about is your classes and your students and how successful you are. Have you ever, even once, considered that I didn't *get* that chance?"

He can't say he had.

"I had Davy when I was twenty-six, asshole," she reminds him. "Guess how many career-furthering opportunities there are for moms who need to be home by 3:00 p,m. or pay out the nose for a babysitter?"

"I thought that was what you wanted. That's why you didn't go on after your master's, right?"

She snorts. "Right, my lowly master's. I don't know; I thought it was what I wanted. You ever consider that Mom gave up her job to raise us?"

Daniel blinks, leaning against the railing next to her, staring at the dark yard. He can barely make out the shape of the swing set. "No."

"She got great grades in college. But she had us, and she stopped working when we were little. And when we were old enough to take care of ourselves, everything she learned before was outdated, and all she could get were admin jobs."

"That sucks."

"Yeah. And when her only son refuses to visit more than twice a year and acts like his career is the only important thing in his life, it's kinda like he's spitting in the face of everything she gave up."

Daniel opens his mouth and then closes it again. "That's not my intention."

"Yeah, well, it's your effect." Meredith pushes herself off from the railing and goes back inside.

Daniel sags against the porch railing heavily. Is there anything to what she said? Does he really make his parents feel like that? Daniel refuses to believe there's no homophobia in the way his dad has kept him at arm's length ever since he came out junior year of college. That was when he started flying home less and less too. He started putting down roots on the East Coast, and the more roots he had, the harder it got to leave them. Daniel's always been an overactive gardener, drowning his plants.

Maybe he was overcompensating for neglecting his earlier roots.

Maybe he wasn't the only one neglecting them though.

He can't believe Meredith still thought he was planning on moving here again someday.

It's not that Daniel categorically denies the possibility, because that isn't how jobs work in academia. Sure, he looked mostly on the East Coast when he was first applying for teaching positions after his PhD, but either way, as an academic, you take what you can get. He hasn't ever explained the process in detail to his parents, though, because they never asked and never seemed to care overly much.

The longer he thinks about it, the more uncomfortable he gets.

To avoid it, he pulls out his phone.

It's actually kind of horrible, he texts Tony. *Hope yours is better.*

aw that sucks, Tony replies only seconds later, followed by a string of unhappy emojis.

Tony, are you drunk? he asks, a smile pulling at his lips.

g2g, kisses. Tony follows that with a kiss emoji.

Daniel sends him a string of question marks, but he doesn't reply. Weird. It's not like Tony being tipsy on the phone would be a problem.

Unless he's worried about keeping secrets from Daniel.

With a sigh, Daniel heads inside. He pops his head into the kitchen, but it's only the aunts at this point, gossiping and drinking wine. The dishes are long-since done. He swipes a glass of wine off the counter and drinks it as he walks toward the living room; he's old enough to enjoy red wine because it makes him mellow and sleepy, and in combination with the turkey and the chronic sleep deprivation, he'll fall asleep before seven at this rate.

Someone or other would probably take that as cause to accuse him of avoiding his family.

He settles on the floor next to Davy, who has his back to the couch, his impressively clunky cast resting carefully on the tops of his bent knees.

"How's it going?" Daniel asks him.

"Shh." Davy frowns. "This is my favorite ad."

Daniel holds up his hands in surrender. Favorite ads. Who knew? Kids these days.

To his surprise, they're not watching sports or a documentary that prominently features a factory line. Instead, it's a local station interviewing retail workers about their Black Friday preparations.

"Nuts," Daniel's dad mutters, and Daniel is surprised to find himself nodding in agreement.

"Did you know people *die* at these things every year?" Aunt Silvia asks, vaguely disgusted.

There's a low murmur of agreement.

"They do this crap in New York too?" Daniel's dad asks gruffly.

"Yeah." Daniel is startled into honesty by his father's interest. "I mean, the big chains, like everywhere. Rhinebeck does a lot of advertising for Small Business Saturday these days."

"Well, that's something."

Daniel counts it as a win.

They watch in joint horrified silence as various cashiers and other retail workers prepare by putting up Plexiglas shields to keep from being attacked and stocking tons and tons of goods. If Daniel hadn't just eaten way more stuffing than his stomach can comfortably fit, he would feel disgusted at the excess; right now, he only feels vaguely disgusted with himself.

A shrill noise breaks through the cozy food coma of the living room.

It takes Daniel three rings to realize it's his phone. He never turned the ringer off after he missed Colette's call last week.

"Sorry," he mutters and answers it, stepping out into the hallway. He doesn't look back to see everyone's expressions; he's sure they're all various degrees of censure.

"Hello, Daniel Rosenbaum speaking?"

"Daniel?" Colette asks. "Daniel, have you heard?"

There's an unfamiliar urgency in her tone, and panic grips Daniel. "Was there another murder? Has there been an arrest? Have they found the killer?" What if they arrested Tony? What if they think it was him, and he lied to protect Gianna? What if they arrested Gianna, and Tony is miserable, and that's why he's so drunk?

"No," Colette chokes out. "No, it's Lily Peterson."

"Lily?"

"She's in the hospital. They found her in her room, unconscious. She— Daniel, she took pills. She left a note."

"Oh my god." Daniel leans against the wall. He should have given Lily that extension, no questions asked.

He shakes his head. That doesn't make any sense. It wasn't their anthropology class that made Lily do this. He should have followed up. He should have emailed her again, asked how she was doing.

"The police came again." Colette's voice is shaking. "They were... much less polite."

"Oh fuck. Did they—was it—I mean, police officers in America—"

"It wasn't about race." It would be more comforting if Colette didn't sound so scared. "At least, it wasn't explicitly about race. They seem to think I'm hiding something about Mario. They think what Lily did is connected."

"Is it?" Daniel hates himself for even thinking it.

"I don't know," Colette bursts out, frustrated. "She left a letter, and it said *something* about her and Mario, and no one is *telling me any-thing*."

"Okay. Okay. Here's what you should do. Call Stacy."

Dead silence on the other end.

"I'm not kidding," Daniel barrels on. "I know you can't stand her, but she's a middle-aged white woman. She can call the manager like you wouldn't believe. I bet she can get you information."

It takes a while for Colette to respond. Finally, with her voice so low Daniel almost doesn't hear her, she says, "I'm afraid they actually might arrest me."

"I'll bail you out." Daniel has no idea how to bail a person out, or if that's even something he could do. He'd figure it out.

She laughs. "It's a homicide, Daniel. Do you realize how high the bail is?"

"No. I don't care. I'll figure it out."

"I wish I had come with you." That's the first time she's said that. Daniel always offers to take her home for Thanksgiving, even when he was dating Jeff, and she always turns him down. According to her, it's the most productive weekend of her academic year. And according to her, in France, people have the decency to act ashamed of their imperialism instead of creating a holiday around it.

Daniel can't argue with either statement.

Eventually, when the silence stretches for too long, Colette announces, "I'm sending flowers to Lily. Shall I sign for you?"

"I'm coming home early. And yes."

"You just left yesterday."

"One of our students nearly killed herself, and you're being framed for murder."

Backlit by the dim glow of the TV, Daniel's mother's shadow drops a wine glass.

It shatters to pieces on the big, flat tiles of the hallway floor. Daniel never liked those tiles. His feet get cold.

"Murder?" his mother whispers, her eyes wide.

"I gotta go," Daniel mutters into the phone. "I'll text you when I get in."

He hangs up, but not before he hears her heartfelt *thank you*. Then, he gets the dustpan from the cupboard by the kitchen door, crouches, and starts sweeping up the glass.

"Oh, Danny, you're a guest. You don't have to," his mom starts.

"I'm a guest who's going to have to leave early. It's the least I can do."

"Leave early?" Meredith repeats from the living room door, where a whole crowd has gathered. "Are you serious? You haven't even been here twenty-four hours."

Daniel takes a deep breath to explain, but before he can even try, his mother does it for him.

"There's been a *murder*."

"Seriously?" Meredith asks.

Daniel rocks to his feet, holding the dustpan full of glass shards. "My colleague Mario was killed a week ago." No one responds, so he powers through. "That was my friend Colette. She was the last to see him alive, and now it's looking like the police think she's a suspect. She said…" He swallows heavily, trying to parse it. Lily, with her pink-tipped hair and the wrist tattoo and her exceptionally quiet voice whenever she does manage to speak in class. "She said one of our students attempted suicide. And it's connected."

The whole family is crowded around the door to the living room, staring at him.

"Well," Dad says. "Guess we'd better find you a flight back."

Daniel nods wordlessly and trudges upstairs to his laptop. He doesn't want to stay in the living room with all those eyes on him, especially with Meredith looking at him like she thinks this is somehow his doing.

There's an email from the college president in the work email tab Daniel left open with the subject line "Urgent: Lily Peterson." Daniel doesn't click it; he clicks another tab and opens his personal email instead. He does a keyword search for Jet Blue and tries to figure out if his flight home on Sunday can still be refunded, but the tiny script makes his eyes cross.

Finally, he does the unthinkable: he dials the customer service hotline. It's only about five minutes of listening to the call waiting jingle before he reaches someone. By some stroke of luck, whoever happens to be manning the Jet Blue call center on Thanksgiving Day is remarkably competent, and within minutes of him explaining there's been an emergency, his flight has been rebooked at only a minor increase in expense.

Daniel packs up the few things he got around to unpacking; he'll have to head for the airport at the crack of dawn tomorrow morning.

Finally, he takes out Emily's carefully, but still somehow sloppily, wrapped birthday present. It's on Saturday, and they were going to have a little party. Now, he'll be the uncle who missed her birthday as well as the uncle who's never around. His only saving grace is that Benjamin is an only child, thus depriving the kids of competent aunts and uncles.

A knock on the door interrupts his preparations.

"Hiya." His mom slides in through the crack of the open door.

Was she always this thin? This frail?

She takes a seat on his bed. "Did you find a flight?"

"Yeah. Early tomorrow morning. I'll take BART. I don't want to—"

"We'll drive you," she tells him firmly.

"Mom, I don't want to make you and Dad drive all the way around the city on Black Friday."

"And I don't want you taking BART all by yourself after a holiday." She smiles a little ruefully.

Daniel relents. "If you're really sure."

"Positive." She picks at a loose thread on the quilt her mother, Daniel's grandmother, made at some point long before Daniel knew her when her hands were still steady enough for sewing. "Daniel, honey..."

"Yeah?" Daniel already fears an accusation or an invitation for

Christmas.

"Why didn't you tell us?"

He blinks. "Huh?"

"Why didn't you tell us all this was going on? You could have canceled."

He shakes his head instantly. "I don't see you enough anyway. And I thought... I don't know; I thought it would make things awkward. You've never met Mario or Colette, so I kind of figured..."

"We wouldn't mind knowing your friends."

"Yeah, well, you'd have to come out to see me sometimes for that." A hint of bitterness escapes with his words, and Daniel wishes he could put it back.

She looks up from the quilt. "You've never invited us."

"Oh." It's true, probably. He assumed they wouldn't be interested.

"What time is your flight?"

"Seven thirty."

"We'll leave around five thirty, then," she decides. "Set an alarm?"

"Yeah."

Daniel goes to bed as soon as she's gone. He can't face the email about Lily; he can't stomach thinking about what he should have done to help her. Staring at the wall of his childhood bedroom is a vastly preferable alternative.

His 5:00 a.m. alarm rings much too soon. He drinks too-weak black tea standing in the kitchen and assures his mom twelve times that he can get breakfast at the airport. The drive to SFO is uneventful, almost too fast. Sitting in the passenger seat, Daniel checks in on his phone as his dad shakes his head at the number of people already on the roads and sips coffee from a thermos.

He's surprised when his dad pulls him into a quick, rough hug before he gets in line for security.

The problem with morning flights is that Daniel can't even attempt to sleep through them. The in-flight entertainment isn't offering much besides six whole episodes of *Diners, Drive-ins and Dives*, and right now, Guy Fieri's voice, presence, and enthusiasm for deep-fried food is like a cheese grater to the inside of Daniel's skull. He can't stop thinking. What if Colette's been arrested by the time he lands? What if her one-day absence from life wasn't a breakdown she didn't want anyone witnessing but a signal of guilt. What if—

Daniel pushes the thought away. He's already driving himself insane wondering about Tony and Gianna, which he shouldn't be doing. He can't start questioning Colette as well. She's his best friend, he *knows* her. She wouldn't.

That, of course, leaves room for other thoughts—wild, fantastical ones about Lily Peterson and Mario. Midway through the flight, he abruptly can't stand thinking about it anymore, and he shells out the money for in-flight internet access. He opens the email and skims it.

Dear Members of the Faculty,

I regret to inform you that one of our students, Lily Peterson, attempted suicide on the college premises early on Thanksgiving morning. Due to the campus being empty, it was several hours before she was found, and then only at the insistence of her roommate, who was concerned when she stopped responding to messages. Lily is currently in the intensive care unit of Dutchess County Hospital. It is unclear whether she will recover. In a letter addressed to our recently deceased Professor

Lombardi, Lily described her motives for this attempt. While these motives are of a very personal and sensitive nature, we have decided to share them with a select group of colleagues who taught Lily, as you will likely be questioned by the police regarding them.

She wrote that she couldn't imagine managing her course load without Professor Lombardi's guidance, and that she could not imagine loving anyone as she loved him. It is unclear as yet whether or not her feelings were reciprocated and what that might mean for Professor Lombardi's death. Over the course of the next weeks, the police will seek you out as other members of faculty with whom Lily had relationships. Depending on the outcome of the criminal investigation, it is also possible there will be an ensuing internal Title IX investigation.

Sincerely,

Professor Ernest Kaufmann

President of Lobell College
Professor of Ethnomusicology
Lobell College
30 Lobell Road
NY 12504
ernest.kaufmann@lobell.edu
845-596-7903

With a shaky sigh, Daniel closes his laptop.

He doesn't know what he was expecting.

To know Lily was alone, probably for hours, before someone finally found her and got her help... It's awful. It's heart-wrenching, it's upsetting in a way Daniel understands so well, and he doesn't know how to process it.

Somehow, it's easier to parse the other part of the email, to turn the complexities over and over in his mind. Lily wrote that she was only managing her course load with Mario's support, but he wasn't her academic advisor. As far as Daniel knows, she only ever took one class with him. That day in the car, when Daniel mentioned her, Mario talked about her with the detached air he would use to discuss any student.

That could mean that whatever was between them was all on Lily's side, that this was a standard crush on a professor exacerbated by Lily's mental health. On the other hand, if Mario was providing her with so much guidance, and there was nothing shady about it at all, why would he not say as much when the subject came up?

Almost clinically, Daniel tries to find ways to make it not Mario's fault as the plane descends over JFK. He supposes it would make sense for Mario not to mention Lily's feelings for him; he wouldn't want to jeopardize her relationship with Daniel and Colette. Likewise, he probably wouldn't want to admit anything because it's a really bad look for a male professor to have young, impressionable female students fawning over them.

At least, in Daniel's book, it is.

He thinks of the faculty retreat summer before last when it was put to a vote whether the college would institute a rule forbidding sexual relationships between faculty and students. Daniel thought it was a no-brainer and that it would be an easily decided question. It was 2016 at the time, and he had believed—naively, it turned out—that no one in this day and age still thought it would be a good idea for professors to date their students. It turned into a heated debate very quickly.

What about the master's students? was the first line of argument. They were older and more mature. Surely it would be an offense to act as if they had no agency. And really, the BA students were all over eighteen; they, too, should be exempt. On and on the debate raged. Daniel had long-since cast his vote for the proposition of forbidding professor-student relationships and spent most of the retreat fervently wishing for a drink.

He was surprised at the time that Colette seemed undecided. Of course, she agreed on principle that a professor ought to keep their hands off their own students, she had said, but what about students to whom they were not connected through classes or advisory positions? She was concerned the whole debate was another example of American purity culture gone rampant. "Who are we," she said, "to tell people who are legally of age who they can and can't be with?"

Daniel argued about the power imbalance inherent in such an age gap and the mismatch in institutional power, but Colette wasn't convinced that gave them any right to decide on the personal lives of faculty and students alike. Daniel argued that tenured professors were basically unfireable, and therefore, any wrongdoing they committed would inevitably be overlooked. The whole system was stacked against student plaintiffs in an internal investigation such as a Title IX investigation. Colette then conceded the point but argued that she and Daniel were lucky to have nabbed tenure-track positions in the first place since secure places for academics were thin on the ground these days and panic over possible private wrongs in intimate relationships threatened those jobs. Jeff was noncommittal, though he thought Colette made good points, especially because he himself wasn't at Lobell on a tenure-track position, and his time there had a very clear expiration date. The whole thing was so galling to Daniel he mostly remembers being annoyed at them both.

He didn't even remember how Mario spent all day playing devil's advocate to both sides, just because he could, until Stacy mentioned it. At the time, Daniel assumed it was because he thought the whole thing was as ludicrous as Daniel did. Maybe he was wrong, and Stacy was right—maybe Mario was prolonging the discussion on purpose. Maybe Mario had something to hide.

It's an hour on the subway from JFK to Penn Station, and he spends it staring blankly at the other passengers, wondering what secrets they have. Is the mother rocking her baby's stroller back and forth monotonously sleeping with her babysitter? Is the guy in matching sweats and a hoodie with a baseball cap pulled low over his head stalking his professors? Is the girl staring out the window with her headphones jammed into her ears secretly in love with someone totally inappropriate?

He gets a soft pretzel at Penn Station, not because he's hungry but because he thinks he'll get nauseous if he doesn't eat. Holding both his pretzel and his bag, he gets elbowed to the side twice on his way to the tracks. Penn Station is overwhelming at the best of times, but right now, the noise all around him, the crowds of bustling people—all of it is too much, and Daniel feels like his ears and eyes are shutting down in self-defense. He loiters around the main hall, waiting for his train to be announced, trying desperately not to give in to his worst impulses (yelling at the young mom with three overactive kids that she needs to get them under control). Not that you can really hear the tinny announcement for the Amtrak up to Boston in the overcrowded hall, but the track number doesn't show up on the switchboard before the announcement. Mario used to head up to Boston for breaks when he was still dating his ex-girlfriend, Laura, more than a year and a half ago now. He and Daniel never got the same train because they were headed in different directions, but sometimes, they split a cab to the station, Daniel taking the southbound train and Mario the northbound.

It's a beautiful stretch of track up to the Rhinecliff Station. The season's first freeze hit over the single day Daniel was gone, and the Hudson is majestic with it, all ice chunks crashing together, angry and stormy. He watches the little coast guard boat dart across the water, breaking up the biggest chunks. It must feel futile to be out on the water alone, trying to fight the full force of nature on a day when everyone else is at home with their families or beating one another half to death over the best sale.

His phone buzzes in his coat pocket. Daniel pulls it out.

Sorry about last night. Family Thanksgiving and all.

He smiles before he can stop himself. Tony was definitely drunk yesterday. It's kind of sweet that he feels the need to apologize.

Tony's kind of sweet.

For a long moment of relief from the noise of his brain, Daniel allows himself to think about that kiss down by the Hudson less than a week ago. There was such an honest potential to it that he finds himself wishing Tony didn't have a sister, that he met Tony utterly independently from the rest of his life, just to savor that sweetness. He wants to cling to it, to that moment of connection, of clarity, with only the two of them and the cold winter air and the beauty of the world around them.

He wonders what Tony would think of this new possible revelation about Mario. He imagines Tony listening to the radio at the garage when a newscaster suddenly announces that Mario Lombardi's death is being investigated in context with inappropriate affairs he was having with his students. Tony would shake his head, maybe scoff in disapproval, and his sister would—

His sister. His sister, who used to be a student at Lobell, who took a class with Mario and was so shaken by his death she spent a whole day crying.

If Lily's feelings were requited—if Mario was using her like that— who's to say he wasn't doing the same to other students?

It's an ugly, unkind thought about a dead friend. It's an even uglier thought about a new lover's sister and what it might do to her to see her professor-turned-paramour go after a classmate. Daniel draws his jacket tighter around himself even though the train is plenty warm. He stares down at his phone, the text from Tony reading suddenly sinister.

Turning to the window again, he snaps a picture of the frozen Hudson.

Had to head back early, but the view is great.

He's not going to use Tony, he decides. If Tony wants to meet up again, he won't turn Tony down, and he'll try to discover more about Gianna in the process, but he won't instigate it. Maybe that will be enough to calm the wildly spinning compass needle of his conscience. He puts his phone away again and resolutely doesn't check it for the rest of the trip.

Colette picks him up at the station looking exhausted. She hugs him tightly, rocking up on her tiptoes to reach, and she drives them both home.

"Should we go visit Lily?" Daniel asks as they pass the hospital.

Colette doesn't answer, but she also doesn't stop.

"Do you think he did it?" she asks finally, once she's pulled into the parking lot that no longer has red tape blocking off the alley where Mario died.

"Did what? Sleep with Lily?"

Colette nods tightly.

"I don't know." Daniel's whole body feels heavy as he drags himself out of the car. "I wish I did."

"I feel like I would have known. I feel like I *should* have known."

"At the very least, he kept her feelings from you. He knew about that, right?"

"I don't know." Colette starts to toy with one of her braids and then abruptly crosses her arms across her chest as if to stop her own vulnerability. "And going to visit Lily when I was...complicit in whatever happened to her..."

Daniel could say that she wasn't complicit; she didn't know. Mario had kept it a secret; she *couldn't* know. At the same time, he feels it as well: the guilt of having looked right past a student in need, a student suffering and reaching out for help in the worst ways.

"It feels wrong," he agrees.

Colette swallows visibly and looks over at him. "I'm scared."

Daniel rests a hand on her shoulder. "Me too."

Chapter Eight

Daniel wakes to a pounding headache. It takes him muzzy moments to realize that some of the pounding is on the door. Slowly, he remembers he's not at home in his own bed. He's sacked out somewhere unfamiliar, and his neck is folded at an awkward angle, his feet pushed out from under the blanket and freezing.

Groaning, he pushes himself upright.

He's on Colette's couch, the scratchy material and the hard cushions reminding him just how very French she is. Daniel's couch is designed to be lain upon for hours at a time; Colette's punishes you for sloth.

He's slow, stumbling toward the door. The renewed sound of the buzzer as he's opening it makes him cringe.

"Detective," he says. Taylor is standing in front of Colette's door, looking harried.

"Professor Rosenbaum." She sounds neither surprised nor pleased. "Don't you have your own apartment?"

If he were marginally more awake, he might manage some witty repartee about how he would be there if Taylor didn't make Colette feel like she was a second away from being arrested for murdering one of her closest friends.

Detective Taylor pushes her way in, regardless of the fact that she was neither invited nor especially wanted. "Where's Professor Ravel?"

"Still asleep, as far as I know. Are you here to scare her some more?"

"I'm here because our coroner has officially ruled Professor Lombardi's death a murder."

"Oh. Should I wake up Colette?"

Taylor sighs heavily. "In a minute. I don't suppose you can tell me anything about Lily Peterson first?"

Daniel shakes his head. "She emailed me to ask for an extension last week. I invited her to my office hours if she was having trouble, but then..."

"Right." Detective Taylor pauses before adding, "My intention isn't to scare your friend, by the way. But until we have more information, pretty much everyone is a person of interest and that includes both of you."

Her suit is wrinkled, he notices. There's a coffee stain on the sleeve peeking out from under her blazer. Her Thanksgiving was probably even worse than his, especially if she actually wanted to spend it with her family.

"I'll wake Colette up." Daniel doubts she'll be especially thrilled.

Taylor nods sharply.

Daniel wakes Colette up with a cup of her strong, black coffee and the news, and hangs around through a brutally awkward conversation between Taylor and Colette in which no new information is gained but it does become glaringly obvious there's no love lost between the two women.

After, while Colette processes the news that Mario was definitely murdered, he heads up to his apartment.

The one good thing about coming home early from Thanksgiving is that Worf spends less time in an empty apartment. He's already waiting by the door to greet Daniel. Last night's pit stop to drop his bags and pour more dry food into Worf's bowl was way too short to provide adequate butt scratches.

"Hey, boy," Daniel croons as Worf weaves in between his legs. "I missed you too."

He gives Worf some of the mushed-up tuna from the can to make up for how bad a cat dad he's been the last few days, and then he falls asleep on the couch for three full hours.

In the back of his mind, Daniel knows he has a stack of essays he hasn't touched yet and a syllabus for next semester he has to write. He was going to take care of at least some of that on his flight home, and now he's lost time. But his brain is mush, and the thought of forcing himself to work makes him want to scream and cry and get it over with until he feels like an empty, dried-up husk of himself, but at least his to-do list is empty.

It's not a healthy feeling.

Instead, he watches three episodes of *Criminal Minds*. It's way too early in the day. The light from the windows reflects off the screen making the dark scenes almost invisible. It helps though, or Daniel would be way too freaked out by the fact that he saw a real dead body a week ago. Now that the first shocking numbness of Mario's murder has passed, it turns out procedural crime shows are less comforting than they were that first night.

It scares him when the buzzer goes off.

He presses pause and heads for the door. It's probably Colette, ready to talk again or in need of some company. But when he opens the door, there's no one on the landing. Daniel presses the door buzzer, sliding his apartment door most of the way shut so the cat doesn't get out. It's probably not the murderer, returned to finish the job. He hopes. Maybe Colette went out and forgot her keys? It's not like her, but it's also been a rough few days.

He loiters by the door, waiting and also guarding Worf, until there's a hesitant knock at the leaned cracked door.

"Yeah?" he calls into the hallway and then shakes his head at himself. It's not like the murderer will announce themselves.

It's really a testament to how seldom he gets unannounced visitors. Maybe he should start getting out of the house more.

"Daniel?" Tony's voice comes through the door.

A thrill shoots down Daniel's spine. He quickly opens the door fully. Worf speeds away to hide under the couch. "Tony! What brings you here?"

"I, uh…" Tony rubs a hand across the back of his neck. "I maybe looked up your address on our client files? Sorry. That was weird and invasive. I just—"

"I came to your place of work four separate times." Daniel shrugs. "Come in."

Tony comes in. He toes off his shoes and leaves them by Daniel's coatrack. For an aching moment, Daniel imagines what it would be like if he did that regularly, if he had a hook specifically for his coat, if his shoes regularly mingled with Daniel's on the floor beneath it because Daniel can't be bothered to get a whole shoe shelf for his four pairs of shoes.

"I just…really wanted to see you," Tony says.

There's something so honest and almost hesitant in his voice and expression, as if he's expecting Daniel to turn him away, that Daniel can't resist any longer. In three long steps, he's right in front of Tony, and then they're kissing.

Daniel's forgotten, in only a few days, how Tony's mustache scratches and tickles the skin of his upper lip. He smiles into the kiss involuntarily and drags Tony closer by the hips.

"I missed you." He keeps Tony close, dragging his against Tony's skin as he says it.

Is he leading Tony on? Is it cruel to say that when he's spent the last few days debating whether or not his sister might be a murderess?

He thinks of Tony's hair blowing away from his face, his cheeks red from the wind, down by the water. He thinks of the Hudson.

"I missed you too." Tony ducks his head, shy, and Daniel snakes his arms around Tony's waist and kisses him for all he's worth.

When Daniel pulls away, Tony's eyes are a little hazy.

"I've been looking forward to being alone with you again."

A thrill shoots down Daniel's spine. "Yeah?"

"Yeah."

It's romantic in a way that's not premeditated, not calculated, just Tony being open with how much he wants Daniel, how much he's been wanting Daniel.

Daniel takes him by the hand and leads him to the bedroom silently.

"I like your place." Tony looks around the room as Daniel closes the door.

Daniel remembers Tony lives with his parents. He probably doesn't get to do stuff like order decorative tables he doesn't need from Urban Outfitters because the stand looks like giant bird's feet and then spend all evening drinking wine while he tries to put together furniture with only the help of instructions in languages he doesn't speak. Daniel wonders if it's something Tony wants, the little independence that frustrates you when you have to muddle your own way through. He wonders if Tony wants to have that with someone else, if he'd like to look over Daniel's shoulder and tell him he's reading the instructions wrong and tease him about not knowing a flathead from a Phillips head screwdriver.

Tony would be really handy to have around for stuff like that.

Daniel's getting ahead of himself.

"Thanks," he says. "I like you in my place."

There's something novel in how easy it is to be direct, to run his hands under the hem of Tony's Henley, to lift it up and help him strip it off.

"You too," Tony demands, and when Daniel's emerged from taking off his own T-shirt, he finds Tony watching him openly, appreciatively.

They leave their pants on even when Daniel tugs Tony toward the bed. He's not sure why. It's not a question of modesty, it's...it's nice. Daniel pulls Tony over him and cranes up to kiss him. Tony responds immediately, leaning down to meet him. As they kiss, Daniel runs his hands up Tony's back. He likes how solid Tony is, how broad. He's not huge or anything, but he's strong, and the planes of his body are smooth and soft.

He makes a noise into Daniel's mouth as they kiss, a little groan. Heat sparks in Daniel's gut.

Tony stops kissing Daniel's mouth to kiss his neck instead, and Daniel tilts his head to give Tony more access. The scratch of Tony's beard makes him smile.

"What's so funny?" Tony asks into his collarbone.

Daniel shivers. "Nothing. Just feels good."

He can feel the curve of Tony's smile against his skin.

There's something nice about how slowly Tony goes, kissing his chest, his nipples. It doesn't do much for him, having his nipples sucked, but watching Tony do it is incredibly pleasant. No one's ever pressed gentle kisses to Daniel's stomach or run callus-rough hands over his ribs and hips. Possibly that's because Daniel mostly knows academics with soft hands. Possibly it's because he's never been touched like this, like it's a pleasure just to be touching.

Eventually, they do get further; eventually, they undo their pants and push them away, laughing a bit as they get tangled, as their belt buckles click together.

"What do you want?" Tony asks, and Daniel flushes at being asked.

"Um," he tries.

For all he's attended a lot of queer socials where asking, consent, and communication were writ large, his actual experience has been more fumbling, less suave, and less clearly communicated than he'd prefer. He's been hoping he and Tony could continue to coast on those electric first meetings where talking was an afterthought because doing was so imperative. At the same time, he's glad Tony asked. He wants that with Tony, to talk about what they like and don't like, what they want and don't want. He looks Tony over, the slight swell of his belly, the defined curve of his pecs, his strong arms, his hair coming out of its ponytail in wisps.

Never once has Tony made him feel self-conscious or as though he's fumbling in the dark for the right answer.

"Could you hold me down?" he asks.

Tony licks his lips. "Yeah. Yeah, I could do that."

Daniel ends up on his back with Tony above him, kneeling between Daniel's spread legs as he kisses Daniel and grinds their hips together languidly. Tony has both his wrists gripped in one hand, pressing them into the mattress.

"Just," Daniel gets out between kisses, squirming in Tony's hold. "Just..."

"Just?" Tony asks teasingly, eyebrows raised.

"Just fuck me," Daniel begs.

For a breathless moment, Tony pauses above him. "Lube? Condoms?"

"Drawer." Daniel gestures vaguely in the right direction.

Tony takes care of it. It means he leaves Daniel alone for an instant, his wrists once again free to move. He itches with the desire to move, to upset the fragile balance they had.

"Be good and stay still for me," Tony demands, settling between Daniel's legs.

"Okay," Daniel breathes. He watches as Tony rolls the condom down his cock and slicks it up with lube.

Cool fingers press gently at Daniel's rim, slicking him up carefully. "You want more?" Tony traces the pucker of his hole delicately with one finger.

Daniel shakes his head. He wants Tony blanketing him. He wants to be opened on the blunt force of Tony's cock. He wants to be held down and taken care of.

His wish is granted without him having to say it. Tony's hand is still a bit wet with lube when he returns his grip to Daniel's wrists. There'll be lube in the sheets. Daniel will have to change them. It will be worth it.

"Good job, baby." Tony's voice is low and gravelly by Daniel's ear as he aligns his cock at Daniel's hole. "Stayed so still for me."

"Yes," Daniel agrees hurriedly. "For you."

He catches the flicker of Tony's smile before his eyes slide shut on instinct as Tony presses into him carefully.

"Okay?" Tony asks.

"Uh-huh." It's a concerted effort to relax as Tony presses in further and further.

"You feel so good," Tony whispers to him.

Daniel tries to stretch and finds he can barely move, pinned by Tony's hands and hips and cock. "Fuck."

Tony pulls out a fraction and rocks in again. His stomach brushes against Daniel's hard cock.

With nowhere to move, all Daniel can do is groan.

"This will not take long," Tony gets out through gritted teeth.

Daniel opens his eyes to watch as Tony fucks him, almost steadily if the arm holding him up—the one not holding Daniel down—weren't shaking.

He clenches down deliberately, and Tony speeds up.

Each thrust forces breathless gasps and hungry cries out of Daniel. He feels helplessly surrendered to Tony, to the movement of his body, his own, a receptacle for pleasure.

"Feel good," Tony slurs.

"Fill me up," Daniel demands.

Tony's hips stutter.

"C'mon, come in me, fill me up, I want it," Daniel breathes. The air between them has gone hot and sticky, and he feels desired in a way he was utterly unprepared for. He's going to ride the wave for as long as he can.

With a long groan, Tony comes. Daniel can't feel it through the condom. He wonders hazily about going bare next time.

Once he's done, Tony barely takes a moment to recover before he lets go of Daniel's wrists and slides down the bed.

"Hold on to the sheets," he demands, at eye level with Daniel's cock. "Don't move."

Daniel whines as Tony's mouth slides down around his cock, hot and wet and with no barriers between them.

In a matter of seconds, Daniel's shaking against the sheets, trying desperately not to move against the onslaught. Tony's mouth is perfect, and his tongue is quick, and Daniel feels like a fraying rope holding a heavy box from falling.

Tony's calloused hand joins his mouth on Daniel's cock, and the rope snaps, the box hits the floor. Daniel buries his hands into Tony's hair as he comes and comes and comes, arching up and barely able to breathe.

There are stars glittering in his eyes when he finally manages to come down.

"Wow," he breathes.

Tony grins a little sheepishly, sitting up. "Yeah?"

"Yeah. Fuck."

Tony reaches down with a grimace and gets rid of the condom, already slipping off his softening cock. He pads out of the room to the bathroom fully naked to put it in the trash, and Daniel watches his ass as he walks, completely unable to look away.

Eventually, he forces himself to his feet and follows after.

They shower together, awkward in the too-small space, all elbows and knees.

About a minute in, Daniel's brain comes back online, and he blurts out, "I don't have any...um. I mean, my last tests were negative."

"Oh." Tony stares at him blankly through water-beaded eyelashes.

He has the prettiest eyes.

"I mean, because you...without...you know..."

Tony's eyes go wide for a split second, and then he buries his face in his hands. "I'm sorry," he says, muffled. "I didn't even think about…"

"It's okay. I kinda thought… I mean, I was pretty carried away too."

When he takes his hands away from his face, Tony's blushing a little. "Yeah?"

"Yeah. And like I said. I don't have anything, so it's definitely fine."

"If, um…" Tony looks at him for a second, then looks away immediately. "If I get tested, maybe we could do it again some time?"

"I'd like that." Daniel isn't lying, he barely thought about it in the heat of the moment either, and giving a blowjob with a condom is a lot less fun.

Tony darts forward to kiss him.

There's a different intimacy to it, kissing now the sex is over, naked together as if it's normal and not exceptional to share space with someone you hardly know in a state so vulnerable. Daniel revels in it, thrilled and comforted at once in a way the sight of his parents' house used to achieve when he was away from home for less long.

Daniel gets water in his eyes from kissing under the spray, and eventually, Tony admits he's exhausted and needs to sit down.

"Oh, shit." Daniel shuts off the water. "Of course, you did all the work. Hey, do you want to stay for dinner?"

The question surprises him; he thought he'd think it through more, or at all. It just slipped out, looking at Tony with his wet hair plastered to his skull, the tiny red mark at his collarbone that Daniel left there.

"Sure." Tony smiles. "I'd like that."

They make pasta together, Tony sitting at the kitchen table and chopping onions with lethal precision. Daniel watches enviously as he defrosts spinach in the microwave. He's not terrible at onions, but there's always a tricky phase toward the end of the onion where it starts slipping out of his fingers and gets harder and harder to control.

Tony has no such issues. "Impressed? He wiggles his eyebrows as he moves on to the garlic, which he's also annoyingly precise and quick about.

"A little," Daniel admits.

"Perks of never moving out. I get to learn all my ma's cooking tricks."

Daniel laughs. "I don't know how you do it. You couldn't pay me to live with my parents again."

Tony shrugs sheepishly. "It's...I don't know. We're not *actually* Italian or anything, but it's still a lot more normal in our family than in American-American families to keep living at home."

"I guess that makes sense. And you must save a ton on rent."

"Yeah. It's supposed to be, like, a future investment, for whenever I get married and buy my own place."

Daniel's hand slips on the pasta, and he ends up pouring the whole pack into the boiling water. Oh well. There will be leftovers.

"I know." Tony sounds apologetic, even though it's a completely normal thing for a person to say outside of the academic bubble Daniel inhabits. "I know."

"Is that something you want?" Daniel's back is turned to Tony as he stirs the pasta into the water, attempting and utterly failing to sound casual.

The barstool Tony's sitting on creaks as he stands. He heads to the sink, runs the cutting board and knife under the water, and cleans them with the sponge. "Your sink is clogged."

"I know."

Tony sets the cutting board and knife on the drying rack by the sink. He comes over to lean against the counter by the stove, right beside

Daniel. Daniel keeps studiously looking at the pasta and not at him.

"Yeah." Tony crosses his arms, an unconscious movement that brushes his upper arm against Daniel's. "I mean, I like the idea. I like it a lot. I...don't really like it the way my parents think of it, I guess."

"Oh?" Daniel chances a look over at him.

Tony smiles wryly. "Yeah. I don't think they picture me with a man."

Well, there's that hypothesis proven. "Must get rough, still living with them." Daniel bumps his shoulder against Tony's.

Tony laughs a little. It sounds bitter. "Bet you're wondering why I do it?"

"Yeah." Daniel thinks of his parents and how little he tells them, how much he keeps quiet. He doesn't even have any specific reasons for it. He started one day, and now he can't quite stop. That's a far cry from all the very valid and awful reasons someone might decide not to come out to their family, and it still makes Daniel's stomach tighten up with regret and pain at how much it hurts. How much it hurts them and him, sometimes, when he's not there; how much it hurts when he is. "You don't owe me any explanations, you know. I may not get it, but I'm sure you have your reasons."

Something like relief washes over Tony's face. The lines in his forehead ease. "Thanks. That's the first time someone's been nice about it."

They don't talk while Daniel's frying up the garlic and onion in oil, adding the spinach and tomatoes and a bit of cream. Tony grates probably too much parmesan to go on top, but Daniel's not complaining. They plate the pasta and sauce and head for the couch. Normally, Daniel would eat on one of the stools in the kitchen, but with no pants on, their legs would get stuck to the plastic, and the only other table in the apartment besides the coffee table by the couch is the one Daniel keeps in the study to pile up his extra papers on.

At the smell of food, Worf emerges from under the couch.

"This is not cat food," Daniel tells him.

"And who is this?" Tony asks once he's swallowed around his bite of pasta.

"Don't try to pet him." Daniel winces internally. There goes any good impression he's made today, trampled under the cat's paws. "He'll make you think you can, but it's a lie; he'll attack you. His name is Worf."

Tony's eyebrows shoot up.

"What?" Daniel asks.

"You're a nerd," Tony says with glee.

"I feel like this should have been obvious." Daniel sniffs and returns to his food.

Having overcome his shyness for now, Worf winds his way between Daniel's legs, purring.

Tony holds out his hand for Worf to sniff. "You're a little unoiled motor, huh?"

Worf sniffs at Tony's outstretched fingers carefully, then slowly rubs his cheek against them. Foolishly, Tony takes this as the okay to scratch behind Worf's ears. Worf immediately hisses and bats his hand away with a claw.

"Wow, you were not kidding." Tony laughs.

With supreme dignity, Worf turns his back and trots away. He stops in front of his cat tree, looks up at the first ledge, wiggles his butt, and makes his usual squawking noise as he leaps up onto the second-lowest platform. Under him, the tree wobbles dangerously. He starts licking his side judiciously.

"Sorry." Daniel grimaces.

"Are you kidding? He's amazing. He always do that little noise?"

"Huh?"

"When he jumps on things, that little cat sound."

"Oh." Daniel takes a little smidge of parmesan on his finger and holds it out to Worf. "Here, boy."

Spotting the food, Worf scrambles upright on his perch before jumping off the cat tree with another little *quack*. His belly jiggles as he runs over, and he licks every smidge of cheese off Daniel's finger, purring as he does it. Daniel loves this stupid cat so much.

"It's like his bumper activates every time he jumps." Tony sounds delighted.

"You are not turning my cat into a car!"

Tony shrugs innocently. "If the shoe fits." He grins around a massive forkful of pasta.

Daniel's about to say something scathing and hilarious, probably, when Tony swallows and continues talking.

"I was going to move out."

"You don't have to—"

"I know." Tony is calm about it, like he has no problem letting Daniel see all of his issues. It's more than a little humbling. "I was going to move out, a couple months ago. Get my own place, maybe a cat." He smiles down at Worf, sitting decorously at the corner of the carpet like he's not desperately hoping for some more cheese. "I even toured a few places, and I was gonna talk to my parents, but then—"

He's interrupted by a pounding on the door.

Daniel looks at Tony. Tony looks at him.

The knocking continues.

Daniel sets his plate on the coffee table. "Colette?" he calls, getting up. "Is that you?"

"Yes," she calls.

"Now's not a great—"

"I don't care."

Daniel looks to Tony again. Tony gestures toward the door, indicating Daniel should open it.

"I want to hear more about this," Daniel tells Tony. "I promise."

"Some other time." Tony waves him off.

Daniel opens the door to Colette and, beside her, Stacy. He winces. Colette has seen him lounging around in his apartment in sweatpants or boxers plenty, but if he'd known she wasn't alone, he would have at least gotten Tony some pants.

"Hi." Stacy somehow manages to convey both sympathy and genuine excitement at seeing Daniel despite having seen him last on Wednesday. "I brought some Christmas cookies."

"It's still November." This should be obvious, but Daniel feels the need to point it out anyway. He wonders if she knows you can show up places without food.

"Oh, I like to start early." Stacy pushes past him into the apartment.

Daniel wants to point out that, furthermore, he doesn't celebrate Christmas, but by then, she's already in, kicking off her shoes and making herself at home.

"Well, hello." Colette spots Tony on the couch and immediately waves far too enthusiastically.

"Hi." Tony waves back with his fork.

"Um—" Daniel hurries past Stacy, who is slipping out of her shoes awkwardly with the cookies still clutched in her hands. "So, Tony, this is my friend Colette. She lives downstairs. And this is Stacy. She works with us."

Tony, Daniel realizes, is wearing boxer shorts and a T-shirt he borrowed from Daniel.

"So you're all professors?" Tony asks.

Colette nods. "And what is it you do?"

"I'm a mechanic."

"Oh, that's great," Stacy enthuses. "You know, I have an uncle who's a mechanic over in Poughkeepsie. Maybe you know him."

She bustles over and sits on the couch next to him, then offers him a cookie.

"I'm, uh—" Tony gestures to his half-empty plate. "—still on the main course. Where does your uncle work?"

"It's this great little shop," Stacy starts and then describes at length what sounds to Daniel like literally any other car repair shop he's ever been to. Midway through her first sentence, Tony picks up his plate and continues eating as if this is totally normal. He makes appropriate listening noises, and it turns out he doesn't know Stacy's uncle, but he does know a coworker of his that Stacy's met once.

Daniel takes the chance to continue his dinner.

Tony must be great at customer service. Tony was great at customer service the first time they met, Daniel remembers, but they got sidetracked by relentless attraction to each other.

"So?" Colette asks in an undertone, nudging her elbow against Daniel's.

Daniel shrugs. He's not sure he can or should say anything if Tony's not out to his family, even if the evidence is fairly damning. Colette knows him well enough to be aware he doesn't often have casual acquaintances over for dinner in their underwear.

As he sets his plate on the coffee table, Tony smiles at Daniel. "This was really good, by the way."

Daniel takes a cookie to hide his smile in return.

"So are these," he tells Stacy. "What's in here, nutmeg?"

"And allspice." She takes one of her own. "I really love those seasonal flavors."

"Me too," Tony and Daniel say simultaneously.

"Well, that's disgustingly adorable." Colette looks between them.

Far from being upset, Tony looks thrilled.

Daniel's heart skips a beat. This is probably what it's supposed to feel like, a new relationship. Jitters and excitement.

"Look, I really hate to bring down the mood." Stacy shifts in her seat. "But I did come over for a reason."

"Aw, I thought you missed us," Daniel teases lightly.

Colette looks like she wants to murder him.

"Of course I did." Stacy looks heartbroken that he would doubt it. "I've been thinking of you both ever since...well, you know. And I've been talking to the president."

"Of the university," Daniel explains hastily at Tony's confused expression.

"Right, yeah." Stacy flashes a smile at Tony and then quickly refocuses on Daniel and Colette. "We were thinking of holding a memorial on Wednesday."

Daniel swallows. A memorial. A memorial for Mario, who was murdered. Possibly over his involvement with his students. Including, maybe, Tony's sister.

"And I was wondering whether you two wanted to speak at it," Stacy concludes.

"Speak," Daniel repeats.

Stacy picks at a loose thread on her knee-length wool skirt. "I know you three were...close. You spent a lot of time together. I can't think of anyone better to give a fitting eulogy for our colleague."

"Is that really..." Daniel trails off.

Everyone looks at him.

He clears his throat. "Is it really a good idea to have the memorial now? With...Lily and everything?"

"Does Mario not deserve a fitting farewell just because he may have been imperfect in life?" Colette asks sharply.

"That's not what I'm saying." Daniel tries to keep his voice calm, even though a part of him wants to yell. "I mean, the police only recently ruled his death a murder. We have no idea who did it, and we have no idea if it was only Lily or if there are other students on campus who might have also been involved with him. It might be a little...soon?"

"I'll do it." Colette's mouth is a firm, thin line. "Whatever else he was, he was my friend."

Daniel holds his hands up. "Fine. I don't really feel comfortable with it."

"Hm," Stacy considers. "Do you think we shouldn't do it at all?"

"Absolutely not," Colette snaps. "Mario was well-liked, and the community deserves to say goodbye to him."

Daniel doesn't respond.

"Do you disagree?" Colette asks him icily.

"No. I...feel like there's a lot we don't know yet. I mean, what if we host this thing and the murderer shows up?"

"Well, according to the police, that could be me." Colette's voice is shuttered and distant. "And I want to go."

"Colette, that's not what I—"

"The police will be there anyway." Stacy is cheery, as if that's a good thing. "They want to get a feel for the community."

Colette turns on her. "They want to *monitor us*?"

"Um, I think I should probably go." Tony stands.

Daniel winces.

"I'll only be a minute." Tony heads to the bedroom. Daniel watches his retreating back regretfully.

"Sorry." Colette doesn't sound even a little sorry.

With a sigh, Daniel pads over to the door on bare feet and waits for Tony to emerge only minutes later. "I'm sorry about this." He tries to keep his voice so low, but his apartment isn't that big. He can feel Stacy and Colette's eyes on them and does his best to ignore them.

"It's okay." Tony attempts a smile. It's nothing as warm as it should be. "Heck, I might even come to your memorial if Gianna wants to go."

"Oh. Right."

"This seems like something you need to figure out...without me."

For a minute, Daniel considers asking his opinion or what he thinks Gianna's opinion would be. He doesn't, conscious of Colette's continued surveillance.

Instead, he presses a soft kiss to the corner of Tony's mouth. "I'll see you soon?"

"Count on it," Tony tells him with a half-smile.

Chapter Nine

The evening of the vigil is cold and clear. Stacy has outdone herself; electric candles light up the high windows of the little campus chapel. The pews are packed, professors sitting toward the front and late arrivals standing up against the walls. Daniel's getting a little choked up just looking at it. He's still not sure this is the right move, but it is a tangible, aching reminder that Mario had a home here and was loved.

Detective Taylor is leaning casually against the wall between two windows in a dark suit indistinguishable from her usual attire.

Stacy taps the mic at the front. "Hi everyone. And thank you so much for coming out tonight. I know it's cold, and we've all got finals coming up way sooner than we'd like. Easy for me to say, I know." She smiles over at the students crowding the walls. There's a brief murmur of polite laughter through the room. The laugh lines around Stacy's eyes deepen.

She takes a deep breath and the lines soften and clear as her expression becomes serious. "More than that—"

The door creaks open. Gianna, wrapped in a thick scarf and an enormous winter coat, sneaks in, Tony close behind her.

"Sorry," Tony whispers.

"Come in, come in." Stacy beckons them inside. "We're open to everyone. As I was saying, more than the cold, more than the time of year, I know there are a lot of questions. The investigation into Professor Lombardi's death is still ongoing, but it has, unfortunately, been deemed a murder. No matter what we know or don't, right now, I'm so glad we're all here together to think of Professor Lombardi and what he meant to all of us. There will be time tonight for everyone who wants to share their favorite memories of Professor Lombardi, but first I'd like to open the floor to Professor Ravel to tell us about his life."

She steps to the side, and Colette glides into place. She's wearing all black, elegant and understated, no makeup and her reading glasses. She's demonstrating grief loudly for anyone watching but most especially for Detective Taylor. It's effective, but it makes Daniel's stomach turn a little with how calculated it is.

"Mario Lombardi was born in 1982 in Yonkers, New York," Colette begins. "He leaves behind two brothers and his parents, who were sadly unable to be here tonight."

Daniel swallows. Would his own parents fly out if he died?

Of course they would. He can't even think about it twice. Of course they would. And Yonkers is only an hour away. Why on earth isn't Mario's family here? Maybe it's because it's not a real memorial service? They're probably Catholic, and this is the least religious funeral Daniel's ever been to.

"It might come as a surprise that Mario was not a good student in his youth," Colette continues. "He used to say that asking an art aficionado to care about chemistry was a hopeless prospect, and so he abandoned it from the get-go."

Shaking his head, Daniel snorts a little. Mario did used to say that, especially about the myriad of science classes for nonscience majors at Lobell. "Why on earth should students getting an art degree need The Physics of Climate Change?" he'd ask, mildly drunk and sprawled over half of Colette's couch.

When Daniel defended the class, arguing that scientific literacy and a well-rounded education were important, Mario scoffed and called him a goody two-shoes.

As Colette goes on to describe Mario's childhood and early education, Daniel wonders if maybe he never actually liked Mario that much. He often felt on the defensive in Mario's presence, like he had to stand up for his opinions and positions. On the other hand, there is an urge Daniel can't deny to pretend that he and Mario were never friendly, that he never laughed at Mario's dumb Super Mario impression, that he hadn't genuinely wanted Mario to like him. Just because it's possible Mario was hiding things, that he was, under the surface, perhaps not such a good guy, doesn't mean Daniel knew it all along. There were some situations where he disagreed with Mario, that's all.

Colette skims through Mario's high school years, his undergrad degree at USC in California. His family, she tells the crowd, was estranged from him. That explains their absence, although Daniel would have thought death would be one thing to breach an estrangement. Still, it tracks with Mario's rare and acerbic references to his family; all Daniel can remember are jokes about Italian Americans and Jersey Shore. It's weird to think about now that Daniel's met Tony. Tony's family seems so close-knit and wholesome.

Unless of course they're way too close-knit and covering for each other.

Colette catches Daniel's eye briefly, and Daniel chastises himself for thinking that. Tonight is about Mario's life, not his death. Colette covers Mario's master's and PhD in New York and then talks about his tumultuous relationship with his ex. It doesn't escape Daniel's notice that she speaks about Laura Cunningham, an up-and-coming academic star at BU, in far more respectful terms than Mario ever did. He'd never been offensive about it, but after the breakup, it was clear when he mentioned her that there was no love lost between the two of them.

Finally, she begins to speak about Mario's time at Lobell.

"When I first became a member of staff at Lobell," Colette says, looking out at the audience over the rim of her reading glasses, "I was extremely nervous."

This is, in Daniel's opinion, not true. Colette was, from the beginning, highly competent and effortlessly put together. He loves her dearly, but he sometimes wonders how on earth she does it.

"Not about teaching, or about my job," she continues, "but about being alone in a new country. It can be a scary thing for us academics to follow the paths our career opportunities take us. However, on my first day as a member of the teaching faculty here, two people made me feel welcome. The first was Daniel Rosenbaum, who offered me a ride from Rhinebeck and showed me where the registrar's office was."

Colette smiles at Daniel, and Daniel can't help but return it. Jeff was miffed all day that Daniel interrupted their regular schedule to talk to their new neighbor. But Daniel was pissed at him as well for some reason he can't quite remember, and Colette was so effortlessly cool even in the back seat of Daniel's somewhat shitty car that he immediately knew he wanted to be her friend. He's glad it worked. He's glad she's demonstrating no hard feelings for his concerns about speaking positively about

Mario at a time like this.

"The other person was Mario," Colette continues, "who saved me from going to the dining hall on my first day and told me instead where to find edible food on campus."

There's a low murmur of laughter. It's common knowledge the dining hall is only something approaching good on parent's weekend to provide the impression that they are paying thousands for their children to be well taken care of. Daniel has been known to sneak in for a bagel and schmear, but that's because he's from the West Coast and wouldn't know a good bagel if it smacked him in the face (according to his grad school friend Paul, who has never lived anywhere but New York and is, to Daniel, the platonic ideal of someone who has never lived anywhere but New York).

It hurts something in Daniel's chest to hear Colette talk about Mario's presence at Lobell. How he would come to class two minutes late with a cup of coffee but stay longer if the discussions were good; how he would tirelessly arrange for film screenings open to everyone on campus. How he would always manage to loosen up tense faculty council meetings with a joke. He liked his popcorn with salted caramel, and it was probably him and him alone keeping the tiny independent movie theater in Germantown afloat.

Mario isn't going to pop up in Colette's office anymore and distract Stacy when everyone else is too uncaffeinated to interact with her. He's not going to enter with, "It's-a me-a, Mario!" He's not going to slide into a booth at the café in the student center next to Daniel and say, "Hey, Rosenbaum, what's cooking?" before stealing some of Daniel's fries.

The lump in Daniel's chest moves to his throat. Tears burn behind his eyes. Beside him, Linda from French Literature is sobbing into a hanky, and Daniel knows there's nothing wrong with crying, but he still tries to stop himself.

Colette comes to the close of the story of the last night she and Mario spent together, drinking wine at Terrapin and comparing their Oscar predictions for the year. She picks up her notecards soberly and tells the audience, "Thank you for being here today," before stepping away from the podium.

"What about Lily?" someone calls from the back.

Colette freezes in place.

"Lily Peterson," the voice calls.

Daniel turns and finds most of the people in the room have turned with him. It's a student, a girl with a nose piercing and turquoise tips at the ends of her dirty-blonde hair.

"Mario Lombardi took advantage of her."

Daniel hasn't heard it said that bleakly, that obviously before. But if her friend says so—if her friend thinks so—how could it not be?

"And she tried to kill herself. Are we all just going to praise him like that didn't happen?"

A murmur goes through the hall. Teaching staff trade wary looks. Of course everyone already knows; faculty gossip is about as fast and hard to quash as a California wildfire. The president might have had good intentions in only emailing a few members of staff, but those intentions were obsolete the moment email forwarding became a possibility. That it reached the students as well... Daniel's willing to bet that girl is Lily's roommate, the one who found her letter. He certainly hopes no one from the faculty is gossiping with the students, not about this.

He really hopes counseling services are taking care of the roommate. It must be an incredibly traumatic situation for them.

"Professor Lombardi would never," another girl claims staunchly, this one with dark hair and a strong, set jaw.

"So what if he did?" a male student chimes in. "This is a memorial service, not a character assassination."

There are so many responses to that Daniel can't even hear them all. Detective Taylor peels away from her pillar, looking alert for the first time all evening.

Stacy taps the microphone at the front so loudly it screeches unpleasantly.

"If I may call everyone to order." She gives the audience a terse smile.

The din quiets down a little, but the atmosphere is less somber than it was to begin with. More whispers, more quiet shifting and people messing with their jackets.

"Investigations into Professor Lombardi's death and his relationship to Miss Peterson are ongoing." It can be easy to forget why Stacy's the dean of the department. Right now, Daniel remembers. "There's not much we can say about that right now. All we can do is remember the member of our community as we knew him. Rest assured that should something untoward in Professor Lombardi's behavior come to light, the college will do whatever we can to support the police and instigate our own Title Nine investigation. Right now, we simply aren't there yet."

Murmurs and comments break out again, people talking over one another. Detective Taylor moves toward the front of the room, badge shining on her hip.

Daniel swallows dryly. The back of his neck is flushed and hot. Rationally, he knows no one here cares about him or his opinions, but he can't help feeling like there are eyes on him, judging him for having been friends with Mario. When students start standing up, discussions getting heated, Daniel uses the confusion to slip out a side door.

Someone probably saw him, but he can't entirely care. He needs some air. He needs not to be asked to weigh in on this yet.

Night has fallen, the lit windows of the chapel and the student center down the road the only illumination on the path. The snow from the weekend has all melted, of course, but the air is still crisp and cold, and the darkness surrounding him makes Daniel feel almost as invisible as he wants to be.

Behind him, the door creaks open again, and Daniel starts.

He turns around to see Gianna's striking dark-red lipstick and big, cozy parka. Behind her, there's Tony, his hair tied up more haphazardly than usual.

"Hi." Daniel tries to meet Tony's eye in the dark.

Tony waves awkwardly. "Gee." He turns to his sister, "Are you—"

"I need a minute." Gianna pushes a hand through her dyed-black hair. "Just...I'm... Can you..."

Tony looks at her like he would move mountains if she asked him to, but she hasn't, so he stands there holding up the Catskills by himself.

"Have you ever had the mozzarella sticks in the student center café?" Daniel blurts out.

The lines around Tony's eyes crinkle up in pleasure and, Daniel thinks, gratitude. "Why? Are they that good?"

"I mean, not authentically Italian good, but they are pretty amazing. Not that the mozzarella stick is a heritage food or anything. Um. Want to get some?"

"Sure," Tony agrees. "Gigi, will you—"

"I'll come find you," she says. "Thanks, Tony."

"Thank Daniel." Tony gestures vaguely toward Daniel as if he's a person Gianna is supposed to recognize.

The fluorescent lights of the student center are shocking, almost dazing. Daniel feels like he's ordering their food through a layer of wool covering his eyes and ears. But somehow, they end up with two piping hot trays of mozzarella sticks and marinara sauce and navigate their way to a booth in the corner of the café.

There's a raised red bump at the line of Tony's beard as if he trimmed it this morning and irritated the skin. For a minute, Daniel lets himself imagine jostling for space in front of the bathroom mirror, dabbing shaving cream on each other.

"Is your sister all right?" he asks.

Tony sighs and dunks a mozzarella stick into sauce. "Not really. You know how I said she knew your friend?"

Daniel nods, taking a bite of his own food. Hot cheese explodes in his mouth and burns his tongue. He struggles to swallow around it and nearly misses Tony's response.

"Yeah, well, she knew him *really, really well*, if you catch my drift."

Eyes burning, Daniel chokes out, "What, like..."

"Like, she dropped out because he got her pregnant."

Daniel drops his mozzarella stick.

"Sorry." Tony winces. "I know he was your friend, and you're like...mourning him and shit. I'm just having a hard time having generous feelings about him." He takes a vicious bite out of his own mozzarella stick. "Shit," he says, mouth full, "these are really hot."

"I didn't know." Daniel feels this intense need to justify himself, even if he doesn't technically owe Tony any explanations. "About Mario, I mean. We were friends, or at least friendly, but I didn't know he..."

Tony swallows and licks a fleck of marinara sauce off his lips. "What would you have done?"

Daniel looks away. "I have no idea," he admits eventually. He finishes the mozzarella stick he first bit into. The cheese has cooled and congealed enough to be edible without causing severe injury, and it's crisp all around the outside on the breading.

To his surprise, Tony laughs.

"Yeah." Tony leans back into the booth. "I like to think, y'know, if Gigi had told me earlier, I'd have been the classic Italian older brother. Gone down to the college, threatened to rough him up a little if he didn't make an honest woman out of her, or whatever."

"But?" Daniel prompts when Tony pauses to eat another mozzarella stick.

"These are really good, by the way." Tony gestures with his bitten-into mozzarella stick. "But she's twenty-two years old. She makes her own decisions. When she told me, we drove to Planned Parenthood. And then we sat there in the parking lot for two hours before she told me she didn't want to do it."

"Shit." Daniel casts around for anything else he could respond but comes up empty.

"Yeah. She didn't want him around either though."

"Did he know?"

Tony shrugs. He twirls his second-to-last mozzarella stick in the marinara slowly. "She won't really talk to me about it much. She claims he never pressured her or...forced her or anything, but he didn't want to hear about the baby at all. She was still talking to him right up until it happened, and I...I thought I'd let her work it out because I didn't know the guy, and maybe it would all end up all right." He laughs hollowly. "I didn't want to push. I'm an idiot."

His fingers drum against the linoleum table.

"I was gonna move out last summer." There's the thread they had to drop the other day in Daniel's living room, when everything was so much more comfortable and so much less complicated. "Before she told me. But then she did, and she dropped out, and she told our parents she doesn't even know who the father is. They're so fucking disappointed it's killing me, but she kept saying the truth would be worse, and then the asshole had to go and die, and I have *no fucking idea* what to do anymore."

Daniel reaches out and lays his hand over Tony's. "So, this is going to sound insane, but do you want to go to the city with me this weekend?"

The corners of Tony's mouth quirk in a smile.

"I have this talk I have to give," Daniel barrels on, "and then I'm meeting up with my friend Paul for a party, which could be terrible, but it's a weekend away, and it sounds like you've been under a lot of stress, and I don't know. Maybe it would be good."

Tony flips his hand over under Daniel's so they're almost holding hands. "I'd like that."

Out of the corner of his eye, Daniel catches sight of Gianna's oversized parka just before she rounds the corner into the café, and he draws his hand away. The mystery of why she's always wearing oversized clothing is solved, at least.

Behind her, trailing like a lost puppy, is Andrew Clayfield.

Tony straightens when he sees her. "Hey, Gigi." The way he smiles at her is so unspeakably gentle that Daniel thinks he might disintegrate into his component parts if Tony were to look at him like that.

Gianna rolls her eyes, but her mouth quirks in half a smile in return. "Can we go?"

"Sure." Tony glances over at Daniel. "Thanks for the mozzarella sticks."

"Anytime. I'll pick you up on Saturday?"

Tony ducks his head a little, looking pleased. "Yeah, text me the time."

One of Gianna's thick, dark eyebrows shoots up her face, but she doesn't comment.

"Bye, Gianna," Andrew mutters.

"Seeya," Gianna tells him over her shoulder, but she doesn't look at him.

Chapter Ten

They leave for the city around midday on Saturday. In part, Daniel's hoping to miss out on the weekend traffic by leaving as late as they can; in part, he's unwilling to bend to the part of his id that wanted desperately to see Tony as soon as possible because it feels like he's getting too attached too soon.

Tony slides into the passenger seat outside a squat, two-story house in Kingston. He smells like he just showered, and he's wrapped up in a red-and-black scarf and a quilted jacket. From the porch, a woman with his dimples waves goodbye.

"Have fun, boys," she calls.

Daniel's jaw twitches.

"Don't start," Tony warns him.

"Wasn't gonna," Daniel lies.

"I feel like I'm a kid going on my first sleepover," Tony tells him as they take the freeway exit south.

Daniel shrugs. "I guess it's not that different."

"No, I mean… This is my first time doing something like this. Going away for the weekend. With, um…"

Catching his meaning, Daniel picks up the sentence before Tony can come up with a label, or worse, ask Daniel what label he'd prefer. "I sure hope my boring talk won't be a disappointing first, then."

"Are you kidding? Hot professor being all smart and professional? No way."

A flush creeps up into Daniel's cheeks, and he turns the car's heating down a bit. "Hot professor?"

"I said what I said."

This time, Daniel couldn't keep the shit-eating grin off his face if he tried.

"So," Tony says pleasantly. "What the fuck are we listening to?"

It's one of Daniel's carefully curated mood playlists, which he can't answer without sounding like an idiot or an asshole. "Um, I think this is the Bleachers." He chances a look over at Tony's blank face and restrains himself from adding a whole swell of words about who the Bleachers are and why he likes them.

"Can I take a look?" Tony indicates Daniel's phone, settled in the holder on the dashboard.

"Yeah. Just let me know if I'm about to miss my turnoff."

"Sure."

It's not that Daniel is ashamed of his taste in music; he knows who he is. He's a nerdy liberal arts professor who likes nerdy indie music. Actually, the Bleachers are pretty cool in terms of Daniel's taste in music. It's not a secret or anything what kind of music he listens to. Something about Tony scrolling through his Spotify makes him incredibly nervous all the same.

There's a little frown line in the middle of Tony's forehead when he looks over briefly.

After what feels like an eternity and is probably less than three minutes, Tony announces, "I have never heard of a single one of these bands."

It's not a judgment, so Daniel will take it. "You can pick the music on the way back," he offers.

"I'll take you up on that. This isn't, like, bad though. I'd need something faster for driving is all."

Daniel doesn't mention that in comparison to some of the other stuff he listens to, this playlist is pretty up-tempo.

He has to turn the music down when they reach the city anyway. It's always weird, how loud noises somehow make it harder to see when, by rights, the two things should be entirely different mental processes. Driving in the city is the worst. By the time they get to the hotel, his grip on the steering wheel is white-knuckled, and his jaw is clenched tight.

"You okay there?" Tony asks lightly, almost amused.

"I hate driving in the city."

"Who doesn't?"

Daniel squints over at him in the dark garage. "You're a car guy, though, aren't you?"

Tony snorts.

Daniel flushes, and he looks away. "Sorry…"

"No, no, I get it. You just keep saying that as if it means anything besides that I know how they work. I can drive us out tomorrow if you want?"

"You'd do that?"

Tony shrugs. "Sure. It's not fun in the city or anything, but it doesn't get me all…"

He doesn't finish, and Daniel's thankful they don't have to have a conversation about anxiety or that it's Daniel's natural state of being.

"Should have taken your car," Daniel jokes.

"Oh, I wouldn't dare." Tony flashes him a grin as he unbuckles his seatbelt and gets out of the car. "Last time I drove more than fifty miles, I had to take a two-hour maintenance break."

"Seriously, why are you still driving that car?"

"You know that saying about cobblers always wearing the worst shoes? Anyway, it's been more than ten years, and you don't just quit on that kind of relationship.

Daniel mulls that one over while they check in and freshen up. Is Tony's relationship to his car somehow indicative of how he feels about dating? Relentless loyalty? That would be nice. Or is this a class thing, and Tony's not in a place to easily buy himself a new car?

In the hotel room, they barely have enough time to use the bathroom and for Daniel to change out of his warm coat and into a blazer suitable for the talk. Under his own coat, it turns out Tony's wearing a dark-blue button-up with lighter pinstripes. It stretches across the expanse of his pecs in a way Daniel would describe as "unfair."

"I'm sorry about this." He adjusts his tie with a wince.

"Are you kidding?" Tony bounces on the balls of his feet. "I can't wait to see you in your element, Professor." He wiggles his eyebrows ridiculously, and Daniel can't help but laugh.

The hotel is only two subway stops from NYU, which is why Daniel chose it. The event Paul invited him to speak at is barely a conference—the Northeastern Digital Humanities Conference is, between the lines, an excuse to get wasted with their grad school buddies. Otherwise, Mari would have stopped getting invited when she accepted an adjunct position at UC Santa Cruz. It's also why Daniel feels comfortable showing up for his own talk and the dinner afterward and none of the other events. There was a panel yesterday evening, and it might have been interesting, but he feels awkward enough about dragging Tony to one day of this.

Anyway, he's so drained by everything that's happened recently. Surely that makes it defensible to miss out on one panel in a subject he knows backward and forward.

Paul doesn't give a shit either way, so long as Daniel makes it to drinks tonight. He greets Daniel with an exuberant hug, at least three espressos deep into the afternoon. "Danny! Perfect timing."

Danny, Tony mouths over Paul's shoulder.

Daniel tries to make his displeasure known without words.

"And who is this you've brought?" Paul looks Tony over with far more interest than Daniel is comfortable with.

"Tony." Tony holds out his hand to be shaken. "I'm Daniel's...uh..."

"My friend," Daniel adds quickly, letting his arm brush against Tony's and hoping he doesn't take the title personally.

Paul's eyebrows do a little dance anyway. "Nice to *meet* you."

Tony's elbow knocks against Daniel's, and Daniel decides to assume it's okay.

His talk is scheduled for forty-five minutes, fifteen of those a discussion section. For the first part, he outlines the Hudson Valley soundscape project and plays a few examples, among them the recording of Tony's garage. He's careful not to look at Tony as he plays it; he might do something unforgivable like wink.

In the second half of his talk, Daniel fleshes out future potentials for digital mapping in social and literary studies. He presents his half-formed notion of an interactive map of real and fictional violent crime and what that could do both to demonstrate the sensationalizing of violent crime and the way media tends to act as though it's a question of individual mental illness rather than structural violence.

The question session nearly goes over. At least five different procedural cop shows get mentioned. Three different people suggest collating crime statistics with reports of police violence or gross police incompetence.

It turns out Daniel struck a nerve with this one. He's definitely going to have to write that grant.

In the obligatory mingle before dinner, a whole bunch of people flock to Daniel to talk about it. And they're not even only people he got drunk with in grad school, although Mari and Paul hang around plenty.

"It's like you're a rockstar," Tony murmurs, too low for anyone else to hear. He has a champagne flute, the stem pinched delicately between his thumb and forefinger, and something about the filigree glassware in his broad, strong hands is relentlessly appealing.

"You're going to inflate my ego," Daniel warns quietly, lips almost brushing Tony's ear.

He can see the goosebumps that break out on Tony's neck. Flattering.

"All right, lovebirds," Paul says loudly, forcing them apart. "Time for dinner; flirt later!"

Daniel asks Tony as they head toward dinner, "Do you mind that he's... Um. So obvious about us?"

"I mean, I think it's pretty clear I'm here as your date."

"Yeah, but you're not..."

"Out?" Tony nods. "True, but what are the chances of anyone here telling my parents about me?"

"Fair."

"So," Mari asks, taking a seat across from Tony in the dimly lit restaurant Paul chose for the evening. It's covered by NYU, so Daniel's willing to bet it will be stupidly expensive. "What did you think of Daniel's talk?"

"It was super interesting." Tony unfolds his napkin. "I never used to think about how my work *sounds*, but when you listen to it, it's actually kind of nice."

"Oh, that was your place of work we heard?" Mari leans forward.

"Yeah. That was me working, actually."

Looking between the two of them, Mari asks, "How did you two meet anyway?"

"My car needed fixing." Daniel wills her silently to drop the line of questioning.

"Do you not find your work *nice* in general?" Paul asks, sliding into place next to Mari and taking a long sip of his wine. How he got a glass of wine already before they've even ordered is anyone's guess.

Tony shrugs, loosening his tie. "I like it. It's just— You know. Loud and dirty."

"Loud and dirty," Paul repeats slowly, savoring the syllables.

Daniel throws a napkin at him.

Tony turns to Daniel. "They don't meet a lot of nonacademics, do they?"

"Sadly, no, we waste away here in our ivory tower, never going amongst the masses," Paul intones. He's at NYU with an anthropology professorship, and given everything Daniel's learned about participant observation since he started working with Colette, the irony is rich, although it's lost on everyone else at the table.

"Ignore him," Daniel says. "Please."

Mari laughs. "Please do. We're only teasing. Daniel never brings anyone to these things."

"That's not true. I brought Jeff."

Paul waves a lazy hand. "Jeff got his own invite. He was on the panels about copyright and other boring legal stuff sometimes, remember?"

"Shit, he's not *here*, is he?" The thought is mildly horrifying. While Daniel wouldn't mind showing off that he's moved on, Jeff would almost certainly be an ass about Tony's job.

Paul shakes his head. "No, he's at a much more prestigious conference somewhere in Wisconsin."

Mari snorts. "If it were prestigious, it wouldn't be in Wisconsin. Anyway, where's Dolores?"

Paul sighs melodramatically. "She's doing fieldwork in Costa Rica. We're on a break."

While Mari drills Paul for further details on Dolores's research, Tony leans in close to Daniel.

"Jeff is..."

"My ex. Also, an academic. And a lawyer, I guess, but mostly he teaches political science and human rights classes. We broke up a year ago."

Tony nods.

"Is this too weird?"

Tony's eyes crinkle a little, as though he's about to smile, but he's not quite happy enough. "It's not. These are your friends, right?"

"Yeah."

They chat easily about work and life over dinner. Mari is slowly working her way up the ranks at Santa Cruz by virtue of being the most organized person Daniel knows while also being too nice to say no to responsibility. She's the Stacy of California. Paul got funding for a truly batshit project that involves attending an ayahuasca retreat, and he's due to start a special diet for it after Christmas, apparently. Who knew you had to fast before taking drugs for maximum effect? Around them, the buzz of the dinner continues through the appetizers and the main course.

Tony eats slowly and steadily, only commenting occasionally. Under the table, though, his fingers brush Daniel's often enough that Daniel feels reassured this isn't going awfully.

Some of the older guests leave around dessert. It's already almost nine, and a few people are in the city with their families or looking to get home tonight. The younger group remains, drawing closer around the remaining tables. Daniel knows most of them, not as well as Mari and Paul, but well enough in passing that he can make conversation about recent publications and current news.

He's only drawn out of a drawn-out discussion about how ridiculous it is that the right to have an abortion is once again in question in the US when Tony's fingers clench around his and then suddenly let go.

Daniel remembers, suddenly, what Tony admitted only the other day. That he drove his sister to get an abortion, and she decided against it.

"Wanna get some air?" he asks in an undertone.

"Yeah." As they get up to go outside, Tony undoes his top button as though it's strangling him.

"Sorry," Daniel says when they get outside.

Tony laughs. It doesn't sound as joyful as Daniel remembers. "For what?"

"Um..." Daniel runs a hand through his hair. "That all my friends are academics and start talking about politics like it doesn't affect people's lives. That I didn't remember about...your sister."

"It's not like I don't have the same conversations with my friends. Or like I've never been to the city before."

That surprises Daniel for a moment, which is shitty of him. Of course Tony has friends. Of course they talk about these things.

"Y'know, I do have an associate's degree," Tony adds, which has nothing to do with anything except that Daniel didn't know.

"Okay." He wonders if he should add anything, but Tony keeps going before he can.

"And I kinda feel like a token uneducated person in the room just because I've had a conversation with a Republican in the last two months."

Daniel winces. "I'm sorry," he repeats.

"I don't mean... Ugh, *I'm* sorry. Look, I have a bunch of hang-ups about stuff, I guess, and I don't want you to think...anyway. It was getting a little much in there. And, yeah. Made me think of Gigi."

Daniel lets himself reach out, grasp Tony's arm with his hand, and stroke slowly along the tendons. "We can go back to the hotel room. Call it a night."

Tony breathes out slowly and leans into Daniel's space. He kisses Daniel, a soft whisper of a thing. "I already promised Paul we'd go out with him."

"Paul can live with the disappointment. I have disappointed him many times." It would be disappointing to Daniel too. Going out with Paul once in a blue moon when he makes it down to the city is the only holdover from his partying days. Standing under a streetlight, dwarfed by the giant buildings in Manhattan and shivering in the cold, Daniel finds he'd rather disappoint himself and one of his oldest friends than Tony.

"Nah." Tony smile weakly. "I wanna see you cut loose a bit. I just need to stop feeling self-conscious."

Tony shouldn't have to feel responsible for managing his response to being the only tradesman in a room full of stuffy academics. Daniel wants to reassure him about that, but he doesn't know how to untangle that line of thought without it sounding either condescending or way too invested in Tony's emotional wellbeing.

"Here's a suggestion," he offers instead. "Alcohol."

They make a valiant attempt, downing their wine and topping it up as soon as they get back inside, but in the end, it's only two drinks before Paul has either scared off or enticed the remaining group into following him to one of his haunts.

Paul has a way of finding places that seem incongruous to his aesthetic. He embodies a waifish, scarf-wearing hipster look that was stylish for a moment when they were still students and has become eccentric now they're professors. The club he takes them to is a barely converted warehouse with R&B thumping from the speakers. The bouncer barely checks their IDs, and the beer costs four dollars. Daniel's pretty sure it's Dolores's influence as he vaguely remembers Paul being aloof and artistic in a very white way when they met—before she sat down next to them in their first-ever graduate seminar and spent half of it muttering about intersectionality under her breath. He's never known much about their relationship, not least because neither Paul nor Dolores are the kind of people who like to label their own genders, sexualities, or relationships, but he loves what they bring out in each other. He does wish Dolores were in the country. He misses her.

"Cheapest beer in the state," Tony yells in Daniel's ear as he slides his wallet into his pocket. He got a glow-in-the-dark bracelet from a group of girls who are way too drunk to be so happy on their way to the bar. He looks lighter around the edges since they talked, even though they didn't clear anything up at all. He looks happy to be here.

The beer is served in red solo cups, sloshing with every movement, so they drink quickly. Daniel can't quite help the way his nose wrinkles.

It's really bad. Bud Light levels of bad.

Grimacing, Tony nods and chugs the rest of his.

Mari cheers. Being a reasonable person, she got a bottle of water.

"C'mon, Danny." Tony grins. "Finish yours so we can hit the dance floor."

It's probably that Daniel doesn't drink this much that often, so he's already tipsy, or that Mari and Paul are rooting for him, or that he's feeling young and stupid in general, but he manages to down the beer in four big swallows.

"Sweet!" Paul crows. "To the floor with us!"

He leads the way, neon bracelets glowing on either wrist. He's still wearing his checkered scarf, and he dances like he used to, all knees and elbows. Weirdly, it seems to work for this crowd because after barely two songs, he's already made friends with three different groups on the dance floor.

Mari bops along to the music, sipping at her water. She throws her hands up when the lyrics tell her to, and she spins and laughs and, to Daniel, looks almost exactly like she did at twenty-three. She's got one of the other academics they brought by the hand, with a third bopping his head along awkwardly next to them.

It's as nostalgic as it is strange how much Daniel feels catapulted ten years into the past. He's spent so much time telling himself he's happy with his quiet life that he almost forgot he wasn't always like this. He does like things restful for the most part, but there's a place for this kind of throwback, for music that was popular when he was a teenager, drowning out his usual cacophony of overthinking.

Daniel doesn't feel guilty at all when Tony's hand migrates from his arm to his hip, when he pulls Daniel in close and Daniel turns away from the group to dance with only him. He loops his arms around Tony's neck, lets himself press close.

He wasn't sure what this would be like, with Tony. It's not as if Kingston is a hotbed for the clubbing scene (although it is, according to one of the weirder staff emails Daniel's gotten, part of the heroin trail between New York and Montreal). Adding to which, Daniel's never done this with…well, anyone but his friends, really. It wasn't Jeff's scene, and before Jeff, Daniel came to places like this to find someone for a one-night stand or to hang out with Paul, Dolores, and Mari all night while their eardrums got destroyed.

He likes how familiar and warm Tony's hands are at his hips, even though he's way too hot already. He likes how Tony throws his head back and laughs when Daniel can't quite help but mouth the words to an Usher song from 2001. He likes how good it feels to move with someone else like this. Neither of them are great dancers, but Daniel can keep a beat, and Tony knows how to use his hips, and Daniel's heart is racing and he's grinning and he feels unbelievably alive.

When he reaches up to cradle Tony's head in his hand, Daniel's struck by the feel of the close-shaved part of his hair prickling against his palm, soft and sharp at the same time. A swell of something unspeakably tender overwhelms him, and he drags Tony in for a kiss.

Daniel tastes the cheap beer on Tony's tongue, and he doesn't give a shit. He wants to kiss Tony all the time. He loves the way Tony's mustache scrapes across his upper lip. He loves how Tony draws him in, wraps him up, holds him close. He barely notices it happening, but one, maybe two songs pass before they've lost the group, before he's got Tony up against the wall and they're not even dancing anymore, just making out to the sound of 50 Cent asking a girl to *take him to the candy shop*.

"Wanna get out of here?" he asks, right in Tony's ear.

Tony shudders, and Daniel feels every little tremor.

"You trying to seduce me, Professor?" Tony's smiling enough that his dimples are showing again. It warms the pit of Daniel's stomach, and his earlier unease is gone.

"I thought you were a sure thing."

They're both laughing as they stumble out of the club, shoulders and hands brushing the whole subway ride to the hotel. Daniel's tipsy in that warm contented sweet spot where he's feeling it but not too much, and with the way Tony's looking at him, all unguarded wide-open eyes, he's probably feeling pretty similar.

For all he's been to a lot of conferences, Daniel's never done the out-of-town hookup cliché, making out in the elevator and stumbling to his hotel room with his fingers tangled with someone else's. Maybe it will wear off, this thrill at every mundane experience he shares with Tony.

He hopes it doesn't.

They tangle up against the door of the hotel room once they're inside, trading sloppy kisses and pushing and pulling at each other's clothes.

"Sweetheart," Tony mumbles into Daniel's lips as Daniel pushes his shirt off his shoulders.

"Fuck you're hot." Daniel traces his fingers across Tony's pecs.

A flush spreads across the skin Daniel's mapping, as though Tony's *embarrassed* or something, and Daniel grabs Tony by the belt buckle and pulls him back toward the bed. When he's got Tony where he wants him, settled above him, Daniel says, "You must know, right? You must know how good you look."

The flush reaches Tony's cheeks. "I, uh, um..."

Daniel grabs him by the nape of the neck, pulls him in, and kisses him with all he's got. "Can't believe I got lucky enough someone who looks like you likes me," he gets out between kisses so frantic they've gone sloppy. "Can't believe someone so *kind* likes me."

With a desperate noise, Tony buries his face in Daniel's shoulder, collapsing to his side beside Daniel, tugging at his belt.

They kick off their pants gracelessly, and Tony squirms closer until he's got a thigh hooked over Daniel's hip. Until they're pressed up against each other everywhere that matters, so close a sheet of paper couldn't fit between them.

"Baby," Daniel gasps when Tony ruts against him.

For the second time that night, he gets the pleasure of feeling Tony's full-body shudder against him.

With an expression bordering on desperate, Tony looks at him, cheeks red, eyes wide. "You gotta stop talking, sweetheart." His voice borders on desperate. "You're going to ruin me."

I want to ruin you, Daniel thinks selfishly. He wants Tony all to himself, for as long as he can get him. Instead of saying that, though, he kisses Tony again, grinding his hips until they're aligned. He snakes a hand down and makes enough space so he can jerk them off together, held tight between them.

Maybe it's the alcohol, maybe it's the frenzy of emotion this night kicked loose in them, but it's not long at all before Tony's groaning in Daniel's mouth and shooting off in his fist, wet and warm and beautiful. He whimpers in the aftermath, oversensitive, with his hips still jerking helplessly into Daniel's grip. Daniel feels powerful, almost ridiculously turned on that he reduced Tony to this, and that thought and the added lubrication of Tony's come sends him hurtling over the edge into an orgasm so powerful it makes him dizzy. He presses up tightly against Tony's skin, riding the waves of it out, balls clenching and unclenching so hard it almost hurts.

He flops onto his back, finally done, breathing unsteadily.

When he gets his eyes open, Tony's staring at him.

For a long moment, they just look at each other. Finally, Daniel manages, "That was...different."

"Uh-huh. Um."

They look at each other for a long moment, and then, unsteadily, they both begin to laugh.

"I think I'm gonna shower." Tony looks down at himself. Most of their mess landed on his stomach, matting the sparse hair on his lower belly.

"Yeah." Daniel snickers. "Yeah. I'll be there in a sec. Once my legs work."

"Yeah," Tony agrees, still laughing a little as he makes for the bathroom.

Daniel gives himself a moment to bask, stretching out in the sheets before he forces himself upright. There's a moment of headrush that tells him he should probably drink some water, and then he hears the shower turn on.

His pants are a crumpled mess at the foot of the bed, and he picks them up to get out his phone to check the time.

Quarter to two.

He's officially not entirely an old person yet if he's up this late.

He's also officially still drunk and really tired, and it's making his head swim.

Shit, there are three missed calls from Colette blinking on his lock screen.

Guiltily, he remembers how they left things and hits the button to call her back before remembering the time.

She picks up on the third ring.

"Daniel?" she asks down the line incredulously.

"Sorry," he hisses, trying to keep his voice down. "My phone was on silent. I'm…"

"Are you *drunk*?"

"Maybe a little. Tipsy."

"Who are you even."

"I'm at a conference."

"Ah. I take it this is a bad time to talk about Mario."

Daniel lets himself slump down onto the bed. "I brought Tony."

"All right."

"I brought Tony, and I like him *way too much*, Colette."

She sighs heavily down the line. "It's not a bad thing to start a relationship."

"Mario got his sister pregnant," Daniel tells her as quickly and quietly as he can. Even as he says it, he feels the weight of the secret lifting off of him, tension releasing in waves. He's spent all weekend forcing himself not to think about it, not to search for gaps to talk about it, because he wants Tony to himself, because he wants this to work. It's a short-lived relief. Within seconds, the weight of the secret makes way for the guilt of not having told anyone. "And we haven't talked about it. Not really. And I *really* like him, and I'm scared that…"

"Daniel?" Tony calls from the bathroom.

"I gotta go. Colette, I don't know what the fuck I'm doing." He disconnects the call and follows Tony to the bathroom.

Chapter Eleven

Someday, Daniel will wake up to birdsong and sunshine. Someday, it won't be a pounding on the door or the incessant, shrill, beeping noise it is today. It's still dark out. It might be early December, but waking up in the dark is still inhumane.

"Tony." He bumps his hips back against Tony's because, apparently, Tony slept wrapped around him like a kid with a stuffed toy.

Tony grumbles and rubs his nose against Daniel's neck, burrowing deeper into the covers.

"Tony." Daniel jostles Tony again, and oh, hey, that's Tony's erection bumping up against Daniel's ass. That's a nice thought. They could—

Tony shoots straight up. "Fuck," he mutters, clawing through the covers.

An involuntary noise escapes Daniel as the cold air hits his bare skin. Fuck, they went to bed naked last night? He never does that.

He remembers stepping into the bathroom with the weight of the murder case lifted off his shoulders after telling Colette. He remembers rubbing soapy hands up and down Tony's body, gentle and laughing. He remembers getting out of the shower with Tony, drying off, unable to stop smiling at each other, falling into the sheets. He remembers kissing until they were too tired to keep moving. At some point, they must have fallen asleep pressed close together and just...stayed like that. As a life-long bad sleeper, Daniel is shocked at himself.

He's also hungover.

Slowly, he sits up, rubbing at his temples as Tony rummages around their clothes on the floor to get at his phone.

"Yeah," he croaks into it hoarsely once he's finally managed to pick up.

In an instant, his entire demeanor changes. Tony stands up straighter; his eyes widen. "What?" he asks sharply.

Then, quietly, "Yeah, I knew."

Finally, "I'll be there in two hours."

Daniel freezes, staring at him. Tony hangs up and starts grappling for his clothes.

"The police took Gianna in for questioning." He pulls his things on roughly. He digs a T-shirt out of his backpack.

Wordlessly, Daniel slides out of bed and starts getting dressed.

They check out without breakfast, and in the elevator down to parking, Daniel silently mourns the opportunity to get to know Tony's breakfast preferences. He's probably a coffee drinker, and Daniel wonders if he likes it black or if he drowns it in cream and sugar. He wants to know. He'd get a coffee machine for Tony instead of the half-empty jar of instant he keeps in one of his cupboards for guests.

"Are you okay to drive?" he asks when they reach the basement.

He's not sure why it matters anymore. They'd agreed to this yesterday; he can drive perfectly well even if he's a little hungover. Maybe Tony needs some peace and quiet. Daniel should offer. Still, it feels safer to stick to the status quo.

Tony nods.

That's that, then.

Daniel hands him the keys, throws his things into the trunk, and slides into the passenger seat.

They drive out of the city in silence.

It's Sunday morning, which means traffic isn't as heinous as it usually is. Daniel doesn't dare ask if Tony wants some music on or if he needs Google maps. Tony seems more than confident as he winds his way out of Manhattan, past Hackensack, and toward the highway. They're past Woodbury before either of them speaks.

"She didn't kill him." Tony's voice is tight.

It would be entirely out of the blue if Daniel hadn't been thinking about it for hours..

Daniel hesitates a moment. "I didn't say she did."

"Were you thinking it?"

Daniel's entire body flushes hot. He doesn't answer.

"Because my mom told me the police showed up saying a *Lobell professor* told them about...about..."

Letting his head thunk against the headrest of the passenger seat, Daniel closes his eyes. "Fuck."

"Did you?"

"No. But I told Colette." The missing pieces are easy enough to put together. She must have called the police last night after he hung up on her or early this morning. Turns out the peace of mind brought by telling her was short-lived.

"Great." Tony shifts, staring out the windshield stonily. "Fucking...great."

They're quiet again for a while, passing by signs for Walden and Wallkill and Poughkeepsie. It's worse, this time, not only tense but accusatory.

Maybe that's Daniel's conscience.

New Paltz is coming up, and he can't help himself. "The police were gonna find out eventually anyway."

A bitter laugh bursts out of Tony. "Gee, thanks, Professor." It sounded a lot nicer, yesterday, him calling Daniel that. "You think I haven't been telling her that since day one?"

"I—"

"You think I haven't been *trying* to get her to see that before something like this happens and our parents find out? I know I'm not as smart as you, but I'm fucking trying!"

"I never said—"

"You didn't have to. I know I'm, like, some exciting little fling on the wrong side of the tracks for you or whatever."

"Tony..."

"Look." Tony speaks with an air of finality, as though all of this is a foregone conclusion and not the first time Daniel's ever considered he might feel like this. "I was fine with that. I thought I'd get what I could take, but I didn't realize you thought this was some James Bond bullshit where you were trying to catch my baby sister red-handed or something."

"And how sure are you she's so innocent?" Daniel snaps. "She was hanging out with the only student on campus who's trying to get access to the fucking corpse."

Tony jerks the car onto the turnoff for Kingston. "Why the fuck didn't you *tell me that*? Am I that untrustworthy? Just because I fix cars for a living doesn't mean I don't understand how bad this is."

Daniel opens his mouth to answer, but there's nothing he can think to say.

When they reach the d'Angelos' house, Tony all but jumps out of the driver's seat, sprints to the front door, and slams it behind him.

Daniel gets out slowly and walks around the car to the driver's side. He wonders if he should stay, if he should try to talk this out.

The front door is open now. Over Tony's shoulder, Daniel can make out his mom's tear-streaked face. He hears Tony saying, "I'm sorry, Ma," over and over again as he hugs her tight.

He gets into the car and starts the ignition.

He'll only be in the way here.

It would probably be healthy to bury himself in work or get some exercise. His workout schedule—by which he means his biweekly guilt-induced jog—has suffered under the stress of the last few weeks. Instead, once he's home, Daniel turns on the local TV news station and watches obsessively, waiting for any report on Tony's family.

There is none, of course. It's an ongoing investigation, and it's not like the police will go to the news stations out of nowhere. They might do it on *Criminal Minds*, but unlike Aaron Hotchner, Daniel's willing to bet Detective Taylor isn't using the media to pull a serial killer out of hiding.

He scrolls blindly through Twitter on his phone while he watches, too jittery to do something productive. Mari has posted photos of last night. In the corner of one, Daniel can see Tony's arm.

As if alert to his state, Worf wanders around the living room aimlessly, squawking every now and again to remind Daniel he's there.

His misery is only interrupted around two in the afternoon when a sudden crash and thundering footsteps alerts him to someone slamming a door and running up the staircase. It's followed by a lot of yelling.

When it doesn't stop immediately, he shuffles to the door and peeks out.

Andrew Clayfield is pounding on Colette's door and shouting, "You *set the dogs* on her! Professor, you need to *listen to me—*"

"Andrew, that's enough," Daniel snaps, abruptly done with all of this.

Andrew's face when he turns to look at Daniel is pale and drawn as if he hasn't been sleeping. "Gianna d'Angelo is innocent!" he yells. "Gianna didn't do anything wrong. I made sure of that. She *promised* it would work. Professor Ravel needs to—"

"Professor Ravel doesn't need to do anything. You need to calm down."

"It wasn't supposed to *be* like this." Andrew shakes his head. "Gianna—Professor Lombardi— It was..."

Abruptly, he turns on his heel and then runs back down the stairs.

When the building's front door slams shut below, Colette opens her door.

"Thank you," she says.

Daniel sinks onto the steps, rubbing his forehead. "At least call the police on him too."

He listens from his seat on the steps as Colette makes the call. She describes Andrew's special interests again because, apparently, no one followed up on that the last time she did. She explains how Andrew was pressuring Mario before his death, how this is the second time he's accosted her. Daniel wonders how it ever got this far. How have none of his professors said anything before? His RAs? Shouldn't there have been some intervention? Involuntarily, his mind goes to what Colette and

Mario discussed that last day when everything seemed like a joke. Corpses and cannibalism. He shudders.

She promised it would work. Daniel wonders what Andrew imagined. What did Gianna promise him? What if Daniel was right all along, and Tony will end up disappointed in his sister? He's sure, now, that Tony was never covering for her. He was only trying to help her. He was the only person trying to help her, given that Mario abused her trust to flagrantly. The idea that, after all that, Daniel was right and Gianna is the killer is grotesque and heinous. Far from being a comfort that Daniel torpedoed his best chance at a relationship in years over a real concern, just the thought of what it would do to Tony makes him want to scream.

After she's done with her phone call, Colette comes out of her apartment, climbs up the stairs, and sits next to him. "I got you in trouble with your friend, didn't I?"

He nods wordlessly, leaning against her.

She strokes a hand up and down his back.

"I think I got myself in more trouble," he admits.

They sit there for quite a while before she tells him, "I think I was wrong about Mario."

"Want to order pizza and get drunk?"

Colette nods. "I think..." She sighs heavily. "I can't believe I'm saying this, but I think we should invite Stacy."

That gets a little smile tugging at his lips. "You feel that guilty?"

"The detective visited her three separate times this week. She deserves to know what we do."

With a groan, Daniel gets to his feet. "Tell you what. We'll do penance together. You invite Stacy, and I'll make a much worse phone call. Meet here in ten?"

"Put some wine in the fridge." She disappears into her apartment.

Daniel swallows, takes a fortifying breath, and unlocks his phone.

There are no messages from Tony, which is a given. Instead, he calls his mom.

She answers immediately. "Danny? Is everything all right?"

He closes his eyes and lets the guilt consume him. "Yeah, Mom. Everything's okay. I just wanted to say hi."

"I'm so glad. I've been worried about you."

"I should have called earlier."

"That's okay, honey." He can picture her as she talks, wandering around the kitchen because she can never keep still when she's on the phone, wiping down counters one-handed.

"It's not okay. I'm sorry I left so suddenly, and I'm sorry I didn't call you earlier. And I'm sorry I don't come home as much as you'd like."

There's a huff of static as she exhales loudly into the receiver, a huff of a laugh. "It's not your home anymore, is it?"

"No. I guess not."

He wonders if he should say more about it, apologize for not being clearer, or apologize for having found a home away from her. But she doesn't let him.

"How's your student doing? Is she all right?"

"She's still in the hospital." He then gives her a rundown of the case so far. He's not sure why she cares or what she gets out of it, but she listens and hums appreciatively. Exactly like he did with Tony, he underestimated the power of his own silence to hurt people. If he'd talked to her more from the get-go, she wouldn't have worried. If he hadn't let himself get so caught up in his own brain and his hermetically sealed-off life, he could have had this with her all along.

He asks how she's doing and about his dad, which is how he learns his dad has started work as a senior union rep in his retirement, and his mom has joined a book club. She's reading Junot Diaz this week. He remembers the book from his undergrad years, and they chat for a while about how Diaz uses footnotes.

"Oh, I've missed talking to you about your work," she says as they wind down.

It catches him so far on the wrong foot that he blurts out, "Really?"

She laughs. "Yeah, we used to talk books all the time when you were still in school, remember?"

"It wasn't my work *then*."

"But you always had a talent for it. I loved reading your essays. I knew you would do great in college."

He swallows around nothing. "Just like you."

"Aw, don't flatter me." She laughs.

"I would really love it if you came and visited some time." It's awkward and apropos of nothing, except that he's been wishing it for years.

"I would love that too. How about we talk about it next week?"

"Yeah. I'll call you."

He feels wrung out once he's hung up, as though he said everything he needed to and, at the same time, didn't even scratch the surface.

For a moment, he considers using the momentum to reach out to Tony, but once he's opened his messenger app, he realizes he has no clue what to write.

Instead, he calls up Village Pizza and orders more food than three people should eat. Then, he pours himself a glass of room-temperature white wine and puts the rest of the bottle in the fridge.

Colette was right. Stacy is subdued when she and Colette come in ten minutes later. She gives Daniel a long hug as a greeting. Even her hair seems less bouncy than usual.

"I'm so glad you invited me," Stacy groans. "This has been...the longest week."

"I heard you've been hearing a lot from the police," Daniel agrees into the top of her head. She's so short for so much personality.

"Yeah," she sighs as she falls into place on his couch. "I know they're doing their best, but between them and all the outrage on campus, I haven't done anything this week that's actually in my job description."

"Same." Daniel hands her a glass and the bottle he unearthed on his pantry shelf. "Here, drink this." The wine isn't chilled, but it will do.

Over probably more pizza than any of them were intending on eating, Colette and Daniel fill her in on Gianna.

"Oh, no," Stacy gasps. "His sister? Daniel, aren't you and he..."

Daniel's laugh sounds more unhinged than he's willing to admit. "Yeah, probably not anymore."

"I'm sorry." Colette is earnest and honestly apologetic, neither of which Daniel deserves.

He shakes his head. "It's my own fault. Should have talked to him about it sooner. Or at all." He still wishes she hadn't called the police without telling him. It might have given him a fighting chance to do something about it, but the more time eclipses since Tony ran out of his car, the more Daniel realizes he was a massive dick.

"You *guys*." If Stacy weren't a half glass of wine deep and a little whiny, she would sound almost as stern as her dean-of-the-department persona. "Sorry. I mean guys and gals and everything else— It's no one's fault. It's *Mario's* fault."

Colette, usually a dignified eater, shoves half a pizza slice in her mouth.

Daniel swigs his wine. Tony, at least, is *definitely* his fault.

"I think none of us would like to speak ill of the dead." Colette's tone is very carefully crafted to be noncommittal.

"Yep," Daniel agrees.

"I also think," she continues, "that it is becoming very hard not to."

"Yep."

They all drink again.

"I can't believe no one knew," Stacy says.

"The students knew," Daniel points out.

Colette shakes her head. "Only the ones he was sleeping with."

Daniel snaps his fingers. "No! Andrew knew, didn't he? He was raving about Gianna when he was here."

Stacy inhales sharply. "Andrew?"

"Andrew Clayfield. Remember, the one with the unfortunate...obsession with death?"

"Oh, I know." Stacy's mouth is a thin, grim line. "I just got an email about him resisting arrest. They've declared his entire floor in Norridge House a crime scene. Residence Life and Housing had to force juniors and seniors to double up for the next *week*."

There are two options here, Daniel realizes. Maybe it's the glass of wine on top of last night's hangover and the lack of sleep making him delirious, but he's tired of being in the dark.

"Okay," he tells them. "I know tomorrow is a workday, but hear me out."

Colette raises an eyebrow.

"Either..." Daniel draws the word out, aware he's about to suggest something very stupid. "...we drink both bottles I have left in the fridge and call in sick tomorrow. Or we sneak on campus and find out what's in his room."

Daniel is pretty sure Stacy will nix this idea. It's why he said it, the hope that common sense will prevail. And she does start strong.

"We couldn't," she gasps.

Daniel shrugs. "Probably not."

Colette says nothing, but she leans in, eyebrows raised.

"Unless..." Stacy trails off. "This would be very silly of us; you do know that."

"We know," Daniel assures her. *Silly* is not the word he'd have chosen, but he'll take it. Convincing Stacy feels like being allowed a sip of wine at dinner as a teenager.

In the end, they're all academics out of curiosity and a passion for learning. Apparently, that includes learning about violent crime.

They wait a few hours until it's past anything like reasonable working hours, even for the police. Stacy drives them to campus in her mom van, chattering nervously all the while.

"We're really lucky we have the car tonight, you know. My husband usually needs it in the evenings. He teaches night classes sometimes, but his knee's been acting up. What if we get caught though? What if— The police were already sniffing around Colette, weren't they?"

"Then I suppose I will find a lawyer." Colette doesn't mention that now she's gotten the police to go after Andrew and Gianna, they're probably leaving her alone. Daniel doesn't either, mostly because he doesn't have the emotional energy to risk another friendship today. Especially given that he agrees Andrew and Gianna are both far more suspicious than Colette.

"You're an administrator, not just a professor, Stacy," Daniel argues. "You can always claim it's part of your job to make sure students are sticking to the rules."

"That's a good idea." Colette nods. "You could even tell RL and H you're stopping by to give them a break."

"That is such a good idea," Stacy enthuses. "Here, call Amanda on my phone and put her on speaker."

Daniel does, and then proceeds to witness the most awkward phone call in the history of the phone. Alexander Graham Bell was probably smoother than Stacy.

"Hi, Amanda." She laughs nervously. "How are you holding up?"

"Oh my god, Stace, it's insanity over here." Amanda Polk, the head of Residence Life and Housing and a lovely person, does not get paid enough for this shit.

"Is it that bad?" Stacy has such a big fake grin Daniel practically hears her gritted teeth.

There's some rustling on the other end of the line, the sound of other voices. "Um, yeah," Amanda says. "We have to find sleeping arrangements for twenty students, and they're not even allowed back into their rooms. I have no idea when we'll get to go home for the night."

"Aw, I'm so sorry. This is the absolute pits."

"Yeah." Amanda sounds confused, probably because no one has called anything "the pits" since the 1990s. "The pits. Listen, Stace. I gotta go. I've got five students here, claiming they forgot all the things they'll need for the next week in the blocked-off rooms. I gotta figure out if I can let them go up and grab their stuff or—"

"Oh, no," Stacy quickly interrupts. "I just got off the phone with Detective Taylor—did you meet her?"

"Yeah, she's a real piece of work."

"Um, I thought she was lovely."

Daniel wants to bang his head against the dashboard.

It must show on his face because Stacy quickly continues with, "Anyway, she said we've gotta keep the students out to keep any crime scene photos off social media and whatnot. I'm driving over right now. Have the students make me a list, and I'll go through their rooms with staff and get their things. That will free you up to find rooms and get yourself home for the night, yeah?"

It's such a blatantly false story Daniel is absolutely sure they're about to get busted. But Amanda must either be too stressed to think or have so much faith in Stacy's character that she can't imagine a world where Stacy would be anything less than honest and helpful.

"Oh my god, you're my hero! I'll hook you up with the master key. Let me know when you're here!"

Stacy is shaking when Daniel hangs up the phone. "I lied to her. I lied to her. If she talks to the detective...oh my god, we're so screwed."

"It didn't sound like she wants to spend any more time talking to the detective than she needs to," Daniel points out. "We'll be fine. And she's giving us the master key. That's perfect."

"Except we will actually need to collect the belongings of five students," Colette points out.

Daniel shrugs. "Small price to pay for not doing something illegal."

Stacy's laugh is high and nervous. "I think this is still pretty illegal."

Daniel looks over his shoulder to Colette in the back seat. They're going to have to keep an eye out to make sure Stacy doesn't instantly blab about this escapade to the detective. She's a great administrator and a very bad liar, and probably a much better person than Daniel.

She wouldn't have *not* talked to a guy she was seeing about the possibility that his sister might have murdered someone.

She probably would never have had that thought about Gianna in the first place, and she'd have talked to both of them about it as a matter of course.

There is probably something clinically wrong with Daniel that he didn't do those things, but at least he has something to distract himself with—namely, breaking into an active crime scene.

Amanda is so overwhelmed she presses the master key and lists of things to grab from each student's room into Stacy's hand and turns right back to the incessantly ringing phone. Her expression says it all. Ever since news about Mario's death reached the student body, there have been a lot of calls from concerned parents. Now, there are probably a lot of calls from concerned and enraged parents. Lobell is not exactly an easily affordable school, and one of the few amenities is the guarantee of single rooms for juniors and seniors.

The problem about privately run colleges, according to Amanda, is that parents are super entitled. Alternatively, according to Daniel, the problem is they pay ten thousand dollars a semester and, in exchange, expect their kids to have reliable room and board and also for there not to be murderers among the student body. In his book, higher education shouldn't be a service you buy, but that's a battle he can't win unless he moves to Europe, and Amanda wouldn't care either way, especially not now. Anyhow, he's pretty sure he, Amanda, and the parents can all agree about murderers being a net bad for the student body.

Norridge House is deserted. Technically, only the second floor is a crime scene, but if Daniel were a student living here, he'd probably find somewhere else to sleep for the night too. It's spooky, all quiet and dark.

They get the students' things first, collecting pajamas and textbooks in tote bags one room at a time. By unspoken agreement, they don't split up.

"Man, I do not miss living in a dorm." Daniel inspects the Tibetan prayer flags adorning Susannah Lewis's window. The whole room is narrow and messy, with barely enough shelving space for her philosophy readings, still bearing the college bookstore's stickers on the spine.

Colette shakes her head. "Another American failure to provide for the next generation. Students ought to learn what it means to live in a space that is truly their own, to take care of it, and to provide for themselves."

"That seems a little harsh." Stacy shoves Susannah's little stuffed hippo into the bag along with her laptop. It's not on Susannah's list, but she'll probably appreciate it. "I loved living in the dorms. It was like having a sleepover every night."

"It had its moments," Daniel agrees. "And it was definitely easier than renting when I was eighteen. But I would not want to live there ever again."

For a moment, Colette looks like she's going to fight them on it, but she takes a deep breath and relents. "I would not want to live in my first flat again either. The smoke detector was right outside the bathroom. It went off every time you showered for too long."

They trade mundane horror stories as they make their way through the floor—from Stacy's freshman year roommate with sleep apnea to the time Daniel got home and his roommate had accidentally exploded a jar of tomato paste across the entire kitchen and then neglected to clean it up, and Daniel freaked out, thinking it was blood.

It keeps them from thinking too hard about the room on the middle of the left side of the corridor.

Each student has a board on their door where they can write their name and leave one another messages. Susannah drew flowers all around her name, and Joaquin wrote his name in bubble letters. Underneath, someone's asked him to keep the music down. Steve's has a Tik-Tok handle scrawled on it and a request to follow him.

Andrew's board is blank.

When the last bag for the last student is full, they set them all down by the stairwell.

Stacy draws a deep breath and, armed with the master key, walks up to Andrew's room.

Then, she pauses. "What about fingerprints?"

"I have gloves in my pocket." Daniel been carrying them around ever since his lunch date with Tony by the Hudson, when he wished he was better prepared for the weather so they could stay in that moment for longer.

He doesn't need to keep carrying them now.

Except for break-ins, apparently.

Stacy hands him the key.

It takes a moment, struggling through putting on his slightly-too-tight gloves and fiddling with the key, but then the door slides open, and Daniel's breath comes out of his lungs in quick pants.

They haven't even done anything.

"We probably shouldn't turn on the light," he says, more to himself than them. "So no one sees from outside."

"Here." Colette turns on her phone's flashlight, aiming it low so it won't be seen out the windows.

The room reveals itself to them in pieces, first the dusty floor, the tightly shut closet, the unmade bed. The desk is a mess, all strewn about papers, syllabi, and cramped notes on loose pages of yellow notepad paper. There are at least three different post-its that read "email report!" in scratchy handwriting. Daniel is willing to bet there's a professor somewhere on campus missing a report. They probably just flunked him instead of reaching out.

It smells like mildew and something worse, thick and cloying.

And there, in the corner, almost entirely invisible in the dark, a photo is propped up against the wall. It's a printout of a blurry cell phone image, taken from outside the film studies center. On it, Mario Lombardi is pressing someone up against the window of his office. Her face is turned away from the camera, but Daniel recognizes her thick, dyed-dark hair.

In front of the photo sits the source of the room's smell. There are two bowls set before the picture, both stolen from the cafeteria. One is filled with moldy slices of toast, the other with a dark liquid.

It would be sad, it would be utterly pathetic and disgusting, except on the floor in front of the bowls, Andrew has carved words right into the linoleum in scratchy, unsteady lines: *I will eat your sins.*

Chapter Twelve

Daniel likes his job. He likes it a lot, probably too much.

He has never looked forward to the end of the semester so much in his entire life, not even when he was still a desperately homesick college freshman. There are only two weeks left to go, he reminds himself incessantly as he drags himself to class on Tuesday morning, trying to project a sense of normalcy he doesn't feel.

"How're everyone's projects coming along?" He greets the anthro section with far more enthusiasm than he feels. It's his turn to teach today. Colette sits next to him at the front of the classroom, but her brain is clearly elsewhere. Five students wrote emails that they're not feeling up to coming to class.

Daniel's question is answered with apathy. No one so much as shakes their head.

"Anyone do their recordings yet?"

A few hands rise.

"That's great." He wants to crawl into a hole and never come out. He plasters on a smile so it might seem like he still has some will to live left over. "Lamar, you were going to record a basketball practice, right?"

Lamar nods.

"Any interesting anthropological notes thus far?"

Lamar shrugs.

Daniel stares him down until Lamar rolls his eyes and says, "Well, the team makes a lot fewer gross jokes when they know they're being recorded."

"Awareness of observation." Daniel nods. "Remember, Professor Ravel talked about the difficulties inherent in participant observation in one of our earlier sections. You can definitely work with that for your final essay."

"Professor Rosenbaum?" A junior with pink highlights in her hair raises her hand. He nods to her to indicate she should go on. "Lily finished all her recordings, and she had half her essay written. Can she still...I mean, if she gets better, will she..." She trails off, shaking her head.

Abruptly, Daniel gives up the act.

He lets himself slump into his seat next to Colette and slides his laptop shut. The projector, which previously displayed his PowerPoint for the day, now displays nothing but a blank screen.

"Look," he sighs. "I'm getting the sense there's not a whole lot of point in me going over how to upload your recordings and essays to the website today, huh?"

Headshakes all around. Even from Colette.

"*Et tu, Brute?*" he mutters to her, but a few students hear it, and it gets a weak chuckle. "Okay. Setting up geographic markers and linking them to your results—Thursday. Be there or be square. How about today we just talk about everything that's been going on?"

No one responds, but no one protests either.

"Natalie, to answer your question"—he addresses the pink-haired junior—"I don't know. If and when Lily returns to class, she's certainly more than welcome to hand in any work she does late. I'll be accepting it whenever she's ready to give it. But as it stands, I haven't heard from her or her family or from the dean."

"Was she really having an affair with Professor Lombardi?" asks a sophomore who hasn't said a single word in class before now.

Daniel looks over to Colette. She shrugs helplessly.

"It's possible," he allows eventually.

"We can't really speak to that," Colette jumps in. "We know Professor Lombardi was involved with students in that way, but I think it would be inappropriate of us to speculate about Lily or him."

The student nods, subsiding.

"Did Andrew do it?" Lamar asks.

"Again, we should probably not speculate," Daniel cautions.

"He's super creepy." Natalie clearly doesn't care about whether or not it's appropriate to speculate; she's made her decisions. "He was, like, stalking Lily. He used to wait outside her classes."

Daniel and Colette exchange a glance. This is the first they've heard that Andrew even knew Lily.

"Creepiness," Colette comments with something approaching solemnity, "is not in and of itself a crime."

Two days ago, driving back to Rhinebeck in Stacy's van in pitch-black darkness after obtaining probably illegal access to a crime scene, Stacy said, "He did it, right? I mean, that's...that's...he *definitely* did it." Her voice was high and squeaky and anxious.

"I'm not sure that's enough proof," Daniel hedged.

"It is certainly damning," Colette pointed out.

They didn't say anything else on the subject.

It got so hauntingly quiet in the car that Daniel asked about Stacy's husband's bad knee so there'd be some noise. He knows a lot more about deteriorating cartilage among high school PE teachers than he ever wanted to now.

Weirdly, he dreamt of jogging through the woods and his knee giving way under him two nights in a row. It's strange that it's the part his subconscious got stuck on and not the stalker altar in Andrew's room.

Libbey, a soft-spoken sophomore, raises her hand. Daniel nods to her, hoping it's not about Andrew. "Can we...can we add some sort of tribute on the website for the class? Not about Professor Lombardi or Andrew or anything, just about Lily and that we love and support her."

"And Gianna," a senior jumps in. "We should give her a tribute too."

Daniel glances over to him sharply. The senior hunches his shoulders, looking defiant. "News spreads." Several other students nod.

Daniel really should have thought harder about taking that job in Albany. It's not a huge city or a huge college, but at least the community is big enough that not everyone knows everyone else's business. Then again, Albany didn't offer him tenure.

"Gianna was never in this class," Daniel points out. "We can consider adding special thanks to her family, given that their shop is one of the recordings featured on the site, but I imagine it would be very intrusive to mention anything else."

They spend the rest of the class period drafting a message of support for Lily to be featured on the class homepage as well as a brief message of thanks to the d'Angelo family in the page header, centered on the recording Daniel made of the garage.

Probably, the moral thing would be to take the whole recording down, but Daniel doesn't know how to begin explaining that to his students, so he does what he always does—he takes the coward's way out.

At least he shows the class how to create and style text blocks on the website using HTML and CSS, so they can all pretend something educational came of this class session.

"Ten more days," Colette tells him as they leave the building and she heads for her office.

"Ten more days," he agrees.

He's worried about her. She was holed up in her office all day yesterday working; he's not sure she's eaten since Sunday night's pizza. He wouldn't describe himself as dealing with the situation well, but he was also not as close with Mario as she was, nor is Andrew one of his students.

It must be rough.

"Hey," he calls after her.

She turns.

"Are you flying home for Christmas?"

The last couple years, he's spent the holiday cozied up in his apartment, first with Jeff, whose family definitely didn't celebrate Christian holidays, and then alone. He set up an away message on his email and sometimes even turned off his phone and spent two or three days just watching TV and sleeping. He has no idea if Colette was there or not. Usually, she flew to France at the start of break and returned sometime in between, and he never knew for sure how long she'd be gone because he never asked.

He's beginning to think that wasn't as nice a time as he told himself it was but rather a symptom of him being less happy than he could have been.

"No." Colette pushes her braids over her shoulders. "It's too much this year."

"We should do something together. Something festive." It earns him a ghost of a smile.

"I'd like that," she says, when he turns to head away, then adds, "thank you."

"No problem."

But she shakes her head. "Not about Christmas. About...being so understanding. You have every right to be angry with me."

Caught up short, Daniel freezes. "I don't know about that."

The truth is, some part of him is still angry. Colette calling the police about Gianna—it took away his chance to talk to Tony about things himself, to smooth over his own suspicions before Tony found out. But Daniel's made such a habit of analyzing his own every action to death that he's well aware that even given more time, he wouldn't have started the conversation. He would have waited for Tony to do it, and he'd have lied and hidden his own suspicions. Maybe he would have kept Tony for a few weeks longer, but he'd have hated himself so much for lying that it would have been even worse in the end.

Colette rests her hand on his shoulder.

Abruptly, Daniel finds himself blinking back tears. "I should have told you when the police first started suspecting you. Heck, I should have told the police myself. I could have protected you."

He's so startled by Colette's laugh that he realizes he hasn't heard it since this all started.

"I think," she suggests, "we should both keep away from the investigation. It's neither of our jobs."

"You're right."

"Let me know about Christmas. I can cook."

He gives her a look.

"I can bring alcohol," she corrects herself.

"Will do." They part ways, and Daniel feels, if not relieved, at least less heavy than he has for the last few days.

He's barely settled in his office when the phone rings. He hasn't dared put it on silent since Sunday on the off-chance Tony might call after all.

Not that he would.

Not that Daniel deserves that.

It's Stacy.

"Daniel." She sounds harried. Daniel misses when she was always cheerful and it pissed him off. "I need you to go to the film building."

"Why?" The film building is clear on the other side of campus.

"The police are letting Mario's family come pick up his things today, and I'm stuck in an all-day crisis meeting with the president's office about restructuring the Title Nine office. I know it's a huge favor, but I don't want to ask Colette. She seemed so...well, you know."

He swallows down the hollowness in his stomach. He knows what Colette's been like, and he's hardly been better, but he can still help Stacy. Maybe doing something worthwhile will help him feel less like a spare part. "Yeah. Yeah, of course. I'll head over right away."

"*Thank you*, Daniel. You're such a sweetheart. I knew I could count on you. You can get a key from Buildings and Grounds."

It makes Daniel smile a little. There's the old Stacy from before all this happened, shining through for just a moment.

It's cold enough out that he debates driving, but nothing on campus is farther than a fifteen-minute walk, and he doesn't need to add climate concerns to his ever-growing list of reasons to feel guilty. He's not entirely sure what to expect when he gets there, and the walk might help clear his head. Anyway, Buildings and Grounds is on the way to the film building.

Mario never talked much about his family. When he did, it was needling commentary about Italian-American stereotypes or living in the suburbs of New York City. Daniel took it all at face value; Mario was an educated man and would certainly know best about his own heritage.

Daniel's own preconceptions probably had him assuming that no matter what Mario said, his family was still his family. Maybe what Mario had been saying all along was that he was completely alone.

There's a silver SUV parked in front of the squat, blocky film studies building. It's one of the only buildings on campus added in the '80s, which explains why it's so ugly and why it's so far away from everything else. As Daniel approaches, a middle-aged woman and a man about Daniel's age get out of the car. Both of them wear puffer jackets over jeans and boots. Gray streaks her dark hair; his is cut short and gelled into a style that was probably fashionable ten years ago.

"Professor Rosenbaum?" the woman asks. "Professor Abrams told us to..."

"Daniel, please." Daniel holds out his hand to shake hers. "You must be Mario's family."

"Yes." She has laugh lines around her eyes and mouth so much like the ones Mario was starting to get that Daniel's heart aches. "I'm Stefania, this is my son Enzo. You...you knew Mario?"

For the second time today, Daniel plasters on a fake smile. "Yeah, we were friends. I'm so sorry for your loss, Mrs. Lombardi."

She waves him off. "Stefania, please."

"Stefania, then. It's been...a huge shock to everyone here, I can't even imagine what you're going through." He indicates wordlessly toward the building, and they head to the entrance, out from the cold.

"You're very kind," Stefania tells him as they walk. "To be honest, huge shock captures it pretty well. We hadn't seen Mario for...well, a few years now. I didn't even know he was living so close."

"Oh." Daniel can't really offer anything more intelligent. He should have asked Mario more.

He leads them up the staircase to the first corridor on the left. There's that Far Side comic stuck to the door.

Mario's brother snorts as he reads it.

Daniel unlocks the door and lets them inside.

The air is stale. No one's cracked a window in the last few weeks, ever since it happened. It probably took a while for the police department techs to go through everything here, but Daniel doubts they've returned since. He wonders if they checked it over again after they found Andrew Clayfield's fucked-up little shrine, to look for evidence this was the place he impregnated Gianna d'Angelo.

Probably.

The thought makes Daniel's stomach turn.

As Stefania wanders through the office, inspecting the stacks of papers, the rows of books and DVDs, Enzo turns to Daniel.

"Did he, uh...did he ever mention us?"

"Not really." Daniel carefully doesn't add that what little Mario did mention wasn't complementary. "I didn't know you...weren't on speaking terms."

Enzo sighs. "Yeah, figures."

"Can I ask what happened? I don't mean to pry. It's fine if—"

"We run a restaurant." Enzo looks away to examine a bookshelf full of DVDs of artsy movies. "My parents and me. My dad always saw it as the family business, thought Mario would pick it up. He didn't, and now I'm the business partner, and Mario and Dad never forgave each other for it."

With a frown, Stefania glances over. "That's a little oversimplified, kiddo."

"I don't think Daniel here needs to know the details."

Daniel swallows hard. So that's what Mario meant about Italian-American clichés and being stuck in the past. So that's what he was thinking about when he talked about getting trapped in the suburbs. It's not some mystical backstory explaining away his behavior toward his students; it neither exonerates nor sentences him. It's just the kind of thing that families do to one another.

"I'm sorry you didn't get the chance to reconnect," he says, trying to convey how much he means it. "I know Mario missed you and wished his family could see the life he built here."

"Oh yeah?" Enzo snorts. "And how do you know if he never talked about us?"

"Good point." Daniel smiles with as much equanimity as he can muster. "I'm going to give you some space, but if you need anything, I'll be right downstairs."

He escapes to the staff kitchen to make a cup of tea and stare blankly at the wall for a hot second.

The thing is, he's sure Mario missed his family and wanted to see them again. No matter how many dumb potshots Mario took about them, Daniel is completely convinced because of Gianna. Why else would he go for the girl whose life and family most mirrored his own? Why else would he choose someone so like him in her choice to go to college and leave the family business?

Why would he leave her when she chose family though? Was he totally unaware of what he was doing in going after her? Daniel wonders what it was like for Mario, those last few months, knowing he got a twenty-two-year-old woman pregnant, knowing she wanted to have the baby, knowing he could have the exact kind of family he left behind all over again. The conflict that must have set loose in him...

Then, Daniel remembers Lily.

The brief kindling of sympathy for Mario that had started up in his chest flickers and dies. Instead, he aches with the lost potential. If Mario had lived, he could have straightened things out. Broken it off with Lily. Worked it out with Gianna. Worked it out with his family. Daniel has no idea if that's what Mario would have done, if that's even what he would have wanted, but now he'll never even have the chance.

Still, someone should reach out to Gianna, ask if she wants her kid to have two sets of grandparents. Someone who's not the asshole who got her on the police's radar. Someone who didn't spend a good two weeks thinking she might have killed her baby's dad.

Daniel has no idea who that someone would be.

He drinks his tea in silence and wonders if he should have offered Mario's family something. It's not as if he can offer them any closure, or their son back, but he's pretty sure there are some Milano wafers somewhere in this kitchen. They hide in the recesses of most kitchen shelves at Lobell.

After what seems like an eternity in terms of how often Daniel changes his mind as to what would be the polite thing to do, Stefania and Enzo come down the stairs.

"Thank you for waiting." Stefania is at least polite. It looks like Enzo's anger is here to stay. Daniel wants to point out that it's not his fault Mario is dead, or that Mario hadn't spoken to his own brother in years, but he doesn't think it would be worth it.

"No problem," Daniel tells her. *You're going to be a grandma pretty soon*, he wants to say. *Your son seduced a student ten years younger than him*, he wants to say. *Twice.*

One time, when they were twelve and fourteen and their parents were going through a rough patch, Meredith took Daniel to Tilden Park to get out of the house for a while. There was no one around. It was November and bad weather in California terms, which meant it was gray and drizzly but still above fifty degrees Fahrenheit. They climbed on top of a park bench and screamed as loud as they could, and afterward, Meredith asked him, "Don't you feel better now?"

Daniel did, but he hasn't done it again since then.

Maybe he should start.

"Hey." He tries to be casual about it, as if it were only now occurring to him. "I know this is a really strange time and all, and I understand that if you weren't part of Mario's life this might be uncomfortable, but I think there are some people around here who might want to pay their respects or attend a funeral if you're having one. Would it be okay if I took down your number and let you know about that?"

Someday, he's going to have to reckon with how good he's gotten at telling believable lies.

"Of course." Stefania dictates her number slowly as Daniel types it into his phone. "We'll have to come back with a van sometime soon to go through his apartment and sort out what to keep and what to sell. I'm sure he has friends or, or...well, I'm sure there are people here who might want his movie collection or his books."

"That would be okay with you?" Daniel asks.

Enzo shrugs. "It's not like he left a will."

He wasn't expecting to die young, Daniel thinks. His throat closes up suddenly. "Right. Well, I'll talk to people. If you let me know when you'll be here again, I'm sure we can work something out."

It's probably the last thing Mario would want, his colleagues and friends going through his things and divvying them up like some yard sale. Daniel will ask Colette. She might have the clearest idea of what Mario would want.

If she can stomach the thought of doing what he would want.

What a mess.

He says goodbye to Mario's family and slowly walks up to his own office. There's something bleak and heartbreaking about the thought that he was actually one of the people closest to Mario when he knew so little about the man. It shouldn't fall to him to make these decisions for Mario—who gets what, who knows what.

Then again, it's not like it will make a difference to Mario.

Still, the idea of a life so unfinished, so many loose ends, so many possible regrets...it's haunting. It's not a thought Daniel wants to dwell on. He can't even think about what his own death would look like. The very notion makes him feel like a skittish horse backing away slowly.

He calls Meredith instead.

"Hi." She sounds almost excited to hear from him. He remembers her at fourteen, makeup already on point because she didn't do things by half even then, yelling her lungs out on a park bench to make him feel better.

"Hi," he says.

"I'm sorry."

"Why are you sorry? *I'm* sorry."

"Why are *you* sorry?"

"For being a shitty little brother. I should have been there for you more, and I shouldn't have made you run interference with Mom and Dad."

There's a long pause on her end. Then, finally, "I don't know if you know this about little brothers, but they kinda have to be shitty. It's in the job description."

He would pretend to be upset, but he can hear the emotion in her voice.

"I'm gonna try," he promises. "To be there more. At least over the phone."

"And I'm gonna ask about your life more, instead of pretending it's in California waiting for you to come back."

"About time too," he tells her.

They both pretend he's not getting choked up, and then they spend ten minutes talking about Emily's upcoming ballet recital and whether or not their dad would be interested in a personal Alcatraz tour for his birthday in January.

"He's been four times," Daniel argues.

"Exactly. He's been four times, so it stands to reason he enjoys it."

He tells her he loves her when he hangs up.

He hasn't done that in too long.

Christmas is too short notice, but maybe he should fly home for spring break. He shoots his mom a text to ask if that would be okay before he can second-guess himself, and then he locks himself in his office and lets himself cry for five minutes.

He can't tell anymore if it's from grief or relief.

Once it's over and he's stopped feeling like he's going to burst at the seams, he checks his email. It's a habit more than anything, and even as he opens his laptop, he realizes how absurd it is, but he doesn't know what else he would be doing. He told Colette he'd drive home at four, and it's only one thirty. He doesn't want to try working on next semester's syllabus with his brain feeling like melted garbage, and none of his students have handed in essays yet. All that's left is his grant proposal, and he really doesn't want to think about murder, fictional or otherwise, right now.

Email it is.

There's one from Mari, which is a nice surprise.

Hi Daniel,

I just wanted to let you know it was great to see you this weekend. I've missed hanging out with you. Maybe I'll see you in Cali one of these days! Emails aren't the same.

Also, and this may be overstepping (if so, I apologize), but I liked your new boyfriend. You two seem really good together, and it was great to see you let loose with somebody, I almost forgot how good that looks on you.

Happy holidays!

Mari

Daniel shoves the email into his "to-answer" folder on autopilot.

If he visits his parents over spring break, he could take a day to go see Mari. He's missed her too. It would be nice to have coffee and chat like they used to when they lived closer together.

There are a few more emails in Daniel's inbox he should take care of, something that looks important from the college president about Title IX. He has more than enough work to bury himself in as an attempt to ignore Mari's email and his own ever-circling thoughts.

He's going to regret it for his entire life if he doesn't at least try to talk to Tony.

Mind made up, he grabs his keys, shoots Colette a text asking her to grab a ride with Stacy, and heads for the parking lot.

Chapter Thirteen

Daniel doesn't recognize the guy in the workshop at Angel Automotive. He's wearing coveralls, which is probably on the whole a better call than Tony's jeans-and-tank-top work uniform, and he must be Tony's dad's age. He doesn't have a mustache, or much hair left on his head at all, come to that.

"Excuse me?" Daniel calls.

"If you're here for a fix, it's gonna have to wait," the guy who might be Tony's dad answers. "We're full up today!"

"I was just looking for Tony."

"The d'Angelos are all out sick this week," says the guy who must be the only non-d'Angelo employee at the shop. "Nobody here but us chickens."

Fuck. "Thanks. Sorry to bother you."

There's a wave of a hand over the top of the car the guy is working on, and then he's back at it.

Daniel gets into his car again. So much for his plan.

Not that it was particularly well thought out. All he was going to do was interrupt Tony at work and apologize.

He could go to Tony's house, now he's been there, once he's pretty sure he remembers the way. But that means facing Tony's parents and Gianna, none of whom know about them. Well. Gianna might. He and Tony never really got around to talking about that. Much like everything else. At least about that, Daniel doesn't feel guilty; it had seemed like a subject Tony needed time to find the words on.

Drumming his fingers on the steering wheel, Daniel catches sight of Tony's backpack in the rearview mirror. Tony left it in the car on Sunday, and Daniel forgot it was still there until he and Colette drove to Lobell on Monday.

It's as good an excuse as any.

He's barely aware of the drive, and he feels like someone else's feet carry him to the door, someone else's finger presses the doorbell. It's definitely someone else who smiles charmingly at Tony's mom and says, "Hi, Mrs. d'Angelo, I was wondering if Tony was home? I was in the area, and he forgot his things in my car on Sunday."

She looks at him for a moment. "You must be Daniel."

"Yeah." Is it a good sign that she knows his name?

"Hm." She beckons him inside. "You know, I've met all of Tony's other friends. It's been a while since someone new came around."

Guilt chokes Daniel for a moment. It's such a parent thing to say, even about her full-grown son. Of course Tony's parents noticed when Daniel started hanging around. Tony lives with them. Curiosity is natural. Tony spending the night at a motel must have been noticeable, let alone going down to the city for a night.

"It's nice to meet you." Daniel tries not to sound like the words are strangling him.

She has Tony's dimples when she smiles. "You too. I'm so glad Tony has someone to talk to. He's been going through a lot."

"Uh." It's true, and it doesn't help with his guilt problem, but he didn't expect her to lay it out there like that. Especially when she has another child who has inarguably gone through more.

"He wouldn't want me to say that, I'm sure." She waves a hand dismissively. "He likes to be the one taking care of everyone else, and we love him for it, but I worry, you know? No one can carry that much all the time."

"That's true." If Daniel sounds a little choked up, well, he hopes she counts it in his favor."

"He's upstairs, first door on the left." She points him in the right direction. "Sorry if I overwhelmed you just now. We've all had a tough few days."

"You haven't overwhelmed me," Daniel lies.

She pats his shoulder.

Daniel takes off his shoes because it seems like that sort of house, and on socked feet, clutching Tony's beat-up Eastpak, he climbs the stairs.

Tony's room is over the garage, Daniel realizes distantly. That's why the light was on over the garage. That's why there's a fire escape on the top of the garage. It's like his own little apartment in his parents' house.

He knocks on the door.

"Told you I'm not hungry, Ma," Tony calls.

Daniel opens the door.

Tony scrambles to his feet. He was lying on the floor, a book in his hand. He's wearing sweatpants and a sleeveless shirt, no socks. His hair isn't in its usual ponytail. Instead, it falls around his face, framing the black-rimmed glasses on his nose perfectly.

"I didn't know you had glasses."

Tony opens his mouth to say something, and Daniel can't let him because he needs to get it out first.

"Sorry. That wasn't what I was going to say. I, um…I have to tell you three things, and then I'll leave, okay?"

Tony nods.

Daniel sets Tony's backpack down and closes the door. "You forgot your stuff. That…wasn't one of the things. I'm really bad at this."

"I'm listening, aren't I?" Tony's expression is inscrutable. He doesn't look angry. He doesn't look amused. He doesn't look anything at all, and it's killing Daniel.

"Okay, first, I met Mario's mom yesterday. And I thought—well, if Gianna ever wants to know her, or for Mario's family to know about the baby, she should have the option. So I'm going to give you her contact details." Daniel pulls out his phone and unlocks his screen with shaky fingers. "I'm gonna send you her number. There. That's it."

"That's it?"

"No. The second thing is that you're right, and I'm sorry. I never talked to you about Mario or about Gianna, and I should never have thought there was a possibility she had something to do with his death or…or kept it from you that I was thinking about it. That was shitty of me. And I'm sorry I made you feel like you were less than because of your job. I don't—I don't believe that, you know? I could never do what you do for a living. I should have been…I don't know…"

Tony opens his mouth to speak, and for a moment, Daniel thinks that's it; it's over; he's sending Daniel away. "You should have been what, Daniel?" he asks instead.

Daniel closes his eyes. "I should have been braver."

Tony steps closer. He hasn't shaved in a few days, and the line of his beard is less precise than usual. "What's the third thing?"

Daniel inhales deeply. If this is the last time he sees Tony, he wants to remember it, all of it, the ugly bedspread, the cold of the floorboards seeping up into Daniel's feet, Tony's disheveled clothing, the black frames of his glasses, the mess of his hair, that his second toe is longer than his big toe.

"I really, really like you." He lets himself look right at Tony as he talks, at his warm eyes and the crow's feet that surround them. "And I should have said so from the start, so you wouldn't have felt like this was just—like I was only messing around with you. If I had told you how I felt... But I couldn't because I'm not built like that. I get all in my head and convince myself to do anything but talk to people. For some insane reason, my brain convinced me it was easier to keep seeing you casually and pretend that if something turned up that made Gianna look guilty or...or made *you* look guilty, I could cut and run. And if I had only been brave enough to tell you I want to be with you because I like you and that I've been seven kinds of fucked up ever since Mario died, but you're still the best thing that's happened to me in three years, I wouldn't have hurt you like this."

The words settle heavily in the room. They're too intense for this place, for the Metallica poster tacked to the wall across from Daniel and the rumpled lavender bedspread with ruffled edging.

"You know," Tony says eventually, "not everything is your fault."

Daniel blinks.

"I mean, yeah, gaining access to a possible murderess by dating her brother is definitely the worst plan in the history of crime. But you never made me feel like you didn't respect me. That was all my inferiority complex. You're not the only one who's all kinds of fucked up about things right now."

Unsteadily, Daniel manages a laugh. "It was a really bad plan."

"Mm. I would actually call it the absence of a plan."

"Wait until you hear about my Sunday night. I'm full of bad ideas, apparently."

"I can't wait. There's just one thing I want to do first."

"What's that?"

Tony leans in, quick as a dart, and brushes their lips together. The shock of contact zings through Daniel all at once, and then it's gone as soon as it came, and he's blinking his eyes open to stare at Tony.

"Good apology." Tony is once again a barely respectable distance from Daniel, and Daniel wishes he weren't. "Thanks for my backpack."

Daniel's not sure what noise he makes at the back of his throat when he crosses the distance between them, but he's pretty sure it's embarrassing. He wraps his arms around Tony's middle, buries his nose in Tony's neck, and holds him tight.

Tony laughs as he wraps his arms around Daniel in turn. The sound warms Daniel right through to the core. "You really do like me." Tony sounds as if it's a shock.

"Yeah." Daniel's going to have to repeat it a few more times until Tony believes it.

"Wanna know something?"

"Yeah."

"I really like you too."

"Glad we cleared that up." Daniel clears his throat and releases Tony.

There's an awkward moment where they both look away, and then at each other, and then away again, and then Tony says, "For fuck's sake," and kisses Daniel properly.

Daniel's self-aware enough at this point to know the ball of tension he carries around with him won't melt away, but he feels like *he* might melt away at the touch of Tony's lips. The sure feel of Tony's hand tangled with his, the dip at the small of Tony's back where Daniel's other hand migrates, they're all that keeps Daniel steady.

He wants to touch Tony everywhere, to make sure he's real and solid and means everything they said. He lets his fingers slide under the fabric of Tony's shirt, just a hint, just to tease, and Tony makes a soft noise against his lips and presses closer.

"Boys?" Tony's mom calls from outside the door.

They spring apart instantly.

"I'm about to head out. Do you need anything to eat or drink?"

Tony closes his eyes. Daniel's not sure whether the flush rising up his neck is from the kissing or the interruption. "I know where the kitchen is, Ma. I'm twenty-seven," he calls back.

"Just checking." It must be a mom thing to be that cheerfully impervious to your children's annoyance. "See you later!"

"So." Tony rubs his hand across his forehead as her footsteps retreat down the stairs. "We're going to your place."

"We don't have to—" Daniel starts, but Tony arrests him with a glare.

"We definitely have to. I swear it's not usually like this, but with Gigi and the police, it's been pretty intense around here. C'mon. Take me away from all this." He gestures dramatically around the room.

Daniel snorts. It's not very attractive, but Tony looks delighted.

In short order, he grabs a pair of jeans out of his dresser, shucks his sweats, and pulls them on before pulling on socks and putting his hair up.

He leaves the glasses on.

Daniel's glad; he liked how soft Tony looked before. "You don't have to get dressed up for me."

Tony shoots him a look, half-pleasure, half-embarrassment. "Noted."

He knocks on the door across the hall on their way out. "Hey, Gi. I'm going out for a while, that okay?"

"I'm fine, Tony. You don't need to keep checking," Gianna's voice comes through the door.

"Okay," he says placidly. "You know how to reach me."

As they get into the car, Daniel tells him, "You're a good brother."

Tony shrugs.

"No, seriously. I'm gonna start taking tips from you."

"I didn't know you had a sister."

Daniel nods. "Meredith. She's out in California, I don't see her as much as I should."

"Ah." Tony slides his seatbelt on with a click. "So tell me about your Sunday night."

In broad strokes, Daniel tells the story of their ill-advised trip to investigate Andrew's room, adding in the context of Andrew's obsession with sin-eaters and how he's been incredibly insistent first with Mario and then with Colette.

"Okay," Tony summarizes when he's done. "That is super creepy, and also, you are an idiot."

"Hey!"

"No, no—sneaking into a cordoned-off police area at night with your friends? That's really risky! And what did you gain besides scaring the fuck out of yourself? You don't know any more than the police, now, do you?"

"I know as much as them," Daniel points out. "It's not like they're keeping us updated."

"Yeah." Tony draws the word out until it becomes eminently clear he still thinks Daniel's being an idiot. "Because it's a murder. They're not keeping anyone updated."

"I'm not saying I've been making good decisions. I'm saying my faith in the police as an institution is not exactly huge."

"Fair. But you do know that if me or Gianna had actually had anything to do with it, you would have been putting yourself in crazy amounts of danger? And that snooping around crime scenes is a fun way to run into criminals?"

Daniel does know, and he's not proud of himself, so he changes the subject. "What happened with Gianna anyway?"

Tony sighs. "She has an alibi, you know. Actually, I'm her alibi. We were home all night, playing Monopoly."

Daniel is an idiot. He should have asked. Because then, he would have known that, and he'd never have thought, even for a minute—

Anyway.

"All night?" he asks.

"Look, Monopoly is a vicious game." Tony makes a point Daniel has to concede. "Anyway. She had to answer a bunch of questions about her and Mario."

Daniel raises an eyebrow.

"Like...when and where she was seeing him. How serious it was."

Those are questions Daniel has wondered about as well, but he's pretty sure now isn't the time. Instead, he asks, "And...your parents?"

It takes a while for Tony to answer. The Kingston-Rhinecliff Bridge blurs past around them, the wide stormy waters of the Hudson underneath announcing the advent of winter loud and clear.

"I don't know." Tony looks out the passenger side window, mulling it over. "I can't tell if they're relieved she wasn't sleeping with so many people she didn't know who got her pregnant, or disappointed it was a professor, or just...scared."

"That sounds...rough."

"Yeah."

"Have they said anything?"

Tony laughs. "Nah, all Ma does is try to feed us. It's kind of ridiculous."

"It's probably hard." Daniel thinks of his own mom and her ridiculous Thanksgiving feasts. "When your kids are grown up, and they don't want you to protect them anymore."

He chances a look over at Tony and finds him looking back with the softest smile Daniel's ever seen him wear playing around his lips.

"Yeah," Tony agrees. "It probably is."

It's strange to walk up to his apartment with Tony by his side as though it's something they do regularly, as though they share space like this all the time.

Daniel wants that with a fierceness that scares him.

They toe off their shoes by the door and hang up their jackets. To stave off the urge to say something really stupid, like telling Tony how much he likes it when their shoes intermingle on the floor, Daniel asks, "Can I get you something to drink?"

"Daniel." Tony's voice is fond and firm.

"Yeah?"

"I don't want something to drink."

He wraps his hand around Daniel's neck, his thumb caressing the hinge of Daniel's jaw gently, and then he kisses Daniel like it's the only thing he's ever wanted out of life.

"What do you want?" Daniel whispers when they separate by a bare inch.

Tony laughs unsteadily. "A lot of things."

Daniel kisses him again, deep and slick and promising in a way Daniel doesn't remember kissing being before this, before Tony. Maybe he's rewriting his own history. Maybe he's romanticizing this beyond repair, but he feels as though each touch is new to him. "Tell me," he demands.

With his free hand, Tony toys with the collar of Daniel's shirt, sliding the top button through its hole. "I kinda want...you to take the lead, If that's okay."

"Yeah. Of course."

The hand at Daniel's neck slides up to tangle in his hair as Tony pulls him close again. "Don't...read too much into this." Tony rests their foreheads together. "But in New York, that night...I felt like...I don't know. I felt like you were taking care of me. And I liked it. A lot."

Daniel tilts his head enough to brush a kiss on Tony's cheek and then more down his neck.

"Mm, that's nice," Tony says breathlessly. "If I'm being honest here, it kinda scared me. How much I liked it. How it made me feel. The next morning..."

"It's easier to be angry than vulnerable."

Tony's eyes are almost glistening when Daniel looks at him. "Yeah. I want to be...I want to be vulnerable with you though."

"Thank you." Daniel kisses Tony so thoroughly he's not sure he has any oxygen left in his brain.

He whispers it again when he returns to Tony's neck, to his collarbone, to his ridiculous shoulders in his stupid sleeveless shirt. And, again, when he drags Tony to his bedroom and gets him settled in the sheets with his shirt off and his jeans undone.

"Baby," Tony chides and then sighs in pleasure when Daniel gets his mouth on a nipple. "Don't...oh, Jesus fuck, don't thank me."

Daniel wants to explain he's not thanking Tony for the chance to do *this*. He's thanking Tony for giving him another chance, for trusting him. He also doesn't want to ruin the moment. What he ends up going with is, "I'm just glad you're here with me."

"So'm I."

The way Tony smiles up at Daniel makes his whole face glow with happiness.

Daniel's heart pounds, and he lets it. Doesn't pretend this is anything other than what it is: pleasure and happiness and desire at being close to someone he cares for.

He pulls off Tony's pants and unbuttons his own shirt before pressing close to Tony, bare chest to bare chest. They spend long, muzzy minutes like that, kissing gently and then less gently. Tony's legs shift, and he turns to slide one between Daniel's till they're aligned from knee to shoulder. With each new kiss, each new motion, Daniel learns something: the huff of Tony's exhale becomes more labored when Daniel plays with his nipples; he squirms when Daniel lets his teeth trace across his clavicle; and he sighs in pleasure when Daniel rolls his hips against Tony's.

Daniel will be the first to admit it was exciting, intoxicating, to ask Tony to make him stop thinking, to give himself over to whatever Tony wanted to do to him. He finds that it's different to stay so fully present and attuned to Tony's reactions but no less fulfilling. He feels as though he's been given something precious. His skin is prickly and oversensitive, each new touch a hint of stimulation. He doesn't even want Tony to touch him, or it would distract him too much.

He takes his time with it, caressing Tony's sides, palming the curve of his ass, stroking gently over the swell of his hard cock until Tony's gasping and pleading with him to get on with it. Even then, he's slow, spreading lube gently around Tony's hole, slipping a condom over his own mostly ignored cock, waiting until Tony's shivering under his fingers and pushing up toward him as if that will get Daniel to hurry up.

"Are you ready?"

Tony nods. The movement makes some of his hair come loose from its ponytail, and Daniel brushes it out of his face, dips down for a kiss as he settles between Tony's spread legs, and slowly, slowly sinks inside him.

"Daniel," Tony gasps.

His head is thrown back as he pants for breath, relaxing slowly around Daniel. His chest is flushed blotchy red, and he's gripping the sheets for dear life. Daniel takes a deep breath and keeps his hips still, giving Tony all the time he needs. Truth be told, he needs the time himself. Tony is tight and warm around him, and it would be easy to keep going, to chase down his own pleasure, but he wants to make it last. He leans down toward his favorite stretch of shoulder-to-collarbone and peppers Tony's skin with kisses and bites.

Tony's arms come up around him, vise-tight and holding him close, and Daniel thinks of kissing Tony by the Hudson and of how much he wants to remember every moment with this man.

"You can move," Tony says hoarsely.

"You sure?"

Unsteadily, Tony laughs. "I might get really mad if you don't."

It's strange how little Daniel cares about his own pleasure, to start with. It feels good, and the sight of Tony under him is more than enough to get him going. But above all, what he wants is for this to be good for Tony, for him to feel even one ounce of the tenderness destroying Daniel's ability to think. The pulse of pleasure under his own skin is a hindrance to his goal.

He keeps it slow, a gentle rocking of his hips, letting Tony fall into it. It's just as much for Tony's benefit as it is to keep his own urgency at bay, to tease himself for that little bit longer.

Between their bellies, the stiff line of Tony's cock brushes up against Daniel with every movement.

"Feel good?" he asks.

"Uh-huh."

Daniel pauses to reposition, to grasp Tony's thighs and hoist them over his shoulders. "You should know I think you're gorgeous like this." He's proud he manages to sound conversational, as if this isn't simultaneously one of the hottest and most important things that's ever happened to him. "I mean, always, but now especially."

Tony smiles, opens his mouth to respond, and then all he can do is groan as Daniel moves. It's deeper, a better angle, and the noises Tony makes go straight to Daniel's cock. He can't keep it up forever. Tony's legs are heavy and holding their weight makes it harder to move, but it's so worth it to see Tony struggle to form words. Daniel's breathing hard, and he can feel his pulse in his balls; he's starting to doubt his ability to survive this.

On the tail end of a thrust, Tony clenches down around Daniel's cock, and all the urgency Daniel was trying to deny himself comes surging to the fore. He closes his eyes and grits his teeth, and keeps moving through it as slowly as he can, holding himself back by the skin of his teeth until Tony begs, "Daniel, can you...faster? *Please.*"

Abruptly, Daniel pulls out, and Tony makes a gut-wrenching sound of loss. "Turn over. C'mon—on your knees?"

It takes Tony a moment, an ungainly scramble, and Daniel uses the reprieve to slather more lube onto the condom and take deep, steadying breaths, trying to pull himself from the brink. Then, he kneels between Tony's spread thighs and slides into molten heat, and it's like reality snaps into him all at once, all his efforts at restraint giving way to the urgent thrum of his pulse.

"Yeah," Tony pants, "like that."

Daniel wraps an arm around his middle to keep him steady, pressed against Daniel's chest. With the other, he reaches down to grasp Tony's cock firmly even as he starts up a hard and fast rhythm.

"Fuck," Tony grits out.

"Yeah," Daniel agrees, breathless. Sparks dance behind his eyes. Each new movement makes him want to cry out with how good it feels, how close he is. It's too much, so much he can't hold out.

The wait, the length spent teasing Tony and working him up, the full weight of emotion Daniel's been carrying around with him all day— it's all he can do to wait until Tony groans and spills across his fingers, contracting around him and slumping into his hold.

"Tony," he manages when he's sure he's seen Tony through it, his own desperation in his voice.

"C'mon." Tony pushes back against him, and Daniel lets himself go.

It's nowhere near as gentle as he was trying to be. He's not sure how he could stand it, now he can't anymore. He's not sure how he could ever stop himself from feeling this knife-sharp pleasure as he thrusts up into Tony's body and comes and comes and comes.

Tony makes a sharp sound, something like shock, and another wet pulse of come shoots across Daniel's hand.

He has to bite into the side of Tony's neck to stop himself from screaming.

He feels like he's been turned inside out.

His fingers shake, after, as he gets rid of the condom. His knees are unsteady.

He collapses next to Tony on the bed and burrows into his side.

"Holy fuck," Tony says.

"Yeah," Daniel agrees.

Tony shifts to kiss Daniel and then to wrap his arms around him.

"You're staying, right?" Daniel asks.

"Try to get rid of me now." Tony laughs.

Chapter Fourteen

"**N**ot that I'm complaining in the slightest..." Daniel sets out three plates, silverware, and wine glasses at the kitchen table. "But where exactly do your parents think you are?"

Tony's back is turned to Daniel, and he's keeping an eye on the gnocchi, catching them as they float to the top and depositing them into the strainer. He's wearing Daniel's green apron and a chunky gray sweater, and it's doing incredibly stupid things to Daniel's insides to see him looking so domestic.

"I told them I'd be with you." Tony smiles over his shoulder. "It's fine. My mom likes you."

"Your mom has barely met me. And it's Christmas Eve."

"My mom has seen you three separate times. In her book, you've met. You're on her Christmas cookie list. Anyway, as long as I make it in time for midnight Mass, it's all good. We do our celebrating tomorrow."

"If you're sure." Daniel tries and fails to hide his delight that he's on the Christmas cookie list. So sue him. Last time he picked up Tony, the whole house smelled of toasted almonds and cinnamon.

The last of the gnocchi rescued from the water, Tony wanders over to press a kiss to the top of Daniel's head. "Anyone ever tell you that you worry too much?"

"You, constantly." Daniel leans back in his chair to pull Tony down for a real kiss by the front of his apron.

"I'm a smart man." Tony grins against his lips. "How 'bout that your sink is still clogged and it makes cooking in your kitchen a pain in the neck?"

"Also, you, constantly."

In the two weeks since their...Daniel's been using the word "reconciliation," but he's not sure that covers it entirely. Maybe, if he continues to be as outrageously lucky as he currently is, he'll call it an anniversary in the future. Either way, in the two weeks since, they've barely gone a day without seeing each other. Sometimes, Tony comes over after his shift in the garage; other times, Daniel will meet him for lunch or dinner in Kingston. It's time away from Lobell he would have previously been using to stay caught up on his grading, but he's decided to be nicer to himself and to let himself enjoy this.

He remembers when he got together with Jeff, how after a few dates on the weekend, they'd settle seamlessly into evenings at one of their places, grading and watching TV together. They moved in together not because they wanted each other around that much but because it was more convenient than meeting up in different places all the time.

Daniel is discovering there are some things worth being inconvenienced for, and also he's an idiot.

Colette knocks on the door at six sharp. She has a bottle of white in one hand and no shoes on.

"Merry Christmas Eve," Daniel greets her.

She rolls her eyes and hands over the wine. "Merry Christmas Eve. Thank you for the invitation."

Between their legs, Worf attempts to escape the confines of the apartment. Colette comes in and lets the door click shut behind her.

"Of course." Daniel sets the bottle down on the table. "Since when do you *thank* me. You're here all the time."

She shrugs. "It's a special occasion, and your boyfriend is here."

Tony grins and gives her finger guns as a greeting before returning to ladling tomatoes and garlic onto toasted baguette slices. Daniel is severely impressed at how easily he and Colette have been forgiven for the havoc they've caused in Tony's family. According to Tony, Colette telling the police was the sensible thing, and on balance, he's glad not to be keeping Gianna's secret anymore. Colette apologized nonetheless, and they've been getting along swimmingly ever since.

"And you should be thankful," Daniel tells Colette as they settle down and he pours the wine. "Turns out he's a much better cook than either of us."

"Not a high bar, in my case." Colette sips her wine. "But much appreciated. Would you like some wine, Tony?"

He shakes his head. "I have to drive to Kingston sooner or later for church."

"Ah, the bane of the practicing Catholic," Colette says dryly.

"Hey now." Tony sets the appetizer on the table they dragged in from Daniel's office specifically for the occasion and takes his seat. "Let's not get insulting. I go to Mass to make my ma happy, not because I'm part of the club."

Daniel laughs as he takes a bite of bruschetta. "Bet hearing that wouldn't make her happy."

"Yeah, well." Tony picks up his own slice. "I'm about due a major disappointment. Can't let my sister take all the heat."

Colette freezes, bruschetta in hand.

"How is she holding up?" Daniel asks, kicking Colette under the table.

Tony sighs. "Gigi's tough. She was all set to do this on her own before he died, you know? I think she mostly hates all the attention and that people know now."

"Has she thought about..."

"Yeah. She says she'll call them in the new year. I don't know what her game plan is, honestly. She's due in about two months. Not a lot of time to get to know Mario's parents and figure out if she wants them in the picture, or if they even want to be in the picture."

"I wonder what would have happened if he'd lived." It's rhetorical, more of a thought Daniel hasn't been able to shake loose than a question either of them can answer. "Maybe they'd have worked it out."

"I doubt it. He'd moved on to Lily by then," Colette reminds him.

Right. Lily.

"She got released from the hospital yesterday. I got an email from Natalie—that's another student in our class," Daniel adds for Tony's benefit.

"That's good." Tony bites into his bruschetta. "Maybe she and Gigi can meet up some time."

They chew and contemplate in silence for a moment.

Worf squawks as he climbs up onto the couch in the living room.

"Weirdest support group ever," Daniel decides eventually.

"What would they even call it?" Colette wonders.

"I Fucked My Dead Professor Fridays?" Tony suggests.

They laugh, and then Tony says, "I'm definitely going to hell."

Daniel helps him clear off the smaller plates for the appetizer, and they set about frying up the gnocchi in pesto.

"They still haven't made any decisions about Andrew, have they?" Colette asks, leaning back in her chair.

Daniel shakes his head. "At least, not as far as I know."

"This is corpse guy, right?" Tony asks, dishing up the first plate.

"Yeah."

It's a pretty awkward situation for the college to be in. Apparently, Andrew has been placed in a closed ward for the time being, but no further information has been released about whether he did it. His creepy altar and his borderline stalking of both Mario and Colette haven't been made public, although Daniel wouldn't be surprised if at least a few students had the same bright idea to break into his room. It seems likely he's being accused of something, but there have been no press releases or, according to Stacy, unofficial communications to the president's office.

"Did I tell you Detective Taylor called yesterday?" Colette wrinkles her nose slightly.

"No," Daniel says, and then, "thanks, babe," as he takes his plate.

"This smells delicious, Tony." Colette smiles at Tony. "Thank you."

"Welcome. What did the detective want?"

"To know more about sin-eaters." Colette's tone is dark. She still feels guilty that Andrew continues to be under arrest absent meaningful evidence.

"That's the thing Andrew keeps going on about?" Tony looks to Daniel for confirmation. "Is it some sort of cult thing?"

Colette spears a piece of gnocchi on her fork. "Is the sacramental wine you'll drink tonight some sort of cult thing?"

"Absolutely," Tony confirms blithely.

She glares at him. "Sin-eaters in Welsh tradition weren't that different. The idea was that at funerals, the deceased's family would pay to have someone present who would ceremonially eat a crust of bread and drink a cup of beer, and the person would symbolically take on the sins of the dead, letting them pass on to heaven."

Daniel swallows his food. "That's a lot less creepy than I thought."

"Well, his thesis suggestion was a film about a sin-eater eating the actual flesh of the sinner, rather than a symbol."

"Yeah, but the setup in his room was bread and beer, right?"

"Yes, but I think the more relevant aspect is that he believed in the practice."

Sighing, Daniel turns to his food again. She's not wrong, of course. It doesn't sit right with him; he hasn't seen any proof or much motive. He's also not a real detective, he reminds himself.

"Gianna said she was friends with him last year." Tony directs the words mostly to his plate.

He must feel the weight of both their eyes on him because he looks up eventually, sheepishly. "She won't say much about it, and I'm not starting up with your detective schtick. I just wanted to know. She met him in Lombardi's class. They were both into...you know, spooky shit."

"Gianna's got a kind of goth thing going on," Daniel translates for Colette.

"She said he was nice, but he had a lot of shit going on, and he got pretty weird. Apparently, he was warning her off Lombardi. Call me crazy, but I would have done the same if I'd known."

"Hm," Colette considers. "Perhaps he was jealous?"

"That is a motive," Daniel agrees. "Did you see the police are getting access to Lobell's email server?" It had been the last point of interest in the pre-Christmas email blast, probably squished onto the very end of the email in the hope that no one would see it.

Daniel saw.

Daniel's been thinking about it ever since.

"Which is a stunning breach of privacy." Colette stabs another bite of gnocchi viciously. "Why they couldn't keep it to Mario and Andrew's emails..."

"I'm guessing the answer is missing manpower." Daniel's been debating whether he should offer his questionable skills to help out. "Our IT administrators are basically only Clark from computer science and, well, Stacy. And she has about twelve other jobs."

"The lack of funding in education continues to astound me." It's the start of one of Colette's favorite complaints about the US, none of which Tony has been fortunate enough to receive so far. Daniel's not sure Christmas is the right time to expose him.

"I mean, if Lobell had an endowment..." Daniel starts.

"A what now?" Tony asks.

"Um...most colleges have massive investment funds from the hundreds of thousands of dollars of tuition they rake in every year, but Lobell refuses to do that, so the money doesn't really accumulate much interest and we're always relying on donations. On balance, it's more ethical, but it's a really stupid way to run a college."

Again, it's Worf who interrupts the ensuing silence by trotting up beside the table and meowing loudly in a plea for attention or food.

"This is not a Christmas topic," Daniel decides.

"We should make it a rule," Tony agrees, eyes sparkling. "No murder and no money at the dinner table."

"Boring," Colette objects. "I thought we were going to apply for that crime project, Daniel. That will mean lots of murder at the dinner table."

"So long as you guys stick with fictional murder."

Daniel smiles at the thought that Tony intends to be around for future dinners. "I think we can agree to that."

Still, they manage to steer clear of the topic for the rest of the evening.

It's a more restful holiday than Daniel remembers his Christmases alone being. Maybe it's due to how much stress he's been under, but the contrast is stark. Instead of staying home and turning his phone off, he skypes with his mom and dad and watches them unwrap the gifts he sent. He did wrap them in Hannukah-themed paper, a last vestige of his years-long protest against Christmas, but he's beginning to see that a full boycott was more childish obstinance that hurt his family than a reasonable protest of Christmas capitalism. He goes for a winter hike down to Tivoli Bays with Tony on Boxing Day, unsteady on the roots and icy patches even in their winter boots. It's worth it to show Tony a new view of the Hudson; it's worth it to have a new kiss by the river to remember.

On the twenty-eighth, they make eggnog and gingerbread, mostly so Daniel can give something to Tony's mom in return for the entire box of cookies she had Tony bring him, and Meredith calls while they're in the middle of cutting out the cookies. Daniel doesn't tell her who Tony is to him, but he can tell he doesn't have to by her probing questions. Weirdly, being given the third degree by Daniel's sister seems to make Tony happy.

On the thirty-first, Daniel finds himself outside a bar in Kingston where Tony and his friends have celebrated New Year's since they were of legal drinking age.

"You're really sure about this?" he asks for probably the eighth time.

"Yeah," Tony says easily.

"And I'm not...pretending we're just friends or something?"

"Eh, I'm about 85 percent certain they all know I'm gay."

"Fifteen percent is a really large margin of error. Also, what if it gets back to your parents?"

"You're really worried about that, huh?"

"How are you not worried about that? I don't want to be the guy who fucks up your life by accidentally outing you."

Tony grasps him by the lapels of his fleece jacket and presses a smacking kiss to his lips. "You think too much. It's sweet, but I'm not about to force you into the closet. Have a little hope that my friends won't immediately rat me out."

"Okay. Trusting you."

The bar is cozy in a very Kingston way, a bit cluttered and eclectic as if not sure whether it should be displaying scenic paintings of the river or fishing equipment. It's full to bursting already at barely past 8:00 p.m., given the date, but the bartender still spots them instantly. He greets Tony by name and immediately passes him an amber ale from a local brewery.

"One for your friend too?" he asks, and Tony raises an eyebrow at Daniel.

Daniel shrugs and nods and, beer in hand, follows Tony to a crowded booth in the corner.

Tony's greeted by cheers and hugs from a crowd that looks, to Daniel, not all that different from his students. They're a little older, sure, but not as old as Daniel (which is a bad thought he'll be shelving immediately).

"I brought someone," Tony tells the group, easily audible above the murmur of voices in the bar. "This is Daniel."

Among Tony's friends, there's one person with blue hair who introduces themself to Daniel with a name he forgets instantly and they/them pronouns; two girls with multiple ear piercings; and four guys, two of whom are called Blake and all of whom are wearing some form of plaid.

"Oh," Daniel mutters to Tony once he's been introduced. "I see why you weren't worried."

"Huh?"

Daniel shakes his head. "Later."

They're a friendly bunch. They almost remind Daniel of him, Mari, and Paul when they first met, if they hadn't all been stupid enough to get PhDs at the time. One of the girls (Lisa, Daniel's about halfway convinced) is a teacher, the blue-haired friend and one of the Blakes got degrees in social work and now have jobs in a care home and a hospital, respectively. The other Blake started the brewery that made the beer Daniel's drinking.

It's not half bad.

Daniel chats with Lisa (if it's not her name, it's too late now for Daniel to ask) for a while about the vagaries of working in education before they get distracted by Blake number one and Charlie, which turns out to be blue hair's name, one-upping each other with horror stories about public health.

"And what about you, Anthony?" Beer Blake asks pointedly. "You've been quiet."

"True." Lisa laughs. "Usually, you're the life of the party."

Daniel has the absolute pleasure of watching Tony flush red all the way up to his ears when he sneaks a glance over at Daniel.

"Things have been...kind of a mess recently," Tony admits. "With my family and stuff."

"Yeah, what gives?" Hospital Blake asks. "Last I heard, you were going to move out."

The girl with the cartilage piercing who isn't Lisa groans. "Jesus, Blake, that was in July. Do you not keep up at all?"

Tony shrugs. "Things happened. It got delayed."

Beer Blake shakes his head in disappointment. "I was hoping we'd have a cool place to chill in Kingston that isn't, like, our parents' houses."

"Sorry to disappoint," Tony says dryly.

Charlie shakes their head "Don't listen to them, Tony. Is your family, okay?"

"Getting there. I'm gonna get another round. Anyone want anything?"

"I'll help," Daniel offers quickly.

At the bar, he asks, "You okay?" as quietly as he can while still being heard.

"Yeah. It's just…uh, maybe you were right and this is more than I thought."

"Wanna get some air?"

They go outside instead of getting more beers. Beer Blake will have to forgive them for the wait.

"I don't even know where to start with them," Tony admits. "I mean, I love them all, but I've only told Charlie about the stuff with Gigi. I didn't even tell anyone about you."

Daniel nods slowly. "It's a lot. You don't have to tell anyone anything before you're ready."

"I brought you here because I wanted them to meet you." Tony runs a hand over the top of his head, tugging his ponytail into place.

"You're allowed to change your mind. I will say though, it might not be super shocking to them."

"Hm?"

"It seems like most of your friends are queer."

"Oh." Tony blinks as if that thought hadn't even crossed his mind. "Yeah, they are. They'll be cool about it. That's not…"

"What is it then?"

"You know how you said I didn't have to tell anyone before I was ready?"

Daniel nods.

"Well, I always kinda thought... This is stupid, but I always thought I was gonna wait until there was something to tell. Until I was with someone worth telling about. I mean, I know it's supposed to be about me and my identity or whatever—that's how Charlie and Blake used to talk about it anyway—but I never really wanted to rock the boat, you know? I wanted to work with my dad. I wanted to stay with my family for a while longer after school. I love them. I figured, when it was important, I'd be ready."

"Okay." Daniel tries to parse out everything Tony said to find the right answer. He desperately wants to ask which Blake, but that's probably not the right tack. "So, I'm hearing that I'm important, which I like."

Tony laughs and pokes him in the side.

"You know what one of my favorite things about you is?"

"The 'stache."

Daniel laughs. "Weirdly, yes. But I was gonna say how comfortable with yourself you are."

Tony glares at him. "Do I seem comfortable right now?"

"No. Not like... You're so good at saying what you mean and being who you are, not because you don't care what people think about you but because you've...you've put thought into it, you know? You didn't stay at your parents' place for years because you forgot to move out or something. You thought about it, and you made a decision to wait until the time was right for you. You don't let other people decide who you are, not even me. And I really like that about you."

"Okay." Tony smiles slowly, which is progress. "I'm not sure what you're getting at, but this *is* making me feel better."

"You don't have to leap out of the closet. You can...I don't know... leave the door on the lean. Be who you are with no extra explanations. If someone asks, you can tell them what you just told me, about wanting to wait, but you don't have to. Just because you've thought about it a lot doesn't mean you owe people explanations."

Tony takes a deep breath. "That sounds...workable."

"But, uh, these are your friends. They wanna be there for you. Not only about...me, but about Gianna."

"Yeah, yeah, I guess you're right." Tony takes a deep breath. "Okay. Let's do this."

He slips back inside the bar at the same moment Lisa slips out. She holds up a finger to warn Daniel to stay put.

"So." She has a pleasant, friendly voice, but Daniel gets the impression she's the kind of teacher who knows how to strike a very different tone when she needs to. "Tony's never brought anyone to these things."

"Yeah." It's kind of unfair that Daniel is still getting this talk even if Tony isn't going to actually say anything. "He mentioned."

"And we're all really glad he did bring someone today."

"So am I."

"And if you give him a reason to regret bringing someone, we're all going to be really pissed."

Daniel is very thankful Tony didn't introduce him before New York. "I'm really not planning on it."

"Good." She nods decisively.

"How did you get saddled with that talk?" Daniel asks, mostly out of idle curiosity.

"It's my penance for being the straight friend. Also, Charlie would be way scarier, and we like you so far."

He takes a breath before responding, looking for the right words. "I'll take it. I know you all have known him longer, but he's really nervous about this, and I think he needs you all to...not comment until he's used to it. If that's okay."

It's good for Daniel's ego to occasionally have people younger than him raise their eyebrows at him as though he just said the stupidest thing imaginable. It doesn't feel great, but it builds character.

"Dude," Lisa says, which ruins the effect of her absolutely withering look. "We've been not commenting on Tony's whole deal for about ten years longer than you've even known him."

Daniel tilts his head to the side, trying to formulate a question about that without sounding incredibly nosy. He comes up blank and decides to go for broke instead. "Anything you could tell me about that?" he asks as casually as he can.

It's a good thing there isn't much business in glaring people to death for women about five foot nothing, because Lisa would make a killing. Possibly literally. "I'm sure he'll tell you all about his sordid past in his own sweet time."

"Sure. I'm not asking about who in your group has been with whom." He's betting on Lisa and at least one of the Blakes, but given that she's here with one of the other guys whose name he already forgot, he knows better than to mention it. "I'm asking about his support system, I guess."

Her face softens. "It's waiting in the wings for him. I know Charlie's had a lot of talks with him about...I don't know, gender and sexuality and all that, but they said it was all theoretical. Tony never really talks about himself or his problems. He's too busy listening to other people do that."

"I think..." Daniel pauses so he can get the words right. "I think he's spent a lot of time thinking about things, for himself, by himself. And I think someday, he's going to be ready to talk about it. And I'm here for that, of course, I am. But..."

"So are we." Lisa slips her arm through his elbow and leads him inside. "Definitely got a good feeling about you," she adds, almost as an afterthought.

She must whisper to the others to let Tony come to them on his own time while Daniel and Tony are grabbing that second round (that's now a quarter of an hour too late) because no one presses them. Tony does end up telling Gianna's story once he's gotten another drink in, to general sympathy and not a little rage about Mario. Hospital Blake, in particular, has some choice words Daniel wishes he thought to record.

Tony doesn't kiss him at midnight, but he does kiss him at ten after in the cramped hallway leading to the bathroom. Beer Blake spots them through the partially open door of the men's room and shoots Daniel a thumbs-up.

Really, the worst part of the night is sneaking up the fire escape to Tony's room above the garage while fairly tipsy. Daniel's definitely had too much to drive home, and Tony says he warned his parents Daniel might stay over. It still feels like he's half his age as they pull off the purple bedspread and squeeze into the too-small bed in Tony's room.

"I feel like I'm doing something illegal," he mutters into the back of Tony's neck as they try to arrange themselves in the bed as quietly as possible.

Tony huffs a laugh. "Go to sleep, baby."

Somewhere on the floor, Daniel's phone flashes with a missed call from the sheriff's department.

Chapter Fifteen

Tony is in the shower when Daniel listens to the message.

It must show on his face, though, because Tony immediately asks, "What happened?" when he returns to the room.

Wordlessly, Daniel sets his phone on speaker and replays the message.

Hi, Professor Rosenbaum. This is Detective Taylor. I'm calling to inform you that Professor Ravel has been arrested on suspicion of accessory to murder in the Lombardi case. She's using her phone call to get in touch with you. A public defender has been made available—

Daniel stops the message before she starts going through the legalities.

"Shit," Tony says.

Daniel nods.

"Shit," Tony repeats. "No way. She didn't do it, right?"

For a moment, Daniel breathes. Colette was the last person to see

Mario alive. He was hiding quite a few things from her, his closest friend. She disapproves of several of the things he was hiding, most notably that Mario was taking advantage of students, although not because they were students but because they were taken advantage of.

Daniel remembers her, the morning they found the body, crouched over the gutter and vomiting.

He remembers her completely ignoring him for a full day after it happened and giving only the weakest of excuses for why.

He remembers her doing the utmost to draw the police's suspicions away from herself, from her rehearsed speech at the memorial to the moment she decided to tell the police about Gianna behind Daniel's back.

Colette would never be stupid enough to dump a body right next to their building.

"No." Daniel shakes his head like that will shake off the possibility. "No, she can't—no way."

"Okay. Okay, so we need to get you to the police department."

"Yeah. Um. Okay. I guess…I'll drive over and call you later?"

"Okay."

Daniel must look about as lost as he feels because Tony grabs him in a short, tight hug and holds him close.

"We'll figure this out," he promises, which is only comforting because he uses the first-person plural.

Climbing down the fire escape feels no less weirdly illicit in the morning, not least because Tony's mom is shoveling snow in the driveway.

"Hi Daniel," she calls brightly.

"Good morning, Mrs. d'Angelo. Happy New Year." It comes out with the inflection of a question.

"Happy New Year to you, too! I was hoping you'd stay for breakfast."

This is news to Daniel. "I'm sorry? Something came up. I have to—"

She waves him off. "That's all right, honey. But you had better come over for dinner one of these days."

"I'd love to," Daniel hears himself say.

"Great." She beams. "How about tomorrow?"

"Um, okay." Daniel has no idea what he's doing tomorrow, but given Colette is in prison, presumably he doesn't have plans.

By the time he gets to the bridge, he's thought himself into a panic. What will they even talk about? How Daniel's closest friend has been accused of committing the murder that got Gianna's illicit baby daddy killed? In the parking lot of the sheriff's department, he types out a quick, frantic message to Tony, trying to sound like this is a perfectly normal state of affairs and not at all like he's losing his mind.

He hasn't been here since that first awful morning. Stepping inside, the smell of stale coffee and the fluorescent lighting awakens dread in the pit of his stomach.

An empty chair sits behind the Plexiglas protective wall in front of the reception desk.

"Hello?" he calls. "Anyone here?"

From an office to the left of the atrium, Detective Taylor emerges. "Ah. Professor Rosenbaum."

He's not sure what he's supposed to say to her.

She seems to realize this after a moment of silence in which they stare at each other across the empty room.

"Professor Ravel is in the holding cell at present," She offers eventually. "I'm afraid she's refusing to speak to me without an attorney present, and the state attorney can't make it till later."

"Can I see her?" Daniel asks instead of commenting. He's pretty sure his intuitive response—*good, she shouldn't speak to you*—would be unwelcome.

The detective shakes her head. "Visitation is only possible once a person in custody has been—"

"All right. Well, what can I do?"

The detective sighs. "You can speak on the phone. I'll call your cell phone and put you through to her."

"That's ridiculous. I'm right here."

"I don't make the rules" is all Detective Taylor answers.

This is how Daniel finds himself sitting on one of the green plastic chairs drilled into the wall of the atrium, clutching his cell phone, and waiting for a call from the next room over.

As soon as she knows it's him, Colette begins with, "I'm sorry."

"What?" he asks, alarmed. "Why are you—you didn't—you're not—"

"No, of course I didn't kill Mario. Don't be ridiculous." Her saying it is neither a defense nor is it proof, but Daniel is still relieved to hear it. "I need you to call Jeff."

"Oh. That makes sense." Why he didn't think of it is beyond him. Jeff is the only lawyer either of them knows. He's not the type of lawyer who does murder cases, but at least he's a lawyer. "I'll call him right away."

"Thank you."

Daniel's not sure what the right thing to do is now. He could hang up and get right to calling Jeff, or he could try to commiserate even though it's not his strong suit. "Um, how did—" He realizes he has no idea how to finish. "Why..."

"I don't know." Colette sounds absolutely wretched. "I don't know anything. She said something about new evidence, but she won't tell me more until I agree to speak without a lawyer present. I have no idea if I should just answer her questions to find out or—"

"No. Definitely stick to your guns. Don't answer questions." He's shocked at the surety in his own voice; he's not sure at all. He's read several Twitter threads emphasizing no one should ever talk to the police without a lawyer present, but he's also never had a friend be accused of murder before. He can tell that the last thing Colette needs is to start questioning herself. "Is there anything else I can do for you?"

"If you can find out anything..."

"I'll try," Daniel promises.

He calls Jeff as soon as he's hung up with Colette.

"Daniel?" Jeff answers the phone, sounding incredulous.

"Hi." Daniel abruptly realizes he has no script for this conversation and no clue how to get from the opening to the massive favor he's about to ask. "Happy New Year."

"Right," Jeff answers. "Happy New Year."

Just as Daniel's gearing up to trying to talk about this, Jeff continues, "Don't take this the wrong way, but I didn't think I'd hear from you again. It's been a year."

"I know. It's... Wait, did you *want* to hear from me?"

He can practically see the frown line in Jeff's forehead deepen as he considers.

"I'm really not sure," Jeff says finally.

Daniel almost laughs. It's no wonder they didn't work out.

"It's Colette." Daniel rips off the Band-Aid rather than draw out this discussion. "She's been arrested as an accessory to murder."

"Did she do it?"

"What the fuck, Jeff, of course, she didn't." Daniel guiltily remembers his own moment of doubt this morning.

"I haven't seen her in a year." For a lawyer, it's an incredibly weak defense. "Who is she supposed to have helped kill?"

"Mario."

"Mario's *dead*?"

"It's been a really rough couple weeks, okay? Look, I hate to ask, but Colette doesn't have any family in this country, and I don't want her saddled with a public defender who won't help her. Do you know anyone? Or can you help?"

"Gimme a second." Jeff sounds distracted, and then there's a crack in the line as if he's muted the speaker. Moments later, he's back. "I'll be there by tomorrow. Is your address still the same?"

"Yeah. Thank you."

"Of course."

The line goes dead.

Of course. Bizarre. Daniel hasn't seen or thought much of Jeff in months. As far as he's aware, Jeff hasn't kept in touch with anyone at Lobell. He only lived in the area for a year and a half, and he spent most of that being a homebody with Daniel. Given Jeff hasn't even heard about Mario, that assessment is probably accurate. Daniel's thankful he cares enough to make the effort, but he's more than a little surprised. Maybe it's another instance of people being better than he imagined them.

He thinks of the vigil for Mario and how his family didn't come.

Maybe Jeff would have.

Maybe Jeff, who hasn't seen Mario in a year and didn't really like him all that much in the first place, was closer to Mario than his own family. Maybe Mario had every reason to look for connection and comfort in all the wrong places.

Maybe Mario *was* the reason his family didn't come, and the only reason they're all mourning his death is because they didn't know him well enough.

Daniel leans his head against the wall and tries to breathe. He needs to figure out what evidence Colette is being accused with. He needs to call Tony.

Fuck, he needs to figure out what he can bring along to Tony's parents when he goes over for dinner tomorrow. Tomorrow, when his ex will also be in town and possibly sleeping on Daniel's couch.

This would be the right time for hysterical laughter if Daniel could work up the energy for even that.

Deciding he can't trust himself to call, he types out a second text message to Tony, trying to sound like a rational human and not a ball of nervous energy.

He should have asked about Colette's family and whether he should call them. She doesn't have the easiest relationship with them, but she still goes home for visits regularly. Maybe they could help somehow.

"Daniel?"

Stacy's voice pulls Daniel out of his haze of confusion.

"Stace?" He sits up straight to look at her.

She's wearing a lumpy Christmas sweater under her thick winter coat, and she looks harried, like she's running on empty. Her hair is a mess.

"What are you doing here?" he asks. "You should be with your family."

Stacy sighs. "I wish. The detective called me in because of the stupid email server. Apparently, she needs to see something right now, and she doesn't know how to navigate it properly even with access codes. My husband is losing his mind because it's a holiday, as if he hasn't been gone for every—whatever.”

Colette said she thought it invasive for the police to get access to their emails, a traitorous part of Daniel's psyche points out. Maybe she was hiding something.

“What are you doing here?” Stacy asks.

“Colette's been arrested.”

Stacy gasps. “Oh no!”

Daniel nods.

“Oh, Daniel, this must be so hard for you.” Stacy pats his shoulder, which she can reach pretty effectively when he's sitting and she's standing. “First, Mario gone, and now Colette—oh, you poor thing! You'll have to come over for dinner tomorrow and let us take care of you.”

“I have a dinner thing tomorrow,” Daniel answers absently, glad of the excuse. Then, her words catch up with him. “Colette didn't do it! You don't think—”

Stacy bites her lip. “Oh, well. I only thought—they wouldn't arrest her without proof, right?”

Apparently, Stacy's faith in the police is greater than Daniel's ever was.

“I don't know what I think, but I know she didn't do it.” The more often he says it, the more he'll believe it himself.

Stacy pats him on the arm again. “You're such a good friend.”

Daniel doesn't know what he could possibly say to that. Peevishly, he wants to accuse Stacy of being a bad friend, although he supposes she and Colette were never exactly friends. It doesn't matter anyway; Stacy bulldozes right on.

“I've been meaning to pick your brain. With the overhaul of the Title Nine office, I really think we could use an LGBTQ-plus perspective. And the students love you, so maybe you could stop by one of our meetings in the new semester—"

"Sure, Stacy." Daniel mostly wants to get her to stop talking about work right now. She does mean well. And the Title IX office has been a mess ever since Daniel got to Lobell.

"You're a peach!"

This is not something Daniel has ever been accused of before.

Detective Taylor peeks out of her office. "Oh, Professor Abrams, I'm glad you're here. Come in, please. Professor Rosenbaum, you can leave."

"Can I?" Daniel asks icily. "Can I also speak to Colette again?"

"No." The detective shuts the door behind her and Stacy.

Daniel can't go home.

He considers it for a while, sitting in his car in the parking lot and wondering what he can possibly do. But he has nothing to do at home besides obsess about Colette not being downstairs, and he can't face the thought.

Instead, he drives to Lobell.

It's kind of tragic to be there when no one else is, and the campus is basically a ghost town. Maybe he should wander around and see if he spots Mario lingering, waiting to tell Daniel what the fuck actually happened to him.

He can't seem to settle into his office chair and start anything. He's pacing back and forth through the office when Tony gets there.

"You didn't have to come," Daniel says. Tony texted to ask where he was, and Daniel told him, but he didn't think Tony would be so quick.

Tony gives him a look. "You're freaking out."

"Yeah, and I don't want you to think I'm always like this."

Tony raises an eyebrow.

"Okay, I don't want you to know I'm always like this before it's too late and you can't get rid of me." Daniel grimaces. "Did I tell you my ex is flying in? As if I could make a *worse* impression on you."

"You also said he's a lawyer, and he can help your friend." Tony is so calm. Daniel wonders how he does it. Maybe his brain doesn't run entirely on anxiety. "Come on. Get your coat; we're going for a walk."

Daniel obeys on instinct.

"Take some deep breaths," Tony advises as they exit Condelmuir. What snow there has been so far is piled up on the sides of the pathways, leaving nothing but gravel on asphalt for them to walk through. It crunches under the soles of Daniel's boots, and he tries to think of nothing but that noise.

They've walked the entire loop past the administrative buildings, down toward the student center where they once ate mozzarella sticks before Tony speaks.

"You don't have to worry about me."

"Try to stop me," Daniel tells him grimly.

"I am." Tony shoots him a grin. "Look, I'm a sure thing. I like how crazy intense your brain is. It's pretty sexy when you're not, you know, panicking. Not that I like you less when you're panicking. It's just not—I'm going to stop myself there. You have every reason to be worried right now, and calling your ex is obviously the right thing to do in this situation, so that's not even worth thinking about. Don't add me to the list of things you're worried about."

Daniel takes a deep breath as if that will let him inhale Tony's words and hold them in his heart. "I really, really like you. In case I haven't mentioned it."

Tony bumps their shoulders together. "Ditto."

The student center is closed because it's the first of January, and even the skeleton staff running the café for the few workaholic professors who come to campus during break took the day off. They walk around it instead, to the quad on the other side with its bare cherry trees planted evenly around the wide, empty space no one ever seems to use for picnics, not even in summer. It's probably too close to authority. Daniel's been told the students like to smoke weed when they picnic.

As they round the path, passing by the squat little dorms for freshmen and sophomores, Daniel spots a man standing outside one of them. He's too old to be a student, easily in his fifties, and his body language screams discomfort. The closer they get to the building, the more curious Daniel becomes until he spots a woman of about the same age bustling out through the double-glazed glass door and then holding it open for a familiar face.

"Lily!" Too late, he reconsiders that he probably should have left her alone.

"Hi, Professor Rosenbaum." Lily Peterson looks pale—the dye at the tips of her hair is lackluster as if it needs renewing—but otherwise healthy.

"I'm glad to see you looking well." Daniel wants to kick himself for sounding like a Dickens character. "Healthy, I mean. We've all been very worried about you."

"Thanks, Professor." She tucks her hair behind her ears, and he's struck by how young she is. There are freckles on her nose and a zit under her lips. Then, she squares her shoulders and looks him directly in the eye. "Will you tell me what happened to Professor Lombardi?"

Her father sags against the door, groaning, rubbing a hand across his face. "Lily…"

"My parents won't talk to me about him." Lily lifts her chin, defiant. "But I want to know."

Daniel looks to Lily's parents. Her mother has frown lines drawn tight around the sides of her mouth. Her father's looking at the ground as if he's embarrassed. Daniel can't imagine what it feels like to almost lose a child, nor can he imagine what it feels like to know she was involved with a professor.

He looks over to Tony. Tony can definitely imagine at least some of that.

Tony nods in Lily's direction.

"I'm not sure I know much, to be honest," Daniel says. "A student—Andrew Clayfield, I don't know if you know him—has been arrested. So has a professor. Professor Ravel."

"Not Andrew," Lily gasps.

"So you do know him?" Daniel lets it out before he can stop himself.

Lily nods, her hair escaping from behind her ears and sliding across her face. "We were in the same dorm freshman year. He was...sweet in a really intense way."

"Maybe he was jealous," Tony offers.

"I don't think so." Lily makes a face as if to indicate that the thought is ridiculous.

At Daniel's quizzical look, she adds, "I never got that vibe from him. He never tried anything. He did keep telling me to stay away from Professor Lombardi, but he always said it was because there were things I didn't know about him. And he kept trying to get me interested in other people."

"He probably did know something," Tony points out. "Last year, Professor Lombardi was seeing my sister, Gianna. She was friends with Andrew."

Lily gasps. "He was *what?*"

"Yeah." Tony gives her a gentle smile. "I'm sorry. I don't wanna make things worse. I just thought you should know."

She nods slowly. "Thanks. Is she, um, is your sister okay? I think I met her, once or twice. I haven't seen her around though."

"She's pregnant. She had to drop out."

"Oh my god," Lily groans. "Andrew *knew*?"

"Pretty sure."

"I'm an *idiot*," Lily says.

Lily's father huffs a noise like he wants to agree.

"No, you're not." The words come out more forcefully than Daniel intended, but seeing Lily here reminds him of Stacy's words. It's Mario's fault this has happened to her. "Professor Lombardi was in a position of authority at this college, and he used that to his advantage. It's not your fault you thought better of him."

It earns him a shadow of a smile, both from her and her mother.

"I can ask Gianna if she wants to get in touch sometime if you want," Tony offers. "Might help to talk to someone who's been through it? Her, too, I think."

Lily's eyes light up, and she's nodding eagerly before she thinks better of it and hastily adds, "I mean, it's not the same at all. I was never actually with him. I just thought—he kind of gave me the— Well, I'd love to talk to her. And thank you both for being honest with me."

"Anytime," Daniel tells her warmly. "I look forward to seeing you next semester if you're ready." He debates telling her she can still submit her work from this semester for credit but decides that can wait.

"I'll definitely be back." Lily's jaw is set even though her parents both look more than a little skeptical.

"Your daughter is a wonderful student," Daniel tells them for good measure. "We'll let you get on with things."

He and Tony are quiet almost all the way down the drive past the student dorms.

"It was nice of you to tell her about Gianna." Daniel bumps his shoulder against Tony's.

Tony shrugs. "Now we know Lombardi never slept with her."

Daniel draws to a halt to stare at Tony. "That is impressively sneaky."

"I learned from you."

For an incredulous second, Daniel thinks Tony is being serious.

Then Tony adds, "Mostly what not to do."

"Ha, ha," Daniel grumbles.

They've reached the vast field by the Wordstone Mansion, which is older than most of the buildings on campus. It's shut up for a good part of the year except for rare occasions when especially rich donors stop by and want to be wined and dined, but it's beautiful, throning above gentle slope leading down toward the woods by the river.

They trek down in silence until they hit the woods. One of Daniel's students told him about the little footpath his first year here.

"This is my favorite place on campus," he tells Tony as they reach the large, flat rock looking out over the Hudson.

"Oh," Tony says quietly. It's started snowing a little, nothing that will stick, only a light flurry. The cold is biting. "Can we stay a while?"

"Sure. One condition."

"What's that?"

"You tell me what I'm bringing your mom when I come over for dinner."

Chapter Sixteen

When Jeff rings the doorbell at eleven in the morning, Tony is in the process of unclogging the sink in Daniel's NYU sweatpants and his own T-shirt. His hair is a mess. The TV is streaming Spotify, and it's blasting Bruce Springsteen because he says it's his turn to introduce Daniel to music. Daniel pointed out that he has heard Springsteen before. Tony asked if he's blasted Springsteen at full volume, which Daniel hasn't, and Tony claimed it didn't count.

Frustratingly, Worf, who hates all noises from the TV besides *Criminal Minds*, appears to be thrilled, winding around Tony's legs in the kitchen.

Jeff is, of course, incredibly put together. It's why Daniel was attracted to him in the first place; he gave the impression of having his life totally in order based on how neatly styled his hair was, how perfectly ironed his button-up shirts were, and how consistent his style was. It had seemed, at the time, to match how organized Daniel felt his own life was. Now, it seems fussy and boring.

The value of hindsight.

"Come in," Daniel tells Jeff, standing in the doorway while trying to turn off the music simultaneously.

Jeff has a tiny suitcase with him, and Daniel had been doing a very good job until this very moment at ignoring that he will, in fact, be sleeping here for at least one night. It's unavoidable now, though, and it's going to be so awkward.

"Thanks for coming," he tacks on as Jeff slides out of his dress shoes and sets them beside Daniel's by the door.

"You're going to have to tell me as much as you can as quickly as possible," Jeff says. "I'm not a criminal defense lawyer, and this is way out of my wheelhouse, but I should be able to at least get Colette some better conditions if we can figure out what happened here."

Daniel nods. "We're trying to figure it out. It's…not exactly easy."

"We?"

Tony ambles out of the kitchen barefoot. Later, he'll deny having timed his entrance for dramatic effect, and Daniel will not believe a word of it. "Hi. I'm Tony."

"Tony…" Jeff trails off.

"Daniel's boyfriend." It's not a term they've discussed, although Colette has been referring to them as such, and neither of them have protested. Daniel finds he doesn't really mind. This possessive streak is kind of funny. "Also, Lombardi knocked up my sister."

Jeff blinks. "I really have missed a lot."

"Have a seat." Daniel gestures to the kitchen. "We'll fill you in."

Sitting around the kitchen table with a pot of Daniel's terrible instant coffee, which none of them touch, they go through the whole story. Daniel starts with the night Mario was killed before Tony gets sidetracked explaining Gianna's situation, and Daniel gets sidetracked explaining Andrew's altar. Jeff takes meticulous notes—he learned that from Daniel—and asks questions about timing and dates of various occurrences.

When Daniel gets to the part about going into Andrew's cordoned-off dorm room, Jeff closes his eyes like he's begging for patience from above.

Jeff is the least religious person Daniel's ever met.

"Right." Jeff sighs. "As your legal counsel, I heard none of that, and I beg you to never repeat it again."

"We wouldn't know why Andrew is under arrest if he hadn't done it." It's the first time Tony has come in defense of Daniel's spectacularly poor decision-making skills of late.

"And now we will have to pretend we still don't know." Jeff's voice is a bare facsimile of patience. "What connects Colette and Andrew? Why is she a possible accessory?"

"He was in one of her classes last year." Daniel tries to think back to what she said about Andrew, that last afternoon before Mario died. "And he wrote a paper about sin-eaters that she thought was really good. But he's a film major, so he was mostly talking to Mario before...well..."

"What a mess." Jeff sighs again. "Right. Well, I need to go see Colette, and I got here by cab."

"I can drive you." Daniel gets up and heads to his shoes. "What time is dinner, Tony?"

"Seven." Tony follows them to the door. "But you don't have to—"

"Yes, I do." Daniel refuses to fuck this up.

"Fine. But you don't have to bring—"

"Yes, I do."

Tony rolls his eyes. "All right." He presses a kiss to Daniel's cheek.

"I'm going to try to find out more about Andrew from Gigi."

"You don't have to—"

"Yes, I do." He pats Worf on the head because Worf hates when Tony leaves, and then they all put on their shoes and head out the door.

Tony drives off toward Kingston as Jeff and Daniel head for the sheriff's department.

"He seems nice." Jeff's voice is loud in the quiet of the car.

"He is."

"I can't believe your cat likes him."

Neither can Daniel, but that's neither here nor there. "How's Ohio?"

"Good."

Topics of conversation exhausted, they spend the rest of the car ride in silence. Daniel doesn't even bother explaining why he stops at a florist on their way to the station. Jeff doesn't ask.

This time, Daniel planned ahead; he brought his laptop. While Jeff is somewhere in the bowels of the station talking to Colette, Daniel can at least get some work done on his grant proposal as he spends ages sitting on the dinky little plastic chairs in the atrium. If he's a little bit vicious while typing out a series of reasons why study into the portrayal of violent crime in America is important, especially when it comes to the storied history of police malpractice, well, so be it. The only person he's bothering is Detective Taylor.

"You could wait at home, you know," she says peevishly as he cracks his knuckles after a particularly poignant paragraph.

"Nope." Daniel smiles cheerfully. "I wouldn't want anyone else to have to spend a moment longer here than they need to."

"Commendable," she gets out through gritted teeth. "You know I'm just doing my job, right?"

"I know you're wasting taxpayer money interrogating an innocent woman for forty-eight hours."

The detective rolls her eyes. "I haven't been interrogating her for forty-eight hours. She's in a holding cell. You're going to be pretty disappointed when she turns out to be guilty."

"Or you're going to be pretty disappointed when she turns out to be innocent."

To Daniel's great pleasure, she has no retort. Instead, she takes a very deep breath, plasters on a transparently fake smile, and offers him a cup of coffee.

He says yes, mostly to spite her.

The coffee is as bad as last time.

After several hours, Jeff emerges. He looks like he did when he caught students plagiarizing their essays, which means deeply concerned and slightly hurt. He's carrying a sheaf of papers under one arm and loosening his bow tie with the other.

"Is it bad?" Daniel asks on the car ride home.

Jeff pauses for long enough that Daniel takes his eyes off the road to get a glimpse of his expression. He's staring straight ahead, expression calm and cold. When he told Daniel he got a tenure-track offer from Columbus, he looked much the same.

"I think she did it."

"No." Daniel rejects it instantly. The unwelcome feeling of having been wrong all along crawls across his spine, along with the memory of that day Colette refused to talk to him right after it happened. He pushes it away forcefully.

"Look, I know she's your friend." Jeff has a unique way of making clear that he's being incredibly patient and his listeners should appreciate it. Daniel always hated arguing with him when he got like this. It made Daniel feel like a toddler. "But the evidence is pretty solid. I have no idea how I would even go about fighting this in court."

"What evidence? Last I heard, all they had was that she was the last to see him alive."

"There's plenty more," Jeff tells him grimly. "A whole email trail between Colette and that student—Andrew?"

"He took her class. He was submitting essays."

"Essays were why he sent her photos he took of Mario? I don't think so."

"Photos?"

"Those stalker pictures you mentioned being in his room. Apparently, he was taking them and sending them to Colette."

"Why would he do that though? It doesn't make any sense."

"Why would she encourage him to keep on 'tracking Mario's sins'?" Jeff returns. "Because they're both nuts, that's why."

"No. No way. She's not...she's not *like* that. You know Colette."

Jeff scoffs. "I know she's cold as ice. Remember that faculty retreat where we were supposed to vote on whether professors could date their students, where you said you thought it was morally questionable, and she started playing the logic police?"

"You were on her side!"

"Yeah, and I've been told I need to work on my warmth and personability. Colette doesn't like anyone, and from what I've seen, I wouldn't put it past her."

"What does she say?"

"That she didn't do it. Obviously. She denies all of it. Which is stupid if I'm supposed to be her lawyer, and she did do any of it. I need to know."

"Colette's not stupid." Daniel sets his jaw stubbornly. He's not backing down on this.

"She's not," Jeff allows. "Watch the road."

Daniel swerves slightly; he was too far toward the middle. Jeff is absolutely a cold fish; he's not wrong about that. He's not wrong about Colette either. This is why they didn't work well together. Jeff likes being right more than he likes being nice. Daniel wonders if that one solid day of no contact would speak for or against Colette. Was she so over-whelmed with sadness that she couldn't reach out? Or was it guilt?

"I can't believe that about her." Daniel pulls into the lot under his apartment and parks.

Jeff huffs an exasperated sigh. "I thought you were going to say that. And I can't believe I did this, but here."

He shoves his phone under Daniel's nose. On it is a photo taken of a printout of an email. Because Jeff's cell phone is about seven years old, the photo is grainy, but Daniel can still make out an image of Mario pressing Gianna into the desk in his office, taken once again from the outside. Above it on the image is a three-line email in which Colette en-courages Andrew to keep "counting Professor Lombardi's sins."

He remembers Andrew pounding on Colette's door, yelling that she promised Gianna would be innocent. Daniel remembers all the post-its in Andrew's room screaming *e-mail report*. Was this what he meant? Was it Colette he was reporting to?

Daniel's spent the last few weeks teaching himself to have faith in his friends and family, to reach out to them, and not to let his brain's anxiety spirals dictate whom he trusts. Nothing about this situation is helping him.

"I can't believe it," Daniel repeats, not sure if it's because he's that convinced of Colette or because he's that desperate.

"I can. I don't want to, but I can."

"So, what now?"

Jeff sighs. "I'm going to look into how I can possibly defend her when she won't admit to the evidence that's right there. And I'm going to see if I can find an actual criminal defense lawyer worth their salt in this state."

"How can I help?"

"You can go to your dinner and get out of my hair."

For a moment, Daniel wants to be insulted that his help is being brushed off. Then, he catches the droop in Jeff's shoulders as he gets out of the car and heads toward the building. He must have caught an awful flight to have gotten here so fast. He's probably exhausted, and Daniel and, from what he's said, Colette, are fighting him every step of the way. Jeff's gotten a lot of shocking information condensed in a very short amount of time, and he's trying his best. This is him communicating he needs to work out the next legal steps by himself. It's him being thoughtful, and it's him trying not to fight, and Daniel appreciates it.

"Thank you." He unlocks the door and lets them in.

Jeff nods once and then sits down at the kitchen table with his laptop open and proceeds to ignore Daniel completely.

Daniel turns on his heel and heads back to the car.

He tries to refocus on the drive over to Kingston. He needs to not think about Jeff and Colette and Mario and anything at all but Tony and how much Daniel wants this evening to go well so he can stop feeling vaguely guilty every time he sees Tony's parents.

It would be easier if he could figure out who killed Mario first, though, his traitorous brain reminds him.

With one hand still on the wheel, he calls Stacy and sets his phone on speaker in its cradle on the dashboard.

"Hi, Daniel," she answers, as sympathetic and grating as ever. "Are you doing okay?"

"I—"

"Wanna come over for that dinner after all? We're having meat loaf."

"That's really nice of you, Stacy, maybe some other time. I was wondering... Apparently, the reason Colette's been arrested is something to do with her emails. You don't happen to know what that's about?"

Daniel winces at himself, at how transparently desperate for information he is.

Stacy sighs into the phone. It crackles on Daniel's end, loud enough that he regrets the speakerphone. "Daniel...we should never have gone into Andrew's room. You know that, right?"

"Yeah," he mutters.

"You can't do the police's work for them." Stacy sounds very gentle, as if Daniel is some sort of spooked barnyard animal.

Daniel wants to scream.

"I know you want to help Colette, but there's nothing we can do for her right now. I don't know what the police are looking for in those emails, but I'm gonna be really honest. If I did, I don't think I would tell you. You need to take a step away."

He knows she's probably right, and he hates it. "Yeah. Thanks. I'm sorry."

She clicks her tongue. "I'm gonna tell you what my mom always told me when I was stressed out—Let reality unfold."

"I hate that," Daniel says dully.

Stacy laughs. "So did I. Try to relax a little, Daniel. It's out of our hands."

Daniel hangs up. It's probably a good thing Stacy is head of the department. She has much better impulse control than him.

The potted plant he bought for Tony's mom is strapped into the back seat carefully, and as he drives across the bridge, Daniel checks on it in the rearview mirror.

He's never even bought a plant for a boyfriend, let alone a boy-friend's mom. He has a few himself—a yucca palm tree that's been thriving staunchly since his first semester in New York when he learned how lonely living alone was, and an orchid he got from his PhD advisor when he passed his final boards. Maybe he should get some more or give kitchen herbs a try. Every other time he's given that a shot, he's drowned the basil within two weeks. Maybe having something more finicky to take care of would take his mind off things. Maybe he should try buying Worf cat toys again, although both of them are very unenthusiastic when it comes to playing.

Daniel pulls up onto the driveway by Tony's family's house and gets out of the car. He carefully unbuckles the plant from its seat before heading for the door.

Tony's mom rips it open before he even manages to get to the bell.

"Daniel." She smiles broadly. "I'm so glad you could make it."

"Thanks for inviting me, Mrs. d'Angelo. Uh, I brought you this." He thrusts out the potted plant—an African violet because, apparently, they're unkillable—and the ridiculousness of the situation crashes down on him.

He's over thirty, and here he is, giving his boyfriend's mom a plant so she'll like him. As far as she's concerned, though, he's just her son's friend who stays the night sometimes, as if they're in high school and still have sleepovers.

She must know that can't be the truth.

She must know.

"Thank you, Daniel. That's very sweet of you, although you didn't have to. Call me Kat; everyone does."

"All right." He has no intention of ever addressing her by her first name.

It feels too awkward.

She ushers him inside to a solid wood dining table with five places laid out.

"Boys," she calls. "I told you to move your project to the garage before dinner."

"Sorry, Ma." Tony shoots a wink at Daniel as he clears what can only be disassembled car parts off the coffee table.

She shakes her head, sighing. "I thought I raised you better." There's a twinkle in her eye. The ridiculous urge to tell her exactly how well she did in raising Tony passes across Daniel's cerebral cortex. He manages to resist.

Tony's father comes in not long after and spends three minutes cleaning the grease from his fingers in the kitchen sink while Mrs. d'Angelo pours water into the glasses at the table.

"So, Daniel," Mr. d'Angelo says. "What do you do?"

"I'm a professor at Lobell. I hope you won't hold it against me."

Mr. d'Angelo snorts before his wife shoots him a sharp look. "What subject?"

As Daniel attempts to explain digital humanities, Gianna comes downstairs and settles into her place at the table. She's much more obviously pregnant than she was even a few weeks ago, although maybe that's because she isn't wearing an oversized sweatshirt. Her hair is starting to grow back in its natural dark brown, the black ends contrasting oddly. He smiles at her in greeting.

"Daniel's work is super cool, Pa." Tony sets out hot plates and wine glasses at the table. "He even featured the garage on that project. Remember, I showed you?"

"Right." Mr. d'Angelo snaps his fingers just like Tony does when he's looking for the right words. "That website where you can listen to my son dropping his wrench twice in a row."

Tony flushes.

"Do people actually want to hear that?" Mr. d'Angelo asks.

It's clear he's teasing, but Daniel answers all the same as Mrs. d'Angelo shoos them to their seats, then sets out a salad and an absolutely massive casserole. "I don't know that anyone is listening to the whole clip. But it's an interesting project for people who want to know how individual senses make up a whole, or how a blind person might experience the Hudson Valley."

"Don't tell him about the crime thing," Tony warns. "He'll keep you going all night."

Inevitably, this means Daniel does have to tell them about the crime thing. It turns out Mr. and Mrs. d'Angelo are huge fans of *Without a Trace* and still wish it hadn't been taken off the air, a conversation topic that maintains them all the way through dinner. The casserole is fantastic, rich and creamy, and Daniel makes sure to praise it accordingly.

"Oh, it's all Tony." Mrs. d'Angelo waves him off. "He insisted on doing most of the work."

"Not true," Tony says with his mouth full, which gets him in trouble with Gianna and his mother.

Daniel tries to imagine his own family like this, teasing one another, sticking to the roles in the family they've had their whole lives, and still loving it.

He can't.

It's not a terrible thing, he realizes. He and Meredith are too obstinate and too self-sufficient to be happy to play along with their parents like this. It doesn't mean they love one another less.

He can see, though, why Tony has never sat down and told his parents that he's gay. He can see what there is to lose. He can also see that Tony's parents are more than happy to accept the situation as-is and don't really need or want further information on what exactly is going on between Daniel and Tony. They might even prefer it like this. It lets them continue seeing Tony as more dependent on them than he is, as younger than he is.

Dessert is an incredibly boozy tiramisu which Daniel will absolutely be needing the recipe for.

"Good luck," Gianna tells him darkly over the fruit salad she got instead because she's not allowed any alcohol. "I don't even have that recipe."

"That's because you could burn water," Mrs. d'Angelo returns tartly.

There's coffee after dinner, which means Daniel will probably not sleep tonight at all. It also means he gets to stick around while Tony casually shifts the conversation to Gianna's dorm experiences and whether or not she was responsible for any of the infamous Lobell fire alarms, given her poor cooking.

"Nope." She snickers. "Some idiot in my freshman dorm put his microwave popcorn in for three hours instead of three minutes and then forgot about it though. That was a shitty night."

"Ugh." Daniel can imagine the carnage.

Mrs. d'Angelo tuts. "What's wrong with these kids? Not even real food, and they can't follow the instructions."

"Alcohol and Adderall," Gianna singsongs.

Mr. d'Angelo shakes his head. "That's my cue." He heads for the garage.

With Mrs. d'Angelo occupied with cleaning the kitchen and refusing Daniel's two offers to help, he sits down in the living room with Tony and Gianna. Tony's in the process of asking her if a lot of Lobell students are on Adderall.

Gianna shrugs. "Officially, not that many, but a lot of them share their meds. Or sell them."

Tony makes a face, so Daniel jumps in before he says something judgmental.

"Do you think we need more counseling services?"

"I mean, yeah. Obviously. Especially now. Who doesn't get depressed about the state of the world?"

It's a fair question.

"And anyway," she goes on, "it's not only that. Lobell's counseling services are totally unequipped for anything that isn't, like, anxiety or ADHD. Andrew tried going three different times, and all they could do was send him to a psychiatrist in Rhinebeck who wasn't covered by his insurance."

"It was that serious?" Tony asks, leaning forward.

"He has pretty severe OCD. At least, as far as I know."

"Isn't that, like, cleaning stuff?"

Gianna shoots her brother a disgusted look. He plasters on an angelic smile as if he hadn't deliberately provoked her.

"It's not," she explains. "It's obsessive, you know, *needing* to perform certain actions to feel safe? Like, if you don't, something terrible will happen? He used to check whether his door was locked four times every time we went to the dining hall. His mom got really sick last year, though, and then it stopped being the kind of thing that seemed like a quirk, and it started being...I don't know...more. I think that paper he wrote for Professor Ravel must have done a number on him because he couldn't let the thought of sins go at all. He kept researching it. First, he was tracking his own sins and then other peoples'. It got so no one wanted to be around him."

"Except you," Daniel guesses.

"I thought I could help. Pretty dumb of me, I know."

Daniel shakes his head. "You were getting a degree in psychology, weren't you?"

She nods, her hair swinging back and forth.

"Good. You should finish it as soon as you can. I think you'll be wonderful at it."

He's rewarded with a rare smile.

"Thanks, Daniel. Can I call you Daniel? Now you and my brother are..."

"Okay," Tony interrupts hurriedly. "This has been great, but we better be going, right, Daniel?"

Daniel would point out that he's in no hurry to talk to Jeff again, but Tony doesn't give him a chance. They're out the door and on the road before Daniel can really protest.

"You know," he observes from the passenger seat while Tony drives, "I am 99 percent certain they all know we're dating."

"Yeah." Tony's jaw is clenched. "I know."

"O...kay."

Tony sighs, drumming his fingers on the steering wheel. "The words are a big deal. Or, no, the words make things a big deal. Okay, so you're my special friend I see a lot, and we have sleepovers like we're thirteen or something. It's not normal or anything, but it's not something my mom needs to get in fights with her church friends over, or my dad needs to explain to our regulars. If we use the words, it's different."

Daniel nods slowly. "I get that. And I am in no hurry here. The thing is, if you don't use the words first, other people have a way of finding worse words to use on you."

"I know. I know. I can take it."

"I know you can. Only...your family seems like they'd have those fights for you. And that's worth a lot."

"Yeah," Tony agrees roughly. "It is. So I'm gonna...keep that closet door on the lean. They know, and that's enough for now."

Chapter Seventeen

"Okay," Tony says over oatmeal for breakfast. "OCD doesn't turn people into murderers."

"No," Daniel agrees. "Definitely not on its own anyway. Although, good job pretending you don't know anything about anything to make your own sister talk."

Jeff looks between them and doesn't comment, but his eyebrows raise in a very judging manner. When they got home last night, he was already fast asleep on the couch. Daniel elected to wait until the morning to fill Tony in on the news about Colette, and they followed Jeff's example by falling asleep at ten thirty.

"I'm taking this sleuthing thing seriously." Tony's grin belies his words. "What's the news on Colette?"

To Daniel's relief, Tony doesn't believe in Colette's guilt any more than he does, not even after hearing Jeff's news.

"Sounds like we need to see these emails" is all he says.

"I've seen them," Jeff points out mildly.

"But have you seen all the emails?" Tony asks. "Or only the ones being used as evidence. I bet there's a lot missing there."

Jeff stares at him. "No, they didn't show me every single email on the college servers, only the relevant ones. Because that would be *millions of emails*."

"How do you know they showed you everything relevant, then?" Tony asks.

Jeff doesn't, of course, and given that he's just as much of a control freak as Daniel, it's going to bother him now. He's also way too proud to admit it, so he's going to seethe for a bit.

"I don't see how we can get at those emails though." Daniel's been thinking about it all morning. He blew his chance with Stacy yesterday. He should have offered to help out rather than beg her for access.

"Because it would be illegal." Jeff sounds as if he hopes Daniel will agree but doesn't actually believe it.

"Because we don't have access to the server," Daniel corrects.

"Your friend Stacy does, though, right?" Tony leans forward in his chair, considering. "We could try asking her?"

Daniel grimaces. "I tried that yesterday. She thinks I need to 'take a step back.'"

Jeff eats a spoonful of oatmeal and swallows. "Because she's not insane."

"Hmm." Tony sighs. "Tricky. Can you hack in?"

"What the fuck?" Jeff asks his oatmeal.

Daniel shakes his head. "I taught myself everything I know about coding. I pretty much only use it for building my own websites, not...that kind of thing. I could always try asking her again. Maybe I can annoy her into giving me access."

Daniel's phone buzzes on the table with a text.

Hi Daniel, I hope you're feeling better! I'll be on campus today if you want to grab lunch together and talk shop. Try not to think about it all too much! xx Stacy.

Frowning, Daniel shows Tony the message. "Maybe not."

Tony studies it for a long moment. "Let's do it."

"Huh?"

"Let's have lunch with her. You might not be able to annoy her into anything, but I bet she'll buy that I'm so worried about you and my sister she'll give me *something*."

"You're very devious," Daniel observes.

Tony grins, waggling his eyebrows.

"I don't suppose I can talk either of you out of this," Jeff says, more to himself than either of them. "Will you at least give me a lift to the station again on your way to obstructing justice?"

"If justice is shit..." Daniel doesn't even need to finish, they both know it will be something Jeff has a hard time arguing against. On the one hand, he has a law degree and tries to live as rule-oriented and morally acceptable a life as he can. On the other hand, his mother is from Ghana, and his father is from Togo, and last Daniel knew, both of them were still trying to become citizens despite having lived in the country for more than a decade. It means he has a plethora of first-hand examples as to how much of a mess the legal system in the US is. Jeff and Colette used to talk about it all the time, how backward the whole country is.

Clearly, Jeff remembers this, given the way his mouth draws into a thin line.

After they drop Jeff off at the station, Tony observes, "He's pretty uptight."

"Yeah." Daniel keeps his eyes on the road.

"Relax. I can tell you're not about to get back with him."

"Really. Then why'd you stay over last night?"

Tony pokes his side.

Daniel squeaks. "Hey, I'm driving!"

"It doesn't hurt to make *sure* he feels weird about being at your place. But seriously, the vibes between you two are so awkward I think a straight person would know you guys are never getting together again."

"The vibes, huh? Did you get that from TikTok?"

"No," Tony claims with extreme dignity. "Instagram. Am I wrong?"

"You're not wrong. Don't let this go to your head, but being with you has opened my eyes that it was nuts we stayed together so long in the first place."

Tony doesn't say anything else about it, but he does exude an aura of unbearable smugness for the rest of the morning. With nothing better to do, Daniel grades final essays while Tony reads one of the books on the overstuffed shelves in Daniel's office. He doesn't actually need so many books, the library is pretty well-stocked, and anyway, Daniel mostly reads digitally these days. He just likes how cozy it makes his office. Given how engrossed Tony gets in *Snowpiercer*, Daniel's definitely not changing anything anytime soon.

They meet Stacy at the café in the student center. It's up and running again after the staff's much shorter winter break, which Daniel appreciates greatly. He's been jonesing for a grilled cheese with avocado and pesto, which is a weird order at the artisanal bakery in Rhinebeck but totally normal on a college campus. Tony gets the mozzarella sticks again, and Stacy has a premade wrap from the fridge. The thought of it makes Daniel's skin itch. He doesn't like wraps as sandwiches at the best of times when he could be eating a burrito instead, and the levels of mayo in the ready-made ones are frightening.

"How are you holding up, Daniel?" Stacy asks as they sit down in a corner booth. She looks at him earnestly, and he feels instantly guilty they're going to try to dupe her.

He shrugs. "I'm holding. How about you?"

She sighs deeply and starts talking about the Title IX restructuring, which is interesting to Daniel in theory. It's an important service, and he wants it to be running well as opposed to being a maze of bureaucracy that keeps students and staff affected by gender-based discrimination from meaningful help. Unfortunately, the main administrator in the office is the kind of person who only accepts forms filled in with the right ballpoint pen, and as a faculty advisor, Stacy only has so much say given that the office needs to be able to make decisions independently from academic staff.

A lot of what she's describing is about infighting between people on different ends of the same bureaucratic string, and Daniel witnesses enough of those kinds of debates in faculty council.

He zones out while she talks, inspecting the café around them. It's remarkably clean today. Usually when Daniel is here, there are crumbs or disturbing salt sculptures on at least one or two tables the café staff hasn't gotten to yet. Campus really is a ghost town with no students.

"Daniel?" Stacy asks.

"Huh? Sorry, my brain drifted."

She pats his shoulder. "Aw, Daniel, sweetie…"

"I know. I know. Let reality unfold. Look, I'm gonna go wash my face or something. Maybe that will wake me up a bit." He tries to keep the look he shoots Tony as subtle as possible as he leaves for the gender-neutral restroom.

On his way, he hears Tony asking about how the Title IX office might be able to help Gianna get back into school.

He lingers in the restroom, actually splashing water onto his face and taking a few deep breaths, wondering how long is too long to stay away. If he's learned anything about himself in the last month or so, it's that he despises manipulating people, even if he's not terrible at it.

He returns to his half sandwich to find Tony leaning his elbows on the table, nodding along attentively to everything Stacy says.

Tony turns to him when he slides into his seat. "Feeling better?" He nudges their knees together under the table.

"Yeah." Daniel starts to smile at him, remembering at the last minute that he can't look too happy or risk alerting Stacy. It comes out more of a grimace. "I'm sorry, Stacy. I should have—"

She waves him off. "No, no, don't. We all get it, Daniel."

Tony nods emphatically. "Hey, do you have a lot of essays left?"

Daniel's finished grading, which Tony knows because Daniel submitted the grades to the online database before they came here. "I have a couple essays left to go," he lies, hoping it's the right call.

"Do you mind if I tag along with Stacy here for a bit after lunch? It sounds like she has some great resources for my sister."

"Of course not, go for it." Daniel rests a hand on his thigh and squeezes lightly out of sight. "Text me when you're ready to get going, yeah?"

"Sure thing." Tony sets his hand over Daniel's and squeezes back.

He heads off toward the administrative building with Stacy after they're finished, and Daniel returns to his office, where he fucks around on the internet for a solid hour for lack of anything better to do.

Eventually, Jeff texts that he needs a ride from the station.

I'm going to pick up Jeff, Daniel texts Tony. *I'll get you in half an hour?*

Whatever Stacy's telling him, it had better be good to justify all the driving around.

When Daniel picks him up this time, Jeff looks less exhausted than before, which is probably a good sign.

"Anything new?" Daniel asks as Jeff gets in the car.

Jeff shrugs. "We have a timeline put together that does *something* to invalidate those emails. According to Colette's planner, she set the date to hand in the final essay in her class a week before Andrew's last email about it. She says she doesn't take extensions without a doctor's note."

She doesn't; Colette is a notorious hard-ass on campus for it.

"That's great." Daniel is maybe pushing it, but it is the first decent defense they've found.

"It's good, but not all the emails are about the essay, especially not the later ones. And she could be lying about the extension in this case."

Daniel shakes his head. "I don't believe that."

"We've established that."

Sighing, Daniel tries a new tack. "Say Colette's telling the truth. Who could have faked the emails?"

"There aren't a lot of people with the means. If the digital infrastructure at Lobell is anything like it was when I left—"

"It is."

"Then that's nearly no one, and I can't see Stacy having a motive."

Daniel slams on the brakes, wrenching the car over onto the side of the road.

His ears are ringing.

"Daniel?" Jeff asks. "What the hell?"

"Stacy..." Daniel repeats, "what about her?"

"She's the administrator of the email server, right?"

"Right," Daniel agrees slowly. "She was helping the police the day Colette got arrested."

Jeff makes a face like he's considering against his better judgement. "She has the digital know-how, and she runs digital humanities as well as English, right?"

"She does." Unlike Daniel, Stacy actually did a double major in English and computer science. She's tech-savvy, at least with tech from the nineties. But she would never kill anyone.

She would also never break into a student's dorm room to look at evidence, nor would she lie to a colleague to get at a master key, except Daniel witnessed her doing both those things. A bad idea for him and Colette, certainly. But while those actions are in the wheelhouse of messed-up decisions both of them have been making since Mario died, they're unthinkable for someone as aggressively nice as Stacy.

"Tony's alone with her right now." Unbidden, anxiety crawls up Daniel's throat.

"Tony's a grown man. He's practically twice her size. And I really doubt she did it. What would she possibly have to gain?"

That draws Daniel up short for a moment. What does Stacy want out of life? A husband who actually pulls his weight, but that's unrelated. "They're redoing the entire Title Nine office because of the case. She's been campaigning for that since I came to this college."

Jeff hesitates.

"What if she…"

"I'm sure he'll be fine. Where are they?"

"On campus." Daniel tries to breathe as he merges left onto the road.

Jeff studies him. "You're really worried about him, huh?"

"Yeah."

"You like him a lot."

"Yeah."

Jeff shifts in his seat. "You know, I met someone too."

"Oh yeah?"

"Yeah. Her name's Tatyana."

Daniel doesn't ask, but Jeff keeps going.

"She's a Russian language and lit professor. She makes me go to a dance class with her once a week and takes me on weekend trips sometimes. I'd never tell her, but I kind of love being forced to do things?"

Daniel snorts.

"I think we were really bad together." Jeff's tone is meditative and calm, as though he's thought about this as much as Daniel has.

"Yeah. We were."

"We have too many habits in common."

"Like overthinking."

Jeff snorts. "You overthink. I overplan. We couldn't do anything without me planning it out in excruciating detail and you overanalyzing every moment after it happened."

Daniel allows himself a second to unclench and look over at Jeff. "That's why we stayed home too much."

"But we don't have enough characteristics in common. I'm too logical."

"If you're trying to distract me with insults—"

"You need someone who makes decisions like you do," Jeff continues heedlessly. "Heart-first."

"Oh." Daniel swallows heavily.

"I'm glad you're happy. And I think this whole thing is nuts, but I will help you."

"I'm glad you're happy too."

Daniel's phone buzzes in its cradle, but he threw it off center with his crazy driving before, so he can't see the message. "What does it say?"

Jeff leans in toward the screen. "Don't freak out. Tony wrote that Stacy's driving him home, and that he'll see you tomorrow."

Daniel inhales sharply. "That...no way."

"It's what it says."

"Read it out loud," Daniel demands.

"Sweetie, Stacy's giving me a ride home. See you tomorrow."

"That's not real." The anxiety in Daniel's throat pushes its way out of his mouth.

"Daniel—"

"He wouldn't call me 'sweetie.'" Daniel pushes on the accelerator, hurtling toward Lobell as fast as he can. "You know who would?"

"Stacy." For the first time, Jeff sounds less than calm.

The tires screech against asphalt as Daniel pulls into the faculty parking lot. Stacy's SUV isn't there.

"Fuck," he mutters. "Where would she have taken him? Fuck, fuck." He bangs his hand into the steering wheel. It changes nothing.

"She didn't take him to Rhinebeck." Jeff is still far too logical. It's probably good, given that Daniel is running on panic, but it still grates on him. "She has a family; she knows too many people."

"Campus is empty. Why would she leave?"

"Maybe she didn't. Drop me by the woods leading to Tivoli Bays. You can check by Wordstone."

"Okay." Daniel tries to breathe. "Okay." He pulls out of the parking lot again. He's gripping the steering wheel so hard he's afraid he's about to rip it off.

"Daniel," Jeff says just before he gets out on the north end of campus. "If you find them, call the police."

"But—"

"I'm not kidding, if she did do it, she's dangerous."

"Okay." Daniel gets out between too-fast breaths. "Okay."

Campus speed limit is twenty miles per hour. Daniel drives sixty on his way to the manor on the south end. He leaves the car door open and sprints across the field. Even as he gets out, he regrets it; he should have driven it right onto the grass until he hit the tree line.

He trips on the roots as he races through the forest, tearing open his pants at the knee. It bleeds, but he doesn't care as he tumbles down toward the water.

He's only a few feet away when he hears her.

"Why'd you have to *keep digging*?" Stacy's back is to Daniel. She's standing exactly where he was the day before yesterday when he showed Tony this very spot above the Hudson. "It would have been so much better for you and your sister if you could have left well enough alone."

"There's no need to rush into things," Tony says soothingly. He stands inches away from a steep drop into the water.

Daniel sidles to the left to see them better and has to clap his hand over his mouth.

Stacy's holding a gun pointed right at Tony.

Daniel scrambles in his pockets for his phone, but he can't find it. It must have fallen out when he fell, and if he backtracks now, he'll be too late.

"Stacy!" he calls.

She doesn't turn away from Tony.

"Daniel," she welcomes him warmly. "You scheming son of a bitch. Why couldn't you trust me that was better for you to chill out, relax, and let the police do their damn jobs?"

"You're pointing a gun at my boyfriend!" He steps out from the undergrowth, trying to get close enough to grab her weapon. "And you're framing Colette for murder!"

She elbows him in the solar plexus.

He doubles over, gasping.

"Colette is a-okay with professors taking advantage of their students. Don't you remember what she said at that faculty retreat?" Stacy smiles a sickly sweet smile. "'As long as they're consenting adults.' If you really think about it, all the damage Mario did is her fault too."

"Mario didn't kill anyone," Daniel gets out through panting breaths. If he can throw her off guard enough, maybe she'll be distracted, and Tony can get by. Daniel glances over at Tony, who's frozen in place at the edge of the rock. With Stacy's eyes on him, there's no way Daniel can give him a sign, and he reads nothing but panic in Tony's expression.

"Mario *ruined* two girls' bright futures, and I couldn't do anything to stop him."

"So you had a student *murder* him?" Daniel tries to grab Stacy by the elbow and pull her away from Tony somehow, but she's too quick and now her gun is pointed at him. It's shaking in her grip.

"Don't be silly, Daniel." Stacy shakes her head as if her manipulation of Andrew was the unbelievable part. "I killed him myself. Andrew is a lost soul who came looking for help, and he gave me the proof he deserved it, but I would never do that to a student."

Of course, Daniel realizes. Stacy works with all the Title IX staff, and with the counselling, she must have known about Gianna and Andrew long before the rest of them. She didn't even need to counterfeit those emails. She just changed the sender so it looked as though it were Colette encouraging Andrew's obsession rather than her. She actually thinks she was protecting him and not destroying him.

"Are you hearing yourself?" Tony asks incredulously.

Stacy spins around to point her gun at him again. "You don't know what it's like," she hisses, "when a man has that kind of power."

Fuck.

Daniel thought about it before, how the one thing Stacy wanted was a husband who wasn't useless. How could he have forgotten that Stacy's husband has a good decade on her at least? Or that he teaches high school PE and already did when Stacy was a senior in high school herself? It would be so easy to see him in Mario and herself in Lily and Gianna.

"He flatters you," Stacy continues, "and you think you're so special, and next thing you know you're the one earning the real money. You're the one taking care of the kids. You're the one staying up till three to clean the goddamn kitchen, and he's still sleeping with his students, and he thinks you don't even *know*—"

Daniel learned today that he thinks with his heart first, and apparently, his heart is an idiot because he uses her distraction to surge forward and grab the barrel of her gun, pointing it upward. His feet slip on the icy rock, one leg going wide and nearly throwing them both off balance and toward the river, at least a mile below them.

A bang sounds in the crisp winter air, followed by a whistling noise right past Daniel's ear, and suddenly his hand is on *fire*, and he drops Stacy's gun as she pulls away and runs for the tree line.

He slips, losing his footing. His hand is too slick with blood to grab on to the rock.

It's only Tony's strong grip that keeps him on the rock, pulling him back up as police and medics swarm through the forest toward them.

Epilogue

"**P**ack some bug spray," Daniel suggests, only half-kidding.

"What kind?" his mom asks, sounding as if she's taking actual notes. "Are there ticks? Horseflies?"

"Yes, and yes. But also, I own bug spray. You will not be seriously injured during your one week in the Hudson Valley. I promise." He elects not to mention the Hudson Valley's lesser-known nickname, "the Lyme Disease Capital of the World."

"Hm." She sounds skeptical. "What about your hand?"

"I really don't think you'll be involved in the arrest of a murdering literature professor," Daniel points out. "As far as I know, we only had one of those here. Anyway, my hand's fine."

"You were still wearing a brace in March."

"Yes," Daniel patiently explains, not for the first time, "and it is now June."

There's a scuffle on the other end, and then Daniel's father is on the phone.

"Don't mind your mother. She likes to fret." This is not news to Daniel. "Does our hotel have air conditioning?"

"Yes." Daniel doesn't actually know, but it's not like they can change anything if it doesn't.

"Then I'm sure we'll be just fine. See you tomorrow, son."

"See you," Daniel repeats, shaking his head as he ends the call. He taps out a quick text to Meredith asking her to wish him luck.

She responds with a selfie of herself and the kids at the beach—Benjamin nowhere in sight—with the caption *first parent-free week in 4 years. score.*

They were all more than a little concerned after Daniel got hurt in January, and for a moment there, it seemed as if the incident was going to restart all their concerns about Daniel living so far away. Thankfully, Tony's consistent appearance in the background of video calls seemed to assuage that fear, especially after Daniel's visit during spring break.

"All good?" Tony asks, strolling out onto the porch of his parents' house. He's wearing pretty much all leather, and he must know what that's doing to Daniel because he smirks. The only consolation is that he must be boiling hot.

"Yeah. All good. You know, we don't have to do this. We could watch a movie in a nice, air-conditioned theater or have dinner or something."

"No, no, no." Tony wags his finger. "You promised I could take you out at least once. No backing out. I promise to keep you safe."

Daniel sighs heavily. "Fine."

Tony grins and hands him the spare helmet.

"Have you thought about how we're going to handle dinner?" Daniel asks as Tony pulls his terrifyingly huge motorcycle out of the garage. It's probably normal-sized for a motorcycle, but Daniel is allowed a bit of healthy skepticism about one of the deadliest hobbies in America.

"It's Colette. What's to handle?"

Daniel flicks his ear, then pulls the helmet on so Tony can't retaliate. "I mean on Saturday, with our parents."

Tony shrugs. "Play it by ear?"

"Don't see that blowing up in our faces at all," Daniel mutters.

"Baby," Tony admonishes.

"Hm?"

"Relax. It'll be fine. My parents *asked* to meet yours. They're not gonna run out of the restaurant screaming if someone calls you my boyfriend because I haven't gotten around to it yet."

"Fine. I just don't want my parents to be all...I don't know, WASPy. Not that they're Protestants, only...I worked too hard to get your mom to like me."

"Not true." There's a smile in Tony's voice. "My mom liked you the moment she met you." He pats the back of the motorcycle.

"Lies and slander." Daniel takes a deep breath and swings one leg over the seat behind Tony. Privately, he knows Tony's probably right. His parents have a leg up already in that they're not Mario's parents, who have been alternately overinvested in their granddaughter's birth and early life and entirely uncommunicative. It's a weird situation, of course, and Gianna is doing admirably without their help, but it's still enough to irritate the d'Angelos.

Inside the house, the sound of infant screaming kicks up, and Tony grimaces.

"Liana's still colicky?" Daniel guesses.

"I'm staying at yours tonight," Tony says as if he doesn't sleep over three nights out of four. He starts the motor, drowning out the baby, and then they're off.

Daniel would never admit it, but Tony was right. The breeze is refreshing in the sweltering, humid Hudson Valley summer. The drive across the bridge especially, with the fresh air from the river cooling them off, is wonderful. Daniel's still not going to make this a regular thing. By the time they reach campus, his heart is pounding. The splash of gravel as they pull up beside Wordstone Mansion does not help, and when they dismount, his knees are shaking.

Tony shucks his motorcycle leathers and stows them, along with Daniel's helmet, in the special compartment motorcycles apparently have. He keeps his own under his arm, and together, they head down the field. It's empty once again now the students have all left for the summer. Somehow, during the spring semester, it remained a popular picnic spot despite the pervasive gossip about Professor Abrams trying to kill Professor Rosenbaum here.

Daniel can't say he blames the students. Even he still thinks it's beautiful.

Colette waits for them on a picnic blanket she's had for about two weeks. "I'm trying to go native," she explained when she suggested this for her last afternoon in the Hudson Valley before her two-week trip to Ohio.

She's brought sparkling wine and orange juice as well as a few snacks. Together, they sip mimosas and watch the sun on its steady decline toward the treetops.

"What a school year," she comments eventually.

"No kidding." Daniel blows out a long breath. "Can you believe I'm a dean now?"

"Someone had to do it." Colette's tone indicates that 'someone' had better not be her. "And frankly, better you than the alternatives."

"I don't know. With some of the emails I get, it's no wonder Stacy went nuts."

Tony snorts. He's seen most of the emails; Daniel prints out the funniest ones to stick to the fridge. "I don't see you with a gun when you're scared of Suzy."

"I can't believe you named your motorcycle," Colette scoffs.

"She's a Suzuki." Tony grins. He is absolutely messing with both of them and just waiting for Colette to call him on it.

"Hey," Daniel protests, vaguely offended. "I got on the motorcycle, and I am still the only one of us who *got shot*."

"It was a flesh wound." Colette recovered admirably from her stint in jail and now carries herself without the tension Daniel didn't realize was there before. It's as if the worst possible event occurred and knowing she can get through it has helped her relax.

Maybe it's knowing she has people to help her through it.

The experience rekindled her friendship with Jeff, even though he was fully ready to believe she had done it. She claims his ability to stick to his principles increased her respect for him. Colette's also insufferable about having always been right about Stacy.

"Send Jeff our greetings, yeah?" Tony leans back to stare up at the sky.

"Send them yourself."

"Eh," Tony wrinkles his nose. He was so thankful for Jeff having called the police in time to save his and Daniel's lives that he actually hugged Jeff in the hospital when they were waiting for Daniel to be released. But he and Jeff communicate exclusively via Daniel's occasional text exchanges to him.

Not everything is as it should be, of course. Andrew Clayfield is still in a closed ward, receiving treatment, and Daniel's pretty sure he's not the only one who feels terrible about that. Lily Peterson hasn't returned to campus yet either, although Daniel's heard she'll return next semester. Stacy's family moved to Poughkeepsie, both so the kids would be closer to their grandparents and, Daniel's pretty sure, to avoid the rumors that cropped up about Stacy's husband and his underage students.

It's still a better outcome than Daniel dreamed of that day in January, grappling on an icy rock with blood seeping out of his hand and loosening his grip.

Eventually, Colette packs up the blanket and the drinks. She's taking a late train to Newark to catch her flight at the crack of dawn. "Don't get involved in any murder investigations while I'm gone," she tells them sternly, which they've been saying to one another every time one of them leaves the apartment building for longer than five minutes. Someday, it will stop being funny. Probably.

"I'll try," Daniel promises. "Have fun. Come back rested. I need you for my crime project next semester."

Colette sighs.

It turns out she doesn't hate procedural crime shows because they're police propaganda or because they're senselessly violent, although she maintains both those things are true. She hates them because she's a big baby about jump scares. The crime-mapping project Daniel got funding for involves watching many, many procedural crime shows.

Daniel can't wait.

After Colette disappears up over the top of the gentle slope of the field and her car starts distantly, Tony twists to lean up on one elbow.

"So." He wiggles his eyebrows.

"So?"

"Come here often?"

"Oh, yeah," Daniel says breezily. "Saved a guy's life here once."

"*Really.* Wild. Me too."

"Wow, sounds like we have a lot in common." Daniel inches closer. "Wanna get out of here?"

"Hmm..." Tony runs a teasing hand up Daniel's chest. "I was thinking we could stay."

A thrill shoots down Daniel's spine. "Really? Here?"

Tony shrugs. "Might as well make some good memories."

He dips down to kiss Daniel deeply, and it's not as if Daniel is overladen with common sense when it comes to Tony anyway, so he goes with it. He skims his hands up along the line of Tony's waist and slides his fingers under his T-shirt. Even in the late afternoon heat, Tony shivers.

"Let me." Tony pulls away with a glare.

"Okay." Daniel relaxes into the grass. "Didn't know you had a vision."

Tony mumbles something indistinct that might be, "You *are* a vision."

Daniel doesn't call him on it. Instead, he lets himself enjoy as Tony unbuttons and unzips his pants, settles between his legs and takes the head of Daniel's cock in his mouth.

He's only half hard to start with, given this has all been pretty sudden, but the adrenaline of how easily they could be caught and the sight of Tony, head bobbing between his legs, dark eyelashes fluttering, is more than enough to get him there.

"You're so good at this," he murmurs, cupping the back of Tony's head in his hand.

Tony makes a sound around his cock; the vibration of it rumbles through Daniel.

He tugs at Tony's ponytail, and Tony redoubles his efforts, swallowing around Daniel and sinking deep, greedy for it.

"You love this, don't you," Daniel whispers affectionately. "Love choking yourself on me, like if you can just be good enough, I'll give you everything you want."

Really, he's not doing anything but telling Tony what he wants to hear, himself, if it were him. It turns out Tony appreciates a lot of the same things, giving Daniel a handy advantage in making him lose his mind.

"You can," Tony rasps after pulling away to catch his breath. "You do give me everything."

Daniel bites the inside of his cheek to avoid a mid-sex romantic declaration. He's saving that. Instead, he pulls at Tony's hair again, stroking a gentle thumb over the ridge of his cheekbone.

Tony dives in again, holding the base of Daniel's cock steady and licking circles around the head as he sucks.

Daniel throws his head back and lets himself enjoy it, feel it, the racing of his pulse, the feel of Tony's mouth, hotter even than a Hudson Valley summer. He comes, biting out curse words and flooding Tony's mouth, and when Tony kneels up to look at him, a trickle has escaped past his lips. He licks it up as if he can't quite get enough. In the past, Daniel would have probably thought it was gross, but because it's Tony, he can't stop from surging up to kiss him.

"Please," Tony gasps. "Daniel, I'm..."

Daniel hitches his hips up to rub Tony's hard cock against him. "Got you all worked up, huh?"

"Yeah." Tony nods furiously. "Yeah, please...please..."

It would be fun to tease him a little longer, make him beg a little more. But they are in a very public place, so Daniel tugs at the fly of Tony's shorts until they're down his thighs, and Daniel wraps his hand around him.

Tony makes a noise like he's holding in a sob.

"Wow, you really like this," Daniel says. Tony's already wet, leaking precome.

"I…" Tony trails off into a gasp as Daniel strokes him quickly. "Jesus fucking Christ."

Daniel tuts. "Language." But he doesn't slow down.

Tony claws Daniel's free arm, holding on for dear life as he comes in thick pulses all across Daniel's fist. His eyes are wide and his mouth is open and Daniel has to kiss him through it because he's just too beautiful.

Tony's grip on Daniel's arm goes tight and painful, and they overbalance, falling into the grass. They wind up side by side, laughing and messy, spread-eagled on the lawn. Daniel probably has grass stains everywhere. He doesn't care.

"I feel like I should have known you're an exhibitionist, given our first time," Daniel accuses.

Tony laughs harder. "I swear I'm not," he gets out between giggles.

"Really? Are you *sure*?"

"I promise. This doesn't count; there's no one here. You know I couldn't sleep the whole night after we met because I was so freaked out my sister might have seen something?"

Daniel frowns. "Seriously? You seemed so confident."

"I promise I was not." Tony grins carelessly.

Daniel shakes his head. "What about when I came back, and we—"

"I don't know." Tony looks over at him. "No one was there the time we actually…you know, in the garage. I knew we wouldn't get interrupted. Didn't know whose van we ended up against, but you know…"

Daniel groans. "I'd nearly suppressed that memory, thanks."

For a moment, they stare up at the clear evening sky together, reminiscing.

Daniel lets his pinky link with Tony's. "When we met, I was really...surprised you were interested. I kind of thought you were way out of my league and that you were just that smooth."

Tony turns onto his side with their fingers still linked together and looks at Daniel. His laugh lines crinkle like he's smiling, but his tone is serious. "When we met...I started talking to you, and I liked you so much my brain stopped working. That never happened to me before. Didn't feel smooth to me; felt like I walked face-first into a steep drop."

There are a lot of things Daniel could say. Potshots about how that brain condition obviously stuck around, given he chose to forgive Daniel over thinking he or his sister might be murderers. Jokes about the fact that Tony sweet-talked him into having sex on a very public lawn, which was nothing if not smooth.

Instead, he tangles his fingers with Tony's. "I was the same. Heart-first."

Tony presses a kiss to the side of his head, and together, they watch the sun sink into the trees toward the Hudson.

Acknowledgements

To Laurel, Kaydee, and Allison: Thank you for reading this project when I was barely halfway through. Thank you for giving me great feedback and cheering me across the finish line.

To Toni: Thank you for telling me you always knew I would write a book someday.

To Hannah: Thank you for commiserating with me about all the parts of writing a book no one tells you about.

To Navya: Thank you for listening to me talk about this book way too much.

To Fabi: Thank you for supporting me in this and all things.

Thank you to NineStar Press for thinking this is a story worth telling. Special thanks to Elizabetta for finding the right changes to make the story stronger and for editing what happens to comma placement when an American lives in Europe for two decades.

About the Author

S. B. Barnes attended college in the Hudson Valley, studying English Language and Literature and Anthropology (although unlike her characters, her time there was not interrupted by crime-solving). She grew up split between the USA and Germany, attending university in both countries before eventually settling in Germany. Today, she works as a teacher and lives with her husband and two cats in an apartment with too little shelf space. Fiction has always been one of her greatest loves, as a reader, as a teacher, and as a writer. While S.B. has been writing for most of her life, this is her first foray into publishing her work.

Email
sbbarnesauthor@gmail.com

Twitter
@S_B_Barnes

Instagram
www.instagram.com/s.b.barnes

Tumblr
www.tumblr.com/sbbarnes

Coming Soon from S.B. Barnes

Second Chance

A Hudson Valley Murder Mystery, Book Two

Almost a year after the murder of Mario Lombardi, the Hudson Valley is once again a quiet, picturesque haven for its inhabitants. The start of a new academic year brings familiar faces back to Lobell College: Daniel Rosenbaum starts his first year as dean of the department and takes a hands-on role in advising students. Among them are Lily Peterson and Gianna d'Angelo, both of whom are returning to complete their studies after Mario's death caused them to take a semester off.

Meanwhile, on the other side of the Hudson, Tony d'Angelo is working hard. With his sister back in college, it's all hands on deck to keep his dad's auto shop running and take care of his niece. Still, he spends most nights with his boyfriend, although he hasn't been able to tell his family that's what Daniel is. His life is exactly what he's always wanted it to be—so why does he feel like he's struggling to be himself?

When a Lobell professor is once again found murdered, the idyll of the last months is turned on its head. Can Tony and Daniel stay out of harm's way this time? Or will the fragile new peace they've found together be shattered?

www.ninestarpress.com

www.facebook.com/ninestarpress

www.facebook.com/groups/NineStarNiche

www.twitter.com/ninestarpress

www.instagram.com/ninestarpress